PRAISE FOR
CALIFORNIA CHRONICLES

"The California Chronicles series captures all the history and drama of our glorious Golden State. Generation after generation, two families struggle to tame the land—and one another—dragging my heart right along with them. With rich, descriptive prose and captivating characters, author Diane Noble raises the bar on historical fiction!"

—*Liz Curtis Higgs, best-selling author*

<hr />

"Diane Noble has accomplished much in her work to date, but nothing as enjoyable as her California Chronicles. From beginning to end, I was a willing captive to the drama unfolding before me. So sit back and enjoy a trip away, across time and miles, without ever leaving your living room! You will not be disappointed."

—*Lisa Tawn Bergren, best-selling author*

<hr />

"Diane Noble's works wrap the reader in the delight of surprise and the warmth of hearth and home. *At Play in the Promised Land* promises and delivers both."

—*Jane Kirkpatrick, award-winning author*

<hr />

"Diane Noble writes with a richness of theme, setting, and character that lingers in your heart long after the story has ended. She takes her readers on remarkable journeys of romance, redemption, and faith that can be read and enjoyed again and again."

—*Annie Jones, best-selling author*

At Play in the
Promised Land

At Play in the
Promised Land

DIANE NOBLE

WATERBROOK
PRESS

AT PLAY IN THE PROMISED LAND
PUBLISHED BY WATERBROOK PRESS
2375 Telstar Drive, Suite 160
Colorado Springs, Colorado 80920
A division of Random House, Inc.

Scripture quotations are taken from the *King James Version.*

The characters and events in this book are fictional, and any resemblance to actual persons or events is coincidental.

ISBN 1-57856-091-8

Library of Congress Cataloging-in-Publication Data

Noble, Diane, 1945-
    At play in the promised land / by Diane Noble.— 1st ed.
       p. cm. — (California chronicles ; 1911-1921)
    ISBN 1-57856-091-8
      1. Actresses—Fiction. 2. New York (N.Y.)—Fiction. 3. California—Fiction. I. Title.

PS3563.A3179765 A94 2001
813'.54—dc21   00-067312

Printed in the United States of America
2001—First Edition

10 9 8 7 6 5 4 3 2 1

This book is dedicated to my two special aunts,
who, from the time I was knee-high to a katydid,
showered me with love beyond measure
and taught me the meaning of family blessings.

Doris Talbert
and
Anna Lou Gough

I love you!

ACKNOWLEDGMENTS

Heartfelt thanks to Lisa Bergren, managing editor through all three books of the California Chronicles series. Her extraordinary skill both as storyteller and editor shines brilliantly, from original concept to finished product. Thank you, my friend, for your years of encouragement, guidance, and wisdom.

Hearty hugs to Traci DePree, substantive and line editor for this series. As always, Trace, your editorial direction, expertise, and patience are so appreciated. And to Paul Hawley, my copyeditor. You've done it again, Paul, fine-tuning this manuscript until it shines. You both are the best!

Special thanks to Patty Hostiuk, naturalist and expert on just about anywhere you might visit in the world—from Borneo to Greenland, the Galapagos to the Canary Islands. Thank you, Patty, for guiding me through the jungles of South America and letting me see the Amazon and its tributaries through your eyes.

To my precious friend Liz Curtis Higgs, loving hugs for seeing me through another writing project. Thank you for being "here" with me as I write, praying me through my days in front of the computer and, as always, dispensing wonderful fiction-writing advice and encouraging me each step of the way.

And to Tom, my husband and writing-research partner, deepest gratitude for your endless patience and loving support through my long hours of writing. I truly couldn't do any of this without you.

Finally, beloved readers, thanks to *you* for accompanying me on this journey through California's wild and wonderful early years. God bless you all!

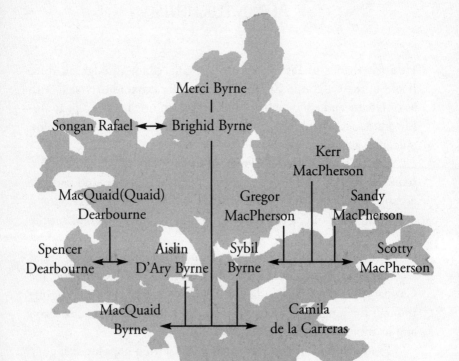

Merci Byrne

Songan Rafael ←→ Brighid Byrne

Kerr
MacPherson

MacQuaid(Quaid)
Dearbourne

Gregor
MacPherson

Sandy
MacPherson

Spencer
Dearbourne ←→ Aislin
D'Ary Byrne

Sybil
Byrne

Scotty
MacPherson

MacQuaid
Byrne ←→ Camila
de la Carreras

Rancho de la Paloma

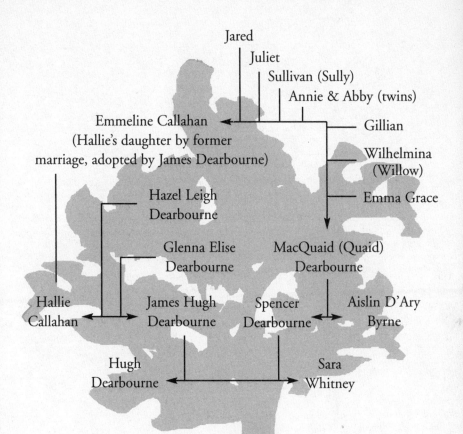

Jared
Juliet
Sullivan (Sully)
Annie & Abby (twins)

Emmeline Callahan
(Hallie's daughter by former
marriage, adopted by James Dearbourne)

Gillian

Wilhelmina
(Willow)

Hazel Leigh
Dearbourne

Emma Grace

Glenna Elise
Dearbourne

MacQuaid (Quaid)
Dearbourne

Hallie
Callahan

James Hugh
Dearbourne

Spencer
Dearbourne

Aislin D'Ary
Byrne

Hugh
Dearbourne

Sara
Whitney

*Rancho Dearbourne,
also called Sunny Mountain Ranch*

ONE

Spring 1915

Abrisk Santa Ana wind rattled the fronds of the tall palms that circled Riverview's new open-air theatre. A full moon promised; its glow already lit the eastern sky above the distant mountains. Beside the theatre dust ghosts whirled upward in a strange dance all their own.

The gusts lifted Juliet Rose Dearbourne's hair as she stood offstage awaiting her cue. Impatiently she fidgeted with her simple leather headband and straightened her long braids. From the orchestra pit the strum of Spanish guitars mixed with the haunting wail of a lone reed flute. Crickets droned from a nearby clump of sage as if attempting to drown the music of the night, wind and all.

Voices from the audience joined the cacophony but only served to make Juliet's heart beat faster in anticipation. She congratulated herself on landing the prized title role of Ramona in this performance of Helen Hunt Jackson's acclaimed story and practiced her lines silently.

Alessandro, my love… How I long for you. I see your eyes in the moonlight, I feel your nearness in the wind, I hear your voice in the bubbling brook…

The music played on. Juliet stepped slightly to the right of the stage, still hidden, but at an angle that afforded her a view of both the set and the audience. To her left rose the freshly painted proscenium with its scenery of sycamores and cactus, the adobe facade of the hacienda, and the pottery fountain in a center courtyard where the first scene would unfold. The wind gusted again, and the footlights that circled the curved stage flickered, casting an eerie light on the painted trees and adobe bricks that made up the backdrop.

She claimed this story with her entire being: lived it, breathed it,

1

dreamed it, especially the tragic role of Ramona Ortegna, half Indian and half Scottish, in love with Alessandro, a noble, full-blooded Indian.

Juliet scanned the crowd, then moved her gaze to the mountains beyond the natural bowl that formed the amphitheatre. Jagged peaks, lavender in the dying light of evening, rose skyward, and just beyond them the faint glow of the rising full moon warmed a navy sky.

The hills. The land. The focus of her family's existence. The source of their strength, her father and mother claimed, as though it were a personal gift from the Creator himself. She shrugged and stifled a smile. The irony wasn't lost on her. Playing this coveted role based on a story about the land was a calculated step in leaving home. Her parents thought that she had taken the part because its themes touched her heart. She doubted they would have let her act otherwise. But she had bigger roles in her future. This was merely a steppingstone. *Ramona* would grant Juliet freedom from her family, from this place, at last.

The music rose to a crescendo. Juliet's cue. Another glance at the audience and a deep breath and she was ready.

Just as she took her first step onstage, she could hear her impish five-year-old sister Emma Grace giggling from where she was cuddled on their father's lap in the front row. Juliet, distracted, studied her family for a moment, their faces illumined by the soft lantern light.

The Dearbournes took up the entire row, Willow, age six, and Gillian, age seven, flanking their parents, with twins Annie and Abby on Gillian's side, and her two brothers, Jared and Sully, on Willow's side. Juliet's mother, Emmeline, mouthed the words *I love you*, and beside her Juliet's father, Quaid, winked and grinned. Emma Grace, leaning against his chest, blew Juliet a kiss, then stuck out her lower lip in a pout when Juliet didn't return it.

The maestro repeated Juliet's cue. The music swelled. The crowd seemed to draw in a collective breath. Juliet tilted her chin upward and strode forward.

An hour and a half later the audience broke into thunderous applause. Juliet stood at center stage and caught her breath as a flush heated her face. The accolades were for her.

For Juliet Rose Dearbourne. *Think of it!*

She bowed. The audience clapped louder. She gracefully out-stretched her arm for the other actors to join her onstage. The crowd stood, and the applause continued. When she stepped forward to take a bouquet of wildflowers from her father, the audience cheered and whistled and stamped their feet. She bowed again, this time holding hands with the other players, her spirits soaring higher than the big round moon overhead. Then standing, she lifted her flowers outward with one hand, and with the other reached for the heavens.

The crowd clapped harder, and Juliet gave them a dazzling smile.

Moments later the theatregoers began to file from the amphitheatre to the romantic music of the Spanish guitars, and Juliet left the stage with the other actors.

A gentle touch on her arm caused her to halt, then turn.

A silver-haired woman, tall and slender, handed her a single crim-son rose. "You have promise, young Juliet," the woman said in a well-modulated voice. "Much promise indeed."

Juliet smiled, pleased that the woman had noticed.

"Someday you'll see, though, that what you *think* is promise, isn't promise at all." Then the woman laughed. She patted Juliet's hand. "But then, no one can tell you or teach you such matters. You'll need to dis-cover them yourself." She waved her fingers toward the moon and laughed again, silken and musical.

Juliet wanted to hear only accolades on this night. Not riddles. "What do you mean?" She decided the old woman must be daft as a doorknob, and judging from the dramatic hand gestures and arrogant tilt of her head, likely fancied herself an actress too.

"Ah, my dear. That's what you must discover. And I pray to God you do."

Juliet shrugged as her smile turned to a smirk. "You fancy to know an awful lot about me, yet we have never met."

"I saw your heart on this stage tonight. And I understood your soul." A gust of wind loosened some strands of hair from the pile atop her head.

Uncomfortable with the old woman's scrutiny, Juliet shook off the light, thin hand, as if brushing a dried leaf from her arm.

"Cherish your family, child," the woman said. "Cherish those who love you."

But Juliet wanted to hear no more. She spun and hurried to the forward aisle where her family waited. And she was again lost in the glory of their congratulations and their embraces.

Willow and Gillian bounced like jumping jacks beside her, yanking on her costume. Emma Grace reached up to climb into her arms. Abby and Annie stood back, looking envious. Juliet gave them a lordly glance to keep them in their places. This was her night, and she didn't hanker to share it with anyone.

Sully, a few years younger than Juliet, curled his lips in disdain, as though he couldn't be bothered with anything so inconsequential as playacting.

Jared, however, grinned and drew his sister into a rough embrace. "You made me proud, li'l sis."

After a moment, they headed up the aisle toward the exit. "Mama," Juliet said as she fell into step with Emmeline, "a stranger just came up to me. Said some of the oddest things."

"I'm sure this is the first of many, Ettie. By the time this play runs its course, all of Riverview County will have seen it. Seen you." She laughed gently. "Be prepared. You'll hear both the good and the bad. People feel compelled to tell you their opinions."

"She talked to me about my promise." She halted, and Emmeline stopped to face her. "She seemed to know me," Juliet said. "Know us. Our family. She almost reprimanded me, though in a way it reminded me of a riddle. I'm wondering if you know her…" She described the woman.

Emmeline shook her head. "She doesn't sound like anyone I know."

They began walking again, then Juliet spotted the woman striding through the back arches of the amphitheatre. "There! There she is."

The woman turned, almost as if she'd heard Juliet speak of her. Her face caught the glow of a nearby gas lamp, and she met Juliet's gaze.

Juliet's mother let out a small gasp. For a moment she didn't speak, and when she did, her voice was hushed. "Didn't you know, child? Why, that's Mairia Garden."

"Mairia Garden?" Juliet frowned. The name was familiar, but she couldn't place it.

Her mother nodded. "I read something about her in *Collier's* years ago. I never forgot the artist's rendition, the slender aristocratic look of her or that glorious halo of silver hair."

"Who is she?" Juliet was more curious than ever.

"One of the greatest opera voices of the nineteenth century," her mother said. "Mairia Garden was a household name in London and New York thirty years ago. It's said that the world-famous Manhattan Opera in New York City was built in her honor. After her voice went into decline, she turned to acting—"

Juliet didn't wait to hear the rest. She hiked her skirts to her knees and ran to the rear of the amphitheatre where she'd last seen Miss Garden.

The crowd had thinned, but the aging actress was nowhere to be found.

Mairia Garden had disappeared.

Juliet stood under one of the tall stone arches, her crossed arms clutching her waist. The wind rattled the palm fronds above her like so many dried bones and kicked up enough dust to turn the moon's glow orange. She shivered.

Her mother caught up with Juliet and circled her arm around her shoulders. "The wind's blowing something fierce tonight," Emmeline said. "A bit unusual for this early in the spring. I worry about the spring blossoms—"

"But Mairia Garden!" Juliet interrupted, unwilling to hear about her mother's beloved trees. "Mairia Garden spoke to me of my promise, and I was rude to her. Now I can't find her." She felt like crying. "I wish I could take it back."

Her mother looked disappointed in her. "I hope your regret is more than simply letting an opportunity pass for her to help you with your career."

Her mother knew her too well. Embarrassed, Juliet didn't answer. Another gust of wind caught Juliet's skirts and whipped them against her legs.

"A wise woman once said that kind words cause endless echoes in the soul—for both the speaker and the listener," her mother continued as they walked toward the carriage. "Unlike the wind, soon to die and leave silence in its wake, the memory of kind words and generous acts reverberates forever."

"Who said that?"

"I did." Emmeline laughed and grabbed Juliet's hand. Together they hurried toward the rest of the family.

At the carriage door, Juliet turned to look back at the amphitheatre just as the stagehands extinguished the gaslights that illumined the stage and the far edges of the arena. It was a strange contrast, Juliet thought briefly. The warmth and laughter of her family spilling from inside the carriage. The shell of the theatre standing ashen and empty in the moonlight.

She shrugged off the thought and settled into the carriage between her mother and Emma Grace.

Two

Emmeline shivered, though the parlor was plenty warm enough. It was the wind, the bane of her childhood, that caused her uneasiness.

The Santa Ana had continued long after the children—with the exception of Juliet, as usual—had trooped upstairs to bed. The soft murmurs and giggles of the older children now drifted from the second floor. The three youngest, Willow, Gillian, and Emma Grace, had fallen asleep in the carriage on the way home and now were tucked into their trundles. Juliet's debut that night at the outdoor theatre had worn them to a frazzle.

Outside the shutters rattled, and inside an occasional draft down the chimney sent ribbons of smoke into the room. Quaid, lost in Willa Cather's *O Pioneers!*, adjusted his round-rimmed eyeglasses, and Emmeline crossed the room to open the window a crack to help the fire's draw.

She held the lace curtain to one side. Juliet, dressed in a long white gown, slipped around the house and headed into the wind-whipped groves. The moon hung high, giving Emmeline a dusky view of the landscape. Spent orange blossoms whirled about her daughter's shoulders, mixing with blowing strands of her hair. Juliet looked like a mirage created by the wind, the moon, the ghostlike gyration of dried petals, as if she could merely lift her arms to leave the earth. Emmeline wondered if such an escape was her daughter's true wish.

The thought had nagged at her before, bringing Emmeline a restlessness of her own. She glanced across the parlor at her husband. As always, the sight of his beloved face calmed her spirits.

His lips curved in a boyish half-grin as he met her gaze. She remembered the first time he'd smiled at her like that. It had been the day she first arrived in Riverview. Here they were, nearly a quarter of a century, two heads of gray hair, and eight children later, still gazing at each other like silly sweethearts, her heart doing flip-flops just as it did the first time Quaid smiled at her.

Merciful heavens! Just to think of it! *Eight* wee ones she'd borne here in the Victorian, two boys and six girls. Jared, the eldest, was nearly twenty-two. A grown man they could be proud of. Stubborn and gentle just like his father. Though now that she considered it, each of their children was as stubborn as the day was long. Juliet, just past twenty, determined to get out on her own; Sully at seventeen wanting to be a man, to prove himself; and the sixteen-year-olds, Abby and Annie, still unsure of their place in the world but determined not to let anyone know.

She'd figured all that stubbornness must surely have come from Quaid's side of the family—the Dearbournes or perhaps the Byrnes. Not that she didn't have a fair share of grit herself.

Quaid laid his book on the table beside his high-backed chair and lifted a brow her direction.

"I was just considering our blessings," she said, then added with a laugh, "all eight of them."

He chuckled with her. "Children are a heritage of the Lord. Happy is the man that hath his quiver full of them."

"A quiver indeed. These growing, gangly children—most still elbows and skinned knees—barely fit into this big house." She crossed the room and sat down again across from her husband. "I'm thinking about one in particular whom I sense won't be with us much longer."

He looked thoughtful, his gaze still on her. "Juliet?"

"I've wondered about it before. But tonight was the first time I felt certain."

"You think she's planning to leave us?"

"I know she is. She's often talked of a career on stage."

"Sometimes I wonder if she wants to be the center of attention." Quaid didn't look pleased. "That's not a trait I admire." Then he shook his head slightly, as if bemused, and laughed. "Of course, it hasn't been easy, being one of eight children."

Emmeline leaned forward intently. "We can't know what's drawing her to this, but can it be so bad to choose such a profession, if that's what she wants? There are wholesome roles she can choose from...such as tonight's *Ramona*."

"Why can't she settle down, find a nice young man to marry? Raise a passel of children. Live on a nearby ranch. I'll give her the land."

Emmeline laughed heartily. "A ranch? Our Juliet?" She laughed again. "She doesn't care a fig about the land. Or finding a husband, for that matter." She sobered. "And as for the grandchildren you dream of, I fear I've depended too heavily on her help with her sisters. She's like a porcupine when it comes to caring for them, even the little ones. Prickly. Haughty. Does only what she's told to do, nothing more. Mostly orders the others around and never with much affection. I suspect she's afraid of getting a new dress soiled or sticky fingers in her hair. Or that she's just plumb tired of caring for three little, squirming girls and listening to the chatter of adolescent twins." Emmeline shook her head sadly. "I fear that a quiver full of children will never be Juliet's lot. She's not yet twenty-one, and already she's had her fill."

Quaid's voice was gentle. "Emmeline, don't blame yourself. You couldn't have raised eight children and built our citrus business without help. It was only proper that you depended on Juliet. In the end, she'll thank you. The responsibilities you've turned over to her have taught her discipline and hard work."

"Perhaps that's why I don't begrudge her dreaming now. Or that it's time for her to follow her dreams."

"You still need her help," he reminded her.

"Not as much as before. The twins are old enough to watch the little ones."

He smiled, removed his round-rimmed eyeglasses, and pulled out his handkerchief to wipe the lenses. "Why do I get the feeling you're leading up to something more than a mere observation about Juliet's dreams?" He replaced his spectacles and peered at her.

Emmeline laughed. "My darling, why is it you can still read my mind after all these years?"

He cocked his head and gave her another of the lopsided smiles she loved. "Perhaps, my love, because I'm fascinated by how your mind works. It's not easy to stay a step ahead. But I try." He laughed softly.

She drew in a deep breath and, letting it out, plunged ahead, "I think it's time to take seriously Juliet's dream to be on stage. She's as stubborn as they come. I think that before she decides to run off with the circus or takes some silly notion—"

He interrupted her with a sputtering sound. "Circus? Surely not!"

"I found a magazine," Emmeline explained, "something about the new moving picture shows. Dog-eared, ink-smeared. Juliet has obviously studied it day and night."

"It's not a life I want for our daughter," Quaid said, "or anyone's daughter, for that matter. From everything I've heard, Hollywood is more of a circus than those with lions, tigers, and clowns."

"Hollywood is less than a hundred miles from here—just on the far side of Los Angeles. But you're right. I've had a nagging concern that her penchant for drama might take her straight into the clutches of that mad world."

Emmeline paused, knowing she had her husband's attention. "That's exactly why I've come up with a plan for Juliet."

"Go on." He arched a brow at her.

"Before she runs off to Hollywood, I wonder if we might give her the chance to prove her grit in a completely different way."

He looked at her sharply. "How?"

"Drama school. Someplace that will allow her to grow beyond her delight in the accolades she receives on stage—but still fits her interests."

A slow smile was dawning. "If I didn't know better, I might think you've already made inquiries."

She grinned at her husband. "One of the best in the nation is in Denver. A serious drama school in the Shakespearean tradition. But more than that, the academic side is impressive. I suspect that Juliet's true love is the story itself, not just her role."

She nibbled her lip in concentration. "I noticed it when she first read *Ramona* aloud to me. There was something in her spirit I'd not seen before. Her questions about the story and characters. The truth about the theme. Her wonder about writing something with such power. None of that had to do with the part Juliet played on stage."

"And this school would give her the opportunity to write…stories?" He frowned again. "Like Willa Cather?" He held up his book.

"Perhaps plays, serious plays, such as the one taken from Helen Hunt Jackson's book. Or *Uncle Tom's Cabin*." She leaned forward again. "Think of it, Quaid. What if our daughter has the potential to change society's views through her writing? Perhaps she could even bring the truth of God's love to the world like Harold Bell Wright did in *Shepherd of the Hills*."

"Now, that's a huge jump, Em—from a girl who tonight gloried in the adulation of a hometown audience to a writer with the ability to change the world." He fell silent, studying her for a moment. "I wonder if you just want to see something in Juliet that isn't there, that there's more depth to her than simply longing for applause."

"I suppose I do long to see a greater calling for her life."

He smiled with his eyes and patted Emmeline's hand. "Tell me more."

"I've heard her stories." She leaned forward in her earnestness. "The one thing she has patience for—telling her sisters tales of wonder. I used to suspect it was merely to keep them quiet. Now I'm beginning to see that those stories are part of the fabric that makes up our daughter. We can't ignore that."

"And this school, the one in Denver…?" He leaned back in his chair, considering her. The lines in his face seemed deeper now, their shadows etched by the glow of the lamp beside him. She wondered if tonight was the time to bring up her dreams for Juliet.

"If we set aside a portion of income from the summer crop, and the winter crop brings in the expected profit…" She considered the rains of early spring, the abundance of blossoms before the fruit set and the winds came. "The winter term would fall into place nicely for Juliet, for our finances."

He leaned back and removed his eyeglasses, held them by the stems, and tapped the frames on the arm of the chair. "It will be difficult if our crops aren't as we expect. After last year's glass-wing attack—we don't know if the pest will return."

"I'm praying that our crop yields will be back to normal, Quaid. God knows our needs, and I am trusting him to provide." She settled back, abashed at using the Lord to back her argument.

Quaid wasn't swayed. "I have serious doubts about letting Juliet go into this world of drama. I understand your reasoning, but I'm not certain that she should attend a drama school. Perhaps we should send her to the university to study literature. Her marks in school were outstanding."

"I would like to mention it to Juliet. Perhaps it would keep her here a bit longer—I tell you, she's ready to spread her wings. Whether we're ready or not."

His smile was gentle. "Juliet has given much of herself to our family—sometimes kicking and screaming, but giving nonetheless. I agree that she deserves to explore a life of her own. But I must tell you, I'm opposed to drama school." He rose and came to sit beside Emmeline, clutching her hand with both of his. "That's not to say I can't be convinced. But we need more time to think this through, pray about it."

Emmeline touched his jaw and smiled into his eyes. "All right," she sighed, "but you'll consider it?"

Their eyes met, the outer edges of his crinkling into easy smile lines as he raised her hand and kissed her fingertips. "Of course."

"I have literature, books and such, on the Denver program upstairs in the secretary. Promise me you'll read through them, Quaid. I think you'll see that it's something that will suit Juliet to a tee."

He chuckled and planted a kiss on her lips. "You can be very persuasive, Em. But I still say, let's wait."

Emmeline considered her husband's words as she followed Juliet's trail through the orange grove. The wind had died to a light breeze, and the dried blossoms had now settled on the ground like new-fallen snow. She knew exactly where she would find her daughter. She stepped from the shelter of the grove and wound along the hillside. Finally, in the distance, she could see Juliet sitting on a boulder, overlooking the valley. Her chin rested in her hand, and she was so lost in her thoughts that she didn't seem to hear Emmeline's approach.

Juliet's light hair glinted in the moonlight. Her profile looked pure and untouched. Vulnerable.

Juliet turned, and the moonlight touched her porcelain skin, emphasizing the largeness of her dark eyes, the perfection of her small, even features.

"Mama...?" Juliet smiled and patted a place on the large stone. "I'm glad you came."

Emmeline brushed the dust from the boulder before she settled onto it.

Juliet grabbed Emmeline's hand, drawing it around her back and leaned against her, the way she used to do when she was a child. "I was just thinking about tonight." She laughed with delight. "I've never experienced anything quite like it."

"You've got another few weeks of performances," Emmeline said. "You may soon be grumbling about the hard work and not feel so overjoyed."

Juliet looked up at her. "Now that couldn't happen in a million years! I'm sure that opening night—especially in my first performance —will always be special, almost magical."

"You say that as though you know this play won't be your last."

She sat up and frowned. "I've always wanted to do this... You know that I have. I mean to make it a career."

"Where will you perform next?" Emmeline felt a stab of fear even as she asked it.

Her laugh was scornful. "I'm not going to stay home forever, you know. I'm nearly twenty-one. That makes me an adult." She lifted her chin with clear annoyance and pulled away slightly.

"Is it the adulation of the crowd that you enjoyed most, or the performing?"

Juliet's eyes darkened in the moonlight. "Obviously it's my craft I love—and do well—otherwise the adulation, as you call it, wouldn't have been so evident tonight." She sounded as if she was explaining the obvious to a child. As if becoming a star was a certainty. A brittle look crossed Juliet's face as she tilted her jaw.

Perhaps those deeper things Emmeline hoped for weren't in her daughter's heart after all. Only a challenge, cold and unwavering, showed now, reflecting something entirely different than what Emmeline had hoped to see.

"Of course, sweetheart," Emmeline said softly, breaking the tension between them. "Your talent shone brighter than the moon itself tonight."

Juliet looked pleased, and her lips curved upward in a sweeter-than-ever smile.

"But I must tell you," Emmeline continued, "the praise of others is short-lived. That's not what will make you happy in the end."

Juliet took her mother's hand again and leaned against her. "I know you mean well, Mama, but these are things I've already thought through. There is something that comes alive in me when I'm on a stage. I've felt that way forever." She paused, looking out across the fields. "Even when I'm merely acting out a story for my sisters."

Emmeline breathed a quick prayer for God's wisdom. If it were up to her, she would give her daughter every desire of her heart. Blurt out her plans right then for Juliet's future. But her own desires might not be what was best for Juliet, might not be God's plan for her daughter.

Juliet grinned as she turned again to her mother. "I was going to keep this a secret until the end of the play, but I think I should tell you now."

"A secret?" Sudden dread seized Emmeline's heart.

Juliet nodded, her look hopeful, eager. She leaned closer and whispered, "I'm planning to leave home as soon as the play ends."

Emmeline tried to breathe normally and smiled as though her daughter's words were the most natural sound in the world. "And where will you go?"

Juliet shrugged. "I don't know." Right then her daughter seemed so young, so naive.

"Have you prayed for wisdom?"

Her daughter chuckled at the idea. "If I ask God for wisdom, I worry that he'll keep me here on this dull land, surrounded by orange groves."

"Perhaps it is God who's placed this desire in your heart?" She hoped her daughter could at least latch on to some aspect of God's care for her.

"I have only one desire, Mama. You know that. And I don't really care how the desire got there."

"Then pray about it. Ask God to guide you."

Juliet stood and walked to the edge of the overlook. "It's easy for you and Father. God gave you what you love, this land. You can't possibly know the suffocation I feel here."

"What if I told you that we've known this? That we want to help you decide exactly what it is you're after?"

Juliet turned, her expression expectant. "I was born for the stage."

"Perhaps you've not explored other avenues for your talent."

"What do you mean?" Juliet raised an eyebrow. Emmeline knew she was baiting her, but she had to find a way to halt her wild dreaming.

Emmeline had promised Quaid that she wouldn't mention Denver to Juliet. That they would discuss their ideas for their daughter at greater length before coming to any final decisions. And they would pray about it. It had always been that way in their family. She wasn't about to change that agreement now.

She reached for Juliet's hand and squeezed it. It felt cold and small, childlike, in the big warmth of her own. "I can only tell you that your father and I know about your restless heart. Please give us time to discuss this. The three of us need to talk about your dreams, your plans, and we need to pray together."

Juliet tossed her hair across her shoulders in a gesture of defiance. She fell silent as she moved her gaze to the valley below them. "I only know I must leave," she finally said behind clenched teeth, "and the sooner the better."

When she turned to her mother, her eyes were dark, unyielding. Once more Emmeline tried to push away the earlier image of her pretty daughter, sitting in the moonlight, so full of certainty about her future, so full of...herself.

"Just promise me one thing," Emmeline said quietly.

"Anything, Mama."

"Don't ever forget this place."

She raised a well-formed brow. "That's an odd thing to say. Of course I won't forget it."

"Your roots are here. It's the land of your ancestors, so protect it."

Juliet's demeanor was serious once more, and her voice dropped. "A moment ago I thought you were about to tell me to fly. To soar where I dared go. Now your words are like scissors."

"Scissors?"

"I once saw an old woman clip a parrot's right wing after the poor thing tried to escape her yard. The parrot could only hop after that. It stayed in her yard all right, adding its bright plumage to her flower garden." She paused, then added, "Don't clip my wings, Mama, before you release me."

For a moment Emmeline held her daughter's gaze, then she nodded. "You're right, my angel. It's time for you to fly." She stood and returned to the house alone.

On the wide veranda of the tall Victorian, rising majestically into the night sky, Emmeline stopped and gazed up at the pale stars.

"Father," she breathed.

"It's time to let my daughter go. I sense it in her. In myself.

"Once, long ago, my parents let me follow my dream and prove my grit. It's time to do the same for Juliet.

"I release her into your care through all her tomorrows.

"Teach her those things she needs to know.

"But, my Father, I beg you…bring my daughter home.

"It doesn't matter that her heart's home may not be here.

"All that matters is that she finds her home in you."

Emmeline breathed in the fragrance of the spent blossoms riding on the breeze and drank in the silence of the deep night.

"All that matters for any of us," she whispered, "is that you bring us home at last."

THREE

We need to include Juliet in the discussions about her future," Emmeline said to Quaid the next morning.

Quaid turned to his wife from across their bedroom. "We still haven't decided if the drama school is the right place for her."

"She's determined to leave." Sitting on the edge of the tall four-poster, Emmeline stepped into her slippers and pulled on her house robe. "Our conversations with her have always led to the same conclusion—"

"Utter disagreement." Quaid sat in the old, scarred rocker, fastening his shoe. "Usually with Juliet stomping from the room."

"I agree. But, darling, this time more is at stake. She's planning to leave, she's told me so, as soon as *Ramona* closes. She said she doesn't even know *where* she's going—she's so eager to be on her own!" The thought distressed her all over again.

Quaid rose and walked across the room to sit beside her on the bed. "Then you're right. Let's talk with her immediately. If nothing else, agree in her presence that we want to help her decide."

He frowned, then sighed as he ran his fingers through his hair. "I suppose we don't have a lot of choice in the matter. At least if she goes to Denver, we'll know she's safe. Of course, ultimately, it depends on our winter crop." He gazed into Emmeline's eyes. "I haven't forgotten how it feels to be twenty."

Emmeline brightened. "It will lighten her heart to know we take her dreams seriously."

Quaid took her hand in his. "Tell her we need to speak with her tonight. We'll make a special effort to convince her that we have her best interests at heart."

He stood and walked to the window and pulled back the damask drape. "I saw her ride out just minutes ago." He turned back to Emmeline. "Sometimes she reminds me of Merci when she was young. She often rode out across the fields early in the morning. There's a stubbornness in Juliet that scares me—knowing what happened to Merci."

Emmeline walked across the room to stand near her husband. "Juliet isn't Merci, Quaid. She's known the love of her father, for one thing. And the stability of a big family who adores her."

"Merci had our grandparents. And Brighid. A mother couldn't have loved a daughter more."

"But eventually—no matter the tragedy of the past—Brighid had to let Merci go. Had to let her child walk the path on which only God could accompany her."

They stared at each other for a moment, then Quaid nodded slowly, a sad smile playing at the corner of his mouth.

Quick tears stung Emmeline's eyes. "I think we just answered our own question. We must let her go."

Quaid wrapped his arms around his wife and drew her close. She felt the warm thud of his heartbeat and the rise and fall of his breathing. "She's the first one to leave," he murmured. "I would give my life to keep her close, to keep her from harm."

"So would I." Emmeline pulled back so she could look him in the eye. "But we won't always be around to protect her, Quaid. Whether we let her go now or years from now, Juliet must learn life's lessons on her own." She pictured the colorful parrot in the old woman's backyard. "There are things worse."

Still arm in arm, they gazed across the fields to the mountains beyond. His eyes were bright when he turned back to her, as if he'd settled something in his heart. He grinned. "Let's ride after her. I have an idea where to look."

She laughed. "I haven't ridden in ages, Quaid."

He caught her hand and gave her a gentle pull toward the wardrobe, then, with a chuckle, withdrew her riding habit. "My favorite. The color matches your eyes."

"You're certain we'll be able to find Juliet?"

He laughed again, his eyes bright. "If we don't, no matter. I'll simply glory in riding with my wife at my side. Just as we used to do years ago."

She reached for the habit and gave him a playful shove to the door. "Out, my man. If it no longer fits, I'd rather discover the calamity myself—not with an audience."

He quirked a brow. "You're more beautiful than the day I met you, Mrs. Emmeline Amity Callahan Dearbourne. It doesn't really matter whether the habit fits like a hand in a glove or whether you must don blue jeans and one of my old shirts. You'll be glorious either way!"

Emmeline descended the stairs a few minutes later. Surprisingly, the riding habit fit. A bit snug here and there but passable for the morning's ride.

Quaid waited at the bottom of the staircase, grinning up at her, his gaze full of admiration. "I've saddled the horses, ma'am," he said with an exaggerated bow.

Three giggles sounded at the doorway leading to the dining room. Gillian and Willow stood, eyes big, watching their parents. Emma Grace scampered across the entry hall and straight into Emmeline's arms.

"I wanna go too," she said, resting her head against Emmeline's neck. "Where are you going?"

Laughing, Emmeline kissed her baby's cheek. "Now, how do you know you want to come along if you don't know where we're going?"

"I just wanna go too," Emma Grace insisted.

"You can't go without breakfast. I baked orange cakes yesterday just for you." She gave her daughter a mock frown as she set her down near the other two. "But you must promise to save one for me."

Emma Grace stuck out her bottom lip. "But I wanna go."

The twins had joined the others in the entry. "Morning, Mama," Annie said cheerfully. She gave her father a quick hug and yawned. "What's for breakfast?"

"Orange cakes," Emma Grace said importantly. "But we gotta save one for Mama."

"And Papa," Quaid added with a grin.

"Where are you going?" Abby asked, her yawn matching her sister's.

"We're going riding," Quaid said. "Hoping to catch up with Juliet. She left a bit ago."

"She rode up to Bald Mountain," Abby said.

"If that's where she headed, that's where we'll go too." Quaid took Emmeline's arm and started for the door.

"There was a rock slide up there last week," Annie said, looking worried. She and the others followed their parents out to the wide porch.

Gillian tilted her head authoritatively. "Jared said it was cleaned up."

"Don't you worry, missy," Quaid said, tousling her hair. "We'll turn around if we come to a pile of rubble." Then he stooped to give each of the girls a hug.

The gesture touched Emmeline. He wasn't afraid to show affection with his children, as some men were. She felt it made him more of a man. Gillian clung to her father's hand as he walked out to the horses, her twisted foot dragging. Her face was dimpled into a smile as her papa tousled her hair again, then kissed the tip of her nose.

Emmeline stepped into the stirrup and swung her leg over the Appaloosa. After settling into the saddle, she blew the girls a kiss. At nearly the same instant, Sully and Jared burst through the front door to join their siblings on the porch.

Jared swung Emma Grace into the air with a toss that caused her to giggle and squeal. The last scene before the horses turned down the road leading from the Victorian was the brood, all laughter and hoots, Emma Grace atop Jared's strong shoulder, Willow poking Sully and scampering away to hide. And Gillian, looking pensive as she leaned against the railing, chin in hands, staring after her parents.

Blessed is the man—and woman—with a quiver full, she thought with a laugh of her own. She nudged the mare in the flanks and quickly moved behind Quaid on his tall sorrel. Though gentle and strong, her mount wasn't particularly nimble of foot, but she felt secure following Quaid and his stout horse.

The sun was on its upward sweep, and the day promised splendor. A covey of quail scurried from beneath a clump of red-barked manzanita. From some scrub pines, jays scolded a ground squirrel, and overhead a hawk soared, its shadow passing over the trail, over Quaid, then over Emmeline.

She shivered at the strange apparition, then lifted her eyes to the creature itself. Its tail gleamed russet in the sun, its wing feathers a golden glint, stretched out sure and strong as they caught the wind.

She studied the hawk, rejoicing in its flight. How would it feel to rise on the breeze? Weightless. Soaring. No longer encumbered by gravity, by the things that anchored a creature to earth. As she watched the hawk catch the thermals and lift even higher, the wind that always had bothered her didn't seem like such a fearful thing. She wanted to laugh at it, the nemesis of her childhood that caused shivers even now.

Emmeline whispered a prayer for her daughter, that she would know the glory of soaring flight. "That she would be lifted," as written in ancient times by Abbess Hildegard of Bingen, "like a feather on the breath of God."

Juliet reached the end of the trail and slid from her horse's back to walk out to the overlook. She stood, facing the rancho lands of her ancestors in the valley far below her, the morning sun beating hard on her shoulders.

Often Juliet came here to write in her journal in the early morning hours, before she was needed to watch her sisters or to help out in the kitchen or gardens. She left behind all thoughts about the ranch, her brothers and sisters, her responsibilities, as surely as she closed the door on the stables every morning.

Instead she recorded thoughts, prayers, even poetry, about her dreams. Her longings. Her desire to leave. She sat on a flat slab of granite and pulled out her worn journal and flipped through a few pages to the place she'd left off the day before.

Today it's a certainty, she wrote. *I will leave soon. For the first time ever, last night I sensed my mother's blessing. I think she finally understands my heart. I can only hope that she'll talk Father into agreeing.*

Now that I've decided when, the question remains, where?

I must find Mairia Garden. As soon as I finish my role as Ramona, I will try every means possible to find her, even if it means hiring a private investigator.

She looked up and smiled at the thought. Private detective? She pictured Sherlock Holmes, from her favorite of Sir Arthur Conan Doyle's books, and giggled. A pipe-smoking, cape-shrouded Englishman was certainly not what she had in mind. Balding, rumpled, frayed collar. She could think of nothing romantic about such a person. But it didn't matter as long as he was someone who could find the aging diva.

Closing the journal with a snap, Juliet stood and stretched, ready to remount for the ride back down the trail. She had a foot in the stirrup, ready to swing onto the saddle, when the sound of horses' hooves and voices in the distance carried toward her.

She turned and walked to the lookout once more. There, below her on the trail, were two riders. She squinted, then grinned. It was her mother and father.

Their timing couldn't be better. She headed back to her horse, planning to ride down the trail to meet them.

That was when the strange rumbling began, faint at first, then louder. The ground shook beneath her, and she crouched, expecting to be thrown to the sun-warmed soil. But just as suddenly as it had begun, the earthquake stopped. Around her the air was strangely hushed. Even the birds had fallen silent.

Carefully, Juliet stood. She laughed nervously, glancing around. Her horse nickered, flattening its ears, and danced to one side.

"It's all right, girl," she whispered, patting the velvet between the mare's eyes. "It's all right."

She mounted and nudged the horse to the overlook. There was no sign of her parents or their horses. Frowning, she stepped closer and noticed a plume of dust rising from one of the switchbacks on the trail.

For a moment she stared in disbelief. Dust? Then she saw the pile of boulders on the trail, covering twisted oaks and broken pines.

She dug her heels into the mare's flanks. They raced down the trail, but before they reached the switchback, the terrible groan of another rock slide carried toward her.

FOUR

Emmeline remembered the first time she'd ridden this trail with Quaid. As bright as day it had been, the moon a glowing orb that rose while they watched, brighter it seemed than a thousand lanterns.

Just like now, she realized, looking into his beloved face as he bent over her. She longed to circle her arms around his neck and bring him closer, this man she'd loved nearly all her life. But she couldn't move. So she caressed him with her gaze. Little things came to her unbidden. How his jaw was sandpaper-rough at night. How he smelled of pine after his bath. How his eyes sometimes held a light that his grandfather said was the hue of Irish seas.

Strange, she'd never noticed the glow that had settled behind him, just as it had on the mountains in the distance, and even through the sky above where the hawk circled still, its wings now golden in the sunlight.

Wild beauty. The words came to her, an echo from the past. *A golden and wild beauty.*

Quaid had brought her to this place all those years ago to teach her something about the beauty of God's creation. And she'd seen it! In the well of stars, the tiny red spider eyes, the deer that bounded through a thicket. In the beauty of the stillness that fed her soul. Quaid's face, touched by the moonlight, the promise of love in his Irish-seas eyes, had changed her world.

She wanted to smile at him now, to tell him what his love had meant to her all those years, meant to her now, but his face was beginning to melt into the golden glow around him, through him.

Now there was another face near his. Juliet, her dark eyes filled with fear.

No, my little one, don't be afraid! Don't ever be afraid again.

23

There is One with you—with you both—who loves you more than I can possibly love you. He is here now. He will remain with you. He will walk with you. He will carry you.

Crying, Juliet touched her mother's face. Father and daughter spoke to each other. Emmeline couldn't hear the words but knew instinctively that one of them would go for help.

She didn't want either to leave. How could she tell them? Her time was short, and she wanted to spend her last few breaths looking on their beloved faces.

Quaid, looking deep into her eyes, seemed to understand. He gave a slight nod to Juliet, and they both moved closer. Emmeline felt her upper body being carefully moved until she was cradled in their arms. Emmeline tried to smile at them. *Dry your tears, beloved! This isn't the time for sadness.* She felt the movement of their shoulders as they held her and cried.

The strange glow became brighter.

Before looking to the source of the glow, she touched Quaid's face with her mind, caressing his temple, running her fingers through his hair. Remembering his smile.

Then her heart touched the sweet profile of Juliet's cheek. Remembering the baby-fresh smell of her as an infant. Her first word. Her first tottering step. Her refusal to cry when she fell down.

Odd, the circle that Emmeline now saw so clearly.

Juliet cuddled Emmeline in her arms as she neared her last breath. Just as Emmeline had held the tiny newborn Juliet moments after she drew in her first.

The light grew brighter, and Emmeline felt herself lifting away from them.

One last look.

Merciful heavens! That smile! Quaid's smile.

He touched her face and breathed, "I love you, Em."

Oh my darling! I love you.

Then with hope, with utter joy, she moved her gaze to the face of Another.

And she was caught by the wind and lifted.

She was soaring, yes, *soaring!* on rolling waves of wind. Powerful waves. Sturdy waves. Cresting, billowing, cradling her.

Wind? Ah, yes, it was truly an awesome, fearful thing. How could it be otherwise? It was the very breath of her Lord!

She threw back her head and laughed, her voice joining the music of the heavens, the choir of angels and stars lifting voices made of purest love. Singing, just as they had from the beginning of time.

"It can't be," Quaid whispered hoarsely. "It can't be!" He moved his eyes back to Emmeline's face, keeping his gaze away from her broken and twisted body, away from the boulder that crushed her. From where he knew the Appaloosa was buried beneath the rubble. "Not now, Em! We didn't have a chance to grow old together. It's not time…"

"We must get someone to help us," Juliet said, her voice a monotone. "You must ride to the ranch. Get Sully and Jared. A wagon. I'll stay here with"—her voice cracked—"with Mama."

Leave? He stared at his daughter, trying to comprehend her meaning. "I can't leave. You go for your brothers." He looked across the valley toward the ranch. "Don't tell anyone what's happened. Especially Gillian, Willow, and Emma Grace. Don't say a word about…" He frowned, unable to finish. For a moment he stared at Juliet, gathering his thoughts. "About what's happened," he finally said. "Just tell them there's been an accident."

Juliet started toward her horse. "We'll bring blankets."

"Yes," he said. "We must keep her warm." Then he shook his head, staring at his daughter, thinking of the ludicrousness of his statement. But how could he not think of caring for his wife, keeping her warm, happy, protected from harm? Wrapping her in a blanket if she was ill. Laying a fire if she was cold. Bringing her a cup of water if she was thirsty. For decades she was always his first consideration. How could it be otherwise? "That's not what I meant, of course."

His daughter turned away from him to swing her leg over the saddle. A moment later the sound of hoofbeats echoed from the trail, then faded and disappeared.

Quaid still held Emmeline in his arms. He rocked her now, bending low to rest his cheek on her forehead.

"Emma," he whispered, "how can I let you go?" Racking sobs shook him. "I can't. I can't." He lifted her close to his heart and wrapped his arms around her. He didn't move until he heard the distant creak of wagon wheels heading up the trail.

He buried his head in her hair and let his tears flow. Then gently, he pillowed her shoulders against a smooth stone. Removing his jacket, he covered her, tucking the sleeves under her, the collar around her beautiful face.

When his sons and Juliet rounded the corner, he rose to meet them. He was calm now, as he needed to be. His children no longer had their mother. It was up to him to see them through these worst days of their young lives.

Five

On the fourth day following Emmeline's death, the Dearbourne and Byrne families entered the family graveyard in small, hushed groups. The wind blew from the east, billows of soft gusts rustling the pepper trees. A gathering of goldfinches warbled from a scrub pine a short distance away, and chipmunks chattered and scurried among the rocks.

Juliet glanced at a scrub jay scolding them from a manzanita bush and wondered how its yammering could be so ordinary, how the haze-brightened sky behind it could be so brilliant in the midst of such dark sorrow.

She stood to one side and slightly behind the others. Arms crossed, she set her lips tight, determined not to let anyone see her cry. Her father was squarely in her line of vision, his shoulders stooped, his hair looking grayer than it had just three days earlier. Gillian clung to his left hand, her twisted foot causing her to lean toward him for balance. More than ever, the girl reminded Juliet of a little gray titmouse, round-eyed and filled with birdsong, too fresh from the nest to be aware of her broken wing, her inability to fly.

Willow clung to their father's right hand with a white-fisted grip. She nibbled on her lower lip as if trying to comprehend the meaning of the casket, the service, the weeping.

To one side of the group stood her Grandmother Aislin and Grandfather Spence, on the other Grandmother Hallie, holding Emma Grace, and Grandfather Jamie, his big arm wrapped around both. Though they weren't weeping—Juliet assumed for Emma Grace's sake—their eyes were red-rimmed and hollow with grief.

Juliet looked away, unwilling to witness the raw need of her family. She was having difficulty enough bearing her own need.

Great-grandfather MacQuaid Byrne's frail, skeletal frame trembled as he took his place near the polished wooden casket, plain but for the spray of morning glories. He pulled out his handkerchief, wiped his face, and blew his nose.

"Aye, my beloved family, we have known our share of sorrow," he said, raising his eyes heavenward. "This day, as we say good-bye to sweet Emmeline, surely I think my heart might break again from the sorrow of it." His piercing eyes watered again. "We must consider the joy in this, our darkest hour. Emmeline joins those who have gone before her.

"There is my beloved Camila standin' at heaven's gates, reachin' out to hug her precious Emmeline. Oh, how she loved our Quaid's wife." He paused, his tears flowing freely and unashamedly. "Aye, and don't forget the woman who'd become a mother to her since Emmeline's own was a continent away. Our dear Aunt Gertie." He smiled. "I'm sure heaven brightened a few shades when Gert Hill arrived." He chuckled and shook his head slowly.

"Emmeline's own Grandmama Sara was there too, waiting to welcome her granddaughter with a joyous embrace as the angels sang." He paused, reaching for his handkerchief to blow his nose. He wiped his eyes, then stuffed the folded cloth back into his hip pocket.

Around Juliet, people wept. Brighid circled an arm around Merci's waist, and Brighid's husband, Songan, moved close to wrap his arms around them both. For more than twenty years Merci had been her mother's closest friend. Her weeping was silent, but her shoulders shook from the effort to contain her sorrow.

"Throughout the decades," MacQuaid Byrne continued, "we have held dear that glorious Scripture from the prophet Habakkuk. We've read it during times of sorrow…also during times of great joy. It was much loved by our Emmeline." He paused. "She never forgot the day she heard me read it first—in the family chapel when we welcomed her into the family and gave her to the Lord. She was a wee child, all of four years herself that day."

He cleared his throat, looked up at the sky, and began to utter the words, his voice filled with more sadness than Juliet had heard before.

"Although the fig tree shall not blossom,
neither shall fruit be in the vines;
the labour of the olive shall fail,
and the fields shall yield no meat;
the flock shall be cut off from the fold,
and there shall be no herd in the stalls…"

Speaking as though the words were carved in his heart, not just printed on a page in the large family Bible, he went on.

"Yet I will rejoice in the LORD,
I will joy in the God of my salvation.
The LORD God is my strength,
and he will make my feet like hinds' feet,
and he will make me to walk upon mine high places."

Several moments of silence followed his words. Great-grandfather turned his big, white-bearded head toward the family, steadying himself with his cane as he peered into their faces, one by one. "Our Emmeline is walking in those high places…places more fragrant than the orange blossoms that cover her trees, places more beautiful than the far hills that frame her beloved California skies."

He paused, then looked down at the children. With great effort, he leaned against the staff with both hands, his heavy-eyed gaze moving from Juliet's face to those of her brothers and sisters. He gestured for them to come nearer.

Jared stepped forward, his shoulders back as though he, like Juliet, refused to cry, to mourn. A moment later Sully followed, white-faced, thin-lipped. His dark-rimmed eyes seemed filled with a strange anger.

The twins and the younger children, after letting go of their father, trailed behind. After a minute's hesitation, Juliet strode to Grand-mother Hallie and took Emma Grace from her arms. She placed the little girl's feet squarely on the ground and led her toward their great-grandfather.

After looking at Juliet for a long moment, he said to them, "Let's bow in prayer."

Juliet noticed that not one of her brothers and sisters disobeyed. Except her. The seven children lowered their heads and folded their hands.

"We bring these our children to you once again," Great-grandfather said. "We give them to you again, asking for your love and protection to see them through this loss.

"We ask that you remind these little ones every day of their lives that their mother loved them more than life itself…and that her prayers for them never once changed. She wanted them to grow in knowledge of you, our heavenly Father, to learn of you, to let your love fill their hearts today and always.

"We ask you too, Father," her great-grandfather said, "to wrap your arms of comfort and strength around all the others who loved Emmeline, especially her mother and stepfather, Hallie and Jamie. Her friend Merci. Her husband, Quaid. Seldom have we seen a love as strong as theirs, as filled with the beauty of your love and theirs for each other…"

Juliet heard her father choke with grief. Without awaiting the remainder of the service, the lowering of the casket into the grave, the first handful of earth to be cast onto the morning glories, she ran. Unheeding of the tears that flowed freely now, she ran as fast and hard as she could away from the graveyard, away from the family chapel, until finally she reached the hillside where she'd spoken to her mother just nights before.

She was breathing hard from the long run, and her muscles ached from the exertion. It seemed insignificant compared to the ache in her heart. She stood for a while and gazed at the mountains, the slant of the setting sun turning them golden. Too numb to cry, to move, to think, she remained as the mountains turned lavender, then gray, and finally midnight blue. Shivering in the growing chill, she thought about heading back down the path to the house where she knew the extended family, from the oldest to the youngest, had gathered for supper and solace, especially to talk of their memories of Emmeline.

It made her angry that her mother wasn't here to join them. She'd noticed the anger on Sully's face at the graveside service too. She didn't condemn him for it; rather, she understood him. God had taken their mother too soon. What would they do without her, this passel of motherless children?

What would *she* do without her mother? Juliet swallowed back the sting behind her eyes and considered her loss. Her mother listened to her dreams, didn't laugh or take them lightly. Who would be there for her now?

The sky was exploding into a canopy of stars. Juliet leaned back and gazed upward, at first wondering about heaven, about her mother and if she might be watching her family now or if she was too busy visiting with those Great-grandfather had spoken of. The thought caused a stab of envy. Why should the heavenly hosts be graced with her mother's presence when she was so needed here on earth?

Juliet felt like raging at God, reminding him of his mistake. Her mother would never have the chance to watch Juliet walk down the aisle in a bridal gown, would never hold the grandchildren Juliet might bear someday.

She would miss watching Juliet follow her dream onstage. Fresh tears flowed. It was so unfair. She studied the dark skies, crowded with stars, that place to the east where the moon would soon rise. After a moment, through her watery veil of tears, she saw a shooting star fall. Momentarily distracted, she breathed a little easier as she trailed it with her eyes. Her mind cleared as she began to consider her own future.

She needed more than ever to get away—to leave this pain behind. At least on a stage she could be someone else, wouldn't have to constantly contend with this aching sense of loss. Last night she had played *Ramona* as if all was well with the world, and for a while it had been. And the wild applause afterward had helped her forget for a moment her sorrow and loss, the emptiness that too often drove her to her knees in deep racking sobs.

The stage brought her such joy. The contrast brought a deep-felt certainty that her plan to leave was right.

If she left, she wouldn't have to see the pale, sad faces of her brothers and sisters, a constant reminder of the vacuum in their hearts. And they wouldn't have to be reminded of the same in her. Perhaps she would be doing them all a kindness by leaving.

She drew in a shaky breath. Of course, that was exactly what she should do. Feeling better than she had in the tragic days since her mother's death, she stood and brushed off her hands.

She would complete *Ramona*, find Mairia Garden to ask for her help, and be merrily on her way. She looked up at the spangled sky once more and turned to walk back to the house, at peace with her decision.

She had taken only a few steps when a rustling in the groves caught her attention. "Who's there?" she demanded.

"Ettie?" a small voice called out. "I been lookin' for you."

Juliet frowned. "Emma Grace? Honey, is that you?"

The sounds of sniffling carried toward her.

Juliet rushed into the dark of the grove, her only thought that her little sister might be hurt. "Where are you?"

The small figure lay crumpled at the base of an orange tree, barely visible in the starlight. She sniffled again.

Juliet hurried toward Emma Grace, stooped, and gathered her into her arms. "What are you doing out here all alone?" The child was shivering, the skin on her thin arms cold to the touch. Juliet gathered her closer and stood to carry her to the house.

"I don't want to go back, Ettie." Her voice was muffled against Juliet's chest, her small arms clinging to Juliet's neck.

"You're freezing. Of course you must go back."

"Mama's not there. It's her I need."

Juliet caught her breath. Since their mother's death, their father had handled the tears and questions and heartaches. She didn't know the first thing about comforting her brothers and sisters. It was difficult enough finding solace for herself.

With a hard sigh, she returned to the boulder and sat down, plopping Emma Grace in her lap. Her sister snuggled closer, still crying softly. Juliet circled her arms around the little girl to keep her warm. She might not know the first thing about mending the child's broken heart, but she could try to keep her from catching cold.

Emma Grace's weepy eyes and running nose were causing an expanding wet circle on Juliet's voile bodice. She tried to shift the child slightly so the dress wouldn't be spoiled, but Emma Grace was too heavy to move without jostling her, so Juliet gave up and rested her cheek on the top of Emma Grace's head. "It's going to be all right," she murmured, not knowing what else to say.

"I want Mama," Emma Grace sobbed. "I'm scared wifout her."

I am too, baby, she wanted to say but thought better of it. "I'm here," she said instead. "You don't need to be scared. You've got brothers and sisters who love you. You've got Papa. You've got me."

Emma Grace pulled back and looked up at her sister with big teary eyes. "Everybody says you'll be going away someday. Even Mama said it."

Juliet didn't answer, just pulled the little girl closer.

"I'm scared you'll go away just like Mama."

At her sister's words, Juliet felt her dreams die a little inside her. "I'm here now," she said weakly. "Isn't that all that matters?"

Emma Grace's gaze was fixed on Juliet's. "Can I sleep wif you tonight, Ettie?"

Juliet considered the myriad elbows and knees, the tossing and turning. "You'll be more comfortable in your own little trundle," she said lamely. "Honest, Emma Grace. You'll sleep much, much better."

Emma Grace's lip trembled, and she looked away without answering. The child's despair made Juliet's stomach twist. She thought she might be sick. "Besides," she went on with false cheer, "your sisters will miss you if you sleep with me."

Emma Grace turned toward her again, and for the first time in three days her eyes lost the blank look of sadness. "I have a idea." She sat up. "Let's all sleep together in your big bed. Gillian and Willow and even the twins."

"There's not room," Juliet said. It might indeed help the girls get through the night of their mama's funeral, but there was no way anyone would sleep in such a pile. She shuddered.

"There is room!" Emma Grace said. "I know there is! Me and Gillian and Willow and you can sleep in your bed. The twins can make pallets on the floor." She actually smiled. "We can pretend we're camping. Just like that time Grandpa Spence took us."

"I don't think so, honey," Juliet said. "I've got an idea," she began, changing subjects. "How about if I practice my lines for *Ramona*? You always liked helping me."

Emma Grace sighed and leaned against Juliet as if totally uninterested. She popped her thumb in her mouth and twisted a lock of her hair with her other hand. Juliet rocked her slightly back and forth and hummed a lullaby that her mother used to sing to them.

"Sing it," Emma Grace demanded. "Like Mama does."

Memories of being held in her mother's lap flooded over her. Juliet bit her lip, then nodded. "All right, but you must sing it with me," she said.

"Sleep, baby, sleep!" Emma Grace murmured the words, her big eyes fixed on the starlit sky. *"Our cottage vale is deep; the little lamb is on the green, with woolly fleece so soft and clean. Sleep, baby, sleep!"*

Emma Grace sucked her thumb noisily and leaned her head against Juliet, her eyelids fluttering closed, heavy with fatigue. The child's sweet warmth filled a place deep in Juliet's soul. A place she hadn't known was there. The threat of tears stung behind her eyes, and she blinked them away before they could form and spill.

"Sleep, baby, sleep!" Juliet sang in a whisper. *"Thy rest shall angels keep, while on the grass the lamb shall feed, and never suffer want or need. Sleep, baby, sleep!"*

She paused between verses, thinking that if her sister slept, she would end the lullaby there. But Emma Grace was now studying Juliet's face, unblinking, solemn.

"Sleep, baby, sleep!" Juliet went on, softly. *"Down where the woodbines creep…"*

"What's a woodbine?" Emma Grace always asked the question of their mother. She asked it again now.

"It's like honeysuckle."

Emma Grace sucked her thumb for a moment, frowning, then pulled it out. "Or like morning glories, Mama says."

"Yes, a pretty vine."

"Vines wrap around things. And stay put, even on a wall."

"Yes."

"And never die. Just like Mama's morning glory."

"Mama planted the one by our porch years ago. Long before you were born."

"It will always be here."

Juliet nodded. "If someone waters it."

"And pinches off the dead leaves. Mama says that's what you have to do to those stubborn ol' woodbines. That's what Mama always calls them. Stubborn ol' woodbines."

"And Mama knew everything there is to know about plants and trees."

The thumb popped back into Emma Grace's mouth. Juliet started to sing again, but Emma Grace sat up and gave her another steady, serious gaze. "If you water Mama's woodbine, I'll pick the brown leaves. Then it won't die. We'll keep it nice for Mama."

"Let's sing the rest," Juliet said softly after several beats of her heart.

Emma Grace lay against her and closed her eyes again. "Sing it like Mama always does, Ettie. I'm tired."

"Be always like the lamb so mild," Juliet sang, remembering her mother's face, remembering the warmth of her arms, the rhythm of her rocking chair, the sound of her voice.

"A kind, and sweet, and gentle child," she whispered. *"Sleep, baby, sleep!"*

Somewhere in the distance a mockingbird called, clear and sweet, above the voice of the breeze. Juliet planted a soft kiss on Emma Grace's forehead. Her hair still smelled of almond and aloe soap from last night's bath. The child sighed and snuggled closer in her sleep, her thumb falling from her mouth as her muscles relaxed.

The mockingbird trilled again.

Six

With a heavy sigh, Juliet pinned a pair of Sully's drawers to the clothesline. Next she pulled Emma Grace's favorite blue-striped Dutch suit from the laundry basket and clipped it into place beside the drawers. The wind sailed through the rows of clothes she'd already hung, snapping them with sharp, wet cracks.

Ramona had closed five months earlier, and Juliet was no closer to leaving home than she'd been before the play started. Every waking minute seemed filled with cooking, cleaning, laundry—either performing the tasks herself or enlisting her sisters and brothers to help. She was too exhausted at night to lift her pen and write a single thought in her journal.

Her responsibilities seemed even more overwhelming since school had begun three weeks ago. The twins, Gillian, and Willow were gone from sunrise to sundown, needing to ride by horseback to the one-room schoolhouse run by Cousin Merci near the hacienda at Rancho de la Paloma. A ways for the younger ones to ride, but the twins, in their final year before graduation, kept an eye on them.

Juliet pinned the hem of Emma Grace's small white gown onto the line, annoyed to realize that she found the fresh smell of the damp garment, with its fragrance of soap and wind-whipped cotton cloth, pleasant. Next she would be finding pleasure in rolling out pie dough, she thought with a grimace, or in peeling red potatoes and snapping beans. She pulled a clothespin from her mouth and jammed it onto the corner of Jared's square handkerchief. And dreamed of the day she would finally leave. She chuckled, hoping it would surely be before she began finding gratification in turning the soil, picking oranges, or some other abysmally dull task.

Secretly, she'd already written to a private investigator, a man by the name of Clay MacGregor, whose name she found in the back pages of the Riverview *Gazette*. The advertisement said that though he was new in town, Mr. MacGregor came with impeccable references and years of experience. She had asked to meet with him at his earliest convenience about the important matter of finding Miss Mairia Garden. The thought of his return letter—and the freedom it might bring—kept her days bearable.

"Ettie, Ettie, Ettie!" Emma Grace ran down the hillside toward the clothesline, her pigtails flying in the wind.

With another sigh, she turned to greet the exuberant five-year-old. Most days the child nearly wore her out. And ever since the night of their mother's funeral, Emma Grace had slept in the same big bed as Juliet. The child was a jumble of elbows and knees and thumb-sucking sounds through the night.

The little girl's cheeks were bright with exertion, and she puffed breathlessly when she reached Juliet, who promptly handed her the clothespin bag.

"You might as well get to your chores while you catch your breath," Juliet admonished, giving the child a stern look. "I had to take on this chore myself because you'd disappeared."

Emma Grace reached into the canvas bag and pulled out two wooden pins, each twice the size of her thumb. Tucking them in her mouth, she picked up a wet nightgown and shook it out with a snap. As she stepped onto a small footstool, the cotton gown dragged across the ground, picking up bits of dried grass. Within a half-second, it twisted into a lump, clinging to the line with the two pins. Juliet didn't want to destroy the look of pride on the child's face, so she left it. She could always return later to brush off the debris and straighten the gown.

Juliet reached for one of Jared's heavy woolen socks. "Now, what's your news?"

"I ain't gonna work and talk at the same time—"

"I'm not going to."

"Gonna what?" Emma Grace reached for the matching sock.

"*I'm not* instead of ain't. *Going,* instead of gonna."

"Oh." Emma Grace hooked the toe of the sock over the line, stuck on the clothespin, stood back, and grinned proudly.

"Go on."

Emma Grace let out a huffy sigh. "I heard Papa say something important. It's a secret."

"He told you it's a secret?"

The little girl shook her head solemnly. "He doesn't know I heard his secret."

"Were you eavesdropping?" She frowned. "You know better than that."

"I didn't mean to hear. I just did, that's all." Her thumb moved toward her mouth.

Juliet caught her hand and, stooping, drew her close. "You sound worried about whatever it was that you heard."

"Papa's gonna go to Brazil." She stared at Juliet. "I don't know where that is."

"Brazil? Are you sure?"

Emma Grace still looked worried, just as she always did when someone mentioned leaving, even when heading to school or to Riverview for supplies. "I'm sure."

Juliet picked up the shirt, her heart pounding a slow beat of worry. "That can't be right."

Emma Grace stuck her shoulders back in a proud posture. "I heard Sully tellin' Papa that there's a new 'riety of oranges in Brazil. They'll make our groves stronger. I heard him say so with my own ears."

"But Father didn't actually say he was going there, did he?" Then she laughed. Emma Grace had the propensity to stretch stories. Lately she'd even begun to make up imaginary playmates.

"I heard him say it, Ettie. Honest, I did."

"Papa wouldn't leave us. Not now, baby." She couldn't imagine such a thing and laughed again to relieve Emma Grace's fears. And her own.

She was wrong. Juliet knew it the minute her father called a family meeting the next morning at breakfast. He said they would talk about something very important the following Saturday night, so no one was to make any other plans.

She tried to catch her father by himself to ask, but he was never without one of her brothers or sisters. So she stewed and fumed and waited, certain that she would be left alone to care for the entire family while he gallivanted to South America. She planned to stand up to him, let him know in no uncertain terms that he could hire a nanny to take her place because she was leaving too.

Then she thought of Emma Grace, how frightened she would be if they both left.

On Saturday night, the family filed into the parlor. The evening was cold, so Quaid set some small sticks of dried citrus in the iron stove and lit the kindling. Though the fire blazed, it did nothing to warm the empty chill of their mother's absence. No one sat in Emmeline's high-backed chair or moved her half-finished quilt top folded neatly by the sewing basket. Even her gold-rimmed eyeglasses remained atop the basket, resting next to the floral-embossed sewing scissors. As if she'd set them there that morning.

The twins took their place on the horsehair sofa and settled back, unusually quiet and looking worried. Sully slumped to the floor, leaning against a footstool made from an old army camel saddle, a gift from Grandfather Spence years before. Emma Grace crawled into Juliet's lap on the settee, and Gillian and Willow scooted in beside them, one on either side, their skinny, stocking-covered legs sticking straight out in front of them.

A hush fell over the room as their father, standing by the stove, turned to face them, hands clasped behind his back.

Before he could speak, Emma Grace said in a quiet voice. "We already know what you're gonna say."

"Going to," Juliet corrected.

The worry lines seemed etched in their father's face. He smiled wearily down at his youngest child. "What is it you're so certain I'm about to say, little one?"

"I heard you and Sully—"

"What have I told you about eavesdropping?" Quaid interrupted.

Emma Grace wound the tip of her braid around her index finger, letting her gaze drift toward the carpeted floor. "Not to listen."

Quaid crossed the room and knelt before the settee. He gently lifted Emma Grace's face, and Juliet saw deep concern in his eyes. Again she was certain that he wouldn't leave them. How could he?

Finally he sighed and said, "It happens that what you heard is right."

Juliet's heart caught in her throat. "It's true then?"

Her father gave her an almost imperceptible nod, then stood and included them all in what he said next. "A long time ago—when Aunt Gertie was still with us," he said, "and your mama was a very young woman—the two of them journeyed to South America to bring back the trees that we now have in groves around our house." He smiled, seeming to be lost in some distant memory. "Thousands of trees were transported here," he mused. "Most of them personally by your mother."

Juliet had heard the story at least a dozen times. She frowned, unwilling to hear it again. At least right now. Not until she was certain of his plans.

"For some time now we've been concerned about the grove," her father continued. "Your mother believed in toughening the young trees by subjecting them to harsh elements, withholding water, even beating the trunks a bit to create resilience."

"She should have done that to Annie and Abby," Jared whispered, giving them a teasing grin.

The tension in the room lessened. Abby threw a needlepoint pillow at her brother. He tossed it back. Annie yanked it away from Abby and threw it again, aiming for his head.

Quaid raised his hand for silence, then stepped to the window, pulled back the long lace panel and looked out. "None of this was enough to fend off the pests. I'd hoped last year's rain would help…"

"It's a glass-winged bug," Emma Grace said importantly. "I've seen 'em before."

Their father smiled, looking pleased that she remembered. "The glass-winged leaf hopper. An insidious little creature." He paused, moving his attention to the others. "I've spoken to some experts who think our crops might be helped by bringing in a new variety of orange from the Bahia region in Brazil."

"I want to go," Willow lisped. "Let me go too. I can help find new treeth. Just like Mama and Aunt Gertie."

Quaid shook his head. "The best way you can help is to watch over the ranch while I'm gone. Jared will oversee the care of the groves—we're between seasons, so the work will be minimal." He looked at his eldest son. "Juliet will run the household—with a lot of help from you younger girls."

Juliet's heart sank. She fought to keep from arguing in front of the others. But she glared at her father, her lips tight.

"But if we all went..." Abby began, then halted. "Wait. You forgot to mention Sully."

"That I did." He nodded to Sully, whose face had turned pale. "That's because Sully is going with me."

His announcement was met by grumbles of protest, including Juliet's.

"But we all want to go," Abby whined. "I don't see why we can't. It isn't fair that Sully gets to."

Gillian looked up at her father with wide eyes. "I always wanted to go to...where is it?"

"Bahia, Brazil," Juliet said with an impatient sigh. "In South America."

"I don't care where it is. I wanna go," Gillian said with a huff.

"Want to," Juliet said.

Sully finally found his tongue. "Me?" he finally breathed.

Quaid, who'd been ignoring the whines and complaints, grinned at his second-born son. "You've always taken special interest in the varieties of citrus around the world. You're truly your mother's son in that respect."

Juliet glanced around the room. Everyone was looking on placidly. It irked her that her sisters and Jared were so quickly getting over their

disappointment. They were talking as though this news had been antici-
pated, something to delight in. They were quite content for their father
and brother to head into the dangerous jungles, leaving Jared and her in
charge of the household and land.

Her father went on to describe the journey, the two months they
would be gone, and when they planned to leave. Six weeks from this
day. *In six weeks they will be off to South America!*

She clamped her lips together, sat back, glaring with grave intensity
at her father until the others had gone upstairs to bed.

Quaid sat down with a heavy sigh. "Now it's your turn," he said quietly. "I can see the disapproval in your face. For all your love of the stage,
you don't mask your feelings well." He smiled and touched her arm.

Her anger melted.

"Papa," she said, using her childhood name for him, "are you certain this is a wise thing to do? To leave us like this. It hasn't been six
months since Mama died."

An unbearable sadness seemed to settle over him like a cloak. She
followed his gaze to the fireplace. A single flame licked upward, moving
as if performing some silent and forlorn dance.

Then she looked up to see that he was watching her. "I have no
choice, Ettie. The projected losses are devastating. We may lose half our
winter crop."

"We've had losses before," she challenged. "How is this different?"

He didn't answer.

"Short of losing the land, nothing could be that bad." She waited
for him to reassure her.

He didn't. "I must go," he said simply. "I understand your concerns.
But they're minor compared to my own."

"We are in danger of losing the land then." It wasn't a question.
"That's why you're going." She didn't wait for him to comment. It must
be true, or he would have said so. "Is all this worth it? I mean, trying to
save the land. Why not just sell? Let's get a smaller place, something—
well, more manageable."

He stared at Juliet for a time without speaking. Only the sounds of the mantel clock and the now-popping fire filled the room. "Since the time I met your mother," he said finally, "I've done three things. Raise children. Raise oranges. And once in a while, write an essay for an obscure wildlife journal. And the latter certainly doesn't bring in enough income to raise a family. The truth is, I must save our groves, save this land. There's nothing else."

She leaned forward. "I could help. Maybe I could be the one to leave…"

His demeanor darkened. "If you're talking about going to Hollywood—"

"Hollywood? The flickers?" She laughed as if it was the silliest idea in the world and the furthest from her mind. "Why, I hadn't given that a thought."

"I have considered this, Juliet, and weighed our choices a dozen different ways. But I must endeavor to save the land and provide for the family. This is the best chance to see that happen. It's something I must do." His gaze was hard as he continued, "And as for the other. Selling the land. I'm surprised that you would consider it. Does this land mean nothing to you? It's the home of your ancestors. Your great-grandparents settled here."

She shrugged. "You know it's always been in my mind to leave. Perhaps I see it as an albatross, not an asset."

He studied her for a moment before speaking. "Someday, child, I hope you find the value of your heritage."

She tilted her chin upward. "I would hope, Father, that the value of our heritage is in who we are individually, not where we live." It was exactly the kind of thing Sully might say, with his matchless air of superiority, but she didn't care.

Quite unexpectedly her father smiled. "If you haven't yet discovered what I mean, I can only pray that you do someday."

He removed his eyeglasses and leaned forward, his tone earnest as he continued. "We've gone through great tragedy, and our mourning isn't over yet. Neither is the change your mother's death has brought to the family."

He studied the fire for a moment as though considering his next words, then he began again. "The night before she died, sweetheart, she spoke to me of her dreams for you. She was so proud of your performance as Ramona."

Warmth flooded Juliet's heart. "She spoke to you about…me?"

"She was concerned that you'd given too much of yourself for the younger ones. She wanted to give you the opportunity to follow your heart."

Juliet willed herself not to smile, but she couldn't help it. "She did?"

Quaid nodded. "When I return, we'll speak more about it."

Juliet gasped. "She had dreams for me?"

He grinned at her. "Of the finest sort. She spoke of drama school, one where you might expand your experience, perhaps explore other possibilities…" He hesitated, then apparently decided to say no more. He waved his fingers and laughed lightly. "If you'll promise me that for the next few months you'll commit your heart and dreams to your sisters and Jared, you'll be rewarded when I return. If all goes as planned, we will hire a nanny and pack you off to the school your mother found for you."

It was almost more than Juliet could take in. For the first time in months she thought she might breathe again…fully and deeply. "She actually took my dreams seriously?"

He was still smiling. "Haven't you figured it out, Ettie? Your mother loved you more than you can ever know. And she believed in you, far more than simply your ability to act on stage or care for your sisters."

"What do you mean?"

Her father threw back his head and laughed, a sound Juliet had heard too seldom since her mother died. "Now that, dear Juliet, you'll have to discover on your own."

<hr />

Quaid watched his family, huddled together on the windy pier, as the ship pulled out to sea. Juliet—holding Emma Grace by the hand, with

Gillian tucked under the same arm, Willow beneath the other—had adopted a more confident demeanor since their conversation six weeks earlier. She stood tall and brave, looking for the life of her like Emmeline. Not in her physical characteristics. Emmeline was robust where Juliet was petite. And Emmeline was dark, her daughter fair. No, it was their spirit, that undauntable, indestructible spirit that made them alike.

Grit, Emmeline had called it. And Juliet had it in full measure. He prayed that God would give her a strong dose of wisdom to go with it.

The children lifted their arms to wave good-bye. Jared gave him a salute. Emma Grace blew kisses; Gillian and Willow jumped and twirled, their hands looking like miniature windmills from this distance; Annie and Abby, faces solemn, waved their handkerchiefs until he could see them no longer.

Sully seemed unaffected by the sight of his disappearing family and headed to their cabin, probably to read about agriculture in Brazil.

Quaid was left alone, leaning against the deck rail, the salt spray in his face, the swift ocean breeze lifting his hair.

Father, watch over my children, he prayed as the pier faded into the gray haze. *Keep them in your tender care, and grant them safety and peace while I'm away. May they learn of you and depend on you for courage and strength.*

The ship moved steadily from the harbor into the wide expanse of the glittering Pacific. Emmeline's image drifted into his thoughts, just as always.

"Ah, my darling," he breathed. "You would be proud if you could see our brood now. They still mourn for you. But brave and good-hearted they are and, at last, filled with a small measure of joy for the future."

He was still staring at the place where he'd last seen them huddled together.

"And our Juliet," he sighed. "You were so right about her. Obstinate as the day is long, but, oh my, how she dreams…"

His daughter's stubborn image replaced that of her mother for an instant. Fiery-spirited, glittery-eyed, sometimes as brittle as porcelain, but prettier than a Rembrandt portrait. He delighted in her. He feared for her. Juliet was a woman now, free to do as she pleased, make for herself the life she pleased.

He only hoped she would wait until he got home to strike out on her own.

⚬⚬⚬

It was late afternoon when Jared headed the farm wagon down the dirt road leading to the ranch. Juliet sat on the bench with her brother, while the others groaned about being crowded amongst the sacks and barrels of supplies.

Juliet held her temper as the whining continued behind her. All five, from the twins to Emma Grace, fussed that they were hungry and tired of the bumpy, noisy, dusty ride from town. Exaggerated coughing and wheezing and groaning grated on her nerves. She silently counted species of birds as they bumped along, trying to keep from demanding that each and every one of the girls, even little Emma Grace, remove themselves from the wagon and walk the rest of the way home.

Finally the big grove house towered in the distance. It needed a coat of paint, and the land around it was sadly in need of water, but it was a welcome sight. The children cheered as one. When the wagon halted in front of the porch, the girls tumbled from it and hit the ground running, their laughter and shouts carrying on the late afternoon breeze.

Juliet hoisted herself from the bench and let out a deep sigh. *Two months of this?* She took her time following, wondering if she could bear it, chasing after her sisters, seeing that they got to school every day with clean drawers and petticoats. Seeing to their meals, their health, their safekeeping. Gillian yelled from the porch, joined in chorus by Emma Grace and Willow. Even the twins were putting up a howl about it being time for Juliet to fire up the stove and start supper.

She bit back her irritation. *As if none of them could lift a finger in the kitchen by themselves.* Another yell resounded from the porch. Through the thick morning glory vines she could see Willow waving a piece of

46

paper. It was probably a recipe the child had found for something new for the evening meal. Lately the family had grumbled openly that she had no imagination when it came to baking. With a heavy sigh, Juliet walked toward the house, vaguely aware of the rattling creaks of the wagon as Jared headed the mule-drawn vehicle to the barn.

Willow ran toward her, still waving the paper. "It'th for you," she lisped. Her tongue played in the space where she'd lost a front tooth the day before. "Jared got it in Riverview. It's a letter from the potht office." She proudly placed the envelope in Juliet's hands. "Who'th it from, Ettie? Huh?"

Juliet turned it over carefully, her gaze landing on the left-hand corner where *Clay MacGregor, Private Investigator* was printed in scroll-like script. She clutched the envelope to her bodice, fighting the urge to spread her arms, click her heels, and dance around the yard.

Only the lineup of curious faces on the porch kept her from it. Instead, she tucked the letter in her pocket and, without a word about its sender, hurried the family in to prepare supper.

SEVEN

Juliet waited until Willow, Gillian, and the twins left for school, then hitched the mule to the family carriage. The old swayback pulled its ears back as she fumbled with the harness and grumbled under her breath.

"Whatcha sayin', Ettie?" Emma Grace said from behind her.

"I was just telling this old mule to watch its manners."

"Why're we goin' to town?"

"I have business there." She yanked the harness too hard, and the mule stamped the ground.

"But why?"

Juliet laughed. "Do you ever run out of questions?" She swept Emma Grace upward and onto the carriage seat. "Did you know that this is the same carriage that Mama and Papa went courting in?"

"What's courtin'?"

"Courting is what it's called when two people fall in love and the man comes to visit the woman. When Mama and Papa fell in love, Papa would ride over on his horse to see Mama, and they would go on rides together, sometimes into the mountains. Other times he would drive this buggy over to fetch Mama and Aunt Gertie for church or a picnic."

Emma Grace looked solemn, obviously thinking it through. "How come no one comes courtin' for you, Ettie?"

Juliet laughed. "Well, now, that's a question I don't have an answer for."

"Jared says you're too pigheaded for a man to tol…" She frowned. "Tol-rate?"

"Tolerate." She popped the whip over the mule's back. "He said that, did he?"

48

"Uh-huh."

"Likely he's right."

Emma Grace's eyes grew huge with wonder. "I've never seen your head look like a pig's." She wrinkled up her nose with the tips of three fingers, imitating a snout.

Juliet threw back her head and laughed. She reached for Emma Grace and pulled her closer, still chuckling. "He meant that I'm as stubborn as the day is long, that's why no young man cares to court me."

They rode along in silence until the quiet of the country gave way to the blasting toots of train whistles, the pops and chugs of motorized vehicles, and the tinkling warning of bicycle bells. The mule laid back its ears in irritation at the cacophony. Juliet never tired of riding into the growing city with its magnificent, domed Spanish Inn, its eight-story brick buildings flanking tree-lined streets, and hillsides covered with citrus groves. It had an excitement all its own. She pulled out the envelope and read the address. She knew very well the location. From the first time she read the advertisement, she'd been surprised that Mr. Mac-Gregor was in a locale considered a shantytown, since it tended to be more rundown than most areas of town. She turned right onto Mission Street, then left onto Park Plaza. They drove another mile or so toward the south side of the city, where the buildings gradually looked older and more unkempt as they headed toward the railroad tracks.

Juliet's confidence fell as she spotted the street number she sought on an abandoned lemon packinghouse near the train station. She wished for the hundredth time that she had contacted a private investigator in Los Angeles instead of the lone man who had advertised in Riverview.

Emma Grace popped her thumb into her mouth and watched solemnly as Juliet hitched the reins to a post in front of the cavernous building. Juliet swung the child from the bench seat to the ground, then, holding her sister's hand, led the way into the edifice.

It loomed, dank and cold. Emma Grace clung to Juliet's hand as they stood in the center of the room and circled slowly, looking up, then downward. Skylights were cracked and broken, some missing completely. Big hanging doors that appeared capable of opening to the world rattled against the outdoor breeze. The floor was covered with what appeared to be grease and grit.

With a disgusted sniff, she followed the trail of grime with her eyes from the swinging metal doors to a huge lump of canvas in the center of the room.

Taking Emma Grace by the hand, she marched to the canvas and lifted a corner.

"Oh my," gasped the little girl. "It's an aeroplane, Ettie."

"It is indeed," Juliet said. Even in the darkness of the place, its bright yellow paint seemed to glow. "We've obviously not found the agency address. This appears to be someone's idea of an aeroplane hangar." She sniffed again, dropped the canvas, pulled out the envelope, and reread the address. This couldn't be the place.

With Emma Grace walking along behind, she headed toward the door.

But a voice from the upstairs landing stopped her. "Ho, there! Can I help you?"

Halting, she looked up. A man leaned against the rail, looking down at them with a friendly smile.

"I'm looking for a Mr. MacGregor," she yelled back at him. "Mr. Clay MacGregor."

He saluted. "At your service, ma'am."

"What are you doing in a place like this?" she yelled back. She figured he must be down on his luck, renting out space to anyone who needed it. Pilots included.

He chuckled, still gazing down at them. "We could yell at each other all morning, or you could come up to my office and I'll tell you what I'm doing in such a place as this." He waved his hand. "Your choice."

"I'll come up," she muttered mostly to herself and Emma Grace.

"Yes, please do. The stairs are to your right." When she looked puzzled, he added, "The acoustics create a mighty fine resonance in here, ma'am." He gave her another mock salute then waited, lolling against the rail as she ascended.

She again imagined Sherlock Holmes and swallowed a smile. And here was this arrogant, smiling private investigator, no more than ten years her senior. If that. He obviously hadn't had time to garner the experience he'd touted in his advertisement. And instead of a decent building for his agency, the man sleuthed out of a packing plant, of all things. And rented out space to bring in income.

She obviously had wasted her time driving into town, and she definitely should have looked for an investigator elsewhere.

"My name is—"

"Let me guess," he interrupted. "Miss Juliet Dearbourne."

"You must not have many clients," she said under her breath.

He ignored her comment and stooped to shake Emma Grace's hand. "And you are…?"

"Emma Grace," she said with a small curtsy.

He gave her a dignified bow. "I'm pleased to make your acquaintance, Miss Dearbourne."

Her forehead puckered, Emma Grace looked up at Juliet. "Maybe he could come courtin' us."

Juliet felt a blush begin at the roots of her hair and creep downward until it flooded her face and neck. "We're here on quite a different matter, Emma Grace." Her words were clipped. Then she turned to MacGregor. "Please, may we go into your office to discuss my business?"

He grinned. "I was just about to ask you if you'd care to come in." He gestured toward a pebbled-glass door to their left.

She nodded briskly, hoping her face had returned to its creamy hue. When she reached the door and read the agency sign, her trepidation grew even more intense. It stated, in ornate lettering:

MacGregor Enterprises
Aeroplane Rides & Expert Lessons
Stunt Pilot & Private Detective

"You do all this?" she croaked, wondering how he could devote enough time to do any one well.

"Yes ma'am," he said, standing back to allow her to enter with Emma Grace. "MacGregor Enterprises at your service. 'Fly 'em or find 'em,' that's my motto." His grin was too charming to endure.

She let her gaze drift from his face to the dusty window behind a beat-up desk as he seated himself. Shelves with haphazard stacks of books lined the walls. She settled into a spool-back chair and pulled Emma Grace onto her lap. The chair teetered on its uneven legs.

MacGregor leaned back, hands laced behind his head, the springs in his wheeled chair groaning in protest. The man was big, rawboned, and rugged. She could see him equally at home riding the range or in the boxing ring. Or piloting an aeroplane, for that matter, walking on a wing, scarf trailing in the wind.

She blushed again, surprised that the thought struck her as utterly romantic. She cleared her throat. "How did you know I was the one who wrote to you?"

"You signed your name to the letter you sent," he said, studying her face. "I remembered it from *Ramona*. Thought it might be a coincidence. But as soon as I saw you, I knew you were the actress I saw perform."

She waited for him to say something more—a remark or a compliment about her performance. When he didn't, she pushed disappointment aside and plunged ahead, getting right down to business. "I assume you've already begun the investigation. About Mairia Garden, I mean, since it's taken you so long to get back to me."

"I don't work without my fees being paid up front, Miss Dearbourne."

Heat started to creep into her face again, and she cleared her throat. "Well, of course not. It's just that you didn't get right back to me."

"I do have other clients. The last required travel." She pictured him in his aeroplane, scarf fringes fluttering.

"How soon can you start? Working for me, I mean?"

"What's he gonna do for us, Ettie?" Emma Grace said, looking worried.

"He's going to find someone, sweetheart," she said absently, keeping her eyes on MacGregor.

"May I correct you?" He proceeded to do so without Juliet's answer. "I don't ever make promises I can't keep. I will only say that I'll try to find your Mairia Garden."

Juliet bit her tongue to keep her quick retort to herself. "When can you *try* to find Mairia Garden for me?"

"I have time now, and I can work it in. Provided, of course, you can give me the advance."

Juliet swallowed hard. The family really didn't have the extra money, but she had set aside a small amount left after purchasing supplies. She drew in a deep breath and rummaged in her tapestry drawstring bag and pulled out three bills. "Will this do?" She hesitated, her face warming yet again. "For now, I mean?"

She met his gaze, almost daring him to laugh at the small amount. He didn't laugh. He merely pulled out a desk drawer, lifted from it a flat metal box, opened it with a key, and dropped in the money.

Next he pulled out a pad of paper and dipped a pen into an inkwell. "Now then," he said. "Tell me all you know about Mairia Garden."

"Had you heard of her before I wrote to you?"

He looked up. "Yes. Former opera diva who's past her prime and down on her luck. Worked for a while on stage in New York. Laudanum and drink became more important than any role she tried to play. I hear she doesn't want to be found."

"She came to see me when I performed in *Ramona*. She said…some things that, well, meant a lot to me once I found out who she was. I must find her again."

"What is the purpose of the search?" He leaned back again, studying her. She was struck by the nonchalant grace of his movement.

"You must know in order to find her for me?"

"It's a standard question."

"I thought she might have connections. I mean, she liked my work in *Ramona*." She didn't want to say more in front of Emma Grace.

MacGregor hunched his shoulders and made some notes. "So she was in Riverview six months ago. She may still be here. I'll make inquiries."

"Thank you. It would mean a lot to me if you found her."

"You said she might have connections, meaning she could help you. Your plan then is to make acting a full-time career?" His pen was poised, ready to write her answer.

The question was innocent enough, but Juliet's heart beat rapidly. Not because he waited, but because she heard Emma Grace's breath catch when he asked it.

The child clutched Juliet's hand and held on to it as if she'd never let go.

"Someday," she said and added nothing more.

The little girl relaxed her grip as MacGregor went on with his questioning. Finally he stood, shook Juliet's hand, and bowed elegantly once more to Emma Grace, who giggled. She pulled out the edge of her skirt and dipped, grinning up at him as if he'd just hung the moon.

"I want him to come courtin' us, Ettie," she said before they were out of earshot.

He had been right. The place did have good acoustics. Juliet could hear him chuckling as they descended the stairs.

One of the most appealing letters Clay MacGregor had ever received was that from Miss Juliet Rose Dearbourne. Not because of the intrigue of her request or the charm with which she'd asked for his help. Though both had endeared her to him before she set foot in his agency. No, it had been more than that.

He leaned back in his chair, ignoring the squawking springs, hands behind his head, elbows akimbo.

He'd seen Miss Dearbourne in *Ramona* on opening night. One look at her when she stepped onstage and he knew he would never forget her. For days afterward, the musical tone of her voice stayed with him, the manner in which she took command, the utter joy with which she delivered her lines.

He'd stood with the others when she finished and applauded and whistled, taking an almost personal delight in the rosy flush of her cheeks when she realized, with obvious surprise, that the applause was indeed for her.

That same week he'd read the account in the Riverview *Gazette* of her mother's untimely death, and he'd grieved for her, a young woman he knew only from afar.

And he'd prayed that he would one day see her again. When her letter arrived, it seemed that God had answered his prayer.

Now that he'd heard the once joy-filled voice darkened with sorrow, had seen in her face the hope of finding Mairia Garden mixed with the pain of her loss, his heart twisted with an ache he couldn't identify.

He only wondered what the future held for the gifted Miss Juliet Rose Dearbourne. Indeed, the elusive Mairia Garden wouldn't be easy to find.

Lost in thought, he pulled his jacket from the hat tree, tossed it over his shoulder on the crook of his finger, and locked the door behind him.

He could only try.

Eight

The first letter from their father and Sully reached the family in early December. Quaid described their voyage, the ports they visited on Brazil's east coast, and their search for the elusive trees. His words were filled with hope and with longing to return to California as quickly as possible.

The second letter reached the family in mid-December. They waited as Christmas approached for a third. When it didn't arrive, Juliet and Jared tried to brighten their siblings' spirits by suggesting that surely their father and brother were sailing home. That they would drive up the lane any day, full of hugs and surprises from the faraway lands they'd visited.

On each Sunday of Advent, Jared drove the family into Riverview to church, where they sat in the family pew with Brighid, Songan, and Merci. On the Sunday before Christmas, Grandmother Aislin and Grandfather Spence drove down from the Valley of the Horses to join them. Afterward they gathered for dinner at the old hacienda where Merci lived alone.

The day was warm for December, and after their meal the family retired to the courtyard to sit in the shade of the century oak. The children ran to the barn to play, and the twins headed to the corral to saddle and ride the only two horses now kept on the ranch.

Once the topic of conversation moved away from Quaid and Sully, Merci drew Juliet away from the others. They walked back into the house and through the wide foyer to the veranda that wrapped around the front of the adobe.

Settling onto the top step, Merci patted the space next to her. "Sit!" she commanded with a smile.

With a heavy sigh, Juliet did just that. It was a relief to have a moment's conversation with another adult.

Her father's cousin leaned toward her. "Now tell me how you're really doing. When anyone asks, you sound as though everything is running as smoothly as when your mother was alive and your father was home." She narrowed her eyes. "I know you, Juliet, and I know that you're holding this family together with a glue made of devotion and affection that you didn't know you contained. I also know your insides must be ready to burst from the confinement of heart and spirit."

Juliet's smile turned into a laugh. "You're the first one to notice." Then she shrugged. "But it can't be for much longer. Father said they'd be away just two months. It's been that."

Merci nodded solemnly. "I know you'd hoped to hear from him by now."

"He has to return soon. Our finances can't hold out much beyond the time he planned to be gone." It was the first time she'd uttered the worry to anyone but Jared.

Merci studied her carefully. "As close as your father and I have been through the years, he didn't mention a need for money."

"It's the crop. The income we expected won't happen. We've seen it coming, so that's not a surprise. Father borrowed against the property, though, for the voyage. He made the first three payments before he left, expecting to be home in time for the next."

"When is it due?"

"Right after the first of the year."

"I'll help." Merci took Juliet's hand. "I have a small savings…"

Juliet shook her head. "No. Father is a proud man. I'm certain he would object."

Merci laughed. "Pride runs in the family, not to mention that it goeth before a fall. Listen, Ettie, he owes it to me to let me help. You realize, don't you, that your father gave me this land?" She patted the banister rail. "This house and everything around it? He can't have so much pride that he wouldn't accept help from me."

"Thank you for the offer, Merci, but we may not need help at all."

She looked up as Jared opened the front door and stepped out to the veranda, a glass of lemonade in his hand. "If he will just tell that sea captain to sail a few knots faster, maybe he'll be here in time."

Jared leaned his lanky frame against the rough-hewn post by the steps, crossed his boots at the ankle, and listened politely as their conversation continued. "If he is delayed, child," Merci went on, "you come back to me."

Juliet nodded, though she had no intention of doing so.

Merci, whose gaze was still intent, laughed again. "I suspect you, my dear, have more pride than all the members of this clan rolled together—with the exception of your brother." She tossed a teasing glance toward Jared.

He smiled in return, though his tone was as firm as Juliet's had been. "We thank you kindly, Cousin Merci, for the offer. But this family will take care of itself. We aim to make our father proud that we've done it without help once he arrives home."

Juliet smiled at her brother. He gave her a nod, and she noticed how he'd grown up in the few weeks he'd been in charge of the groves and fields. He rolled his shoulders back and fixed his eyes in the direction of the Dearbourne property. "The way I see it, we'll all have to pull our weight to get by if Father and Sully have reason to tarry."

Juliet's smile faded. "What do you mean, 'pull our weight'?"

He turned back to her, his expression serious. Anxiety twisted her stomach.

"I figure," he went on, "that good wages can be made in the packinghouses. When ours was in operation, you used to love to help the transients wrap purple tissue around the fruit. I figure that you and the twins can get work at another. You're all three able-bodied and strong."

"It was a game, Jared. We were children playing." She looked down at her hands, feeling a creeping horror, hot as a fire iron, start at her toes and move to her head. "I wouldn't allow the twins to take on such…" She found herself sputtering, and stopped to breathe evenly for a split second. "Menial labor," she growled, again finding it hard to breathe. "I wouldn't allow it for them—or myself, for that matter."

"It may never come to that, Ettie. But you must admit, it will be a way to keep our home from falling into the hands of the bankers."

She cocked her head. "And what about you, Jared? Do you plan to play the gentleman rancher, sending the little women out to work for your supper?" Her tone was meanspirited, but she didn't care. She couldn't fathom that he would concoct such a plan.

His smile faded, and beside her, Merci shifted uncomfortably. Probably preparing for flight before Juliet and Jared's words exploded into a real argument.

"You know better than that, Juliet," he said, his voice a clipped monotone. "I'm simply trying to figure out a way to keep our home. I would work right beside you if nothing better is available."

"So you would try to find *better* employment for yourself but you're willing to send your sisters to the packinghouses along with the migrant workers."

"You're a woman. What else is there?"

She stood, her fists clenched. "I'm a woman?" Her voice came out in a squeak. "A woman?" She glanced down at Merci for support.

Her father's cousin looked ready to explode with laughter. She stood and brushed her hands. "If you two could just hear each other…" She laughed. "Your father and I were more like brother and sister than cousins." She walked over and took each of them by the hand. "Fought like cats and dogs more often than not. And you'd be surprised to hear many of our arguments were over some very similar topics." Her face grew wistful. "Just be sure you don't ever part without forgiving each other first."

Only half listening, Juliet still glared at her brother. He had the grace to look sheepish. "It's only an idea," he said, "not a certainty."

"It just so happens I have plans too." She tossed the words as though they were bricks. "I've made inquiries, and I'm merely waiting for the proper timing." She lifted her nose in the air.

"What inquiries?" Jared demanded.

She lifted her nose higher, betraying none of her disappointment that the last letter she'd received from Clay MacGregor had informed her that he hadn't found Mairia Garden and that his best advice was to give up her search. He didn't want to waste her money, he said.

⋖══➤

On Christmas Eve morning, Jared and Juliet did their best to make the occasion one of celebration. But nothing could mask the fact that this was their first Christmas without their mother. And their disappointment about their father and brother not yet returned from South America settled over them like a cloak they couldn't shake off.

Jared had taken Gillian and Willow to the pine forest in the mountains to cut a Christmas tree. And while they were gone, Emma Grace tied an apron around her waist and set about helping Annie and Abby as they rolled out pie dough and cut up apples.

As Juliet chopped onions for the wild duck stuffing, she tried to push the memory of her mother in the kitchen on Christmas Eve from her mind. But Emmeline remained as surely as if she had been with them now. Juliet remembered how she carefully toasted the cornbread in the oven, how she cut the onions into tiny, perfectly square pieces, and how she crushed the dried sage in a speckled bowl with a wood-carved pestle. And how, after she boiled the giblets and added the flour for gravy, her face would get flushed and she'd look so pretty as she stood over the stove lifting lids and stirring.

Juliet blinked back her tears and glanced at her sisters, ready to blame the onions. Their long faces told her their memories were the same.

"Let's sing!" Juliet said with false cheer. "How about Christmas carols? Anyone have a favorite? *God rest ye merry gentlemen...*" she began.

"I miss Mama," Emma Grace said in a small voice. "I want Mama to come back."

Shoulders stiff, the twins kept rolling dough and chopping apples. Annie sniffled, and Abby wiped her wet cheek with her apron hem.

Juliet put down her knife and nodded to the kitchen table. "Let's talk," she said, having no idea what to say or where to begin.

Annie's bottom lip trembled. "It's not right doing this without Mama. It makes me miss her more, not less."

"I just want to forget Christmas this year," Abby added. "It's worse with Papa gone. I thought for certain he would surprise us and arrive just in time for today."

"Me too," Emma Grace said, eyes ready to overflow.

"Then I have an idea," Juliet said, sitting down and sliding Emma Grace onto her lap. "Let's give away our Christmas."

All three faces turned to her in surprise. At least her announcement stopped the tears. She quickly formulated a plan. "Cousin Merci always invites the children from her school to spend Christmas Eve with her. I think we ought to take our Christmas to them."

"Take everything?" Emma Grace looked uncertain. "Them are poor little children from the Indian school."

"They," Juliet corrected.

"They are poor little children," Emma Grace said solemnly.

"That's why it's such a good idea. We'll cook our dinner, just as planned, then wrap it in heavy cloths to keep it warm. And we'll string popcorn all afternoon, so that when Jared gets home with the tree, we'll load up candles and popcorn and put the whole caboodle in the wagon."

"Doesn't Merci have a tree?" Annie asked.

"No, she's always just decorated with pine boughs. We'll surprise her with her very first tree."

Emma Grace clapped her hands together, then turned and gave Juliet a tight hug and a smacking-loud kiss on the cheek. "I love you, Ettie! Let's make Christmas for Merci."

The twins gave Juliet a look of admiration, and she was surprised at the pleasure it gave her.

"How about some paper snowflakes?" Annie gave a conspiratorial nod to Juliet, then turned back to Emma Grace. "How does that sound? When Gillian and Willow come home, we'll get them to help."

"We'll have to be *very* careful wif the candles and them snowflakes." Emma Grace tilted her chin, looking proud that she thought of it.

"Those," Juliet said.

Emma Grace grinned up at her. "*Those* snowflakes."

The afternoon flew by, and once Jared arrived home with the ceiling-tall pine, it was apparent that all seven children were relieved that they could give Christmas away this year.

It wasn't until long after midnight that Juliet allowed herself to cry. Out of loneliness for her mother and worry about her father. She even admitted to herself that she missed Sully. She sat by her window, blew her nose soundly, and stared out at the bleak landscape.

Her mother and father always said the distant hills gave them strength in times of trouble, that the majestic peaks and pine-covered mountainsides were a reflection of the Creator's beauty. That the magnificent hugeness of his handiwork put their troubles, their lives, in better perspective. But tonight they only reminded her of the pain in her heart.

God, I don't even know you, she cried silently.

I don't know that I want to. Not after what you've done to our family.

I want to ask you for help, but I'm afraid my words will return to me empty.

Like an echo, or a boomerang.

Unheard.

That the faith of my ancestors is an illusion at best, a joke at worst.

But how do I find my way? How do I find peace in a heart that can't be still?

Sometimes I walk to the end of the road and want to keep walking. Running. As far and as fast as my legs will carry me.

I don't want to care about the little clothes that must be washed and ironed. I don't want to care about the hungry stomachs of my sisters. I don't want to care that they cry in their sleep and that I must be here to comfort them.

What about me? What about the comfort I want? The solace I need?

What about me, Lord?

She glared into the heavens, her breath burning in her throat.

Finally, in desperation, she folded her arms on the window ledge, buried her head, and sobbed until there were no more tears to cry.

⟿

On a cold, bleak day toward the end of January, Juliet saw a Model T bump and rumble up the winding road to the house. It sputtered to a halt just beyond the porch, causing a hidden covey of quail to squawk and flutter into the lower branches of the pepper tree. A goose that had recently taken to roosting in a large flowerpot at the end of the porch waved its wings and shrieked in alarm, flapped to the rail, then to the ground.

A few minutes later, Ervin Baugh, head of the family bank in Riverview, knocked on the front door. He glanced at the still-squawking goose as if he thought it might attack him. Through the oval glass, Juliet could see that his expression was anything but pleasant. He obviously wasn't here for a social call.

After greeting him with polite grace, she led him to her father's office and seated herself behind the polished cherry-wood desk. Mr. Baugh sat opposite her.

"Don't you think your brother should be present?" He obviously didn't think the little woman had a mind for business.

She bit her tongue. "He rode into the high country today," she said sweetly. "If we'd known you were coming, we would have arranged for him to be here."

"Your brother should have come to see me weeks ago. We have pressing business matters to discuss."

"You're speaking of our father's loan. I'm fully aware of the details and am at liberty to discuss it. In fact, Jared likely would prefer that I handle the family business entirely." That was a stretch, but she wanted to make a point. "Truly, we expected our father to return by now." She smiled at him. "With the needed funds," she added, adopting a meeker tone.

"I know it's been a difficult time for your family. But I'm afraid my people can't wait any longer."

"Your people?"

"The loan officers. You see, my dear, your father's loan is in arrears."

"My brother is trying to make up for the deficit from our crop losses by rounding up some rogue cattle." Her words nearly caught in her throat even as she spoke. She and Jared knew what cattle he could find certainly couldn't be sold in time to make the bank payment.

"Have you kept your grandparents advised?"

Juliet sighed. "Of course." They had visited the ranch several times since Quaid and Sully left. But the disposition of the ranch…all the land…was always secondary to their concern about their son and his whereabouts. Besides, she and Jared did agree on one thing: They would take care of matters themselves.

Juliet stood and moved to the window. She stared out across the land, thinking about how she'd always wanted to leave the Big Valley. She'd thought she would choose to leave. Not be forced to because of the circumstances that now weighed on her shoulders like rocks the size of the world.

She turned again to face Mr. Baugh. "You're talking about foreclosure."

He nodded sadly. "Yes, I'm afraid we have no choice. You aren't the only ones in trouble. The glass-winged pest has taken its toll on many. The bank is taking a loss as well. I'm sorry."

"How long do we have?"

He regarded her quietly for a moment. "I can perhaps stave off the officers for a few more weeks, but beyond that…I fear all will be lost. Do you understand what that means?"

Of course she knew. The bank would take over the property. The family would be left with nothing. She didn't say the words aloud.

He let his gaze drift over her shoulder to the window. "You might consider selling off the strip of land your father kept as a wildlife preserve. If a developer could be found with some vision for what the land might yield—besides oranges, that is—perhaps you could keep the house and the land it sits on."

"I wouldn't do that to my father."

"I'm merely presenting your options. You stand to lose it all—the family home, the groves. All of it. By selling a portion, you could at least keep the home and surrounding yard intact."

"And look out on a sea of houses or factories." She was surprised that she cared. Surprised that her words were so like those her father might say.

Mr. Baugh gave her a moment's hard stare, then, hands on either chair arm, hoisted himself to standing.

"How long do we have?" she repeated as she walked him to the door.

His hand on the brass knob, he turned to her. "I might squeeze another month's grace because of your family name and history in the area. Perhaps two. No more than that."

She stared at him for a moment, an idea forming. "Since the money we're talking about is substantial, might the bank consider sending an investigator to Brazil to find out what they can about my father and brother's whereabouts?"

He scowled, his lips curved downward. "That in itself would cost a pretty penny."

"But it might pay off in the long run. If they're found, I mean." She noticed too late that she'd said *if*, not *when*. When he didn't respond, she rushed on, "Suppose we add the travel costs of the investigator to the loan. What would that hurt? We would get a full and accurate report. It seems that if my father and brother have run into trouble of some sort, the investigator could help them out. When they've all returned, your people will be paid, we'll have our new crops, and all will be well." She gave him a confident smile.

He surprised her by smiling in return. "You might just have something there, Juliet. There are myriad reasons your father and brother could be stuck in the hinterlands of Brazil. For instance, some foreign governments—Brazil may be one of them—take delight in incarcerating Americans, holding them for ransom—"

At her shocked expression, he halted in midsentence. "I'm sorry. I didn't mean to frighten you."

She followed him to the Model T, refusing to let go of the idea. "Please," she said as he opened the door of the vehicle, "will you consider it?"

He patted her hand, then sat heavily on the horsehair seat. "Your family is among the founders of our community. We need to remember that during these hard times. I'll see what I can do."

"Thank you."

When he'd gone, Juliet leaned against the pillar on the front porch, watching the cloud of dust behind Baugh's new Model T until it disappeared down the palm-tree-lined driveway.

She walked to the big pepper tree at the edge of the yard. An old wooden swing hung from one of the low, spreading branches. She sat in it and swung listlessly, remembering the years before her mother died, remembering how her father pushed her into the heavens when she was a child.

She didn't think her heart could ache more than it had after her mother's death. But now, wondering what might have happened to her father, to Sully, she knew it wasn't true.

The sounds of laughter and yelling spilled through the open windows of the house. Someone dropped something that shattered. Someone cried. Someone yelled. Someone sang.

The sound of hoofbeats carried toward her, and she looked up to see Jared riding in. There were no cattle with him, and his shoulders were slumped.

Wearily, she headed out to meet him, to tell him about Ervin Baugh. She hoped her stubborn refusal to keep herself and the twins out of the packinghouse would convince her brother that his notion was folly.

It was late spring when the banker returned.

"Our investigator has returned from Brazil," he began, his face drawn.

"I can see by your demeanor he didn't have good news," Juliet said, following him into the parlor.

Baugh sat heavily in the chair the children had agreed to reserve for their father upon his return. But she didn't tell him to move. Jared was sitting on the edge of the settee, obviously as impatient as she to hear the news.

"Apparently," Baugh said, "your father and brother decided to head into Peru. They had a guide and a small skiff. Their trail was traced to a tributary and into the remote headwaters of the Amazon."

"That wasn't their plan." Juliet felt her heart begin to speed up as her anxiety grew.

"I realize that, but it seems they changed their mind after they arrived in Brazil."

"What happened to their guide?" Jared asked.

"No one knows. The man left a wife and three small children. His friends say that he wouldn't have taken unnecessary chances because of his family. If there was any way possible to return home, he would do it. He was experienced. Responsible."

Juliet turned away from Mr. Baugh, unable to bear the pity she saw in his eyes.

"We can't just give up," Jared's voice was firm.

"We've done all we can reasonably do, Mr. Dearbourne. I'll give you a full written report as soon as it's ready," he said kindly, which only made the pain worse. "It will give details."

"And the loan?" Jared pushed on. Juliet couldn't look at the little man—she knew what he had to say already.

He cleared his throat. "As you know, the private investigator's expenses added a substantial sum to the already hefty encumbrance against your property."

"How long can you give us to catch up with the money due?"

"I'm afraid I've given you as much time as we can spare," Mr. Baugh said. His expression grim, he leaned back in their father's chair. "The officers plan to start proceedings immediately."

"Proceedings?" Jared and Juliet asked as one.

"Foreclosure. You must vacate the premises by the end of the month."

NINE

We must consider our options, Juliet." Jared sat at the kitchen table while Juliet stirred gravy for the biscuits. Tonight there was no meat to add to it. They'd killed their last hen the week before, and in vain Jared had searched the hillsides for stray cattle. His rifle was propped by the kitchen door, ready for the buck he promised he'd find by twilight. Or maybe a rabbit, he'd conceded.

"It's out of the question. I will not work in a packinghouse. I won't allow Abby and Annie to work there either."

"Even if it means losing the land?"

She clamped her lips together to keep Jared from guessing how scared she was. What if their father didn't return? Ever? She stirred the gravy with a vengeance, blinking back her tears. Her words to Mr. Baugh about refusing to sell were grand and glorious, but the reality of no roof over their heads wasn't.

It was time to face reality, but she was willing only to go so far. Sell the land? Yes. Work in a packinghouse? No.

"Sell the land, Jared," she finally growled. "Put it on the market now before it's too late. Sell it all—at least we'd have some money to buy a roof over our heads!" She glared at her brother. "If we advertise this week, maybe we'll have a buyer before the bank takes over."

"I say if the four of us take paying jobs, no matter how menial, the officers will see how serious we are about making our payments. They'll give us more time. We'll keep our home, the land, everything." He hesitated, his eyes pleading. "You know as well as I do, Ettie, that our land has little value right now except to developers. Do you think it's right that we sell out? After the crusade Father has led against them all these years? Father would be ashamed to call you his daughter."

"He's not here and obviously won't be soon," she threw at him. He blanched, and she was immediately sorry, though she didn't say so. "It's up to us to care for the children now. Likely we're all orphans. Has that occurred to you?"

He stared at her, his freckles showing in relief against his white face. "You don't mean that! We've agreed that we won't believe they're in danger—or worse—until we hear for certain. The private investigator's report was inconclusive."

She ignored him. Thinking about what might have happened was too painful to consider. "I say we sell the land and split the money between us. We can arrange for care for the children. A governess. A nanny. Someone. Anyone who knows how to care for them. Someone to teach them all the proper things that young women need to know." She stirred the gravy angrily. It was sticking to the bottom of the pan. The pungent smell of scorched milk filled her nostrils. She jammed the wooden spoon faster around the pot.

"You're taking good care of them, Ettie," he said softly. He stepped over to the stove and adjusted the damper. "They don't need anyone else."

"Maybe it's time for me now. Father promised me I wouldn't be stuck here—that I could pursue the things I wanted. Well, maybe this is all a sign of what's to be done. It's a relief, really. Like putting down a burden made of stones. Five stones to be exact!" Her voice had gotten shrill. She laughed bitterly. It was better than crying.

"Five stones?" He frowned, then as the realization dawned, he turned even whiter. "You mean the girls."

"Exactly." She didn't look at him.

"You want to walk away from it all. The land. The girls." His laugh was as bitter as hers. "You want only your cut of the money," he said, incredulous.

She stirred the spoon so hard the gravy slopped over and sizzled on the hot steel of the range top. "For months we've struggled to keep the family going. Food on the table, the children in clean clothes." She threw the spoon down, and it bounced off the stove onto the floor. She didn't bother to pick it up. It lay in a pasty puddle, rocking. "Do you have any idea the time and hard work it takes to scrub the clothes and bedding for seven people, hang them to dry, iron them, fix meals when there is barely enough food for us all, help the little ones with their readers and ciphering?"

"I don't deny it's hard work, Ettie."

She crossed the room and sat down beside him. "Don't you see? We can go on. Losing the house, our land, is a blessing, the way I see it. Mama and Papa, neither one would have wanted this for us."

"You're wrong. Neither of them was afraid of hard work. And they loved the land. They would have done anything to keep it."

"I'm leaving," she announced, standing again and taking off her apron. "You can figure this out on your own. Go to work in the packinghouse, put the whole family to work if you'd like. Let them slave from dawn till dusk wrapping fruit in tissue paper for folks better off than us. I will not be part of this plan." She threw her apron on the floor beside the spoon and stomped through the open doorway.

She rounded into the dining room and stopped short.

There between the foyer and the dining room her sisters stood staring at her, as if not believing the horrible things she'd just yelled at their brother. Emma Grace was in Annie's arms. She sucked her thumb in a tight rosebud mouth. Abby had both arms wrapped around Willow and Gillian, who immediately let their gazes drift away from her face.

She wanted them to reach out to her, gather her into their arms, tell her how much they loved her and needed her. But they stood there as if too stunned to cry. Too sorrowful to speak.

Without a word she headed upstairs, taking them two at a time, to her bedroom, fell onto the window seat, and stared at the miserable far hills. Then, without hesitation, she pulled her large satchel from the closet and began to pack every article of clothing she owned.

"Just let him see what it's like," she muttered as she worked. "A few days trying to care for this brood himself, and he'll come begging me to return. He'll see I was right all along. We'll sell this place, get a nanny for the young ones, and begin a new life someplace else. If he can find me, that is! Ha!"

She folded her two finest dresses, both made of organza and lace, one pale lavender, the other ivory, realizing as she did that she hadn't worn either for more than a year. Fresh tears filled her eyes. It wasn't right for a young woman of marriageable age to be saddled with five younger sisters and a sanctimonious saphead of a brother. Not that she wanted to get married or was even looking for a husband. Far from it! Even Emma Grace wondered why no young men came courting. She sniffled.

Who could blame them? With all the encumbrances she had wrapped around her neck like millstones? Who would spend ten minutes with her on the front porch swing when five younger sisters were the sole content of her dowry?

She threw her night robe and sleeping gown on the top of the pile. Next came her stockings and middy skirts. Her bloomers, corset, and petticoats.

She picked up a portrait of her parents from her bedside lamp table. She started to drop it into the satchel, but halted, staring into their faces. Her anger gave way to sorrow, which didn't surprise her. The sorrow was never more than a single thought away. She dropped to her knees, clutching the pewter frame to her chest. Grief flowed over her in ocean waves.

Finally she allowed herself to cry for her father and Sully, for the little girls she loved, for her brave brother and what he was trying to do for them all.

She would wait by his side until the bankers evicted them all. How could she do otherwise?

Jared found work as foreman in a grove on the south side of Riverview. A late frost hit, and because he was overseeing the setting out of smudge pots, he didn't come home for two weeks. When he finally came up the road leading to their ranch, Juliet stood on the front porch with her sisters, each with a small satchel beside them. Knowing what was coming the day before, she'd instructed each to pack everything they would need to stay at their Aunt Merci's. She would see them settled there and help decide which sisters would go with which relative.

She hadn't spoken to Jared about it. In truth, they hadn't exchanged more than ten words for weeks. But she supposed each of the great-grandmothers would take one of the twins. Great-aunt Sybil and Uncle Scotty in Monterey might take one. Perhaps Gillian. That left Willow and Emma Grace. She sighed, looking at them now. The two youngest. Also the two who required the most attention. She hoped she could talk Merci into keeping them, perhaps with help from Great-aunt Brighid. They could attend the Indian school and maybe help out as they got older. Or maybe Grandmother Hallie and Grandfather Jamie would travel to California to fetch them. The girls would want for nothing in Washington.

Could she bear to walk away, knowing that someone else would raise them? The thought was too sad to consider. But how could she, without a job or place to live, think about taking them with her? It was foolish, irresponsible, to consider it for longer than a heartbeat. She put it out of her mind.

Jared rode up to the porch and swung off his saddle. He looked tired and drawn, then angry when he saw the satchels. He tousled the hair of his youngest sisters and nodded to Annie and Abby.

His lips were tight when he moved his gaze to Juliet. "What's the meaning of all this?"

"Ervin Baugh stopped by yesterday. We need to leave today. He'll be here shortly with a sheriff to present the papers and some of the officers to explain the proceedings."

"I was paid today…" he began.

"It's too late, Jared," she said.

He glared at her. "It's what you wanted, isn't it?"

"No, it's not." She refused to cry in front of the girls. "It's for the best though, Jared. You'll see. It's been too great a burden." She turned away from the rage and grief in his face.

He grabbed her shoulder. "You could have helped."

She stared at him, again nearly overcome with fear for them all. "It wouldn't have made a difference."

"It's your fault," he growled. "If all of us had tried to help out, we could have staved them off."

Emma Grace was crying now, and Willow joined her. "You're scaring the girls," Juliet said quietly. "Stop and think what you're doing. From the time Papa left, it's been out of our hands. The only thing to do now is go on with our lives."

"Just as you wanted," he repeated.

"It's hard for me too."

A short, bitter laugh erupted. The girls began sobbing in unison, clutching Juliet. His expression changed, and he knelt down to pull Willow, Gillian, and Emma Grace into a hug.

"We're goin' to Merci's to stay for a little while," Willow lisped. "Ettie says it will be a growin' up experience."

"It will indeed," Jared agreed. He didn't meet Juliet's gaze over the top of the child's head. "Cousin Merci will enjoy having you stay." He was talking to all of them now. "You'll find all kinds of things to do there."

"We'll be separated," Abby said in a monotone.

Annie gave her twin a sad look. "It will be the first time."

Gillian sighed and turned away. Thinking her heart might twist in two, Juliet headed to the child and pulled her close. "Gillie, it's only for a little while." Even as she said the words, she knew she couldn't promise such a thing. "Honey, I will come see you as often as I can."

Gillian looked up at her with eyes that always seemed to look clear into a person's soul. A sprinkle of freckles covered her nose, emphasizing its pretty tilt. Juliet hoped that whoever took her in would notice daily and tell her how pretty and smart she was. She might lag behind when her playmates skipped and ran and played, but her nimble mind put all the rest of them to shame. Even Sully.

She looked up at Jared, hoping he would forgive her for her next words. "I think it's best that I take the girls now before Ervin Baugh and the sheriff arrive."

He stared at her for a long moment, then nodded. "You're going to Merci's, then?"

"Yes."

"Will you stay?"

"Only until the girls are settled." She turned and told the girls to go to the carriage. They trudged off.

"I'll see you at Merci's," he called after them. Shoulders slumped, they nodded. He turned back to Juliet. "Where will you go?"

"I'm going to the theatre district in Los Angeles. See if I can get a part in a play. As soon as I can, I'll start sending money for the care of the girls." They walked together to the carriage. From a distance came the sound of a Model T backfiring and rattling along the dirt road. "And you? Where will you go?"

"There's a bunkhouse for transients near the grove. I'll stay there." He kicked the dirt with his boot toe, looking anywhere but at her face. Juliet thought about telling him she was sorry for the bitter tirades she'd spewed, but figured with Ervin Baugh and the sheriff nearly there, it could wait.

"Good-bye, then," she said with a nod.

"We'll go over the documents from the bank tonight. Decide what to do next."

There was so much unspoken between them, but Juliet merely nodded. "Yes, tonight."

"You got the rest of the money?"

"It wasn't much."

"You keep it. You'll need it for rent and such. Until you get your feet on the ground."

"All right. I can pay you back."

"No need."

Here they were, standing in front of the only home they'd ever known, on land that had been in their family for over a half-century talking about money from a sugar bowl. Speaking to each other in pleasant tones as if they were at a tea party.

Juliet wanted to wrap her arms around her brother and howl about the injustices of what had happened to their family, their mother's death, their father and brother's disappearance. Her fears. Her anger. Her worry about the girls. About Jared. She wanted him to be angry at Baugh or heaven or both.

Jared did none of those things. He stood there toeing an anthill and talking about his plans to earn enough money to buy back the land. His eyes were flat and dull as the sound of the Model T grew nearer. The image of the sheriff putting them off the land made Juliet glance toward the girls, waiting inside the carriage. She didn't want them to witness their eviction.

"We must go," she said. She took two steps, then halted and nodded to the wagon, parked near the carriage. Piled in the bed was a rocker hand-made for their mother by their father, a big trunk brought by Great-grandmother Sara by ship from England now filled with a dozen quilts sewn by Aunt Gertie Hill. The girls had helped her carry the box of blue willow dishes and their father's favorite blue-speckled coffeepot and matching mugs. Juliet had added three of his treasured books and the old family Bible, tucking them among the quilts in the trunk.

"I've packed some things, keepsakes, that shouldn't be left here," she said to Jared. "I figured you could drive the wagon to Merci's."

He nodded, following her gaze. "I'll take care of locking up."

They both knew that it was unnecessary. Rancho Dearbourne no longer belonged to them.

A moment later she clucked to the horse, and the carriage jerked forward. The girls, dry-eyed and silent now, settled against the seats, Emma Grace and Gillian beside Juliet on the driver's seat, Willow, Abby, and Annie in the back.

The horse shied as they passed the Model T. Juliet kept her eyes straight ahead; she didn't venture the slightest glance toward Ervin Baugh or any of the others. She just kept driving, almost forgetting to breathe, until they reached the end of the lane and headed down the road leading to Rancho de la Paloma and her sisters' temporary home with Cousin Merci.

The arched iron gates loomed ahead, a black slash against a cloudless sky. She braced herself, figuring there would be a scene, tears shed over what they were leaving, over the uncertainty of what lay ahead. Her shoulders erect, she popped the reins above the horse's back.

Sure enough, as they passed beneath the arch Emma Grace started to cry. Followed by a wail from Willow. Then Annie began to sniffle. And Abby sobbed loudly. Only Gillian remained silent. Without looking, Juliet knew Gillian's eyes were huge and filled with silent pain, her little lips clamped together.

She halted the horse and turned to her sisters, looking from one small face to the next, then finally to the tragic expressions on Annie's and Abby's faces. They clung to each other, unable to bear the thought of separation, ever.

Juliet let out a sigh. "We must all be brave," she said, feeling the sting of tears begin somewhere behind her nose and threaten to burst into her eyes. "Very brave."

"I don't wanna be brave, Ettie," Emma Grace sobbed.

"I'm tired of being brave," Willow cried.

"Me too," Gillian whispered. "And sad. I don't want to be sad anymore."

"Stay with us, Ettie," Annie sobbed. "Don't leave us."

"You're all we've got," Abby sniffled. "I know we haven't said much, but it's been you who's kept us together."

The sting behind Juliet's eyes now made her nose ache, and she swallowed hard. "If I stay, it won't accomplish anything," she said. "This way I'll find work. Send you money for clothes and food. I can't do that if I stay at Merci's."

She lifted the reins and flicked them to get the mare to move. But the animal, as stubborn as the rest of the family, snorted and danced sideways, shaking her mane slightly. "I can't stay," Juliet repeated. "I can't."

For a moment they all stared at a dust ghost circling skyward in the distance. It picked up speed and sand and skittered across the road in front of the carriage. The horse nickered, one ear flicking forward, the other backward.

"Then let us come with you," Gillian said calmly.

"That's impossible," Juliet said.

"Why?" all five chorused.

"Why?" Juliet repeated in a sputter. "Why? I'll tell you why." She lifted the reins again and clucked to the mare. "Because where I'm heading is no place for decent young ladies. I plan to land a role in another play. That means long hours and hard work. I'll have no time for washing and ironing and fixing meals or helping with ciphering and readers. And we'd have to live as poor as church mice because it might be a long time before I see my first paycheck." She popped the reins with greater force this time, and the mare finally lumbered forward. "You see, it just isn't the life for young ladies. You'll be much better off with Merci."

"We're not all staying with Merci," Gillian reminded her. "We're going to be scattered everywhere."

They rode along the La Paloma drive, the *clop-clop* of horse hooves filling the silence. Just over the next knoll, the hacienda would rise from the dusty landscape.

Emma Grace reached for Juliet's hand. With a sigh, Juliet looked down at the sweet round face. "Please," she said, "I wanna go wif you."

"Pleathe," Willow lisped.

Juliet halted the carriage and craned in the seat to look at her sisters. She let out a long sigh.

They grinned at her.

"I will need help," she said sternly. "Annie and Abby, you'll need to take over some of the chores. Actually, most of the chores. Cooking and cleaning and washing and ironing."

They nodded vigorously.

She moved her gaze to Willow and Gillian. "And you, young ladies, will need to do your share too. You will need to mind Annie and Abby just as you mind me. You will help fix meals and help watch Emma Grace. See that she gets her naps. You will teach her nursery rhymes and play with her."

Their heads bobbed up and down.

"We will, we will!" Willow yelled, bouncing on the carriage seat.

"I'll teach her to read," Gillian said.

Next Juliet looked at Emma Grace. The trusting look on her face made Juliet's tears flow at last. She gathered her little sister into her arms as hoots and hollers went up from the others. They knew they'd won.

They turned the carriage around. The chatter and laughter lasted long after they pulled into Riverview. They headed first to the livery, where she sold the mare and carriage for enough to pay their first month's rent in Los Angeles. Next she purchased six one-way train tickets to the Union Station in Los Angeles.

As they waited for the train, she considered sending a letter to Jared, explaining her decision. Just as quickly, she dismissed the thought. He might try to stop her. And once she made up her mind about something, she almost never changed it. She looked down at the contented expressions on her sisters' faces. This time would be no exception.

By sunset, the Big Valley lay behind them as they headed west. Emma Grace sighed contentedly, snuggling against Juliet's arm. The others sat on the edges of their wooden benches and peered through the windows at the passing scenery, now fading in the growing dusk.

The train's rhythmic clacking of rods and pistons matched the nervous beat of Juliet's heart. What could she have possibly been thinking to take on this brood?

A small hand touched her face, and she looked down. "I love you, Ettie," Emma Grace said.

Juliet rested her cheek on top of the child's head and closed her eyes. She only hoped she would prove worthy of such love and trust.

TEN

A week later, Juliet leaned back into the settee at Miss Thelma Osgood's Home for Proper Young Ladies. Emma Grace, Willow, and Gillian nestled close, their eyes wide as they stared across the room at their father's cousin Merci Byrne.

Merci, fire in her eyes, sat in a high-backed chair, a cup of tea in one hand, its saucer in the other. "Be reasonable, Juliet. You can't possibly keep the children here." Her stare was hard. "Think of the little ones. What's best for them. They need proper supervision." She paused, studying the children's faces. Her voice softened. "I know the dangers of the big city."

"I can't separate them. It's bad enough that Papa and Sully are someplace in Brazil and that we were forced to leave the ranch. But here, at least we can be together."

"You know that I came here to bring the children home with me."

"I figured you did."

"Can I convince you that it will be for their own good?"

"You're too late. The girls have convinced me that being together is in their best interests. I agree." She sounded more confident than she felt. Willow looked up at her and smiled. Emma Grace leaned against her and snuggled contentedly. Gillian sat with her shoulders back and her hands folded, fingers laced. The girls were confident that Juliet would take good care of them, and it frightened her to death. "I have an employment prospect I'll find out about soon."

Merci lifted a brow.

Juliet looked down at Gillian. "Take Emma Grace upstairs for her nap, will you, honey?" Gillian put her shoulders back importantly and pulled on Emma Grace's hand. The younger child's head bobbed sleepily, but she allowed herself to be led toward the stairs.

"You too, sugar," Juliet said to Willow. "You need to help Gillian watch over Emma Grace." Reluctantly Willow ascended the stairs.

Juliet waited until the first door on the right closed with a click. Then, turning back to Merci, she drew in a deep breath. She had to divulge her plans sooner or later. It might as well be now. And of course, Merci would tell the rest of the family. No doubt visits from irate aunts, grandparents, and cousins would follow.

"So it's an audition?" Merci took a sip of tea, watching Juliet over the top of her cup.

Juliet laughed. "As if I could keep my 'prospects' from being found out. Yes, it's an audition. But for nothing shady. It's Shakespeare. *The Tempest.*"

Merci leaned forward earnestly. "Shakespeare or not, you know the family will disapprove. Just the idea of exposing your sisters to such people."

"I don't know anyone in theatre, so I can't comment on 'such people.' But I agree. The family will disapprove. I expected it the minute I drove away from La Paloma."

"There's already word of taking the children away from you. Aunt Sybil and Aunt Aislin may be getting up in years, but they plan to be down here to collect the girls faster than you can shake a stick."

"I won't allow it." Juliet sounded more confident than she felt.

"You may not have a choice."

"The girls will put up a fuss. And I can't blame them. This is where they belong."

Merci sighed and settled back in her chair. "I'm more concerned about the twins than about the younger girls. At sixteen Annie and Abby are so vulnerable, Juliet. I fear for them in this world."

"They are better off with me than separated. All of them are."

"Then God be with you, child," Merci said at last. "I'll try to convince the others, and we'll all help as best we can. Maybe we can take the girls from time to time? Just for visits?" she said with a tender smile. "Especially after you land that starring role."

"Thank you, Merci," Juliet said. "I needed you to understand… Have you heard anything from Jared?" she ventured.

"He was furious when he got to my place and discovered you'd gone without even talking to him about the girls. He was ready to come take them from you himself if I hadn't talked him out of it." She smiled. "Convinced him my velvet touch would be better for all than his iron one." Then Merci looked into Juliet's eyes. "He loves you, you know."

Juliet set her chin in a defiant tilt. "That doesn't give him the right to judge my decision."

Even as Juliet walked her father's cousin to the door, she knew Merci would return, likely with the full battalion of great-aunts, cousins, and grandmothers.

The next day just past noon, Juliet stepped into the audition line behind a large velvet curtain at the left side of the Globe Theatre stage. The small, ornate house fairly glistened, from its polished birch stage floor to its rows of luxurious crimson velvet seats.

Juliet tried not to think how desperately she needed this job. If she dwelled on her need instead of her part, she was certain she would make an utter fool of herself. Her hands trembled as she read the script for the hundredth time since picking it up two days before.

Three women spoke their memorized lines one after the other, voices clear and loud, gestures dramatic, then moved off the stage. Then a young man stepped to the center of the stage and recited his lines. He finished with a flourish, then gave a sweeping bow to the director, a squat balding man named Montgomery Locke, who was sitting ten rows back, writing on a pad of paper.

"Miss Juliet Dearbourne," Locke called out without looking up.

Juliet smoothed her damp hands on her skirt, cleared her throat, and stepped to the center of the stage. Her palms turned even clammier.

Her fingers shook as she held the script closer. Unexpected fright took over her senses, from the quaking of her knees through the rapid beating of her heart to the perspiration that beaded on her forehead. *Ramona* had been nothing like this. But then, she'd played that part for the sheer joy of it, not because she needed to put food on the family's table.

She swallowed around a dry lump in her throat, closed her eyes, and tried to slow her breathing.

"Miss Dearbourne?" Montgomery Locke said again.

There was tittering from the actors and actresses queued behind the curtain.

Juliet looked up to see Locke's eyes boring in on her with a puzzled expression, at once condescending and arrogant. She didn't think it possible, but her already red-hot cheeks flamed hotter.

"Go on, Miss Dearbourne," Locke said flicking his fingers toward her. His watch fob reflected the stage lights as he checked the time.

She nodded and cleared her throat. "Yes sir. All right," she managed finally and cleared her throat again. Again she tried to focus on the script. If only there had been more time to memorize the part. Her hand trembled, and the words blurred on the page.

She lifted her head, gave Locke a brave look, and, squinting, began to read the part of Miranda. *"If by your art, my dearest father, you have put the wild waters in this roar, al...*um*...allay them..."*

She stumbled through a few more words, cleared her throat and began again. *"The sky, it seems, would pour down stinking* pinch...I mean...*pitch, but that the sea, mounting to th' welkin's cheek, dashes the fire out. O, I have..."*

Her knees trembled now so violently that she thought she might fall. She swallowed and glanced up at Locke. To her horror, he looked ready to laugh. Pressing her lips together to keep from crying, she went on. *"Dashes the fire out. O, I have suffered with those that I saw suffer!"*

There was an explosion of sound from Locke. She glanced at him again. His face was red—either with mirth or anger, she couldn't tell which. But she didn't wait to find out.

Clutching the script with one hand, she covered her face with the other and ran from the stage. She didn't stop until she reached the door at the rear of the building. She threw it open and headed into the alley. She kept her eyes closed and leaned against the brick wall, gulping in huge breaths of air and wondering if she would ever have the courage to try again.

ELEVEN

A few days later, Juliet again strode through the entrance of the Globe. She hadn't slept more than a few hours since her audition, staying up long after the girls were asleep each night to memorize the role of Miranda in *The Tempest*. Today the dog-eared script was tucked under her arm as she marched along. She could recite it word for word, with perfect inflection, stage movement, and artistic representation for the innocent Miranda.

She put on a confident smile as she walked to the reception area, now being guarded by a young assistant. "Yes?" the man asked, his voice bored and disinterested.

"I'm here to audition for *The Tempest*."

He scrutinized her face and frowned. "Weren't you here last week?"

As she gave him an arrogant stare, the script slipped from beneath her arm and landed with a thud on the floor. "My name is Juliet Dearbourne, and I'm here to read for *The Tempest*."

"Once you've been eliminated, you aren't given a second chance." He looked amused as he bent to retrieve the small booklet.

Juliet forced her heart to stop its nervous flutter. "I was ill-prepared last week. I have studied the script for days, and I am now ready to read for the part." She swallowed hard and plastered on another confident smile. "Please," she added.

He looked down at the worn script as he handed it back to her. "Perhaps an exception could be made." He shrugged, then disappeared for a few minutes, looking bored once again, when he returned. "Mr. Locke is just finishing the auditions for a different role. He said he'll listen to you."

Juliet swallowed hard. "A different role? " Her confidence melted.

The young man nodded. "Ariel."

"Ariel?" she squeaked.

He wore a smirk. "Follow me."

Minutes later, she again stood on the empty stage, Mr. Locke sitting in his usual tenth row seat before her. "Ariel," he said with a flutter of his fingertips. "Go ahead."

She pressed her lips together and stared at him.

He again waved an impatient hand at her. "Please read. I haven't much time."

She knew Miranda's lines backward and forward, upside down, right side up, every which way possible. But she hadn't bothered with Ariel, the harpy—a foul monster with a woman's face and body, but the wings and the claws of a bird. She swallowed again and nodded mutely. The director might as well have asked her to ride a horse to the moon.

She drew in a shaky breath and gave the man a decisive nod. She tilted her chin upward and willed her fingers to stop their trembling.

"You may begin with Ariel's arrival in act three. Do you know the place?" he asked.

She nodded quickly. "Of course." She thumbed through the script until she found the page. Then closing her eyes, she imagined what it would be like to be lighter than air in a grotesque body. Then she smiled to herself. The body might be strangely configured, but who said the spirit herself was ugly? She pictured wings. Gossamer, she thought. And claws, delicate but strong. Others might see Ariel as a monster, Juliet preferred to see the creature as beautiful. Drawing a deep breath, she began, looking slightly above the director's head as though there were an audience behind him. *"You are three men of sin, whom Destiny, that hath to instrument this lower world and what is in't, the never-surfeited sea hath caused to belch up you; and on this island, where man doth not inhabit; you 'mongst men being the most unfit to live. I have made you mad..."*

Her voice rose with passion as she continued railing against the imaginary men to whom Ariel spoke. She was engrossed, becoming Ariel—the spirit, angered and passionate. *Grotesque and beautiful. Strong and graceful.* She lifted her head and stared at Montgomery Locke, forgetting he was anyone but a member of her imaginary audience.

After a moment of silence, he broke the spell. He moved up the aisle, strode the stairs onto the stage and took a stance near her.

He began to speak, and she recognized his words as the part of Prospero. *"Bravely the figure of this Harpy hast thou performed, my Ariel..."*

Juliet wondered if he might be speaking of her performance, not Ariel's, and she gave him a small nod of gratitude.

"Now skip to act five, scene one," he said. "I will again speak the part of Prospero."

She nodded and found the place as he began to speak. *"Say, my spirit, how fares the King and 's followers?"*

Juliet followed, concentrating on his exquisite delivery, the mood he was setting. When she spoke, she again became Ariel. This time her tone was sorrowful, rather than triumphant. *"Your charm so strongly works 'em, that if you now beheld them, your affections would become tender."*

Montgomery Locke spoke Prospero's part again, softening his voice as he continued, *"Dost thou think so, spirit?"*

Juliet willed her eyes to fill with tears, and she inclined her head slightly to deliver the final line. *"Mine would, sir, were I human."*

She stood for a moment, letting her tears slide down her cheeks and splatter onto her bodice. When Montgomery Locke nodded his head in a slight bow, indicating the completion of the reading, Juliet thought she might collapse.

The director handed her a handkerchief. "Rarely have I heard someone so unprepared give such a moving performance." His tone held a mirthful tone, as if he would laugh at her if she weren't standing beside him.

"But I did prepa—" she began, feeling her face warm with fresh embarrassment.

He held up a hand. "Hear me out." She gave him a nod, and he continued, "You have promise, of that I have no doubt."

"Then you'll hire me?"

He considered her for a moment, his eyes narrowing. Then he

shook his head. "I'm sorry. There are no speaking parts available. I've cast them all, large and small."

Juliet's breath caught as if she'd been socked in the stomach. "You said I had promise—"

"You mistook my meaning," he cut her off again. "By promise, my dear, I meant that you have an aptitude for melodrama. Though not Shakespeare." He chuckled as she blew her nose. "Vaudeville, maybe. Not serious theatre. Surely you don't have such grandiose thoughts…"

"I can learn. I promise I'll work hard to overcome whatever handicaps you think I have. If it's melodrama you see in me, I'll…I'll…well, I'll stop being melodramatic. I'll learn the actions, the intonations—whatever it is called—of the Shakespearean method."

Still the director shook his head. "As I said, Miss Dearbourne, even if I thought you might fit into this production, I have no part for you at this late date." He turned toward the stage stairs to leave her standing dumbfounded onstage.

Juliet didn't move. "I'll work. I'll mend costumes or build sets. I can paint. I know how to use a hammer and saw." She followed him, mutely imploring him to reconsider. "I need the work," she said, hating herself for begging. "Please. I have a family to feed. And I'll watch the actors. And learn." Now she was groveling, but she hadn't a choice. "I promise, I'll learn everything I need to know."

He glanced at his pocket watch again. "I will check with the costume department. We're always looking for quick and able seamstresses. That's all I can do for you at this time. I'm sorry."

She nodded. He had just destroyed her dreams. Not by refusing her a part. But by laughing, by calling her skills melodramatic. It was time she woke up to reality. The lead in *Ramona* had been a big part performed for a small town, her hometown. No wonder the audience clapped and cheered.

"Follow me," Locke said, and he led Juliet to a door at the end of the hall.

With a brisk nod, she trailed him to the costuming room. A smudged window broke the lines of the painted brick wall in the sewing area. Bars of late-afternoon light slanted through its panes, causing dust beams to cloud the hot and stuffy room. Row upon row of costumes lined the walls, seeming almost alive to Juliet.

The room felt too small, closed in. Juliet thought she wouldn't be able to breathe if she stayed another minute in this dreary place.

An older woman sat in the corner, bending over a drape of purple silk, her needle clicking against the metal of her thimble.

"Cornelia?" Locke said.

The woman turned, and Juliet gasped, instantly recognizing her as Mairia Garden.

Locke didn't notice. "Cornelia," he said, "meet your new assistant, Juliet Dearbourne."

The woman smiled gently and rose to shake Juliet's hand. "We've met," she said. "Some time ago." Her voice reminded Juliet of silk.

"I'm pleased to meet you, er, Cornelia," Juliet said in wonder.

The seamstress looked back to Locke. "I saw Miss Dearbourne perform in *Ramona*. She was stunning, utterly stunning."

"Really," he said, obviously dismissing the news as coming from a woman who knew nothing except costuming and sewing.

The older woman's attention was focused on Juliet. "So you've come to the city to seek your fortune after all."

"Not a fortune. Just enough to keep my family together."

"In theatre?" She glanced at Locke and laughed, though not unkindly. Looking back to Juliet, she went on, "So you came here today to audition and landed a job as a seamstress."

"Yes." She didn't know the half of it.

"Not a bad starting place," she said. "I've known stars who swept floors or worse before finding the right play, the right part at just the right time."

If stardom were her only objective, the news wouldn't be so disheartening. If she'd had a single word of encouragement about her audition, she might have the heart to persevere. "I need the money," she said. "Just tell me my duties. And my salary, please?"

"A dollar a day," Locke said from the doorway. "Sundays off."

She felt the blood leave her face. "That's all?" she managed. She was paying seventy-five cents each day, seven days a week, to Miss Osgood for room and board. It would have been more, but all six of them were crowded into one bedroom. There would be precious little left over.

"Take it or leave it." Locke shrugged. "You're lucky to get this much. Cornelia's the best," he added. "She's worked on Broadway, costuming some of the most famous actors in the world."

She's played on Broadway, Juliet corrected silently.

"I have a family of six I must care for. That's not nearly enough."

Locke looked her up and down, obviously not believing her. She stared at the man, wanting desperately to turn and stomp from the room.

"Take it or leave it," Locke said again.

She had no choice. "I'll take it," she said quickly.

"This isn't where you belong, child," Mairia Garden said once Locke had closed the door behind him. "You must leave as soon as possible." She gestured for Juliet to sit down opposite her sewing table.

"I know who you are," Juliet said.

"I thought so," Mairia said. "I could see it in your eyes."

"Once I thought if I could only find you…" Juliet hesitated. "I thought you might introduce me to some directors, producers, and such." She shrugged and laughed nervously.

Mairia didn't laugh. "What changed your mind?"

"I hired a private detective, though he finally gave up. Said he was stealing my money by continuing."

Mairia didn't explain why she was going by a different name or why she was working as a seamstress; Juliet didn't ask. "And now?" Mairia asked simply.

"I'm overseeing the welfare of my five sisters. Had I come here alone I would likely be on my knees by now, begging for a part in the production." She laughed lightly. "I was willing to go anywhere, do anything, to be onstage. A dollar a day is more than I had yesterday. I suppose I should count my blessings. It will have to do."

"Why are you caring for your sisters?"

Juliet met Mairia's gaze with a sigh, and to her dismay her voice broke slightly when she answered. "My mother," she began, then cleared her throat. "Mother had a tragic accident just after I met you last…"

Mairia let a moment of comfortable silence fall between them before asking, "Yet you came to audition today. You must have still held your dream close."

Juliet walked over to the room's single window, pulled back the dingy plaid curtain, and peered out. "It was my second audition for the play. I failed miserably at both. Locke laughed me off the stage the first time. The second time he ridiculed me."

She turned back to Mairia. "In the last hour, I've concluded that I won't subject myself to such humiliation ever again."

"Because you didn't get the part?"

"Because he called my reading melodramatic."

Mairia rose and walked across the room to stand near Juliet. Every movement was as graceful as that of a doe. She was beautiful, ageless with her elegant twist of silver hair, high cheekbones, piercing sapphire eyes. Juliet was surprised she hadn't noticed the woman's beauty when they met at her performance in *Ramona*.

"Have you considered that he might have been testing you?"

"Then I failed miserably."

Mairia chuckled. "No, child. I don't think you failed at all. Sometimes doors are closed for a reason."

"So that I can work in here, sewing for a dollar a day?" Her laugh was short, brittle. A shadow crossed Mairia's face, and Juliet was sorry she'd scoffed at the job. At least it was work.

"No, I think you belong elsewhere. That's all." Mairia turned to go back to her sewing table.

Juliet trailed and sat again across from her. "You speak in riddles. You told me last year I would someday find that what I think is promise, isn't promise at all." When Mairia didn't comment, she continued, "And just a moment ago you told me that I don't belong here. That I should leave as soon as possible."

Mairia studied her for a moment before answering. "Both things are true. You hold dear your gifts, but your gifts aren't what you think. You may also recall that I said only you could discover them."

"And you said to cherish my family."

"Yes."

"My mother died the following day."

Mairia's face fell. "Oh, my dear. I'm sorry. So sorry."

"Then everything changed," Juliet continued. "Our family is scattered from South America to migrants' sheds to a sewing room behind a theatre. And it doesn't seem to matter anymore about cherishing anyone or dreaming dreams or anything else. All that matters now is making it through each day, putting food on the table for five children who have me and no one else to care for them, seeing to their clothing and schooling and all the rest." She hadn't meant to go on about it.

"One role missed and you've decided to feel sorry for yourself?" Mairia sat back, her piercing eyes stabbing through Juliet.

Juliet caught her breath. "I'm merely telling you how it is."

"You've decided to sew for your supper instead of trying again? And again? And again? For you see, dear, that's what it takes."

Juliet felt a long-forgotten anger start at her toes and spread upward until she was certain her face was bright red. She leaned forward, her words clipped when she spoke. "You may think this is easy. But let me tell you, Miss Garden, it isn't. I'm doing my best. I could have left my sisters with relatives. Life would be a lot easier right now if I had. Then maybe, just maybe, I'd be more courageous."

"Unless your sisters are your excuse for accepting less than what you've been called to do."

"I've never backed away from a fight in my life. This"—she gestured around the room—"this is the best I can do right now."

"Is it?"

"What are you doing here? Why have you settled for this and given up your gifts?" Her voice was shrill, but she didn't care who overheard.

Mairia surprised her by laughing. "Ah, my dear. I see a bit of fire remains in your soul." When Juliet didn't speak, she continued, the mirth still evident in her voice. "What if I told you that I still have connections in New York? Would you be willing to go, to explore what that world might hold for you?"

Juliet stared at Mairia in astonishment. "New York?"

"New York. The theatre section. Serious theatre, not vaudeville."

"I can't possibly." She imagined the bright lights, the music.

"Because of your family?"

"It's too risky." But her pulse skipped a beat as she pictured herself walking—no, dancing—across a Broadway stage.

"Any more risky than here?"

"Of course more than here," Juliet said, trying to calm her now-thumping heart. "Besides, I haven't the money to get myself there, let alone the others."

"Ah, yes," Mairia sighed. "That's true. And I don't think you've the desire either."

"I do! Of course I do," Juliet protested. Even as she spoke, her bright fantasy turned to ashes.

"Or the courage to try again, even after you've fallen on your face. Or think you have."

"Tell me what I need to do to start," Juliet said with a sigh.

"On your journey to the theatre?"

The woman was merely toying with her dreams, Juliet decided. She had no idea of her heavy responsibilities. She couldn't know. "My work for you here. Tell me what you would like me to do."

"Yes, of course," Mairia said. She pulled a pair of cloth slippers from a high shelf and handed them to Juliet. "You'll need to cover these with sequins. Not even an eighth of an inch of cloth can show." She handed Juliet a tin box filled with the shiny disks.

Juliet spent the rest of the afternoon and evening stitching sequins. The light was dim in the room, and her eyes ached by the time she told Mairia good-bye and left the empty theatre.

That night Juliet couldn't sleep. She sat in the small bedroom, staring from the window into the darkness. Behind her, her sisters' soft breathing rose and fell.

Emma Grace sucked her thumb, a small clicking sound, and Willow giggled in her sleep. Across the room, Gillian sighed and turned over, pulling the covers close to her face. Moonlight spilled through the window, illuminating the child's features. She smiled, clutching the edge of the bedclothes, much as she'd held her baby blanket years before, rubbing it against her nose.

The sweet look of them was almost too much to bear. Juliet turned to the window again, staring out into the dark expanse. Gaslights flickered in neighborhood windows, and a row of electrified globes glimmered along each side of the street below.

Mairia Garden's words came back to stir something inside her. The joy she'd felt onstage in Riverview rekindled for an instant, drawing her as surely as a moth to flame. Foolish daydreams, that was all they were. And the old diva's empty promises were likely just that. Empty.

Quickly she put aside the alluring image. She would remain a seamstress until something better presented itself, sewing sequined slippers and watching the actors and actresses from the sidelines, if that remained her lot.

But New York? Imagine! Juliet couldn't help but wonder.

TWELVE

Sully Dearbourne woke to the night sounds of the jungle. He shivered and squeezed his eyes closed, trying to shut out the fear that made him quake from head to toe. "Oh, God," he whispered, "help me abide another day in this forsaken place." Tears slipped from the corners of his eyes, slid along his cheeks, and dripped onto his earlobes, finally creeping onto the woven palm hammock.

Alone and scared, he felt any courage he tried to muster during the light of day dissipate like vapor into the heavy and wet, mosquito-filled night air. Try as he might to keep the terror at bay, it was with him every night. And oddly enough, it was his own lack of courage that haunted him the most.

It had been that way since the night his father had been taken at spearpoint. The tribal elders, dressed in ceremonial garb, had danced wildly through the night, chanting over a caged puma. Finally they killed it, ate its flesh, and painted themselves with its blood. Then they came for his father, wordlessly commanding him to go with them.

The dancing had continued with the same heavy beat, and the wailing, the chanting. It stabbed at Sully as he lay there in the dark that night, wondering what had happened to his father.

It was far into the night when the dancing and wailing stopped. He saw the shadow of movement through the jungle, dugouts gliding into the ink-black waters of the Napo below his poled hut. But all was silent, the moonless night too dark to see, so he thought perhaps it was his imagination.

The following morning, the natives returned.

His father wasn't with them.

Sully refused to think about what might have happened to his father. Instead he dwelt on the fear of being alone, being without his father's courage and direction to guide him. He would grieve some other time, he told himself every day. Every night in the dark just before dawn.

In the corner of the hut, a rat scampered up the pole and into the thatched palm-frond roof. The dried leaves rattled as the creature moved. Sully cringed, praying it wouldn't drop on him, as one had done just a few nights ago. For at least an hour he lay there, listening to the rat, imagining its droppings falling onto his elevated sleeping mat. Judging from the rustling racket, he figured the creature had been joined by at least two others. Maybe more. Or perhaps it was the movement of one of the seven-inch, mammal-eating tarantulas that sometimes made a hunting trek through the ceiling fronds, looking for a rat small enough to paralyze with its venom. He shuddered.

Eerie jungle sounds were accentuated by the surrounding silence. A rattling squawk. A scream. A faint screech. Farther into the jungle, the wild howling of bushdogs prickled the hair on Sully's neck. Though Sully knew their favorite prey was the paca, their yipping and growling terrified him; he pictured himself treed by the pack. For a long time he lay in the dark, trying to erase the image of bared teeth and wild eyes from his mind.

Daybreak's thin, gray light began to creep into the hut. Sully looked around the cubicle that had been his home for the past two and a half months. He detested it more every day, especially the empty hammock where his father had slept the first weeks after they were taken captive. Now it was a reminder of his loneliness. Also of the truth that he would never be rescued from this place.

Feeling sorry for himself, he turned on his side and stared out at the ashen dawn. He rose and stretched and looked out the opening to the river below. The seasonal floodwaters were subsiding, and soon the ground would show—or so he'd read when he and his father first left for Brazil.

When they'd first been brought here, the river was at its height, and the villagers traveled from hut to hut by dugout canoe. Then they'd had no reason to bind their captives. They'd merely put them in one of their huts at the top of palm-tree-trunk poles and drifted away in their canoe.

Sully and his father had no means of escape, so here they'd stayed, subsisting on grubs and a tapioca-like paste made from manioc roots.

To pass the time, they had talked of home, laughing about the tales they'd have to tell Juliet, Jared, and the others once they reached California again. They talked into the night, while the Yagua held tribal council, their torches casting a golden glow around the compound of stilted houses, their drums beating that ominous rhythm. Quaid told Sully stories that had been passed down to him by his mother and father and grandparents—about his grandfather's seafaring days and the early times at the rancho.

All the while they avoided talking about the one thing that separated them: Sully's feelings of guilt that he was responsible for them coming to this, their capture by the Yagua. When the elusive pest- and drought-resistant orange trees had turned out to be nothing more than myth, Sully had suggested they travel upriver to Iquitos and put their money into part-ownership of a rubber plantation.

At first his father had been against it, but Sully had convinced him that he'd heard people were making fortunes on such ventures. He knew that if not for the fear of losing the land back home, his father never would have agreed. Now, as the mist laced through the foliage beside the river, Sully leaned against the crude opening of his hut, idly watching the village come to life. A hundred times a day, he wished he could relive that day they'd hired Indian guides to paddle them up the wide, muddy Amazon to Iquitos, the center of the rubber industry, instead of heading downriver to the steamer that would take them home.

They would have returned to California penniless, but he and his father would have been with the others, figuring out how to save the ranch. With all of them working together, surely they would have found a way, even without the new species of citrus.

Now? He laughed bitterly and turned away from the river. Now Jared and his sisters were likely desperate to save the ranch. And no doubt they'd given Sully and Quaid up for dead.

A shout from below the hut ripped him out of his reverie. A young Indian man steered his dugout to the ladder and tied it to the nearest pole. It was the same every morning. Someone brought him a reed bowl filled with the pasty native tapioca, then waited while he ate.

Sully stood back while the young man entered and handed him the bowl. Sully lifted it and scooped the mush into his mouth, using two fingers like some strange curved eating utensil. He handed the container back to the Yagua, but this morning the young man didn't turn to leave. Instead he pointed to the floor and nodded his head, jabbering in the strange, clicking language that Sully couldn't understand. Didn't want to understand.

Sully slumped forward, and with a half-hearted shrug, seated himself on the woven fiber mat. "You should know by now, my good man, I can't understand a word you're saying."

The man continued on as if Sully understood. He gestured toward the river, made more clicks and grunts, then looked back to Sully expectantly.

Sully sighed and shook his head. In times such as this, he thought he should attempt to learn the language. But acknowledging his need for it was acknowledging that he would never leave the place. So he planned to stay ignorant of everything around him. Flora. Fauna. The heathens. The language. It dulled his pain to ignore them all.

The man stood over him, frowning and gesturing even more wildly. He pointed upriver, then to the canoe, then upriver again. When Sully said nothing, did nothing, the Indian moved around the hut, pointing to Sully's dirty, torn clothes and the mildewed satchel that he'd shoved under his hammock.

The Indian, growing more irate by the minute, finally grabbed the satchel and threw it from the hut. It landed in the canoe with a dull thud.

Sully was on his feet in a second. "Why'd you do that, man?"

The Indian walked to the doorway, gesturing to Sully.

Sully looked him in the face, trying to read his expression. Wishing he knew where the Indian was about to take him. Finally he shrugged and followed the young man down the ladder to the canoe.

It didn't matter where they were taking him, he decided. Even if they killed him and cannibalized him, he figured it would be better than the dead existence he faced in no-man's land. Settling into the front of the canoe, he sat with his back straight, his face toward the Indian who was poling the dugout into deeper water. Too weak to do much else, Sully's only movement was to swat at mosquitoes swarming around his head like a thick, gray cloud. He grimaced, imagining that they blended into his straggly reddish beard and long, unkempt hair, making him look decades older than his eighteen years. He'd always been thin, with angular features, but now, after weeks on the near-starvation diet, his ribs protruded and his knees and elbows jutted out from his limbs like the sockets on a skinny clown doll that Emma Grace played with.

Sully and the Indian were farther out into the river now. At the edge of the native village, a few men had climbed into their own canoes. He'd watched them leave every morning, with spears and poles. They always returned when the sun was high over the river with enough fish in their canoes to last the day. Sometimes they would bring in a fish so large it took two men to carry it to the village. That night the tribe would celebrate, and the fishermen stayed in the village for several days before fishing again.

The canoe glided along in silence. From time to time a fish jumped, showing its gleaming side to the morning sun.

"So, where are you taking me?" Sully asked after a while. Not that he expected an answer.

The Indian said something in his strange clicking language. His tone wasn't threatening, so Sully relaxed.

The river was wide, and the sun beat down hard and glinted on the coffee-colored water. After a time the Indian guided the dugout into a lesser tributary, and after another hour or two—or so Sully reckoned from the slant of the sun—into a still smaller branch. It narrowed, and the jungle closed over their heads.

It became so dark that it might as well have been dusk instead of midday. The sounds of the jungle rose to a ratcheting din. A haunting cry carried from the branches of a kapok tree, towering above the rain

97

forest at a distance. The creature cried again, a tremolo that reverberated across the water. A shudder spidered up Sully's spine.

The Indian laughed. "Tinamu," he said. "Tin-a-mu." The young man at the far end of the canoe smiled, white teeth showing against his dark bronzed skin. "Tin-a-mu," he said again, and flapped his elbows like a bird, or more accurately, like a chicken. The sight was so silly that Sully laughed and repeated, "Tin-a-mu." Then he mimicked him, which caused the young man's smile to widen.

"What is your name?" Sully asked.

The Indian stared at him.

Sully thumped his chest. "Sully. Sul-ly. My name is Sul-ly."

"Ja-ca-ré." The Indian thumped his chest. "Jacaré."

Sully nodded. "Jacaré."

They drifted in silence along the dark, narrow river until they came upon a village just before darkness fell completely. Frogs croaked and gurgled and barked, sounding larger than any tree frog or toad Sully had heard. A dozen or more flickering torches created a glow in a clearing just beyond a stand of palms and a stretch of beach. Jacaré poled the canoe into a shallow, sandy cove. When he stepped out of the boat to pull it to shore, Sully hopped out to help him. The physical movement and having laughed for the first time in months felt good.

A group of Indians moved into the clearing around the two men. Jacaré spoke, gesturing toward Sully a few times, then looked back toward their village. The tallest of them stepped forward, jabbering and pointing, sounding angry. Finally the apparent conflicts seemed to be settled, and the group proceeded to the clearing.

As they approached the silent villagers, Sully's heart pumped overtime. Blood rushed through his temples, pulsing with each beat.

Flames from a central fire flickered into the night sky. Around the perimeter stood a group of fierce tribesmen in full ceremonial garb—bodies painted, grotesque masks on their faces—just as they had been dressed the night the puma was killed. The night his father was taken.

It was his turn.

Sully hadn't one courageous fiber in his body. Of that he was certain.

But now, faced with certain death of the most horrible sort, his calm surprised him. He stood taller, knowing his father would have faced death in such a manner.

He followed Jacaré and for the briefest moment wondered how the man could have laughed with him in the boat earlier, knowing he was leading his companion to the slaughter.

The drums were beating a slow rhythm, and the dancers had begun their slow steps and sways. A low chant filled the air, quickly growing to a crescendo. Soon the young women joined in, their voices blending with the men's.

Jacaré nodded to Sully when they reached a hut on the far side of the clearing, then he stood back, indicating that Sully was to enter.

"God, help me," he breathed, praying he wouldn't cry no matter what they did to him. Courage mattered. Even when no one he knew was watching. He hadn't realized it until now.

With his bearded head held high, his bony shoulders tall, Sully limped into the dark, thatched hut. For a moment he stood there, letting his eyes become accustomed to the dim light. He blinked and stepped backward to the doorway, clutching it to keep from falling. He stood there staring, too stunned to move.

Outside, the drumbeat quickened, and the chanting grew louder. More villagers had joined the ceremony, their voices reflecting a near-frenzied state.

Sully had prayed he wouldn't cry. But he couldn't help himself. "Father." The word came out as a hoarse sob.

He fell to his knees beside the skeletal figure, put his hands to his face, and wept.

THIRTEEN

On three separate occasions Merci traveled by train from the Big Valley to Los Angeles to see the girls, warning Juliet that her grandparents and great-aunts had a fierce concern for their welfare. While Juliet truly didn't want them to worry, she didn't want their help, and most of all, she didn't want them demanding to take her sisters home. She finally convinced Merci to intervene on her behalf. Her father's cousin did just that and held the peace—at least temporarily—while Juliet struggled to keep her sisters together.

Jared's disparaging words about her stubborn refusal to help him save the family home still stung. Just because she didn't see eye to eye with his way of doing things didn't mean she didn't care. She fumed just thinking about it.

She would show him! Oh yes, she would show everyone she had her sisters' best interests at heart. She never wanted to see sadness shadow their little faces again the way it had the night she betrayed them, the night she and Jared exchanged their bitter words. Like a mama grizzly, she would fight to protect her sisters. Most of all she would fight to keep them with her.

On a Thursday just two weeks after she was hired, Montgomery Locke summoned Juliet to his office.

"I'm sorry, but I am going to replace you," he said without preamble.

Juliet's cheeks reddened. "What do you mean?"

"I'm sorry," he said simply.

"I've been putting in extra hours, even taking work home with me to complete at night." She leaned forward with a frown. "Why would you want to replace me?"

"It's Cornelia's decision. I assume you're not doing an adequate job.

But you'll need to bring that up with her." He stood and handed Juliet an envelope containing a few bills. She didn't bother to count them. She turned away without another word and fled to the hallway, breathing hard. From a distance she heard the voices of the performers rehearsing their lines onstage, the strains of the orchestra, the pounding of hammers as the sets were nailed into place.

Without stopping, she strode to the costuming room and threw open the door. As if expecting her, Mairia looked up calmly from her sewing table.

"You've sacked me." Juliet moved to stand in front of her, hands on hips.

"I have."

"Why?"

"I no longer have need for you, my dear." Mairia didn't even have the grace to apologize.

"Haven't I been going beyond what you've required?"

"Yes, truly you have." Her voice was even, almost kind.

"Then, why? You know how much I need this work," Juliet said, her voice rising.

"I do."

Juliet sighed and fell into the chair across from the sewing table. This woman could be so exasperating. "I need this work."

"No, actually you don't."

She looked up in surprise. "What do you mean?"

Mairia pulled a letter from a small drawer at the top of the table. "I took the liberty of writing to a friend of mine in New York. Oscar Hammerstein."

"Oscar Hammerstein?" Juliet squeaked.

"We go back. But that's another story." She smiled. "He opened the Victoria in 1898, then turned it over to his sons the following year. It's fallen on hard times, but they're trying to make a go of it. For a while they put on freak revues and novelties, but in the last two years they've turned to a type of show that's selling well in New York these days."

"Why kind of show?"

"Have you heard of Flo Ziegfeld?"

"And his Ziegfeld Girls. Of course."

"The Hammersteins are patterning their shows after Ziegfeld's. Of course, it's not nearly as grand, and the stars aren't well known. But, Juliet, it's a starting place for you." She tapped the envelope on her palm. "I received Oscar's response this morning. He has already talked with his sons. You are going to New York, child. And without delay."

Juliet was stunned. "I can't!"

"You can't turn this down. It's a small role, but it's a start. And it's legitimate theatre."

Juliet swallowed hard, biting back the hope that threatened to spring from her heart. "What is the role?" she whispered.

"You will be in a variety of roles. Parodies of Shakespeare, for one thing. Song and dance, for another."

"Vaudeville, you mean."

"No, there's a difference. At the Victoria there are no freak shows. It's a clean-run place with good people—from the actors to those running it."

"It's impossible, even if I wanted to go."

"Because of the money?"

"Yes."

"I will make you a loan. Enough to get you and your sisters to New York and settled."

Juliet stood. "I appreciate the offer, but I can't accept it."

"Because you don't believe in yourself?"

"Because I'm not foolhardy enough to believe I can traipse across the country with my five sisters in tow and make a life for us. It's impossible. But I thank you for going to all this trouble on my behalf."

"Is sewing sequined slippers for me making a life for your sisters now?"

"We're getting by." She paused, then said, "I can't take your money. You're placing dreams in my head that shouldn't be there, that I'm just not capable of attaining—Mr. Locke was right. And by firing me, you're forcing me to return home to work in the packinghouses."

Mairia gave her a steady look, and her voice was as quiet as flowing water when she continued, "That kind of labor is beneath you? What must you think of my choice to serve others for my supper? What must you think of honest, hard-working laborers with mouths to feed who have no choice but to break their backs in the packinghouses?"

"It's dull," Juliet protested.

"And this isn't?" She held up a small sequin-encrusted shoe.

Juliet didn't answer.

"Go to New York," Mairia said softly. "Follow your heart."

"I'm scared."

"Ah, I thought that was it. You're afraid of failing once more."

"I had high hopes. I thought I would walk right into the first theatre I came to and land a starring role." She laughed bitterly. "Instead I lost my grit, as my mother always called it. And my dream."

"It happens to us all, child. But it doesn't mean you must give up."

Juliet let out a deep sigh. "Why didn't you contact someone here in Los Angeles. It would make things easier."

Mairia studied her for a moment. "You have surely heard about my past. All of it, the good and the bad."

"Yes."

"New York is my home. Where I'm known. It also holds memories I'd rather forget."

"You ran away."

The older woman lifted a silver brow, then smiled. "Yes, I did. I disappeared in a place where I could stay near the burning desire of my heart—theatre—but remain unknown. I adopted a new name, but I'm close enough for my heart to beat wildly every time I watch a show come to life. Or when I discover new talent."

She slowly tapped her small sewing scissors against the scarred desk. "I have remained purposely anonymous to producers, directors, actors and actresses here so that I can go on doing what I enjoy without the temptations I'm not certain I've overcome in New York.

"You said you once hired a private investigator to find me. You seemed desperate to see if I might help you, introduce you to the right people. Had you found me then, dear, and had I suggested the same Victoria Theatre and Oscar Hammerstein, would you have gone?"

"Yes," Juliet whispered, thinking how vivid her dream was then, how brightly her hope burned.

Mairia leaned forward. "And let me ask you this. Had you discovered my whereabouts before you were laughed off the stage by our Mr. Locke, would you have taken me up on my offer of financial help?"

"Yes," she had to admit.

"Even considering your sisters' care?"

Juliet let out a long sigh, nodding slightly. "Yes."

Mairia looked satisfied that she'd made her point. "You see, dear, what's holding you back?" Before she could utter a single word, Mairia continued, "There's one more thing, child, that I've also made inquiries about."

"Besides theatre?"

"You've told me so much about your sisters that I feel I know them as well as I would my own family.

It was true. While they sewed, she'd told her friend everything, from the twins' growing pains to Willow's lost teeth. Everything about the family ranchos from the original Byrnes and Dearbournes to the youngest of the clan, Emma Grace.

"I heard about a surgeon in New York who works wonders with crippled limbs, especially with children. I can't promise he's ever seen a case such as Gillian's, but he's said to be the best."

"Gillian? A doctor?" The remark stunned her so that Juliet thought she might never breathe again. She'd never heard of such miracles.

"I asked Oscar to see if he's still in practice in Manhattan. And he is."

Without another word, she reached into a valise beside the table and pulled out a small leather drawstring pouch. Handing it to Juliet, she gave her a gentle smile. "You'll find quite enough for passage to New York for all and to get you settled. Also for the doctor's visit. You must promise me you'll write as soon as you get there. Tell me where you've landed, how your audition goes." Next she picked up the envelope and put it in Juliet's hands. "Everything you need to know is in here."

"An audition? I don't think…" She couldn't finish. Her failures flashed through her mind. Then she thought of Gillian, of all Mairia was doing for them. She bit her lip. "You really believe I—we—can do this?"

"I know you can, my dear. I saw the spark in you months ago, and I'll see it again."

"You'll come to New York?" she said, before remembering Mairia's comments about the temptations there.

"Perhaps," Mairia said, walking Juliet to the door. "There's one more thing."

Juliet hesitated. "What is it?"

"Don't lose yourself in this new life. The dangers are many. The temptations that stardom brings are far worse than you can imagine."

"All I want is the joy of acting."

"You think that now, but the lure of stardom is heady. Mistakes are too easily made, the oil of joy you have now quickly replaced with ashes."

"It is possible that what I think is promise," Juliet murmured, "isn't promise at all."

"Your memory serves you well," Mairia said with a laugh. "Go now, and don't forget to write."

Juliet woke before dawn and, staring through the boardinghouse window at the hazy, filtered light, listened to the *clop-clop* of horse hooves on pavement and the clink of bottles as milkmen made their way from house to house.

Emma Grace crept from her bed to join her, crawled in and cuddled close to Juliet. Her hair smelled a bit like puppy dog, and a tiny speckle of sleep was stuck in the corner of her eye.

"Why are you smilin', Ettie?"

"Today's a big day, sweetheart. Let's wake the others to tell them the news."

"What's wrong?" Willow rubbed her eyes and sat up in her trundle.

Gillian, in the step-up bed beside Willow, crooked her elbow so she could lean on her hand. She stared at the others with a worried frown.

"Hurry, children. Get up, and get moving." Juliet laughed as she folded Gillian's, Willow's, and Emma Grace's little pantaloons and dropped them into their valises. "We haven't much time."

"Where are we going?" Abby stretched, yawned, then stretched again noisily. She scratched her shoulder.

"Don't scratch," Juliet said, still folding clothes. "It isn't ladylike."

"Why are you in a hurry?" Gillian asked, now that she was awake. She sounded grumpy.

"It's not even light yet," Annie persisted. Gillian threw a pillow at her. She howled and tossed it back. Her bottom lip protruded. "I want to go back to sleep."

Juliet clapped her hands to get their attention. Immediately silence fell over the crowded room. "Yesterday I heard about an opportunity in New York. Something that pays better than anything here."

"New York?" Abby whispered in awe. A chorus of sighs escaped the lips of the others.

"New York." Juliet sat on the edge of her bed and patted the comforter beside her. The girls gathered around, their eyes wide. Emma Grace twisted her braid, and Gillian nibbled her bottom lip. They were sitting the closest, and Juliet reached for their hands.

Willow drew her knees to her chin and wrapped her feet in her sleeping gown. "Whath in New York?" Her lisp was still prominent. At that moment Juliet thought it was the most beautiful sound in the world.

"But we must leave now. I made inquiries yesterday. The Santa Fe leaves Union Station at noon."

Sunlight was now streaming through the window, and Juliet stood. "We have a lot to do before we catch the trolley. Faces must be washed, behind the ears especially, and hair combed, the sleep removed from the corners of your eyes. You should wear your best traveling clothes. I want you lined up by the door in one hour, straw hats in place."

"Horithontal with the ground." Willow grinned, showing her shiny, toothless gums.

Juliet thought her heart might sing at the look of their excited faces. "Yes, hat brims horizontal, ribbons straight," she said, a warm glow flowing through her.

Promptly at ten thirty-seven, the girls lined up at the door in stair-step order, beginning with the smallest, Emma Grace, and ending with the twins. Juliet stepped to the side of the doorway as they exited. In the parlor she paid Miss Osgood for their meals and lodging, then took Emma Grace's hand and headed down the street to the trolley stop. They passed putting Model Ts and buggies bouncing along on squeaky springs. Bicycles, bells ringing, whizzed by, dangerously close, their enormous front wheels looking ridiculously out of harmony with their tiny back wheels, cyclists precariously balanced on top.

The city had never looked so charming, Juliet thought with a grin. Strange she hadn't noticed it until now, when she was leaving. Perhaps it was due to her suddenly buoyant mood.

The trolley stand was at the end of Miss Osgood's street, just beyond an outdoor fruit and flower market. Juliet halted the girls and gave the twins enough money to buy a sack of apples for the trip, one for each day for regularity.

Emma Grace reached for one hand, Willow for the other. Annie, Abby, and Gillian fell in behind as they headed to the trolley bench. All the girls jabbered nonstop about the train trip, New York, where they would live, when they would return. They had asked at least a thousand questions since sunup and seemed full of at least a thousand more.

They were still asking questions when Juliet strode to the ticket counter. Within minutes the tickets were purchased, and the group waited on the platform. A train's lonely whistle blew in the distance, and soon the reverberating clack of pistons and metal wheels on the track could be heard coming toward them.

For a fleeting moment she considered turning on her heel, grabbing the children, and returning to the safety of home and those who adored them. Instead, she lifted Emma Grace onto the stairs and helped her scramble up. The others followed, one by one, the twins taking up the rear, carrying their valises, hat brims horizontal to the floor.

They had settled into their seats, Emma Grace in Juliet's lap, Gillian on one side and Willow on the other, the twins in the bench behind them. Juliet leaned her head back and let her eyelids drift closed. The train soon lurched forward, and the rhythmic clacking of wheels on rails settled her spirits.

Until Emma Grace spoke. "Ettie?"

"Uh-huh, Baby," Juliet murmured, her eyes still closed.

"Look at me." Emma Grace reached up and put her hand on Juliet's cheek the way she had when she was two.

Juliet smiled into Emma Grace's round eyes. Her little brow was furrowed, her expression troubled.

"What if Papa can't find us?"

Juliet was instantly awake. "Oh, honey! When he comes home, we'll come back to California."

"But how will we know?" Emma Grace nibbled on her bottom lip. "I want Papa," she said and turned to look out the window, leaning her head against Juliet. She sighed and popped her thumb into her mouth.

"We'll write to Papa in care of the post office in Riverview. That way, when he gets home, he'll know exactly where we are."

Emma Grace put her head on Juliet's shoulder as if satisfied. But Willow and Gillian were gazing into her face now too, with their own unspoken questions.

No one knew where she was taking the children. Or why. No one would be able to find them until they were settled. Then she planned to write with the news of their success. Hers on Broadway. The children's health and happiness. Until then she wanted no one to interfere with her plans.

Fourteen

Sully squatted beside his father and touched his neck. His father's skin was hot, his breathing shallow. Sully dropped his ear to his father's chest and listened to the soft fluid rattle in his lungs.

"Father," he whispered, "I'm here." He rocked back on his heels, his courage failing. Too long he'd been dormant, like a winter-dead tree or hibernating animal, unable to move, to act. He wondered if he could change.

Staring into his father's face, he uttered his first real prayer in weeks. Not for himself. For his father.

With a flash of recognition, like the remnants of a dream come morning, he pictured his heavenly Father holding his earthly father in his arms, carrying him. Just as quickly the image disappeared, and Sully was left with an even bleaker sense of loneliness, for it was surely a premonition of his father's death. He shuddered.

"Father," he said again, "I'm here. I'll take care of you. I'll get us out of here, get you medical help." He didn't believe the words himself, but it didn't matter. His father couldn't hear him anyway.

Quaid didn't open his eyes or move.

Jacaré stood by the exit. Sully wasn't sure if he was guarding it or merely staying to help. He walked toward the young man he thought might be his friend. "Jacaré?"

A singular, swift nod downward acknowledged his name.

Quaid had been with the villagers for weeks; perhaps he'd taught someone a few words. A phrase. Anything. Sully pointed to his mouth. "English?" He made a clicking sound and pointed to Jacaré's mouth. "English," he said, again putting his fingers to his own lips. "English."

Jacaré uttered a strange word, pointing to himself. Then he pointed to Sully. "Eeeen-qlich."

"Yes." Sully nodded vigorously. "En-glish." He pointed to Jacaré again and uttered the same clipped word Jacaré had spoken. Then he stepped to the doorway and made a sweeping gesture toward the villagers. "English?"

Jacaré moved from the hut to the clearing outside the small dwelling. He shouted something. Once. Then again. A hush fell over the group, and they turned, their black-and-white masks in place. He jabbered, the clicks and grunts coming faster now, and gestured to Sully, to the doorway, then back to the group. The word "Eeeen-qlich" was uttered several times as he pointed to his mouth.

When Jacaré had finished, he looked back to Sully. The group, some sitting cross-legged near the fire, others standing behind, was silent.

No one had come forward, so Sully returned to his father's side. He knelt down.

Then a young voice spoke behind him. "Faaa-th-er?"

He turned with a frown as a slight-figured girl walked toward him. She wore a garment of palm branches and several necklaces made of gourds, pods, and kapok seeds. A pleasant rustling sound accompanied her as the fronds of the skirt swayed, and the dried pods around her neck clicked together in rhythm with her footsteps.

"Faaa-ther?" she said again, looking to the place where Sully's father lay dying. She walked to the side of the mat and knelt. "Sick," she said softly. "Long time sick."

Sully knelt beside her. "English! You speak English?"

She frowned and pointed to his lips. "Slow."

Enormously relieved, he managed a smile. "Too…fast? I speak too fast?"

She watched his mouth with a frown, then looked to his eyes, confused. With her deep-bronzed skin and black eyes, she didn't resemble his sister one bit, but there was something in her puzzled expression that reminded him suddenly of Gillian.

"Did my father teach you English?"

Her brow furrowed, and she remained silent, watching the movement of his lips and frowning.

If his father had taught her English, of course, she hadn't had time to learn more than a few words before he grew ill. What little courage he had drained away, and he sat back on his haunches with a heavy sigh. The rattle in his father's chest filled the hut. Sully bowed his head in thought.

When he looked up a moment later, the girl was gone. He let out a noisy breath. "What good am I? I don't know what to do, where to turn...if there is a place to turn to for help." He wished that his father had chosen Jared to come with him to Brazil. Jared was the son with courage and valor—starch in his spine. Not Sully.

His shoulders slumped forward. Had God brought him here only so he could say good-bye? Taking his father's hand, he held it awkwardly in both of his. His inadequacies had never been more clear. Staring at his father, he let the waves of helplessness and self-pity overtake him.

Suddenly he felt a tap on his shoulder, a touch as light as a moth's wing, and he looked up in surprise. It was the girl.

She pressed a gourd filled with water into his hands. Then without a word, she moved to Quaid's head and struggled to pull him to sitting so he could drink. Sully remained motionless as he watched her lift his father's neck and head and hold it between her hands.

He lifted the gourd to his father's lips. "Drink," he said. "Drink, please."

His father swallowed as the thin-sided implement touched his lips. He choked, then swallowed again. Water slopped into his beard. The girl spoke in the dialect of her people, almost a crooning sound, as if it had been her duty to care for Quaid since he'd fallen ill.

To Sully's surprise, his father's eyelids flickered, and his face seemed to relax at the sound of her voice. The girl said no more. She laid Quaid's head gently on the mat, then moved in barefoot silence away from the sleeping pallet.

Sully stared at the cup a moment, then looked back to his father.

Then he did the only thing that came to him. Ripping a small piece of cloth from his shirt, he dipped it into the gourd, squeezed it, and brought it to his father's face. Gently he wiped his brow, along his protruding cheekbones, and across the bridge of his nose.

The lines on his father's face softened. Sully repeated wiping the wet cloth across his brow, then down one thin arm and the other. Two bony feet stuck out from his father's dirty and torn trousers. Sully knelt beside them, and lifting one, then the other, poured water over them, then wiped each with the cloth. The girl was standing beside him now and took the empty gourd. A few minutes later she returned with fresh water. With her this time was the boy, Jacaré.

"My father needs food," Sully said. Then he scooped his fingers, spoonlike, toward his mouth.

"Food," the girl said.

Sully wearily motioned again, and said, "Yes, food." He pointed to his father, hoping she would understand that he must have something soft, drinkable. Jacaré moved toward the girl and they spoke for a moment, then left the hut together.

Outside drums were beating in a low, slow rhythm and the chanting had begun. Sully no longer felt he was in immediate danger. The villagers had kept his father alive for some reason, though he had no idea why. And they seemed to have brought Sully here to tend him. He understood none of it and was becoming too fatigued to think logically.

She held out another gourd, this one a little larger and oval in shape. In it was the familiar tapioca paste. Only less dense. He smiled again. She had understood.

He pressed it into her hands so that she could feed his father, but she refused. "You," she said, pointing toward him. "You."

Sully shook his head, frowning. "No, it's my father who needs nourishment."

She moved between him and his father, shaking her head emphatically and speaking rapidly. Off to one side, Jacaré was grinning, his white teeth showing in the dim light of the hut.

"My father needs food," Sully insisted, trying to pushing past her.

"No," she said clearly. "No!"

Sully felt his ire rising. "Get out of the way. My father will die if he doesn't have food."

Lips pressed together, the girl refused to budge.

In exasperation Sully stood to his full height and reached down to pick her up under her arms. She couldn't weigh more than a sack of feathers, but his knees threatened to give way beneath her weight. Apparently she took pity on him, for she finally moved of her own accord. Jacaré was still grinning in the background as Sully once again crouched toward his father.

"Come, hold his head," he commanded the girl.

She stared at him without moving, but there was comprehension in her eyes.

"If you're not going to help me," he said, nodding toward his father, "at least help him."

She moved closer and gently cradled the angular, bearded head in her arms. Sully moved to the opposite side, and using his fingers as a scoop, placed a small amount of the gruel on his father's lips.

Through reflex, or perhaps because he was closer to consciousness, Quaid drew in the nourishment with his tongue and swallowed. Pleased, Sully repeated the action again and again.

He was congratulating himself for succeeding in feeding his father when a sound worse than death erupted from Quaid's mouth. It was followed by a vile liquid that spilled from his father's mouth, and a moment later, more liquid from his bowels.

Sully turned his head, unable to bear the stench. Then he stood and walked briskly from the hut into the fresh air outside.

He stood near the doorway, staring at the glow of the fire and torches, as the girl cleaned his father. The one thing he'd thought might help had worsened his father's condition. He felt a presence near him and turned as a thin, gray-haired man approached. He held his mask between his inner arm and his bony torso.

"You come from far," the man said, his black eyes fixed on Sully.

Sully didn't think he'd heard right and stared at the man, dumb-founded.

The man nodded. "I attended missionary school. Long time ago. I was a child."

"Missionary school? Near here?"

The man stared sullenly. "Nothing near here."

"You spoke with my father?"

"We spent much time talking."

Sully drew in a deep, shaky breath, trying to comprehend. "Why was my father brought here?"

"You do not know?"

"Of course not." How could he have known?

"Your father a healer. Has special powers."

Sully thought he was hearing things. It was an incongruous assessment of a man who lay near death himself. "A healer?" he finally croaked.

"He healed the sick. We have seen him take away fevers and heal our elders of swelling joints."

"You must be…" *mistaken,* he started to say, then thought better of it, considering that the misconception might have been all that kept his father from being killed.

"What is it he suffers from now?"

"A curse of the pink dolphin." His expression was taut and fearful. "The river dolphin."

"The pink dolphin?" Sully leaned against the side of the thatched palm hut for support, trying not to think of the creatures he might disturb. A wolf spider, a tarantula, possibly a scorpion. He stood upright again.

The man's dark eyes glittered in the firelight. "The whole village will be cursed if he does not leave. None of us can take him from our village, or we too will fall beneath the dolphin's spell."

"That's ridiculous!" Sully spat the words, staring at the man as a gradual understanding dawned. Now he knew why he had been brought from the other village. "He has a jungle fever, that's all. I suspect he has malaria. I need to get him to a doctor…a hospital."

"There are signs you do not understand."

"How far is it to a city with a hospital?"

The man shrugged without answering.

"Iquitos. Can you take us there?"

"Our people cannot leave when you go."

"I'll never find it alone." Sully's heart was pounding so hard he thought the Indian probably saw the rise and fall of his chest. "You must send a guide with us. I insist."

The native stared at him with those unblinking, glittering eyes. "We will be struck down by the dolphin god. Cannot go."

"We have no choice!"

"You must go."

"We need a guide! Can't you see?" Sully's voice rose, becoming shrill in his panic. "Send someone with us. He can stay in his own boat, if necessary. That should take care of the curse." He was pleading.

"You will leave tomorrow at dawn." With that pronouncement, the Indian turned and moved silently toward the fire. Soon the drums quickened their beat. Dancers shuffled, holding torches, masks in place, and the sounds of shaking, seed-filled gourds obscured their chants. Wisps of a narcotic-laced scent mingled with the already heavy smoke-laden air.

Sully entered the hut just as the girl finished bathing his father. Jacaré had been standing near the doorway, and Sully looked him in the eye. He sensed that the boy knew everything, had known all along.

He walked to his father and knelt beside the pallet. The girl and Jacaré moved silently from the room.

It was just as well. Sully felt betrayed by everyone in this village, especially by the two he'd thought might befriend them. How could he ever help his father now? Surely they would both die, lost on a jungle river.

In a still and silent dawn, as fog lay thick on the river, Sully was escorted to a strip of beach. The unconscious Quaid was stretched out on a ten-foot raft made from the branches of a kapok tree and tethered with twine to one of two poles supporting a thatched roof.

Its construction was substantial, and it surprised Sully that the villagers would give up such a large and useful craft. Not that it mattered. He was fully aware of their chances for survival on the river.

His head hung in resignation as he climbed aboard. A container made from woven palm fibers had been placed in one corner. He figured it was food, but even that wouldn't matter. Not without a guide.

Before the men shoved the raft into the river, Jacaré handed Sully a steering pole. Long and unwieldy, it felt awkward in his hand. He stood in the center of the raft, uncertain what to do as the villagers stared and chattered among themselves.

Then they hit a current and spun around. Soon the raft gained speed and turned wildly again, tipping on one side, then the other, as it glided downstream. The village was soon out of sight. Only the river's black waters remained, and the jungle that threatened to close in on them from both sides.

His father stirred, and Sully turned to him, praying only that he could relieve his suffering until death overtook him.

Overtook them both.

FIFTEEN

S on?" his father whispered. "Son?"

Fighting to keep balanced against the sway of the current, Sully made his way across the raft to his father's side and knelt next to him on the smooth kapok branches. The raft tipped, and the coffee-dark water rippled in waves across the corner.

His father's eyes remained closed. The rattle in his lungs was louder now. Sully bent closer as Quaid's lips moved. "Water."

They had been on the river for several hours, and the sun was directly overhead. Sully needed to pole the awkward contraption to shore and look for fresh water, but each time he had headed for a landing place, he thought of the jungle creatures, the piranha at the water's edge, the scorpions that crawled among the rocks.

But now that his father was awake, it couldn't be put off any longer. "The river water isn't safe to drink," he said. "I must go ashore."

Quaid squinted against the glint of sun on the rippling river, his gaze boring into his son. "I'm glad you're here." His eyes were sunken in his head, with bruise-hued circles beneath them. "I prayed you'd come."

Sully let out a quick snort, which caused his father to look at him again. "As if I can do anything to get us out of this fix." He shrugged and looked out at the thick foliage that lined the river.

He had entertained the brief thought that the way to the first village might return to him, and perhaps from there, they could find their way back to the Amazon and civilization. But the dark river was deceiving with its identical tributaries. He had already discovered that what appeared to be a continuation of the river wasn't always so. Because the high-water season was over, many of the inlets led to shallow black-water pools where rafts and canoes got stuck in the thick ooze.

117

"We're together," his father said weakly, as if reading his thoughts. "And we're free. That's all that matters."

Sully guided the raft closer to shore. He searched for a stretch of smooth, sandy beach. After gliding and poling along the riverbank, he spotted such a place just before a bend in the river.

He attempted to maneuver the raft just as Jacaré had done. But for him the method was awkward. He dropped the pole in the water, then, cursing under his breath, grabbed for it before it floated away.

His father closed his eyes again and didn't seem to notice when Sully at last poled the unwieldy craft onto the strip of sand. The only extra twine to tether the raft was what the Indians had used to tie his father onto the cot so he wouldn't roll into the river.

Sully unfastened the twine and, with a grunt, rolled his father away from the edge of the raft. Then, hoping he wouldn't encounter piranha, he stepped into the water and tugged the raft to shore. After he had secured it to the slender trunk of a palm, he stepped onto the beach and looked around.

He had no weapon. No shoes. Nothing with which to carry water. If it hadn't been for his father, he would have sat down and given up hope altogether.

Instead, he looked down at his feet, bony, insect-bitten, and callused, and started to chuckle. Could it get worse? He supposed it could. But for now just finding fresh water and getting it to his father was the only thing that mattered.

Ahead of him, away from the river, lay thick foliage. When he'd traveled with Jacaré, the young Indian had easily found natural springs bubbling with sweet water. It seemed the boy knew by instinct where to look. Years of travel on the river must have taught him. But Sully had no such experience.

Sully took a few steps toward a plant with leaves the size of two elephant ears, then stopped.

He remembered that each resting place had always been near a beach. Perhaps the Indians had a pathway they had used for decades. Centuries.

He studied the dark foliage. The hint of a footpath seemed to take off just to one side of the tall elephant-ear plant. He glanced at this father to make sure he hadn't moved, then, pulling aside the giant leaves, stepped into the cool damp jungle.

Surprised, he halted. There before him was the definite trace of a path. Even the greenery had been cut back recently. He followed the path slowly, ever on the lookout for snakes in tree branches or slithering from out of the fern carpet to each side of the path.

He jumped, startled, when a monkey swung through the canopy of trees above him. The little creature pointed its comical face at Sully and scolded. Sully couldn't help the grin that took over his face. Behind the monkey a flock of bright-hued parakeets chirped and carried on.

Sully chuckled, again surprised that he was actually enjoying his walk in the jungle. He strode on along the path, paying close attention to his whereabouts to make certain he could find his way back.

He walked for several minutes before he heard the distinctive trickle of water mixing in with the sounds of birds and animals. Picking up his pace, he made his way around a clump of vines hanging from the branch overhead and through another stand of the elephant-eared foliage, and stepped into a clearing.

Stunned, he halted, almost afraid to breathe. The place contained a beauty so startling it was almost painful.

Around the sunlit lagoon rose the swamp forest, medieval and mysterious. And in the clear, rain-fed waters of the pond grew giant lilies at least six feet across. He stepped closer, stooped to taste a handful of clear liquid, and let his heart and soul devour the beauty surrounding him.

Oh, Lord, he prayed, *the beauty of your creation...I'd forgotten.* He scooped more water and swallowed huge gulps from the cupped palms of his hands. It was sweet to his palate and satisfying. He sat on his haunches, more at peace than he'd been in months.

A macaw squawked, breaking into his reverie. Sully took in its hues of royal blue and sunlit yellow, the sheen of its feathers. It cocked its head, watching him with an unblinking eye. Sully grinned, wishing his little sisters could be here to see this place, the giant lilies of the palest pink, the bird with its magnificent sweep of wings and tail.

The macaw fluttered from its perch in the upper branches to a slender twig that swayed with the weight of the bird's body. It kept its keen gaze on Sully, who suspected that with a little coaxing, the bird might land on his arm, perhaps take fruit from his fingers.

Then he began looking for something to use to take water to his father. And finally he found a cannonball-shaped nut from a nearby tree. Breaking it open, he scooped out the fruit and filled it with the sweet water. His heart was light as he headed back to the raft, humming, the makeshift canteen in his hands.

He parted the leaves to step through to the black-soil beach, then stopped.

And listened.

Voices drifted toward him from the direction of the raft. He faded back into the brush and crept around the side until he had the raft in view. As he moved a big leaf to one side, his heart dropped.

Three Indians, dressed in a different tribal garb than that of the Yagua villagers, had boarded the raft. One was pillaging through the food basket at the corner; another was rolling his father to the edge of the raft as if to push him into the water. The third man, slightly smaller than the other two, drew out a knife as if to cut the raft loose. Sully looked beyond and saw a fourth Indian waiting nearby in a dugout canoe. They were stealing the raft.

Quaid groaned and lifted his arms, attempting to shield himself from the pokes and kicks as the Indian moved him toward the side of the raft.

Sully didn't stop to think, to plan. His rage was instant.

He howled like a banshee and leapt into the clearing by the raft. The three Indians near his father stopped and stared.

Without a knife or spear, he had nothing to use for defense. Except his wits.

He yelled again, an unearthly sound. He shook his hands at the group, and chanted the only thing he could think of, a lullaby sung by his mother to him, to them all, years ago. He lowered his voice very suddenly, and began to chant, narrowing his eyes with great menace, hoping it resembled a curse. *"Sleep, baby, sleep! Our cottage vale is deep..."*

They stared at him, eyes wide.

He crept toward them slowly.

"The little lamb is on the green," he growled, *"with woolly fleece so soft and clean. Sleep, baby, sleep!"*

If he hadn't been so scared, he would have laughed. They backed away from him, moving toward the far edge of the raft. The Indian who'd been ready to cut the tether still held a knife in one hand, a spear in the other. He didn't look as frightened as the others. But Sully kept on, menacingly. Fearlessly. By now, the man in the canoe had drifted closer.

"Sleep, baby, sleep," Sully sang, his voice soft yet threatening. *"Thy rest shall angels keep, while on the grass the lamb shall feed, and never suffer want or need. Sleep, baby, sleep..."*

He placed his hands above his head, fingers splayed and wiggling. The horrified looks on the Indians' faces almost made him laugh. He roared, and they shrank back again. Now even the Indian with the weapons looked ready to run.

Sully danced a quick jig in a circle, waving his arms like some sort of supernatural tree in the wind, glad for once that Jared and the others weren't here to see him. He would never hear the end of it.

"Sleep, baby, sleep." With each ominous word, he moved closer to the raft. *"Down where the woodbines creep."* On the word *creep,* he lurched forward. The Indians jumped back in rhythm. *"Be always like a lamb so mild, a kind, and sweet, and gentle child. Sleep, baby, sleep."*

He leaped onto the raft, hoping he looked enough like a madman to give them pause. With hollow eyes, dirty beard, and wild tangle of hair, emaciated limbs, and ragged clothes, he certainly could have passed for a lunatic. He stifled another laugh, fighting to keep his look grim, waving his arms and growling like a wild man as he sidled toward his father. Even if he couldn't coax the marauders off the raft, at least he would be there to catch his father when they rolled him into the river.

The three men now stared at him from where they huddled in one corner of the raft. Before Sully could blink, the canoe drifted closer, and the men leapt in, never once taking their wide-eyed gaze from Sully.

He heard a raspy grunt as the dugout canoe glided away from them, and he gave another wild shout until they had paddled out of sight.

"Sleep, baby, sleep?" His father's whisper was hoarse. "You scared off the savages with your mother's lullaby." His shoulders shook in silent laughter. *"A kind, and sweet, and gentle child?"* He coughed with the effort of talking. "They were anything but…"

Sully knelt beside him and lifted the round nutshell. "I brought you water." Then he turned it over. Not a drop fell out. The water had apparently sloshed out during his wild antics. He stared at his father a moment, a plan formulating.

"I found a good resting place for us tonight. We can't stay on the raft." His father opened his feverish eyes. "You're in charge, son."

The words frightened him, but he hid his fear. He gave his father a quick nod, as if leadership was the most natural thing in the world for him to assume. Quaid needed him to be a man, and the more his father could relax, the quicker he would recover.

An hour later, Sully led his father, whom he'd half-carried, half-dragged, into the clearing by the clear-water pool. The sun was on its downward slant, its golden-pink rays transforming the little cove into an ethereal wonderland. When he had his father settled to the ground, Sully glanced at his father's face to see if he was awake enough to appreciate the beauty of the place.

But his father had curled into a ball and was clutching his stomach in pain.

Frowning, Sully moved closer. "Father, what is it?"

Quaid didn't answer. Beads of sweat covered his face, and he began to shake uncontrollably. When Sully touched his father's face, his worries increased. The fever had risen again, this time higher than before. Without hesitation, Sully ripped what was left of his shirt from his back and plunged it into the water.

As darkness thickened, Sully continued washing Quaid's body with the cool cloth. Twice he pulled his father into the water and held him afloat until the fever subsided and the shaking lessened. It took only a few minutes, though, until it rose again and the violent convulsions continued. By dark, his father was delirious, calling out to Emmeline as though she stood next to them.

"I love you, my darling," he uttered, looking into the dark foliage. Then he ranted about citrus groves and wild lands, about his cousin Merci and how he had to find her. He tried to rise, and it took every ounce of Sully's strength to keep his father lying down.

"Father, keep Merci in your care!" Quaid mumbled over and over again. "I can see your arms around her! Don't let her go." Sometimes he sobbed, his brow wet with perspiration, and he tossed this way and that, his face grimacing in pain.

Sully was afraid to leave him even for the few minutes it would take to return to the raft and retrieve the basket of food. Without it, they had nothing to eat, at least nothing that he was certain was edible. Then he remembered his father's reaction to the food the last time he had eaten and decided to wait until dawn.

The night sounds rose to a racket, and Sully shivered in fear. He sat in the dark, listening to the rattle of his father's breathing and occasional wild ranting. He had only a stick the size of his leg to keep anything at bay that might attack. So he remained at his father's side, keeping watch over him as the bleak darkness wore on.

He had heard the story of his father's cousin Merci years ago, but he'd been too young to pay it any mind. Now, as he listened to Quaid's delirious ravings, the story returned. His father had felt responsible for Merci running off when they were young, and he'd given up everything to search for her, eventually even the rancho that had been his inheritance.

The part of the story that seemed to be Quaid's focus now was his prayer for Merci, how he had never prayed for anyone until that night, just before he left on his journey to find her.

His father had told the children many times how it happened. How when he cried out, telling God he didn't know the words to pray, he'd sat for a long time in the darkness of the rancho library. After waiting a while, his prayer became an image, instead of words. He pictured Merci in Christ's arms, wrapped in his robe…being carried in Jesus' strong arms…borne along even while she was in her "troubles," as they later referred to it. Each image became the prayer of his heart, put there by God. He couldn't have known what was ahead for Merci, where she was, what choices she was making. He only knew to surround her with prayer, his father said, each one lifted heavenward.

Sully listened as Quaid thrashed back and forth and groaned.

"I don't know how to pray, Father." Sully spoke aloud into the jungle night. "I have come to the end of everything, especially of myself.

"I haven't even anger to hold on to. And certainly no courage."

He stared upward, noticing for the first time the brilliant canopy of stars. "You are the God of my father, but I suppose I never thought I needed anyone but myself to rely on."

He laughed. The sound was hollow. "As if relying on myself—someone with greater fears and less confidence than any other ten people—would accomplish anything."

His father groaned again, and Sully reached for the cloth, dipped it in the pool, and laid it on his father's forehead.

He stared into the darkness, the water lilies barely visible in the ink-hued night. "I don't know what to do." His voice sounded like a child's, but he didn't care. And he figured God didn't mind. "I don't know how to save us—my father from whatever illness is eating away at him, myself from the hugeness of this jungle." He paused, letting the words sink in. It felt good to talk to Someone who understood him, Someone who cared. He wondered why he'd waited so long.

"We're not going to make it. But I ask you to take away my father's suffering…"

He halted, his voice breaking. "I don't know how to pray for him. If I pray for his recovery, we'll still be lost in the jungles. Should I pray that we'll be found?" He dwelt on the words for a moment. "How can I know what your will is, Father? If you've already decided that it's our time to die, dare I ask that you change your mind?" He dropped his face to his hands and sat in silence for a moment. "How, Father?"

An image came into his mind, a pleasant image of his father…and his Lord.

"Father," he breathed, "cleanse my mind. Take away all hope, all images of hope, if they aren't from you."

The image filled his mind, Christ carrying his father just as he had seen in the hut the night before. Now they walked beside a sea, the waves laced across the sand in harmony and rhythm with Christ's foot-steps. It was a comforting sight somehow, perhaps because the Christ who walked with his father was the Creator of all things.

All things. Creator of the hills back home, the sea and its creatures, also of this…the giant lilies, the jungle, and its inhabitants. The people who lived here.

Musing on the idea, Sully opened his eyes once more and stared into the night sky. He was no farther from God's presence here than he was sitting on the veranda of the Victorian in the Big Valley.

For weeks now he'd felt so alone, overwhelmed by self-pity. Now he looked down at his father, barely visible in the darkness.

"Forgive me, Lord," he breathed, "for forgetting that you are with me. With us. That nothing happens without your knowledge. That no matter where we go in the world, you are there."

He remembered the words of the psalm that his father often read before breakfast to all the children. Sully had been too young to pay it any mind, so only snatches returned to him now. He couldn't remember where the verses were found or even the exact words. But phrases returned…the impression of the words and their meaning from so long ago.

If I rise on the wings of the dawn,
If I settle far across the sea,
Even there your hand will lead me…
Your right hand will hold me fast.
The darkness will not be dark to you.
The night will shine as the day…
Darkness and the light are both alike to you.

Sully bowed his head, comforted. God was here with him, with his father. He swallowed hard, fighting against a surge of emotion that threatened to pour from him. God had been here all along. It didn't matter whether he was at home, riding across the windswept ranch lands, or here, in this foreign region of God's world.

Sully laid his hand on his father's head, feeling a new strength in himself. A strength that gave him courage to pray.

"Father," he said, "no matter the outcome, I place my life and that of my father in your hands."

Quaid, still unconscious, muttered in delirium.

Sully touched his forehead. "Let him live, heavenly Father. Please, let him live."

He thought of his brothers and sisters at home, and for the first time felt the full weight of his last weeks of moping in self-pity. How could he have thought only of his own discomfort when the little ones were grieving for their father and brother, likely considering them dead?

"Forgive me for my selfishness, Father," he prayed, "and comfort the little ones at home: Emma Grace, Willow, Gillian, Abby, Annie, and Juliet." He grinned, thinking about them, missing them. "And Jared, Father. Give him strength to keep things going until we get home."

Until we get home…?

He threw back his head and laughed out loud. Here he was in the middle of God-knew-where, and he was still thinking about going home.

God knows where we are after all, he thought, relaxing in the strange sense of peace that filled his entire being.

Drawing in a deep breath, he listened to the night music of the jungle, and for the first time since their capture, he actually wanted to live. A small spark of something inside him, something he'd not known was there still now, grew into a flame. Courage, perhaps?

He laughed again. He wouldn't have thought it possible until he'd frightened off the Indians with nursery rhymes…until he'd met his God in this place.

Dipping the cloth in the pool and laying it again on his father's forehead, he uttered a prayer with every breath.

Then he settled down, close enough to hear his father cry out, to sleep if he could, to await dawn if he couldn't.

A heavy mist hung low over the sweet-water pond when Sully awoke. The morning jungle sounds greeted him. He looked immediately to his father, who seemed to be resting more peacefully now, without the groans of delirium of the night before.

They had made it through their first night. But before he could congratulate himself, he thought he'd better see to getting them some nourishment. He stood, stretched his cramped back and arms, and headed down the path to the river.

The raft rocked gently, lifting with the current, then dropping again as small waves lapped against it. He leapt onboard and headed toward the basket of provisions. Just as he lifted the lid and looked in, he heard a sound from behind the dense foliage.

At first he thought perhaps his father must have followed him. Just as quickly he knew it was impossible.

Frowning he turned toward the sound. One of the elephant-eared leaves moved as someone—or something—stirred behind it. Someone watched him. He could sense a penetrating stare.

The hair on the back of his neck stood on end. Very likely nursery rhymes wouldn't work twice.

He stared at the place, hoping his look was menacing. "Come out!" he shouted, his hands in fists. Whispering a prayer, he stood tall, thin shoulders back. "I command you to show yourself!"

Sixteen

Clay MacGregor headed from the Big Valley on his tall bay mare, her black tail and mane gleaming in the sun. A day like today made him glad he'd moved to Riverview. Especially because he was the only private detective in town. He grinned. And he's just been hired by three elderly sisters to find their relative, Miss Juliet Rose Dearbourne. Granddaughter to one, grandniece to the other two. He looked heavenward and chuckled. It seemed God had once again answered his prayers.

He nudged the bay mare to a canter. Just the thought of once more beholding the sweet curve of her cheek, gazing into the flash of her azure eyes, and watching her move across a room with the fluid grace of a deer was enough to make his heart race. He would find her, all right.

Of course, convincing her to return home was something else entirely.

Clay boarded the train to Los Angeles within the hour, then ran to catch a streetcar to the address Merci had given him.

He bounded up the steps at Miss Osgood's boardinghouse and rapped on the door. A prim-looking woman answered.

"Miss Osgood?"

"Yes." Her lips pinched into a sour look even before she spoke.

"I'm here on behalf of Juliet Dearbourne's family."

"I've already answered all the questions one could possibly think of regarding Juliet Dearbourne." She gave him an impatient sniff.

"I realize this is an inconvenience, but perhaps some detail has been overlooked," he persisted.

The woman nodded and stepped back to let him in. He followed her to a small sitting room and took his place near an ornately carved organ. Miss Osgood sat down opposite him.

"Did Miss Dearbourne give any indication the morning she left where she might be headed?"

"The train station. Just like I told one of her relatives. Miss Merci Byrne."

"She didn't mention a location—or even a direction—beyond that?"

"No." Miss Osgood frowned. "I told you, I really have no information about the Dearbournes."

A little girl with bright orange curls skipped by the doorway, paused, then leaned again the jamb, her chin tucked down.

"Run along, child," Miss Osgood said. "This is a grown-up conversation."

"Wait," Clay said, looking at the girl. "Did you know the Dearbourne children? Maybe play with the ones your age?"

The little girl nodded. "Uh-huh."

Clay stood and walked nearer the child, then half knelt, half squatted, rocking on his right boot heel in front of her. "Which one?"

"Two. Emma Grace and Willow." She smiled at him, her nose wrinkling.

"Did you see them the morning they left?"

"Yes." She stooped to fiddle with the buttons on her shoe.

"Did you play together?"

She stood and twisted her shoulders for emphasis. "No. They didn't have time. Their big sister was makin' 'em hurry out of here."

"Did they say why?"

"Uh-huh."

"Why?"

"They was leavin' on a trip. A long trip on a train."

"Oh, that sounds exciting. Did they say where?"

"I don't remember where." She ran the end of her ribbon sash between her fingers and thumb and sighed.

Clay leaned forward patiently. "How about if I name some places and you tell me if they sound familiar?"

"Okay."

"San Francisco?" He raised a brow.

"Nope."

"Sacramento?"

She shrugged and puckered her forehead into a frown. "No."

"Um, how about Denver?" He sighed.

She shook her head and giggled. "This is a funny game."

"Denver?" he repeated.

"Nope." She was smiling at him now, her eyes full of mischief.

"Chicago?"

She shook her head so hard her curls bounced.

"New York?"

"Ummmm, maybe."

"Think hard. It's important."

The little girl wiggled her fingers in the air around her head and ears, pretended to fasten a bow under her chin. "Mama's always tellin' me to put on my thinkin' cap so that's what I'm doing."

He grinned at her. "Good. Now that your thinking cap is on, tell me if New York sounds right."

She puckered her forehead. "I think so."

"New York?" he said again, looking into her face.

"Can you ride a train there?"

"Yes."

"Then that's where they was going."

He didn't want to confuse her by saying she could ride a train to all the other places he'd mentioned. "Did Willow and Emma Grace say anything else about their trip?"

"Nope. We was standin' in line at the privy when they told me. It was my turn next, and they was gone after I finished."

He grinned at her as he stood up. "Thank you, little lady. You've been a big help."

"You believe the child?" Miss Osgood frowned at him as though she'd never believed a child in her lifetime.

He nodded. "Of course. Children can often be the most honest witnesses and forthcoming informants."

With a sniff, Miss Osgood stood to see him to the door.

He ran to catch the next trolley rattling across town to the theatre district. When he stepped from the vehicle, he walked down the street and around the corner to the New Globe.

He was fortunate to catch Locke on his way to rehearsal. The man agreed to discuss Juliet Dearbourne on the walk from his office to the stage.

"I had to let her go," he explained. "She was doing a fine job, but we just didn't have enough work for her apparently."

"What do you mean 'apparently'?" They headed around a corner near some Shakespearean costumes. Snatches of Elizabethan speech carried toward them.

"I let the head of costuming determine her needs. If she decides to sack someone, that's her choice. I don't interfere."

"And her name is…?"

"Cornelia. If you'd like to speak with her, she might be willing to tell you what she knows." He gave directions to the costuming room, then headed toward the players.

Moments later, Clay knocked on Cornelia's door.

The woman who opened it surprised him. Elegant was the first notion that came to his mind. With her thick silver hair twisted into a knot atop her head, aristocratic neck, and a curious brightness to her eyes, she looked nothing like any head of costuming he'd seen before. Not that he'd seen many. His stunt work kept him in the air, not on sets, and his costumes were usually limited to a fringed neck scarf, leather helmet, and goggles.

"May I help you?" She held a length of fabric in her hands, needle poised in midstitch.

"I'm sorry to disturb you, but Mr. Locke suggested I stop by and ask you some questions."

"Certainly," she said, stepping backward. "Come in, please. Sit down." She nodded to a chair across from her small sewing table. "And this is regarding…?" She resumed her work.

"I'm looking for someone who was in your employment a few weeks ago. Miss Juliet Rose Dearbourne."

"Rose," she mused. "I wasn't aware of her full name. That would look very nice on—" She stopped as she tied a knot in the thread and bit off the length.

"You remember her then?"

She laughed. "Oh my, yes. One certainly couldn't forget Juliet." She paused to rethread her needle. "Juliet Rose."

"I've been hired on behalf of the family to find her."

She dropped her needle and fumbled to find it. "Have you now?" she said, and sat up straight.

"Locke tells me you fired her."

"That's true. There wasn't enough work to sustain the two of us."

"Do you know where she's gone?"

"She told me in confidence," Cornelia said, looking at him evenly. Something seemed to dawn in her eyes, and she smiled almost in recognition. "Tell me your name again."

"How rude of me. I'm sorry," he said rather sheepishly. "Clay MacGregor, private investigator, at your service. The best Riverview has to offer." He grinned. "Also the only one Riverview has to offer."

She laughed with him, going back to her stitching.

"I appreciate your keeping a confidence," he said, letting his eyes travel over her small table. Stacks of papers, costume designs, and notes were intermingled with spools of thread, pincushions, and scissors of varying sizes. "I must do the same in my business."

She looked up and nodded.

"But this is a matter of the welfare of young children. Surely you can understand why the family is worried. Juliet doesn't have the means to care for them properly. They could be living on the streets for all we know."

"I can assure you, Miss Dearbourne isn't living on the streets," Cornelia said with confidence.

"You've heard from her then?"

"Yes. But you'll get nothing more from me. I must honor her wishes."

"I know she's in New York."

A shadow crossed the older woman's face, and he knew the child at Miss Osgood's had been right. He leaned forward. "I will find her, but if you could give me a hint as to where she's living, working...anything, it would relieve her grandmother and aunts."

Cornelia seemed nervous suddenly, her eyes darting across the tabletop. She shifted the fabric toward a pile of papers on her right. He stared at the spot, curious about what she was hiding, and when their eyes met, he saw a disapproving expression on Cornelia's face.

"I won't keep you any longer," he said. "I'm sorry I troubled you." He stood abruptly, having found exactly the clue he needed.

She kept her lips in a prim, unfriendly line as he made his way to the door. He turned and gave her a nod. "Thank you," he said, then headed out.

She didn't answer.

Mairia picked up the envelope and fanned her face with it. If she hadn't tried to cover the address written in the upper left-hand corner, the young man might not have noticed *Victoria Theatre* written in large, ornate lettering, with its address—7th Avenue and 42nd Street.

She gathered her things from the small drawer in the center of the table, the remainder of her savings, Juliet's most recent letter, also that from Oscar Hammerstein, and tucked them into her satchel.

There was only one thing to do. Get herself to New York before the private investigator found Juliet.

She turned out the light and headed down the long hallway to find Mister Locke to resign her position. Who knew when she might return? Or whether she would return.

The temptations New York held for her were many, the old life with its old habits and old sins. She pushed the worries aside, thinking instead of Juliet and the children and reaching them in time.

Her only hope was that Mr. MacGregor was as incompetent at sleuthing this time as he'd been on the assignment to find Opera Diva Mairia Garden.

Seventeen

On her sixth week in New York, Juliet stepped into the lights for her third audition at the Victoria. Even the letter from Oscar to Mairia promising special treatment hadn't hurried the process. She had to wait with everyone else for the scheduled audition dates. As each week passed, her anxieties grew as steadily as her funds dwindled.

Gladding McBean—who made it clear he preferred to be called Gladdy—leaned back in his seat in the third row. The director was colorful in both spirit and dress, from his spats to his pink shirt. She wasn't sure which outdid the other. She'd liked him from the first time they met. But she'd known his agreement to let her audition was merely a favor to Mairia's friend, the theatre's founder, not because he thought she might have talent.

"Parade." Gladdy McBean waved his hand, then looked to the orchestra and nodded to the conductor. "Play *Araby*," he said. *"The Sheik of Araby."*

Juliet breathed in deeply and swallowed hard again. Heart pounding, she tried to still her clammy hands. The music began, a heavy Middle Eastern tone and rhythm, and she swallowed a sudden giggle. Strut to *this* with a serious face? She didn't think it possible.

The drums beat their exotic rhythms, and she stared dumbly at the orchestra, wondering how to move, where to move to, and if she should move—all by the time the orchestra hit the second measure.

She looked down at Gladdy McBean's intense expression, and in her nervousness, fought the sudden urge to laugh. She scanned the ornate theatre, the heavy drapes, the gold-and-tile-inlaid ceiling. And beneath it all, the incessant drum music, something no real sheik would likely recognize.

The showgirls she'd seen backstage, many of them sultry, buxom, and heavy-hipped, were cut out for such a parade. But someone knee-high to a doodle bug? as her father used to call her. She giggled again. This was as far from her dream of serious theatre as it could possibly get.

The music continued, and Mr. McBean frowned. "Miss Dear-bourne, we're waiting."

"Yes sir," she called to him. "I-I just wanted to get the right feel for it."

He settled back in his chair and waved his hand. "Then go on. Let's see what you've got."

"Start the music again, please," she called out. "I would like to make my entrance from offstage."

Mr. McBean looked surprised, but he nodded to the maestro who halted the music with a stroke of his baton.

A moment later, she grabbed a feather boa that was draped hap-hazardly from a hook offstage and looped it around her neck. With a dramatic sniff, her head tilted seductively, she awaited the music.

The heavy rhythm began again, and Juliet forgot everything except becoming a parody of the most sultry star she could think of, Theda Bara. She glided onto the stage, lengthening her stride, letting the boa flutter.

Never once did she break character as she moved to center stage, twisted sideways, and fluttered her lashes at McBean.

Grinning ear to ear, he motioned for her to continue. She swallowed her surprise.

Juliet gestured to the maestro to soften the music so her voice could be heard. The strings dropped to a honey-silk rhythm, and the drums thudded softly as Juliet vamped across the stage as if it belonged to her. She motioned for the orchestra to match the beat of her stride, then stopped and looked at McBean.

"You would like me to sing, dahling?" she drawled in a sultry voice.

He lifted a brow and nodded, still grinning. "Go on."

She looked into the orchestra pit. "Do you know *The Rose of Washington Square?*"

The maestro nodded and swung his baton into a faster beat.

"That's more like it," Juliet said, pulling a long-stemmed paper rose from behind her skirt.

As Juliet performed, her body felt lighter than air. Never had she felt more alive, more vibrant. A warm rush of blood ran through her veins as she tilted her head and swayed her hips seductively. Another actress performing the same dance might have brought a grown man to his knees. But from her…?

She watched McBean's expression and knew she'd guessed right. He understood the parody and guffawed. The orchestra members were looking up at her as she strutted across the stage. Some were chuckling out loud, attempting to continue playing.

She sidled to center stage once more. "Now for my finale," she said, "you may play *A Pretty Girl is Like a Melody*." It was the theme song of the Follies as the real show girls undulated across the stage swathed in their acres of feathers and chiffon.

Juliet lifted her head and with her boa circling like a cowboy's lasso, moved across the stage. Halfway, she tripped at the perfect comedic moment, caught her boa around her ankle and tripped again. Stretched prone, she turned to her side, resting her head on her hand, elbow on the floor. She gave McBean a coquettish grin and batted her lashes. As she stood, she placed the rose stem between her teeth, stood and bowed, then sailed to the curtain on the far side of the stage. The music came to a dramatic close at precisely the same time she gave her last bow and swung the rose from her mouth.

Her heart drummed frantically as she brought her cold hands to her sizzling cheeks. She tried to catch her breath and calm her quaking knees.

"Miss Dearbourne," McBean called to her. "Miss Dearbourne, please. Will you return to the stage?"

Juliet swallowed hard and moved back into the lights. She shaded her eyes with her hand to see McBean's face. He walked toward her and around to the stage door, then bounded up the steps to join her.

"I want you to try it this way," he said, and showed her a better angle to carry her body across the stage.

She nodded and followed his lead. The boys in the orchestra laughed. McBean met her gaze. "It's funnier that way. Try it again."

And she did. For a half-hour he showed her steps, refined her timing, and let the maestro suggest different music. He asked his choreographer to join them, and together they had Juliet try some new steps. Then he called the woman in charge of costuming and talked about possibilities for Juliet.

Juliet stood to one side during most of the discussion, certain she was dreaming. Finally, Mr. McBean motioned to Juliet to join him. "How would you feel about going on stage with your act?"

Juliet let a slow smile overtake her face. "My act?"

"The same one you just performed."

She swallowed hard, stared at her toes a moment, trying to collect herself before lifting her eyes again to his. "I feel just fine about it...I mean, if you think it's good enough."

He didn't reassure her that it was. Instead he frowned, and again she worried that he was merely asking her as a favor to Mairia. "We'll let the audience decide. You'll perform tonight. If they accept you, we'll work you into the show on a regular basis."

Juliet's heart was pounding so hard she thought it might burst right through her chest. "Tonight?" she croaked. "What about my costuming, the music...?"

"You just leave all that to us, my dear. All you must do is rehearse your moves, work with Maestro here to learn your cues."

"Tonight," Juliet whispered, almost to herself.

"Tonight," McBean pronounced. Then he nodded to the maestro to begin.

Juliet stood dumbfounded, staring at the empty stage. She should be rejoicing.

This was what she wanted, wasn't it? What she'd hoped for, dreamed about for years!

"Miss Dearbourne?" the maestro called.

She took her position onstage, trying to forget everything except the task ahead.

The nagging worry that she shouldn't leave her sisters alone in the city during tonight's performance darkened her thoughts. She pushed her worries aside for later.

Then the music began.

Boa waving, she strutted from behind the curtain.

Clay MacGregor strolled through the heart of Manhattan's theatre district on his way to the Victoria. On either side of him marquees blazed with the show titles of Broadway's latest musicals, comedies, farces, and revues. Three-foot high posters with the names of the most popular stars on Broadway beckoned theatregoers—to his right, the extravagant productions of Irving Berlin, George M. Cohan, and the Shubert brothers.

Dusk was descending on the city, and the evening air was balmy. It might have been lovely except for the clamor all around. On the street, trolleys and automobiles fought horse-drawn carriages for space. Bicyclists rattled their handlebar bells, and theatregoers, dressed in diamonds and furs, shoved and pushed their way into lines for tickets.

When he reached the agent in the booth in front of the Victoria, he smiled amiably as he passed the man his money. "Who're in the revues tonight?"

The man looked up from under the rounded brim of his uniform cap. "Can't name them all, sir. But it's a good lineup, that you can be sure of." He handed Clay his change and the ticket.

"Anyone new?" He couldn't imagine that Juliet had landed a job so quickly, but it didn't hurt to ask.

The man shrugged impatiently. "The names are listed on the program." He jerked his thumb toward the door. "Inside."

Clay fell in among the crowd and made his way past the ticket taker, who handed him a single-page program. Eager to read it, he hurried into the theatre and took his seat near the rear. The light was dim, but not dark enough to keep him from reading the long list of players. Act One, as promised on the playbill, was the parody of D. W. Griffith's

Intolerance, here called *Tolerance.* Act Two promised three scenes, all Shakespeare parodies, and Act Three would be war skits and a ballet.

His gaze fell on Act Four, Scene Two, a skit titled the *Travesty of Scheherazade.*

But Juliet wasn't listed among the players. He would need to make inquiries in the morning. Likely she was working in costuming again.

The curtain was drawn, but he could see movement behind it. Music drifted from the orchestra pit. He settled back and crossed an ankle over the other knee.

The orchestra leader held up his baton, and for a split second silence reigned. Then the music began. Clay laughed his way through the Shakespearean parodies, *Tolerance,* two ballets, and parodies of the *Keystone Kops, The Perils of Pauline,* and a boxing match. None were risqué, but all were lighthearted entertainment.

Then the music changed dramatically, turning into an exotic beat and the wail of an oboe or two.

Six young men dressed like sultans slithered onto the stage, turbaned heads high, backs straight. They danced-kicked into a semicircle, singing about the beautiful Cleopatra. They extolled her attributes from head to toe, her sultry and statuesque beauty, her honeyed voice.

Clay sat forward. He'd heard plenty about New York's beautiful showgirls, and now he held his breath in anticipation.

The male chorus continued its words of adulation about Cleopatra until finally they faced the right side of the stage, arms outstretched.

The orchestra leader nodded to the percussion section, and a long drum roll was followed by a wire brush on snares in a seductive rhythm. The spotlight crossed to the heavy crimson curtain, stage right.

Clay could almost feel the anticipation in the large, dark theatre. He was imagining the beautiful, curvaceous woman, Cleopatra. Slinky yet slender as an Egyptian reed.

No one appeared.

The maestro lifted his baton again and the percussion section began another drum roll, the wire brush rhythm became louder, and the men in the chorus lifted their arms higher.

The spotlight remained on the heavy curtain.

The drum roll continued.

At the precise moment when Clay thought the actress must surely have missed her cue, a small and delicate young woman stepped onto the stage. She was swathed in veils.

Frowning, he leaned forward, elbows on knees, shoulders hunched so his hands could support his chin. He concentrated on the only part of her face that was visible. Her eyes, luminous and large, struck a chord in his heart. Surely this wasn't Juliet. It couldn't be, could it?

Just as she took her first sultry steps forward, a child's straw hat rolled from behind the curtain on the opposite side of the stage, spun like a coin to a halt on the polished floor. A flash of reddish pigtails, a swatch of navy-blue cloth, the dart of a tiny hand…and the hat disappeared.

It happened so quickly that Clay thought his imagination most surely was working overtime.

The veiled figured didn't miss a beat.

But he kept his gaze on the spot where he thought he had seen the child. He wasn't disappointed. After a moment, a little girl sidled her way to the edge of the heavy velvet curtain. His seat angle afforded a perfect view of the child's face, though she was likely visible to only a few others in the audience and perhaps the actress, should she look. The child, now squatting on her knees behind the curtain, watched with rapt attention, her hands brought together as if ready to clap with delight at any minute.

The woman turned her back to the audience, apparently to shoot a disapproving glare toward the child, and Clay grinned as the child quickly disappeared.

Clay's attention was brought immediately back to center stage. The sultans twirled and kicked as a comic rendition of *The Sheik of Araby* sounded from the orchestra pit. They held large fronds of pampas grass, hiding from the audience's view the center attraction: the young woman actress.

After a few minutes of singing and dancing, the sultans bowed and parted, stepping backward in a half-circle to reveal the woman that they celebrated.

There, on a pedestal, was the young actress. She struck a pose like Theda Bara, chin tilted upward, and fanned her face with a smaller frond of pampas.

She was in complete control, from her sultry demeanor to her slightly husky, melodic voice once she began to sing. The lyrics were perfect for her—incongruous, considering her Mary Pickford-like size and large expressive eyes.

He found himself chuckling as she delivered her lines, guffawing as she vamped and flirted with the audience. Judging from the expressions of the musicians and male chorus, he wasn't alone in his love of the actress's performance. Every movement was perfection itself.

She danced and sang and moved across the stage with faultless comedic timing. When the curtain fell at the end of her performance, Clay leaned back in his seat, still laughing.

During intermission, he walked from the theatre into the foyer and glanced up at the colorful bills depicting tonight's performers. None of the actresses resembled the young woman. He glanced at the playbill once more, then decided to catch some fresh air before returning to his seat.

He dodged a runabout as he crossed the street and narrowly missed a leather-top buggy heading the opposite direction. Both were carrying theatregoers, judging from the men in their double-breasted coats and high winged collars and the women in hats as wide as their hips and frothy, birdlike bows of tulle. Hundreds of others strutted up and down the side walkways, seeming more concerned with being seen than making it to their destination.

The showgirl couldn't be Juliet, he told himself for the dozenth time. Then he remembered the child backstage and knew it had to be. It was too much of a coincidence.

⇐◆⇒

Juliet sat the children down in the corner of the bustling, crowded dressing room and gave them a stern lecture about staying silent and staying put. She narrowed her eyes at Emma Grace and threatened her within an inch of her sweet life if the child again dared to stick her button nose out the door. All around them showgirls applied face paint and draped themselves in costume. Laughter, loud hoots, and murmuring voices filled the air. One of the musicians slid up and down the scales on a saxophone, and the oboist hit a couple of shrill notes, trilled a bit, then played a few measures of *The Sheik of Araby,* practicing for the finale.

The children's eyes were big with awe, and Juliet looked at their faces, wondering if she'd made a terrible mistake bringing them here. All around them were props and costumes. A mirrored dressing table took up nearly half the room, and it was covered with pots of paint and hairbrushes. A feather boa was looped across the top of the scratched mirror. The women chattered amiably and from time to time stopped to tousle Emma Grace's hair.

"I like the feater," she said more than once.

Even the twins chattered like magpies as if this was the most wonderful outing they'd ever had. Juliet warned them again about staying put during the finale, then stepped to the mirror to adjust her veils.

A loud rapping sounded at the door.

"Ettie!" squealed Willow. "It must be time for you to do your dance again! It isn't fair. Emma Grace got to see last time. I wanna see this time."

"Not a chance, pumpkin," Juliet said, heading to the door. Then she turned again to give them each a quick hug.

Pausing, her hand on the brass knob, she drew in a deep, calming breath. Her performance had rekindled the old hopes and dreams long buried in her heart. She closed her eyes for just an instant, knowing that when she moved onto that stage for the reprise, she would give it her all. And after tonight, her life—their lives—would never be the same.

She met their hopeful gazes. "I'll be thinking of you the whole time," she said, "and when you hear this music…" She hummed a few bars of *The Sheik of Araby,* whining like an oboe. They giggled. "When you hear that, it means I'm almost through with my opening night. And on our way home we'll stop and celebrate with ice cream."

Cheers went up just as the knock came again. She blew them all a kiss and turned the brass knob.

Instead of the stagehand, a tall, broad-shouldered man stood leaning against the doorjamb, arms folded across his chest, feet crossed at the ankles. He swept off his hat and gave her a curt nod.

"Juliet Rose Dearbourne, we meet again."

"Clay MacGregor," she gasped, stepping backward.

He looked over her shoulder into the room. "And you are the missing Dearbourne sisters, I presume?" He winked at them.

But when he turned back to Juliet, his look was chillingly disapproving.

"What do you want?"

"Pack your things, ladies. It's time to return to California."

Eighteen

Quaid stepped into a sunlit spot near an old century oak near the house. The light was so vivid, so clear, it stunned him for a moment, and he couldn't move. In the distance, jagged peaks rose against a purple-blue sky, and from the top of a pepper tree, a mockingbird trilled. He grinned as he shaded his eyes and looked up to watch its clownlike antics. Then he remembered. Mockingbirds always turned somersaults and trilled in spring. And it was definitely spring. Orange blossoms covered the ground like fragrant snow, their perfume filling the air. For a moment he stood, eyes closed, savoring the fragrance, the beat of the sun on his shoulders, the calls of the red-tailed hawk soaring overhead.

In the blink of an eye, he stood on a hill overlooking the Big Valley. Below him lay the ranch that he and Emmeline had worked so hard to make a success. Sunny Mountain Ranch, they'd called it whimsically after Emmeline designed a label with the same name for the crates that held their oranges, fruit that was shipped across the nation. The drawing was a rendition of their Big Valley, snowcapped mountains, even rows of orange trees, with Emmeline's graceful Victorian grove house tucked among the pepper trees and live oaks, sheltered by the morning glory she treasured. He chuckled, thinking of her surprise when he entered the label in the State Fair—without her knowledge—and it won first place.

Still chuckling to himself, he walked to an outcropping of granite at the edge of the bald mountain and remembered the night he'd brought Emmeline here years ago. He'd watched her beloved face as she tumbled upward into the starry skies and shared her delight when she spotted the tiny red spider eyes reflected by the full moon.

Where had the time gone? How he would love to see her once more, hold her in his arms, laugh with her. No one else shared memories of their love, the births of their children, their trials through drought and floods and fires. No one else knew the joy of holding each of their babies in their arms for the first time. No one else had watched them grow, rejoicing in every first step, every sweet word added to their vocabulary.

He thought of them now. Sweet little Juliet, all bouncing curls and rosy cheeks, and the boys, rough-and-tumble Jared and Sullivan with his intelligent eyes and gentle ways. Then came the twins, Annie and Abby. He grinned as he remembered them wrapped in flannel blankets, one on either side of Emmeline. He thought their joy was complete. Then came three more babies. His heart swelled as he thought of them, each so unique, so familiar. Gillian, Willow, and finally Emma Grace, named after Emmeline.

His beloved Emmeline.

He stood on the edge of what seemed eternity, sensing her nearness.

"Quaid," she whispered, and he turned, somehow not surprised to see her laughing face.

He moved toward her, holding out his arms. "Emma!"

She laughed again and moved into them with a long sigh. "Oh, how I've missed you, my darling."

She stepped back so she could look into his eyes. The light of her smile seemed to tell him she'd never been gone.

"Then, how…?" he began, but she touched his lips with her fingertips to shush him.

"Oh, if you could only see the children now," he said. "They are so like you."

"I'm sure they have plenty of your courage," she said. "I could see you in them already when I…left."

He didn't want to speak of sadness, of her leaving. "You were known to have quite a measure of grit yourself," he said, laughing. "Do you remember the night you slept by the river, taking care of your baby trees?"

"That wasn't grit," she said. "I was just stubborn and hardheaded."

She paused a moment, looking up into his eyes. "I remember how you played the harmonica that night. I could hear you in the distance, just down the river from me. The music rose in the air and comforted me."

"Some thanks I got. You almost shot me later."

Her laugh was musical. "How was I to know you'd come to stoke my campfire? I thought you were an intruder." She shrugged one shoulder. "Could you blame me?"

He took her hand and led her to the edge of the lookout. "Things haven't changed much. The land is still half wild, half tamed." He pointed across the valley. "There in the distance is Los Angeles. It's a full-blown city now."

"I don't care about the city, Quaid," she said, her tone teasing. "You were always concerned about the land and the city slickers who wanted to take it. What about the children...our home? I don't mean the house...the Victorian that once meant so much to me."

He frowned, trying to follow her meaning.

"Our home was in our hearts, Quaid. It had nothing to do with boards and nails or even the morning glory that climbed our porch. Our home was made up of the children's laughter and chatter. The love between us."

He felt the sting of tears behind his eyes. "Ah, yes, our love, Emma."

She lifted his hand in both of hers and kissed it. "Tell me about our home," she urged again.

His heart caught, and he didn't know what to say. Her clear eyes probed, and suddenly he was ashamed. "I left it behind, trying to save the house, the land," he said finally. "I left our children."

There was no accusation in her gaze, only compassion as if she knew what it had cost his pride to admit it. "Our children need you," she said. "They don't need a house or land. They need you."

"But we had dreams about leaving something of substance to our family. The land has belonged to the Byrnes and Dearbournes for generations. Even you loved it..." He smiled gently, remembering. "The oranges...their blossoms."

"That was then, beloved."

He understood but turned to glimpse the Big Valley once more. "Do you see it, Emma?" he asked, now turning away from her. "There's the Victorian…" He chuckled. "I can see Emma Grace playing in the yard. And there's Willow pushing Gillian in the swing. The twins are on the front porch, laughing and talking. The boys are in the field out behind, Jared watching over the picking of the new crop, Sully studying about the latest pest.

"Oh, and look…there's Juliet. She's standing in the doorway, as pretty as a picture. She's a beauty, Emma. So like you in her courage and determination." Laughing lightly, he turned again to meet his beloved's gaze.

But Emmeline was gone. Only the brilliant sun remained where she'd been standing. Even the snow-peaked mountains and the purple skies faded at the same time the windswept lands melted into liquid gold.

He ran to the edge of the cliffs and fell to his knees. "Emma!" he cried. "Emma! Beloved, wait for me! I want to come with you."

The only voice that answered him was that of the wind.

Sully watched his father thrashing in his bed. He stood, and the room began to spin a moment, then moved his chair nearer. He plunged a clean cloth into a basin that Rebecca Deverell, the young missionary nurse, had placed on a nearby table, squeezed out the excess water, then wiped his father's face.

Outside the small, spare building, the wind howled and rain sliced against the windows. Throughout the compound slender palms bent away from the near-gale gusts, their fronds spinning wildly.

"Emma!" Quaid mumbled, turning his head. "Emmeline!"

"Is that your mother's name?" Rebecca stepped closer and touched Quaid's forehead.

"Yes. She died a year ago. Since he fell ill, he's been calling out to her. Sometimes he talks as though she's standing or sitting next to him."

Rebecca nodded as she straightened the bedding and fluffed the kapok pillow. Sully watched her work, her slender, deft fingers pulling the bottom sheet up tidily under the dead weight of his father. She was a slender woman, yet she had surprising strength. He often watched her when she wasn't looking, refreshed by the rhythm of her movement, the cheerful cadence of her voice as she spoke to the other patients.

The first week following their arrival, he'd been too weak to do much other than eat and sleep. But he would never forget the first time he opened his eyes and saw Rebecca's face as she bent over him. He thought Jacaré had transported him down the river to heaven, not to a remote missionary outpost.

Rebecca fiddled with her hair self-consciously and flushed, aware of his scrutiny.

"How does my father seem this morning?" he asked.

"His temperature is near normal. That's a good sign." She smiled at Sully, and when he looked into her face, he thought the sun had surely come out from behind the tropical storm clouds.

Rebecca reminded him of no one he'd ever known, with her olive skin and golden eyes. Her hair was light brown with streaks of gold—it wasn't as fancy a style as his sisters would choose, but it suited her perfectly, the way it sprang out around her face and smelled of crushed lilies.

Despite her outward beauty, it was her inner serenity that drew Sully. It seemed to fill her to overflowing, like water from a fountain. It was present in her golden eyes and in the song that graced her lips.

Rebecca had come to the compound with her missionary parents, Morgan and Vala Deverell, when she was a child. Her father, a doctor, had died seven years earlier, and her mother, who'd never had formal medical training, had nonetheless taken over tending the Indian patients. She'd taught her only daughter to do the same. Two other missionaries lived on the compound. Collin and Tildie Fleming were an elderly couple who had devoted their lives to the Yagua.

Sully had learned that the compound was run by an interdenominational church group, and their funding was sporadic at best. Part of Rebecca's duties, besides helping her mother at the clinic, was to write letters to the States, to churches, asking for money. Until her father died, she'd told him, they returned home on furlough to speak to churches and get pledges for monthly support. Since Dr. Deverell had died, there hadn't been enough money for the tickets home.

Sully wondered if Rebecca or her mother had left the compound at all in those years. Their supplies were purchased by the mission Indians who traveled by dugout to Iquitos. One week going, less time returning because of the current. He'd noticed a wistful look in Rebecca's eyes as she spoke of it. Rebecca stood in front of him, her hands on her hips, her expression puzzled. When their gazes met, her quick smile brought him out of his reverie. "I just asked if you felt like walking to morning chapel with me," she said. She raised an amused brow, waiting for his answer.

Embarrassed to be caught woolgathering, he merely nodded and eased himself from the chair. He was still lightheaded and more than a bit weak. She helped him regain his balance by grabbing hold of his upper arm. After the room quit rocking, he nodded that he was steady and she dropped her hand.

They ducked out of the rain under one small thatched-roof building to the next as they made their way to the opposite side of the compound. The faint wheezes of organ music carried on the wind and through the downpour.

"Are you always this faithful?" he ventured as they circumnavigated a silt-filled puddle.

She raised a brow. "Are you asking why we don't just wait for the rain to stop?"

"It seems to me that out here in the wilderness, you could hold services anytime you wanted. Sundays, Mondays…" He shrugged. "Afternoons. Evenings. Would it really matter?"

"Ah, but you're wrong, Sullivan." He enjoyed how she'd taken to calling him by his full name. "It does matter," she went on with a laugh. "If we waited for perfect weather, could be we'd never hold another service." She glanced up at him. Rain had settled on her eyelashes, the miniature beads sparkling like pinpricks of candlelight above her golden eyes. Sully thought it was surely the most beautiful sight he'd ever seen. For a moment he couldn't think what to say next.

She eased his shy discomfort by taking his hand to steady him as they made their way toward the chapel, across another couple of muddy stretches through the downpour, then finally to the rickety bamboo stairs. Much like the clinic, the building was made of whitewashed clapboard perched storklike on short, squat palm trunks. It had obviously seen better days, though Sully was aware that the weather probably caused unceasing repair. And if the weather didn't threaten to bring it down, the carpenter ants would.

He stopped midstep, just before placing his foot on the first stair, and squinted through the rain up toward the crude wooden cross atop the thatched roof. For several seconds he studied it, and though he remained there, shivering and soaked to the skin, the sight of it comforted him.

Rebecca seemed to understand and, after pressing her palm against his for the quickest moment, led him up the stairs and out of the rain.

They seated themselves toward the front of the sanctuary, side by side on a rough-hewn bench. To the right of the altar, Tildie Fleming pumped the organ pedals vigorously, playing "Nearer, My God, to Thee" with a flourish as the smattering of Indian parishioners lifted their voices in off-key song. Two other hymns followed, then finally, "Amazing Grace."

Though the congregation was singing in the Yagua language, Sully sang the first two verses in English. When he began the third verse, his heart lifted in response to the images that appeared before his eyes. *"Through many dangers, toils and snares, I have already come; 'Tis grace hath brought me safe thus far, and grace will lead me home."*

The congregation continued the final verse in their soft, clicking language. But Sully couldn't mouth another word. The terror of being alone in the jungle, of caring for his father as his illness worsened, the hopelessness of being lost…all his fears and doubts about himself and his world returned, almost taking his breath away.

Then he remembered the night that he felt God's presence, his grace, while sitting by the backwater pond in the jungle. The memory fell upon him like a warm blanket on a man who knew the fear of freezing. It brought warmth to his soul, too long shriveled and cold.

"And grace will lead me..."

Yes, God had brought him safe thus far. And his grace would lead him home.

"Home."

As he sat on the squat wooden bench in the middle of the Peruvian wilderness and listened to the soft music of the Indians' voices lifted in song—off-key, in a language he couldn't understand—Sully couldn't think of any place on earth that suited him better. He almost laughed with a strange joy that bubbled up inside him.

Home.

The plain wooden cross on the whitewashed wall behind the altar seemed to take on a shimmering glow, though perhaps the simple explanation was that his eyes had filled with tears. He swallowed hard and thought about all that once had seemed important. His feelings of never measuring up to his witty siblings; his dogged determination to prove to his father that he too was strong and capable. Yet it was that same pigheaded resolve, his cockamamie dream about investing in a rubber-tree plantation, that nearly cost them their lives.

THAT BROUGHT YOU HERE, BELOVED.

BROUGHT YOU HOME.

MY GRACE, MY CHILD...

He stared at the cross, certain his imagination was working over-time. What could he possibly be thinking? That God was calling him here? He nearly laughed out loud. Here?

He looked around at the worshipers. If God was going to do a mighty work among the people in this congregation, he needed some-one with a lot greater qualifications than Sully's.

He sighed with relief as he thought about the logic of it. He'd been through a terrible ordeal. It stood to reason that in his gratitude for being saved from almost certain death, he would hallucinate about how he could repay his Lord.

That was all it was. He looked back to the cross, and it was again as it should have been. A plain, wooden symbol—albeit a glorious one—hanging above the altar. It was nothing more.

He was still contemplating his foolish imagination when Collin Fleming moved slowly across the platform, his ancient form bent as though beneath a heavy burden. His white hair was plastered to his head from the rain, his white cloth robe thin and damp.

Collin first spoke a few words in the Yagua language that caused nods and chuckles in the congregation, then he welcomed Sully and asked him to stand. Upturned, smiling faces greeted him. After Sully seated himself again, Collin opened a large Bible and read a passage, first in Yagua, then in English, then bowed his head to pray.

As he prayed, Sully felt a restlessness that wouldn't let him go. It became so pronounced that at the end of the prayer, he mumbled an excuse to Rebecca about not feeling well and hurried up the center aisle to the back door.

Once outside, he leaned against the side of the building and closed his eyes. He sensed a presence near him and looked up to see that Rebecca had followed.

She looked worried. "Perhaps we'd better head to the clinic."

Sully drew in a deep breath. "Yes, yes. I'm feeling a bit lightheaded. I'm not certain why..." He let the words fall off lamely.

"You need rest," she said. "You haven't yet recovered."

They stepped from the stairs onto the still muddy walkway between buildings. The rain had stopped, and billowing tropical clouds filled the sky, leaving a few vivid blue spaces between. The sun slanted from the west, creating a halo effect behind the clouds. Palm fronds glistened with a wet sheen, and on a large rubber tree, rainwater dripped from leaf to shining leaf, creating rivulets that slid gracefully to the bottom leaves then onto the ground.

The beauty of the storm's aftermath was blinding. Sully looked away, focusing instead on the rings in a puddle beneath a low thatch.

After they had walked a few minutes, he glanced at Rebecca. "How do you stand it here?"

"What an odd thing to ask."

"It isn't really. You've been here for how many years now?"

"Thirteen."

"That's a long time to be away from civilization."

She laughed. "I suppose it depends on what you call civilization."

He stopped, turning toward her. "You know nothing of the rest of the world, do you?"

"What is there that's important to know?" But before he could answer, she went on, "Lest you think me ignorant, I need to tell you that my parents have seen to my education. Before his death, my grandfather was a professor at William and Mary. He provided me with texts and papers. And my grandmother made certain that I read the classics, even those more modern works." She smiled, looking a bit sheepish. "Before she too died, she sent me works ranging from Jane Austen to O. Henry. I've read all of them again and again—"

He put up his hand. "Please don't misunderstand. I wasn't questioning your education. Far from it. I suppose what I'm getting at is that you know nothing of our modern world." He paused, not wanting to offend her, but wanting answers to the questions in his mind. "For instance, do you know who's president now?"

She stared at him solemnly. "No."

"Do you know about the modern conveniences of life today? The automobile?"

"Of course I've heard of them. I've just never seen one."

"How about the flying machine?"

"I've heard of that as well." She shrugged one shoulder. "Haven't seen one though."

"A dirigible? A talking machine…or a phonograph?"

She shook her head. "The same."

"And women's clothing…did you know that women's styles now show their ankles?"

She flushed, and he was immediately sorry he'd mentioned such a thing. In his opinion, Rebecca looked beautiful in her plain brown skirt and high-necked blouse.

"My mother and I have a 1902 Sears and Roebuck catalog," she said after a moment. "We sometimes get a bolt of cloth from Iquitos, and we copy the patterns as best we can."

"I didn't mean anything by it..." he said lamely. "I think you look, well, you look just fine." She seemed pleased with the compliment, which gave him greater courage. "Real fine," he added.

After a moment, she said, "There are some things I'd just as soon not hear about. For instance, the unsinkable ship that was lost to the sea just a few years ago."

"The *Titanic*."

"Yes. I could have gone a lifetime without hearing about the tragedy of it. For nearly a year afterward, I imagined the sadness and terror as it sank."

"But those things happen in our world. We can't shut them out."

"I agree. But neither can we presume to think we can fix all ills— especially when we're not called to fix them." She paused. "For example, the tenements in New York City or in Boston. Places where families with little children freeze to death on the streets or starve because they have no food."

They reached the clinic and climbed the stairs. She paused at the doorway, turning to Sully again. "I'm not saying the only solution is to sequester ourselves away from the world. To become monks or spiritual mystics and pretend that we are alone on the globe. But I think God places us in certain parts of his world to do a certain job for him. It could be any job, anywhere."

"The needs are so great, isn't it worthless to try to make a difference?"

"God doesn't ask us to be successful," she said softly. "He wants us merely to obey him." Rebecca then headed through the door and into the clinic. She was a few steps ahead of him as she turned the corner into his father's room.

He lagged behind as the shimmering image of the cross behind the altar came to him again. He had just begun to consider its meaning when Rebecca shrieked.

"Come quickly, Sullivan!" she shouted. "Hurry!"

Nineteen

At the sound of Rebecca's cry, Sully rounded the corner and all but slid into the young nurse as she headed back to fetch him.

"I need your help," she called over her shoulder as she ran back to Quaid's bed. "Hurry!"

Sully limped along behind her. At the far end of the room, he could see that his father's cot was empty. His first thought was that Quaid died while they were in chapel. "We shouldn't have left him," he said.

"We don't have time for that now," Rebecca said as she stooped down behind the bed.

Sully rounded the iron foot board, then halted midstep. His father lay sprawled on his face, limbs twisted. For a moment of stunned silence, Sully couldn't move, his heart aching with the knowledge that his father was surely dead. Then Quaid groaned and moved his head, and Sully could breathe again.

Rebecca rolled Quaid to his side. Sully quickly knelt beside her to help.

Once he was lying on his back, Quaid looked up at him as if trying to focus. "I was about to come looking for you, son." His voice was little more than a whisper. It was the first time he'd spoken since they arrived at the compound. "I'm too weak," he said.

Sully met Rebecca's worried look over his father's head. "You just need some time to recover," she said.

Lifting together, Sully and Rebecca brought Quaid to a sitting position, then with great effort onto the bed. Quaid closed his eyes as though he was too weary to keep them open. For several moments he didn't speak.

Finally he began, "I was worried when I didn't see you. I couldn't remember if you made it off the river." His eyes opened. "I only remembered that last night in the jungle…when you carried me…" His breathing was heavy. He coughed several times, a deep choking that sounded as though his lungs couldn't take in air.

Rebecca drew up the thin sheet and fluffed the pillows behind Quaid's head. "Try to cough again. Contrary to what you might think, it's good for you." She helped him lean forward, then pounded his back in a vertical pattern that caused another spasm of coughing.

When he caught his breath again, Quaid gave her a skeletal grin. "Are you the same angel who's been watching over me?"

"I assure you, I'm made of flesh and bone, Mr. Dearbourne. And as far as the watching goes, it's your son who's been hovering by your bed day and night." She sat down in a chair near the bed as Sully collapsed in another on the opposite side. Lifting Quaid's hand, she pressed her fingertips into his wrist and looked at the watch pinned to her lapel. Then she touched his forehead and nodded slowly. "Your fever is down today." She held a cup of water to his lips.

When he'd finished drinking, he rubbed his jaw. "I knew something was different. My beard is gone."

"Your son took care of that as well, Mr. Dearbourne," Rebecca said. "Every morning as soon as he was strong enough to hold a razor."

"Sounds dangerous." He chuckled lightly, then closed his eyes and leaned back into his pillow. "Sully…?"

"I'm here, Father."

"Tell me how we made it out of the jungle. I never thought you"— he corrected himself—"never thought *we'd* make it."

"Your son's quite the hero," Rebecca said with a look of pride in Sully's direction.

Sully felt his cheeks redden. "There were no heroics, believe me," he said.

"That's not what Jacaré told me, Sullivan."

At Rebecca's use of Sully's full name, a smile played at the corner of his father's mouth. "I'll be the judge," he said. "Tell me how we got here."

"You remember being sent from the village because of the curse?"

For a moment Quaid didn't speak. "The pink dolphin. I remember something about a river god…"

"The myth of the river dolphin is a powerful one among the river Indians," Rebecca said. "I'm surprised the villagers allowed you to live if they believed you'd brought a curse on them."

"I was moved to the upper village because I was thought to be a healer."

"How did they conclude that?" Rebecca asked.

"Simple aspirin crystals. I gave some to a few children and old folks who were suffering from fevers. Of course the fevers subsided, swollen joints returned to normal without pain. Sick children were soon up and playing."

"That wasn't long after we were first captured." Sully frowned, remembering.

"Apparently the word spread. I was taken to the upper village, where an influenza epidemic was rampant." His gaze moved to a window. "Only nothing could be done there. At least, nothing that aspirin crystals could help."

Quaid closed his eyes, fatigue showing in his angular, pale face. "People died. Many people. I had nothing left but Dr. Wilden's Quick Cure Stomach Remedy, Dr. Echols WonderHeart Cure, and Internal Catarrh Medicine." He coughed again, long and hard, then grimaced. Sully stood to pound his father's back just as Rebecca had done. When he could speak again, Quaid continued, "I couldn't save them. Still, I tended to the sick and helped bury the dead."

"That compassion probably saved your life," Rebecca said gently.

"When my father fell ill," Sully joined the story, "they took me to join him in the second village. I was there just hours before they set us loose on the river that morning. It seemed like a burial raft, down to the provisions for a journey into the nether world." He looked across the bed at Rebecca. "Why do you suppose they would do such a thing?"

"It might have to do with the river dolphin, a being they consider a god," she said. "Because the river brought you to the tribe, it was left to the river to reclaim you."

"And it would have, if not for Jacaré," Sully said, remembering the terror of the night.

"Jacaré told me that you were ready to kill to protect your father," Rebecca said. Her eyes held deep admiration.

He dismissed it with a laugh. "I was standing on the sand near where I'd tethered the raft when I heard Jacaré in the brush that night. I was certain it was a panther, its yellow eyes boring through me. I could smell its breath as it stalked me." He chuckled, shaking his head. "Then Jacaré stepped into the clearing."

Quaid, who'd been listening with his eyes closed, spoke up. "I think I would have leaped for the raft and headed into the river, had it been a real panther. That would have been a wise move."

"You lay unconscious by the pond. Had I cut loose the tether, I might never have made my way back to shore—and who knows what state I would have found you in by then. Jacaré took good care of us—found us fruit to eat, clear springs of water to drink. Taught me how to fish for our suppers. It took many days for him to find this outpost, then he disappeared before I could say a proper thank-you."

"He was frightened for his life and for his family," Rebecca said. "I spoke to him, gave him provisions as he pushed off. He was worried that the village elders would think he had interfered with the gods and their plans. He was shaking when he took the pole in his hands."

"He's the brave one," Sully said.

One of the young Indian boys brought a pot of soup. Rebecca took it from him with both hands and set it on the table near the bed. Sliding her chair closer, she ladled the broth into the water cup and held it for Quaid. He closed his eyes and drank deeply.

Sully watched the ritual, wondering if his father had any memory of Rebecca feeding him water and broth each day. Sully had caught her unawares, speaking to an unconscious Quaid as she worked. "Just because you are unconscious," she would say, "doesn't mean your throat can't remember how to swallow."

They talked for a few more minutes, then Rebecca excused herself, taking the empty soup pot with her. "Don't forget to let the patient rest," she said to Sully. "He needs to regain his strength for the journey home."

Quaid studied Sully. His son had grown into a man in just a few weeks. In this place, so far from anything Quaid recognized, his son sat before him, shoulders back, chin jutting forward with confidence.

"I've lost all track of time," Quaid said after a bit.

Sully laughed. "We've been away from home for nine months. We've been at this outpost for only two and a half weeks." He smiled at his father. "Most of that time you've ranted and raved as if yelling at Jared and me for not cleaning out the barn. I would have sworn you'd been transported back to California."

Images floated into place behind Quaid's eyes. Images of Emmeline and the children…Sully. All the little ones. All of them in the golden sunlight near the ranch. He nodded. "I had dreams. Some so real I thought your mother was right there with me." A hot sting rose in his throat, and he turned from his son's inquisitive eyes to gaze through the open window.

Sully coughed, and Quaid turned toward him again. "Father," Sully said, "I take responsibility for all this. If I hadn't had such grand ideas about the rubber plantation, about traveling up the Amazon with so little experience—"

"The guides we hired abandoned us," Quaid interrupted. "That wasn't your fault, son." He settled deep into his pillows, his eyes closed. He was weary, so weary. "Your ideas were good," he said after another moment.

Sully didn't speak, and Quaid thought his son hadn't heard him…or perhaps had left the room. He squinted against the light that now streamed through the window behind Sully. He peered toward his son's face, but Sully's expression was hidden in the shadows.

"Do you still have the bank draft?"

"Yes," his son said quietly. "A bit worse for the wear, but it's legible."

"How about the rest of our money?"

Sully swallowed visibly. "There's very little left. When I was taken from the first village, I wasn't given time to gather my belongings. The lockbox was left in the hut."

"Just where we put it for safekeeping."

"The same." Sully paused thoughtfully. "We're penniless without going into the money we were planning to invest."

"How far are we from Iquitos?"

"A week's journey one way, several days return," Sully said.

Quaid rested his eyes again, feeling a new exhaustion overtaking him. There was too much to say, too much to plan for, in the event he slipped into unconsciousness again. "Perhaps one of the Indians could take you there," he said. "You need to find a bank that will take the draft and give you American dollars."

"It's everything we've got," Sully said. "If we use it to travel home, we can't repay the bank in Riverview."

Quaid studied his son. "I'm not certain I can make the trip." He paused, letting his gaze drift to the open window. "You may need to return home without me."

"The children need you—they don't need the land or our home. *I* need you—so you're not going to dispatch me to save the day," Sully said.

For a moment, Quaid didn't speak. Sully stepped closer, worry etched in his face, but he held his silence, waiting for his father to continue. "One of us must travel home to them. I obviously can't, and you can—as soon as you get the money." He fell silent, letting his eyes rest again. "The house is likely already lost. The best we can hope for is that the bank hasn't resold it. Perhaps with the money left after your passage home, you can reclaim it from the bank. If it's indeed too late, you can use the money to find a small farm to accommodate the family."

"I can't leave you here, Father."

"You must," Quaid said. "Promise me that no matter what happens—even if I slip into unconsciousness again—you will go. And go quickly."

Quaid could see opposition in his son's eyes. "I want you to go to Iquitos immediately. Ask around for a bank that will cash in drafts from a bank in the United States. American dollars are worth more here."

Sully didn't answer, and Quaid closed his eyes, fighting the fatigue that threatened to engulf him. His voice was weak as he continued, "I need to rest now. Godspeed, son. Please go quickly." The conversation had pushed him to the edge of darkness. It folded in on him, and he found himself floating in that place between wakefulness and slumber.

When he at last drifted off, it was a restless sleep. He dreamed of Emmeline standing on the lookout above their ranch. The California winds blew her lovely hair, and she smiled at him. He tried to run to her, but his legs wouldn't move.

"Oh, my darling..." he cried out.

"Don't be afraid," she said. "Don't be afraid." She reached out to him.

He tried to grab her hand, but couldn't. He tried again...and again...until at last he was flying toward her, unbound from earth, flying among the clouds...in the sunlight...toward his Emmeline who waited, loving him with her smile.

A hawk cried somewhere above the compound, and Quaid awoke with a start from his dream.

Sully headed from the clinic to his cottage at the edge of the compound. His father was counting on him to go to Iquitos. He didn't want to leave him for even the two weeks it would take to go to the village. How could he possibly consider leaving him for months to go to America, no matter his father's request?

Then he considered his brother and sisters and sighed heavily. They needed him.

He was still thinking about his father's request when a voice interrupted his thoughts. "Sullivan?"

He turned to see Rebecca hurrying across the compound, her arm wrapped around a large, empty basket at her hip. His world brightened every time she came near. This moment as she walked toward him was no exception. Her hair was in springy ringlets from the rain, her cheeks flushed to a pretty peach hue.

She fell into step with him as they continued together for a moment. When he halted near his cottage, she tilted her chin upward, squinting at him against the slant of the sun. "I'm on my way to the river to fetch the laundry for the clinic. Do you want to come along?"

"I'd like nothing better."

They walked for a few minutes in companionable silence, winding through ferns and dense tropical foliage. The narrow path was flanked by starburst-shaped palms and delicate yellow flowers that Sully, hardly knowing roses from tufts of grass, couldn't identify.

When they reached the river, fields of water hyacinth stretched before them, a carpet of purple and lavender blossoms. Rebecca stepped to the clothesline where several rows of bed linens hung.

"This is one thing that makes us wait for fair weather," she said with a laugh.

He knew she was making reference to his complaint about chapel and their inclement weather. "I'm sorry I left the services without explanation earlier," he said.

She unpinned a thin sheet from the line, held the length of it with arms outstretched, then deftly folded and dropped it into his waiting hands. "You said you were sick."

He dropped the sheet into the basket. After she unpinned the next, he held one end and they folded it together. "It was more than that," he said. "I suddenly felt I needed to get out of there, out of this place, or I might not leave at all."

There was a curious light in her eyes as she studied him. She held a clothespin in her mouth, and said only, "Hmm."

He laughed self-consciously, shrugged, and turned to unpin the next sheet.

"That's why you asked me how it is to live in isolation from the rest of the world?" She was smiling when he looked back.

"Perhaps. Though don't get me wrong, I'm certainly not planning to stay." He laughed again. "Sitting in the chapel, staring at the cross above Reverend Fleming's head, made me go a little crazy. I thought I just might want to. I had to get out."

"Ah, remember what happened to Jonah," she said, raising a brow.

He laughed. "I doubt that God will have me swallowed by a whale."

"If there was ever a place that can grow a fish big enough to swallow a man, it's here." She unfastened another clothespin, stuck it in her mouth, and reached for the next.

"Of that I have no doubt. I've seen their size firsthand." He reached for the corner of the sheet and helped her fold it. "Now enough about me and my hasty exit from chapel. I need to ask you about my father, what you really think about his condition."

She dropped the last of the linens into the basket, then plopped down on top of it, looking up at him. "I thought I saw something in your demeanor that was weighing you down," she said.

"Yes. I know you're being purposely optimistic, probably for both our sakes. But I need to know—because of business that needs to be taken care of here and in the States—what you really think."

When she didn't answer, he went on, "I haven't told you why we're here—or at least why we came in the first place." He explained about the ranch, the years of drought, the financial troubles, the search for the new variety of orange trees in Bahia. "We'd given up on the wild-goose chase for the perfect citrus fruit, when I had the bright idea of investing in rubber. We were heading to Iquitos when our guides disappeared one night and we were overcome by a renegade group of natives.

"Rebecca, I have six sisters and a brother at home, ready to lose everything." He sighed. "They may have already. I must get to them, but I don't want to leave my father. He's urging me to take care of business in Iquitos and make my way back home—the shortest route possible."

"It's a rigorous trip, no matter which way you choose to travel," she said when he'd finished. "And one that I'm uncertain your father can make anytime soon."

He looked away from her, out over the river with its hyacinth carpet. "I was afraid of that." He turned again to face her. "But how can I leave him? Some days I think he won't live till nightfall. If something happened before I returned—"

She touched his arm. "He's in good hands here."

"I believe he'll need someone trained in medicine to travel with him. Someone who speaks the language…"

She frowned and seemed to study him for a moment. "About this medical person. You're thinking of sending someone from the States? I mean, after you arrive there, you'll arrange for someone to return and bring your father home? And you'll need then to hire a Peruvian guide for them both. That is your question?" Her gaze met his.

He smiled. "Actually, I was thinking that perhaps...just maybe... well, you might be ready to take a furlough. That you might be the one to accompany both of us to serve as my father's nurse and as a translator. We would leave as soon as arrangements can be made. And I wouldn't have to leave him here."

"Oh, I could never leave here," she said. "I'm needed. I mean, what would they ever do without—" She grinned at him, the gold flecks in her eyes sparkling in the sunlight. "I suppose it wouldn't hurt to ask," she said finally.

TWENTY

The stubborn woman wouldn't listen to reason. No matter how Clay pled or what he threatened, she told him in no uncertain terms that her sisters wouldn't set foot outside New York. Neither would she, for that matter. She didn't care that her grandmother and great aunts spent a fortune sending him to fetch them all.

So beginning at dawn the day after he found her, he spent a week trailing the young woman and her brood. If they were going to involve the courts in taking the children, he needed evidence to bring before a judge. Some leverage to force her to acquiesce. But he couldn't help hoping the opposite would be proved, that his evidence would show Juliet Rose Dearbourne was fit to raise her sisters.

He learned about the lively neighborhood of rundown brownstones where they lived, the corner grocer where she shopped for fruits and vegetables, the pattern of comings and goings to the theatre and home, sometimes with the children in tow, sometimes without. She performed each night at the Victoria, but at the end of the week she left the children in the care of the twins from afternoon rehearsals and matinees through the late-night shows.

He made note that on four different occasions the twins slipped from the house to a nearby soda shop, then hurried back home. They were never gone longer than a half-hour, but nonetheless, the little ones were left alone.

In a single week he filled an entire notepad for his report to her grandmother and great aunts. Always he weighed whether the children might be in danger. Whether he should contact the authorities. But just when he thought Juliet might be placing her career ahead of their well-being, she surprised him by spending several mornings with the children, rolling hoops in the park, riding bicycles, and, on one afternoon, visiting a museum.

One thing worried him. Two mornings after he began his sleuthing, he followed Juliet and Gillian onto the subway to the outskirts of the city. Juliet seemed aware he was following and darted quickly in and out of the crowd on the platform to lose him as they disembarked. But by the end of that first week, she hadn't made the trip again, he noted. He wondered what had been so mysterious.

On the second Sunday morning, he trailed the troop—the little ones dressed in matching straw hats and navy sailor suits, Juliet in a froth of lace and organza—to a small church in their neighborhood. The hymns drew him inside, and he put aside his worries about being detected and entered just as the congregation knelt to pray. Sitting in the back pew, he slipped to his knees, feeling a sacred peace overtake him.

When the service was over, he felt a reluctance to leave and waited just a moment too long. Juliet turned, just yards in front of him, and met his gaze. Her expression was fiery, and she hurried to catch him, likely to give him a considerable piece of her mind.

With a grin and a salute, he stepped into the crowd outside the church, disappearing just as expertly as she had on the subway platform days earlier. He waited in an alcove nearby until she once again passed him, this time heading for the trolley at the corner.

Juliet led the girls to the trolley stand, still fuming over the sight of Clay MacGregor. She'd sensed his presence all week, and she'd certainly had enough of his slinking around and writing on his notepad with a stubby pencil. Some private investigator! Not only had he been unable to find Mairia Garden, he had no clue that Juliet was watching him watching her.

She had to laugh. If she hadn't been so irritated that he'd followed her to church, she would have taken great delight in the look of him. He was always dressed like a cowboy, though likely he'd never seen the inside of a barn. Cowboy boots, Stetson hat, and blue jeans. Even in church, if one could imagine such a thing! Oh, and the expressions on the New Yorkers' faces when they turned to see the towering cowboy! She was still chuckling to herself when the trolley stopped near Central Park. The family trooped from the vehicle and headed toward the entrance. She wouldn't be surprised to find Clay MacGregor still trailing behind. Didn't the man have anything better to do?

"Ettie!" Willow tugged on her arm. "I want to see the pumas."

"There's a sloth! I see its snout," shouted Gillian, yanking Annie's hand to pull her forward. "Over there. I want to see it eat some ants. Maybe we can find some."

Abby held Emma Grace's hand, and the wide-eyed child seemed speechless with excitement. "There's what I wanna see!" Emma Grace pointed to the lion cage. "Ooh, lions and tigers and bears, oh my!" she said, quoting her favorite book. The twins had been taking turns reading *The Wizard of Oz* to Gillian, Willow, and Emma Grace. They all laughed, including the twins, and repeated the chant.

Then Emma Grace stopped dead, still in the middle of the walkway. "There's that man."

Juliet followed her gaze and saw Clay MacGregor standing near a wheeled cart, buying a hot dog from a man in a striped shirt. "Don't point, Emma Grace," Juliet said. "It isn't polite."

"He's not polite to uth," Willow said. "Not one bit. He said we had to go home to California. But I like it here with the lions and tigers and bears." She turned from MacGregor to look at Juliet. "But I would like a hot dog too."

It was time to talk to the incorrigible man about his invasion of their privacy. "Abby and Annie, I want you to take the little ones around to see the animals while I speak with Mr. MacGregor."

"Just like in *Peter Rabbit*," Emma Grace said, giggling. "Only he was a farmer."

Juliet knelt and drew the younger children to her. "I'm going to ask you questions about the animals." She smiled. "I'll try to stump you…and there will be a surprise afterward if you know the answers."

Their eyes grew big, and they nodded.

"What's the surprise?" Willow wanted to know.

"It won't be a surprise, silly goose, if Ettie tells us." Gillian gave her sister a look that said she knew these things.

Juliet stood. "Abby and Annie, I don't need to tell you that you can't take your eyes off these three at any time. Ever."

The twins nodded, looking almost guilty. But Juliet didn't dwell on it. Instead she watched them fall in with the crowd of long-skirted ladies with parasols and bowler-hatted men, some in fancy striped suits and vests, others in shirtsleeves with black arm garters. A group of school-boys raced by, nearly knocking her over as they headed past. She smiled at their rambunctious abandon, reminded of Sully when he was still in knickers and sailor-suit shirts, his hair in a Dutch-boy cut.

Juliet watched her sisters stop to giggle and point in front of the monkey exhibit. Willow bounced up and down and scratched under her arms. With a whoop, Gillian followed suit. Next, Emma Grace pooched out her lips and made a chattering sound. Soon all three were howling with giggles and laughter, pretending they were monkeys. Abby and Annie rolled their eyes and pretended they didn't know their sisters.

Satisfied she could now speak to Clay MacGregor without being disturbed, Juliet turned away to see him watching her with a curious expression.

"Mr. MacGregor," she said once she was standing squarely in front of him. "We have something to discuss."

Clay nodded to Juliet and struggled to keep from smiling at the antics of her sisters just beyond her left shoulder. "Miss Dearbourne," he said, tipping his hat. "Fancy meeting you here."

She made a noise that sounded like "Hmmph."

Juliet looked into his face from under the edge of a wide-brimmed pouf of a hat, its ribbon band covered with a cloud of silky flowers. As she stared up at him with those glorious eyes, he thought he surely must be gazing into the face of an angel.

He swallowed hard and tried to concentrate on why he'd kept her under surveillance. Since seeing her this morning in church, he hadn't been able to think straight.

And now here she was, standing so close he could touch her if he dared. From the tip of that glorious hat to the end of her pointed, kid-leathered toe, from the froth of cutout violet lace on the collar and pockets to the exquisite handkerchief hem, all was uniquely Juliet. Angelic. There simply wasn't another word for her appearance. It unnerved him.

"What do you think you're doing, Mr. MacGregor?"

He cleared his throat, and when he spoke his voice was gruffer than he intended. "Ah, Miss Dearbourne, as I said to you the other night…in your, ah, dressing room. I have come here on behalf of your relatives. I promised them a full report, which I intend to deliver."

"You also said you've come to remove the children from my care."

"Your grandmother and your great-aunts are understandably concerned about the well-being of your sisters. I am merely making an evaluation before I contact the authorities."

Before he could go on, she stepped closer and pointed her index finger to his chest. "Mister, you will have one bigger-than-life fight on your hands if you try to take a single sister away from me." Her voice was a soft growl, and she now emphasized each word with that same index finger striking his lapel. "You come within a hundred yards of any one of them and I swear I'll have you thrown in jail."

"For what?"

She stopped to think. "For bothering us, if for nothing else."

He laughed, which caused her eyes to glint even more dangerously. "For 'bothering' you?" He laughed again.

"No one is going to take my sisters anywhere."

"Think about what's good for your sisters," he said as he saw something flicker in her eyes. Uncertainty, maybe? He continued, his voice soothing. "Please, let's step over into the shade and discuss this civilly." She allowed him to take her elbow as he nodded to a bench beneath the dappled canopy of a big elm tree, and they walked toward it. A little girl rolling a hoop with a stick ran toward them, and they stepped aside to let her pass. Juliet's shoulder brushed Clay's, and the scent of her sweet perfume floated up. "Now, Miss Dearbourne, let's discuss this like adults." He sat down beside her, and stretched out his legs, crossing his ankles. "We all want what's best for the children. That's reasonable to assume, isn't it?"

She glared at him without answering.

"Ah, I think we can come to a reasonable agreement."

Still she stared.

"Ah, well, I…" She was unnerving him with her silent gaze. He cleared his throat and started over. "You have begun a new career, and judging from what I've observed, you love every minute of it. Being on-stage, I mean. And you do it well."

She smiled at this, then let her eyes drift away as if embarrassed.

"As you move on to bigger and better roles, it means longer hours, more time away from your sisters."

She had turned back to him, and again a flicker of uncertainty shadowed her face.

Uncertainty was good. It would make his job easier, he thought, trying to regain his own emotional standing. Trying to focus on his task and not the dusty pink of her cheeks or the sweet curve of her lips. He rushed on. "Don't you see, Juliet? If I take your sisters home to California, you would be free to pursue your heart's desire without the worry of their welfare."

Before she could comment, he dropped his voice as if divulging a confidence. "Even the other day, I saw that the three young ones were left alone—"

"Alone?" she sputtered. "They've never been alone for a minute. The twins are sixteen years old. They watch the little ones like hawks."

"I beg to differ with you. I'm sorry to tell you that during my observations I've seen them leave for the corner soda shop on four separate occasions."

"Together?"

"Yes, together."

Her cheeks flushed in visible anger.

"You see," he continued, "if you'll just allow me to return them to California, I don't have to go to the authorities. You can relax, and your family will be happy."

"And you'll get paid," she said. "Your job will be done, so you'll get a nice fat paycheck. Isn't that right?"

He swallowed hard, then cleared his throat. "Well, yes, of course. That's part of it. But that's not why I'm here."

"Isn't it?" Her eyes were wide. Angelic again.

He looked out across the park, the children playing with hoops and on bicycles. Why did life have to be so hard for some, such as these orphans he'd come to rescue? He turned back to Juliet. "This is part of what I do for a living, yes. But as you know sometimes I take on jobs for very little reimbursement."

She flushed again, and he was sorry for bringing it up. "Money counts," he added quickly, "of course."

"It does for me as well," she said quietly, letting her gaze drift to the puma cage. "You have no idea what it feels like to bear my responsibilities." There was no anger in her voice. Or self-pity. Only truth.

"I understand."

A burst of an exasperated sigh escaped her lips. "How could you?"

He didn't answer.

"Do you have children, Mr. MacGregor?"

"Well, no, I don't."

"A wife?"

He shook his head.

"Are you responsible for anyone besides yourself?"

He felt his face redden. An annoying malady left over from boyhood. "No one." He played with the rim of his hat, looking at it instead of Juliet.

"There's no way on God's green and gorgeous earth that you can possibly understand what I'm trying to do for my family."

He couldn't deny it.

"Look," she said, leaning forward again and narrowing her eyes. "You have come clear across the country, acting as judge and jury, when you don't know the first thing about me. About how I would die for my sisters before I would allow anyone to take them away from me...or allow anyone to bring them harm."

"Your feelings for your sisters have never been in dispute."

"But the children's living arrangements are still 'in dispute'?"

"My assignment on behalf of my clients has been clear from the beginning." It broke his heart to say it.

She stood abruptly, on her face the angry look of one betrayed. "Then this meeting is over, Mr. MacGregor. You will not take the children! I would advise you to leave on the first train out of Grand Central Station in the morning." With that, she turned and left him standing in the shade of the big elm tree.

He watched until she was reunited with her sisters. Emma Grace tumbled into Juliet's arms, nearly knocking her down. The two other little ones were jumping and giggling and talking at once, with the identical twins hovering watchfully behind.

The single image Clay couldn't get out of his mind was the expression on Juliet's face as she bent over her brood. If he were an artist and could capture the look of curiosity, intelligence, and compassion all rolled together in one beautiful mix, it would be in such a face as hers.

The look of her stayed with him, long after he strode from Central Park.

Juliet turned to watch Clay MacGregor until he disappeared through the open Central Park gates. She would be an idiot not to guess his next move. He would head to a police station, then return to confront her again, this time with an officer at his side.

She didn't know what legal documents her grandmother might have sent with him, but if she had gone to all the trouble of hiring Mr. MacGregor, she was obviously serious about wanting her grandchildren back.

Her sisters were shrieking with joy and laughing about the animals they'd seen. She shushed them long enough to ask questions, and when she was satisfied that they truly had learned everything they could, she led them to an ice cream cart near the children's play area. As soon as she had paid for five double chocolate cones, she headed them toward the exit.

"But I wanna stay," Emma Grace whined. "Pleeeze, can't we stay a little longer?" The child looked longingly toward the carousel.

Juliet glanced at her watch, and calculated the time. Surely Mr. MacGregor wouldn't return immediately with an officer. There would be documents to examine, an investigation perhaps? She looked at her watch again impatiently. As if she didn't have enough to worry about without Mr. Know-it-all, Judge-it-all, Private Detective-Swashbuckler-Pilot, sticking his nose in where it didn't belong.

She looked down at the chocolate-smeared upturned faces awaiting her answer and sighed. "All right then. We'll stay just for a few minutes."

The little ones ran off with whoops and hollers, the twins hurrying along behind. "Watch over them carefully," she called to Annie and Abby. She would speak to them about leaving the children unattended as soon as they all headed home. But for now, the twins waved and ran after Emma Grace, Gillian, and Willow, who were already waiting impatiently at the carousel.

Minutes later, all five had clambered aboard and were sitting atop painted horses, geese, and rabbits. The calliope began wheezing its chorus and the merry-go-round creaked to a start. Soon it was moving smoothly, the animals rocking up and down. Willow waved from atop a white rabbit, her toothless smile spread across her face. Emma Grace blew kisses, and Gillian grinned. Annie and Abby tried to look grown up, but judging from their expressions, they were having as much fun as the little ones.

Juliet tapped her foot in rhythm to the tune, enjoying sun beating on her shoulders. Around her, children played, calling to each other merrily. Squeals of laughter from a swing distracted her for just a moment, and she turned to watch a little girl being pushed skyward by her father.

Juliet thought of her own father. He had pushed her each night after supper in the swing that hung under the big pepper tree by the front porch at home. For a fleeting instant, she glimpsed her own childhood and with it a sense of knowing something she no longer knew— the child she was before the heartache, before real life took hold and swept her away from that story that was hers. When she felt utterly loved by the One who created her. When life meant hope and wonder, and inside her was light with no room for darkness, a shimmering that filled her heart.

Just as quickly as it came, the image, the longing, disappeared. In its place was the work she had ahead for the day, overseeing Sunday dinner for the children and learning a new song for rehearsal tomorrow. Buying new shoes for Emma Grace when there wasn't enough money, taking Gillian to the doctor again this week.

She stood and smoothed her skirts, then turned to head toward the carousel. She stopped, puzzled. The girls weren't in sight. Not one of them.

The music started again. She relaxed, telling herself they must have decided to take another turn. That had to be it. She walked toward the gate to wait.

She'd taken only two steps when her heart caught in her throat. All five of her sisters were speaking earnestly to a police officer. Behind them stood Clay MacGregor, who met her frantic gaze with a steely glare.

Hands on hips, Juliet planted herself in front of the policeman. He actually looked harmless with his walrus mustache, muttonchops, and high-crowned bowler. A bulging double row of brass buttons on his navy coat gave testimony to the rotund stomach beneath.

She frowned at him. "Sir, may I help you?"

He looked surprised. "You help me? Can't say as that question is asked of me very often. 'Tis usually the other way around." He peered at Juliet's face as if trying to read something there. "The name's Officer O'Malley. I just stopped to say hello to the children, Miss Dearbourne," he said, tipping his hat to her, then smiling at the girls. "To see how the wee ones are doing."

"How did you know my name?" Juliet demanded, glaring at MacGregor. She knew exactly how he'd found out.

"Ettie." Willow yanked on her sleeve. "I gotta go."

"Just a moment, sugar." She didn't take her eyes off the officer, half expecting him to make a grab for one of her sisters any minute.

"I gotta go bad." Willow hopped on one foot, then the other. Juliet reached for the child's hand to hold her still.

"Me too," Emma Grace chimed in. "I gotta go too."

Juliet looked down at their little worried faces, grimy with dried chocolate ice cream, flushed with the warmth of the afternoon. Even from the distance of a few feet, she could smell the familiar puppy-dog scent unique to children after play. She gathered them to her and turned to leave.

"Ah, just a minute now, lassie," the officer said. "You see, it's come to my attention that the children might need some extra lookin' after. With you gone all day and such."

She shot a glare at MacGregor, who gave her a steady, unapologetic look.

"I gotta go bad, Ettie," Emma Grace repeated.

"You see, officer, I really don't have time to talk to you about this right now." She backed away as she looked to the twins, willing them to pick up Willow and Gillian so they could all run from the park. She swung Emma Grace into her arms.

"I will just accompany you to your home, then, lass," the officer said. "I'm a mite curious myself about your circumstances."

She shot another piercing stare at Mr. MacGregor. If he hadn't stuck his nose into their business, she wouldn't be in this fix. She nodded at Officer O'Malley. "All right, then, follow me."

Clay MacGregor had told her about the twins leaving the little ones alone; likely, he'd said the same to the officer.

She wondered how soon the girls would be removed from her care.

TWENTY-ONE

I wonder why Mr. MacGregor chased Peter Rabbit out of his garden," Emma Grace said. She leaned her head against Juliet, frowning through the trolley window. She had asked at least a dozen questions about Mr. MacGregor's garden since their encounter with the man at the park.

" 'Cause he wath a mean, mean man," Willow said, sitting to Juliet's right. "He made Peter Rabbit sick." She turned around to stare at Clay MacGregor and the officer, sitting behind them.

Gillian scooted closer to Juliet, looking worried. "Peter Rabbit made his own self sick, silly goose," she said to Willow. "He ate himself sick in Mr. MacGregor's garden."

"I'm hungry," Willow said, "but I don't want any ol' carrots." She sighed noisily, wiggling in her seat. "Ettie, I still gotta go. Bad."

"We'll be home soon," Juliet said.

The trolley rattled to a stop near the brownstone, and they hurried from the car, all six Dearbournes, Juliet in the lead, carrying Emma Grace, and Officer O'Malley striding to catch up with her. Clay MacGregor walked between Willow and Gillian, answering questions about Peter Rabbit visiting his cabbage patch. They walked up the stairs, all four flights, single file, Officer O'Malley at Juliet's elbow. He questioned her about the supervision of the younger children while she was at the theatre, and just as they reached the landing, halted to catch his breath.

"You can understand why I'm concerned, lass," he said. "The big city is no place for little ones to be left unsupervised." He went on to tell her horror stories about what had happened to children left alone on his beat. "Everything from fires to burglaries," he said with a nod. Then he looked over the railing to the landing on the first floor. "Even this is a danger with wee ones. They could fall and be crushed below. Aye, 'twould be a tragedy indeed. You would not recognize them once that's happened."

Willow, Gillian, and Emma Grace gawked at him, wide-eyed, mouths hanging open.

Juliet had heard quite enough. "Please, sir. You're frightening the girls."

"Perhaps it's time someone did," he muttered.

"No one can care more than I do for the welfare of my sisters or be more diligent—"

He went on as if she hadn't spoken. "I'll have someone from Child Welfare stop tomorrow." He moved his stern glare to the twins. "If there's any hint that the younger lasses of this family are being neglected, there will be repercussions, believe you me."

The twins exchanged a guilty look. Annie swallowed hard, and Abby turned pale.

"Child Welfare?" Juliet sputtered. She gave Clay MacGregor a helpless expression. He looked away, appearing almost embarrassed.

Lips clamped tight, Juliet turned from where they were standing in the hall, to unlock her door. Her heart twisted.

It wasn't locked.

"You don't lock your door, lass?" Officer O'Malley asked, looking over her shoulders. "Did I tell you about burglaries?"

"I'm certain I did lock—" she began.

The door swung open from the inside.

Mairia Garden stood there, smiling at Juliet, smiling at them all. "Good afternoon, Officer," she said pleasantly. "Mr. MacGregor." She gave Clay a nod. "And my darling little girls," she said, kneeling to greet Willow, Gillian, and Emma Grace, who were staring at her open-mouthed.

Officer O'Malley frowned. "And who might you be?"

Mairia stood regally, her chin tilted just enough to remain stately without looking arrogant. "My name is Cornelia," she said. "Didn't Juliet tell you about me?"

He shook his head, cast an accusing look at Clay, then looked back to Mairia. "You live here too?"

A silken, honeyed laugh resulted. "Oh my, yes. I'm the little ones' governess."

She was still laughing as Clay and the officer headed down the four flights of stairs. She turned to Juliet. "I hope you don't mind my letting myself in this way."

"How...?" Juliet began.

"I spoke with your landlord, told him that I'd come all the way from California to see my darling girls. I must look honest—he let me in."

Juliet made proper introductions all around, then the little ones ran to the privy at the end of the hall, and Abby lit the stove without being told to begin dinner preparations. Annie put the kettle on for tea, and Juliet offered a seat to Mairia.

"Can you stay here with us, Cornelia?" she asked, hoping Mairia would say yes.

She was disappointed when the older woman shook her head. "I've already inquired. There is another room for let just down the hall."

Juliet grinned. "I don't know what to say other than thank you." She paused. "How did you know that we might need you?"

"Clay MacGregor came to see me while sleuthing for clues to your whereabouts. He saw an envelope on my table with the Victoria Theatre's name on it, and I knew he'd be off to New York in record time. He seemed determined to find you." She leaned forward. "And by the sparkle in his eye at the mention of your name, I think his search might have been for other reasons besides your relatives' hire."

Juliet colored and said nothing. Clay had betrayed her. She supposed he'd defend himself by saying he had no choice. But she still felt betrayed. What a silly thought. As though he was anything but a private investigator working against her.

Willow, Gillian, and Emma Grace burst through the door, chattering and laughing. Juliet sent them promptly to the apartment's single bedroom to rest before dinner.

"I have something for you," Mairia said, pulling a torn piece of newspaper from her pocket. "When I arrived in Grand Central Station, I bought the *New York Telegraph*. Of course I turned first to the theatre news." She laughed. "Can you guess what I found?"

Juliet couldn't imagine.

"It will have more drama if I read it to you."

"All right, then. Please do."

Mairia cleared her throat and held up the paper. Annie and Abby, in the kitchen, and the three young ones in the bedroom, fell silent.

" 'A new star is rising.' " She looked over the clipping at Juliet. "That's how it begins. It gets better."

Juliet gasped. Surely the writer didn't mean her.

" 'A new star is shooting skyward with the speed of a comet. Miss Juliet Dearbourne is the latest addition to the Victoria Revue. We all know that the Victoria isn't the incomparable Ziegfeld Follies, but the Hammerstein brothers sometimes make discoveries of equal import. And it seems that the Hammersteins have found a gem in Miss Juliet Dearbourne.' "

Juliet sat back in her chair, covering her open mouth. "You're making this up!"

"There's more." Mairia gave her a proud look, then dropped her eyes to the clipping. " 'Not only does Miss Dearbourne shimmer with a quality that some call "stage presence," she also can belt out a tune with a voice that makes everyone in the audience sit up and take notice. We encourage the Hammersteins to give her a feature role and get her out from under the veils.

" 'Miss Dearbourne is on her way. New York, she has arrived! Let it be said that we predicted it first!' "

Mairia pulled off her eyeglasses and nodded her head slowly, still smiling. "I knew it from the first moment I saw you perform. This is only the beginning…should you decide the theatre is truly your heart's desire."

"Of course it is," Juliet said quickly. "It's what I've always wanted. I gave it up for a time because of other reasons, not because I lost my desire to perform."

A clatter sounded from the kitchen as the oven door slammed and something dropped from the stove to the floor. Annie howled, and Abby squealed. Juliet jumped up to help, and Willow, Gillian, and Emma Rose raced in from the bedroom.

Mairia held up her hands with a laugh. "I'll leave you to your domestic chores. I'm not really much good in a kitchen."

"Promise you'll come back for dinner?"

"I will," she said.

"About an hour," Juliet said, then surveyed the scattered chicken parts and spilled flour. "Make that two," she added with a laugh.

They had just finished eating when a knock sounded at the door. Juliet opened it to see Clay MacGregor, leaning against the wooden rail at the top of the stairs, ankles crossed, white Stetson low over his forehead. Some things didn't change.

He held a copy of the newspaper in his hand. "Congratulations," he said before she could close the door.

"We have nothing to say to each other."

"I came to apologize." He took a step toward her.

"You turned us in to the authorities!" She couldn't believe his nerve! She wondered what his true motive was now.

"Not in the way you think. I merely stopped Officer O'Malley to ask his opinion."

Her laughter was bitter. "Ask his opinion? What did you think he'd do? Pat us on the head and send us on our way?"

He reached for her arm. "Please, can we start over?"

She whirled to face him. "There's nothing to start over, Mr. Mac-Gregor." Her words were clipped. "You have your job to do. I have mine. Now if you will excuse me…" She moved to close the door.

"I've done some thinking," he said, his tone apologetic. "Perhaps I've been too hasty."

"I've also done some thinking. You're a private investigator. You're trying to disrupt my life, the lives of my sisters. It's as simple as that. You're the enemy, Mr. MacGregor."

"You've got the wrong idea."

She whirled again to face him. "You made it very clear this afternoon what your intentions are, Mr. MacGregor. You even had a police officer bully us. Are you going to deny it?"

"Actually it was Officer O'Malley who knocked some sense into me," MacGregor said.

"How can that be?"

"He's got seven children of his own."

"And…?"

"He said that children belong with those who love them most. You dragged them across the continent with you when you could have self-ishly pursued your own career, your own desires, without all the worries of caring for them. He says that shows your love. And he was hoping to put the fear of God into Abby and Annie by letting them know what they'd done wrong."

The door was still wide open with Clay standing in the hallway. Juliet stood, letting the information sink in, frowning at him. "He put the fear of God into me," she said finally. "He had no call to do that."

"I don't think he had any intention of sending someone from Child Welfare. And when he saw Cornelia, he said Willow, Gillian, and Emma Grace would be in good hands."

"And they will be," she agreed.

"There's more I need to tell you. Would you care to go on a ride in the park with me?"

"I can't leave—" she began, then Mairia stepped up behind her.

"You go on now, child," she said. "I'm here. I'll make sure the girls get to bed on time. You go and enjoy yourself."

She hesitated, then looked into Clay's eyes. She found them sur-prisingly warm, inviting. "All right. I'll go." She turned to lift her coat from the hall tree. "But that doesn't mean I've forgiven you," she said.

He threw back his head and laughed, the sound echoing off the dingy walls. "Then I'll just have to keep trying harder," he said, and laughed again, his eyelids crinkling at the outer corners. He placed his hand beneath her elbow and escorted her down the stairs to the front entrance.

A hansom cab pulled to the curb as MacGregor signaled the cabby, who stepped from his bench and opened the door for Juliet. As soon as she had settled her skirts and leaned back in the plush seat, Clay climbed in and sat down beside her.

"Central Park and back. We're just going for a ride," he leaned around the bonnet and called to the cabby. "And we're in no hurry." The carriage wheels rolled forward, and the seat bounced comfortably as the driver headed his team into the flow of traffic.

Electrified streetlights, just beginning to glow in the twilight, lined the boulevard. Two horse-drawn hansom cabs jangled by in tandem. A Model T putted along in the opposite direction. It backfired twice, then once more, causing the driver of the second hansom to stare furiously at the motorcar as he calmed his horse.

Juliet and Clay exchanged a smile as their cabby grumbled about the turnip-brained drivers of the newfangled vehicles with that "gallderned fireworks" comin' out the rear.

"I have a plan," Clay said after a few minutes.

She leaned deeper into the velvet upholstery, wondering why she was inclined to believe him. "Tell me."

"Your grandmother and great aunts' greatest concern is for the well-being of the children. You yourself said that's true."

She lifted a brow and didn't speak. The hansom pulled into Central Park, tipping slightly as it turned. The buggy bounced, and Juliet caught her balance, looking out at the magical park after dark. On either side of the carriage electrified lamps cast a golden glow across the grassy hills and shadowy trees. Horses' hooves clopped along the brick road. Faint laughter carried from the carriages' passengers, punctuating low murmurs of conversation. High among some distant branches an owl called out; a moment later, it was answered by another deeper inside the park.

"It reminds me of home," Juliet said, still gazing at the beauty of the landscape.

The hansom wheels creaked along, and she breathed in the cool May air with its fragrance of newly mown grass, pond marshes, and night-blooming jasmine. Her heart quite suddenly ached for home, for the scent of orange trees, the starlit skies…the night birds.

"We have mockingbirds," she said, more to herself than to the man sitting next to her. "This time of year they sing so loud you can't sleep at night."

He was watching her with interest.

"Your ad said you were new to Riverview," Juliet changed subjects. It seemed so long ago that she'd sat across from him in the packinghouse he called an agency. "Where did you live before that?"

"Not far from your ranch. My father had a spread out in the San Fernando Valley. Sold it to developers sometime ago. Made a fortune."

"No doubt it's covered with look-alike houses and tin-roofed factories. My parents talked about those who sold ou—" She caught herself and stopped. "I'm sorry. I didn't mean anything by it. It's just that my family has always battled to keep the land wild."

"Please, don't apologize. I couldn't agree more with your point of view. My father acted out of spite." A hard look overcame his face as he turned away from her.

When he turned back, he was smiling again as if the exchange never happened. "This may surprise you, but I miss it too. When I rode out to meet your grandmother and aunts, I was quite taken with your Big Valley."

"It's been no small battle to keep it from being developed. The years of drought, the recent pest infestation, haven't helped."

"California's always had cycles of drought and floods—"

"Earthquakes and fires," she finished for him, laughing. "How well I know. It's the drought that finally sent my father packing to South America. He'd heard about a new variety of citrus that he was sure would solve the financial problems of our land."

"It was the drought that finally forced my father to sell our cattle ranch," Clay said. "It seems he didn't have the gumption or foresight of your father."

"This time my father was a bit shortsighted, it seems," she said quietly. "We lost everything anyway. The bank will likely sell to developers when all is said and done. May have already. I know that no citrus grower worth his salt would touch our insect-infested trees."

"I'm sorry," he said simply. He sounded as though he meant it.

She shook her head. "You were about to tell me your plan?"

He grinned and stretched his arm across the back of the seat. He seemed too big for the small cab, and it struck her that a long ride in this vehicle, charming as it was, truly couldn't be the most comfortable mode of transportation for him.

"Have you thought about writing to your grandparents and great aunts?"

"I'd planned to eventually, of course. I just wanted to wait until things were a bit more stable."

"Will they believe you? About things being stable, I mean?"

"Of course they will. They know me. Trust me."

"But they hired me to find you, didn't they?"

"Good point."

"If I spend time with you, with the children, and see firsthand that they truly are healthy and happy and safe, don't you agree that your family would then believe a report from me, an unbiased party?"

A smile played at her lips. "It's likely," she said.

They rode along without speaking. The rhythm of the horse's hooves, the breeze in her face, the glow of lamplight, all fed her senses.

She glanced across the distance that separated them to see that Clay's face was solemn as he beheld her. The wind twisted loose a strand of Juliet's hair from where it had been fastened. She tucked it behind her ear, and the cab turned onto the street where Juliet's brownstone stood.

"There's another reason I'd like to stay," he said, his voice husky.

The horse halted in front of her building, but the cabby sat looking straight ahead as if he were used to prolonged good-byes.

Juliet smiled into Clay's eyes, surprised at the quick thud of her heart. Leaning toward her, Clay touched her face with his fingertips.

She thought he might kiss her, and was deciding whether or not to let him, when a cry interrupted her thoughts.

"Ettie! Ettie!" Annie, her face stained with tears, ran toward the cab.

As soon as Juliet stepped to the ground, Annie hurled herself into Juliet's arms. "Come quickly," she wailed. "Willow's hurt."

Twenty-Two

"It's my fault," Annie sobbed as the three raced up the stairwell. "It's all my fault."

"I don't want to hear whose fault it is." Juliet panted as she ran. "I just want to know what happened and how Willow is now."

Annie gulped back another sob and bit her lip. "She put her eye out."

"Mothers have been saying that to their children for years," Juliet said calmly, though her heart was pounding. "I've never known it to happen. Ever."

"Can she see out of it?" Clay called up to them from a few stairs behind.

Annie drew in a shuddering breath. "She was crying, so I don't know. Her eye is swollen shut." She sniffled. "It's just the blood scared us all. I said I'd come to find you. We didn't know what to do." She started crying again.

"She's bleeding?" Juliet's heart was racing now. She envisioned a sharp object penetrating Willow's iris and shuddered. "Where?" She kept her voice low and soothing.

"Her eye."

"No, tell me what happened."

"She got hit by a doorknob."

"A doorknob?"

"She was trying to pull out another loose tooth," Annie said. "We tied a string around the tooth, then slammed the door to see if we could get it to come out." She sniffed again. "I guess the tooth wasn't loose enough. Or maybe it's because Willow weighs less than a feather. Anyway, she flew right along with the door. It closed with a slam. She banged into it."

Juliet took Annie's hand in hers. "Is Cornelia still with you?"

"Yes, but—"

"But what?"

"She fainted dead away."

Juliet halted briefly. "Fainted?"

"When she saw the blood. She just crumpled onto the floor. Abby's trying to take care of them both. We pulled Cornelia to the sofa and put an ice pack on her head."

Something told Juliet that Mairia didn't know the first thing about childcare, but she kept her silence about it, afraid Clay might put it in his report.

She didn't even have to place the key in the knob. The door flew open, and Willow flew into her arms, clinging to her waist and sobbing. Up and down the dark hallway people poked their heads out of their doorways, staring and shaking their heads.

"Let's go inside so you can tell me what happened." She wrapped her arm around the little girl and led her gently into the apartment.

Willow, Gillian, Emma Grace, and both twins all started to talk at once, and at the same time, across the room, Mairia moaned and tried to sit up.

Juliet hurried to her side, saw that the color was returning to her face. "How are you?"

Mairia smiled weakly. "I never was one much for trauma of any kind." With a worried look, she rested her gaze on Willow. "Are you all right, baby?"

Willow moved her head up and down as Juliet pulled the child onto her lap, then tipped Willow's head toward the light. There was a small cut at the outer edge of her right eye. A large bruise surrounded it. She touched it gently, and Willow yelped. "Can you see out of it?" Willow closed her uninjured eye and looked around the room.

"Ith a little blurry."

Juliet stroked her hair. "Has anyone put a cold cloth on it?"

Willow nodded. "Yeth. Abby did." Then she looked at Annie. "And Annie ran to get you."

"Now," Juliet said, "tell me what happened. Everything." She kissed Willow's forehead gently.

Willow sat up taller, obviously feeling important. "Well, ith like this," she said. With an index finger, she felt in her mouth for the culprit tooth and tried to wiggle it. She grimaced. "Ow. It hurts." She launched into a long, very detailed story about who'd said what and how the doorknob hit her eye. Halfway through her tale, she clambered off Juliet's lap and acted out the rest of her tale, with her sisters filling in details she'd forgotten.

"Come back here, pumpkin." Juliet patted her lap, and Willow climbed into it. "Do you think we ought to take you to see a doctor?"

Willow shook her head. "No!"

"I don't either. But I want you to lie still and keep a cold cloth on your head until the swelling goes down."

Willow promised she would.

"Something very silly will happen in the morning."

"What?" Her other eye was round and large with curiosity.

"Your eye might not open."

"Really?" Already the eye was swollen half closed.

"I don't want you to be frightened."

"I won't."

"That's my brave girl. Now you scoot and get ready for bed." She now focused on all the girls. "Gillian and Emma Grace, you skedaddle too. Off to bed you go. It's much too late for you to be up."

"And you, young ladies," she said to the twins. "We have something important to talk about. Get ready for bed, and then we'll talk."

They looked sheepish and headed for the bedroom.

Clay MacGregor stood and cleared his throat. "I, ah, think I should be going."

She walked with him out to the landing above the stairwell.

"It's a big job, what you're doing. Even with your new governess." He grinned.

"You don't know the half of it."

"I'm sure I don't."

She turned away from him, letting her gaze travel down the dimly lit, bleak, and narrow hallway. She didn't answer him.

"You have my admiration," he said to her back.

She listened to his footsteps as he descended the stairs. Long after the door on the first floor closed with a thud, she stood, head resting against the closed door. Then she walked across the landing and sat down on the top step.

She should be elated. Her first smashing review, a friend newly arrived to help with the children, and for the first time in what seemed like forever, she felt that they were safe. But the shadows of life still hovered close. She wanted her mother to be with her to share her joy, and she wanted to hear that her father and brother were safe, and she wanted to find that piece of her heart that was lost.

The door behind her opened, and soft footsteps padded across the thin carpet toward her. She waited to see which little sleepyhead would nestle against her arm. It was Emma Grace. Smiling, Juliet circled her arm around the child's shoulders and pulled her close.

"I missed you while you were gone, Ettie," she whispered, snuggling her head into Juliet's waist.

"I missed you too, angel." She kissed the spot on her head where her hair was divided into the two plaits.

"Does Mr. MacGregor still want us to go away with him?"

"No, honey. And he's going to let Grandma and the aunties know we're all happy and well."

" 'Cept for Willow who got hit by a doorknob."

"Yes, except for that."

"And Miss Cornelia who fainted."

"Yes, Miss Cornelia, too."

"She's still resting and talking to Annie and Abby."

"That's all right. We'll let her rest."

"I don't wanna go anywhere without you." Emma Grace cuddled against her with a sigh.

Juliet bent over the child, resting her cheek on top of her head, and closed her eyes.

That night, long after her sisters slept, Willow on one side of her, Emma Grace on the other, Juliet lay awake thinking about the future, the uncertainties for them all, her concerns about her abilities to perform—to be funny and carefree—night after night. Matinee after matinee.

A still, small voice seemed to speak to her from the depths of her heart.

I AM WITH YOU, AND I LOVE YOU.

She laughed at the notion. Why should God care about her after all the years she'd ignored him. But the thoughts persisted and drifted into her soul on the wings of words she'd heard her mother and father read from the prophet Isaiah years before.

> For I will pour water upon him that is thirsty,
> and floods upon the dry ground:
> I will pour my spirit upon thy seed,
> and my blessing upon thine offspring.

She remembered her parents' conversation as clearly as if it had been that morning. Her mother had asked her father if the words meant that God would pour out his blessings on their children because of hers and Quaid's faithfulness.

Her father had taken several minutes to answer. After a bit he said he thought that yes, God would pour out his Spirit, his blessings, on all their children. But as for the children being filled to overflowing, that would be up to each one individually. If they thirsted for God, the blessings would soak in. If they didn't, the blessings would run off them like water off a duck's slick feathers.

Juliet smiled in the dark, picturing her mother and her father. Emmeline had gone then to Quaid, still seated at the big round table, wrapped her arms around him, and laughed softly. First she'd said he needed to be careful of blasphemy, speaking of ducks and God's spirit in the same breath. Then she'd said she was certain that particular scripture was meant as a special blessing to mothers.

Still embracing Quaid, she'd said to the children, "Until the day I die, I will be praying for each of you to thirst after your heavenly Father until nothing else in the world will quench that longing."

Juliet sighed, listening to the loud alarm clock ticking the passing minutes, echoing off the walls in the small apartment. It mixed with the chorus of the girls' breathing, punctuated from time to time by a dream-giggle or a deep sigh.

A tiny smacking sound came from Emma Grace, and Juliet reached over to pull the child's thumb from her mouth.

Juliet finally fell asleep with Emma Grace's little hand nestled protectively in hers.

Juliet stepped through the stage entrance at the back of the theatre. Around her whirled the pre-performance bustle and chatter. Someone was singing a scale offstage, and a row of dancers stooped and stretched, their left ankles resting on the barre, as they limbered up for their number. Onstage a bit player dressed as a traffic cop juggled nightsticks. He raced across the empty space, chased by a tricycle-riding, whistle-blowing fireman who was dragging a fire hose. That night the hose would shoot confetti. For now it was merely a rehearsal prop.

She had been at the theatre for a month now but didn't think she would ever tire of the bustling and noise backstage prior to a show. It energized her.

Desiree Dow, an older actress who was known to be a trouble-maker, followed Juliet beyond the makeup mirrors and rows of costumes to Juliet's small cubicle in the dressing room. Once inside, Juliet tossed her coat onto a hanger, then sat in front of the mirrored table to remove her hat.

The woman's eyes glittered. And for the quickest instant Juliet thought she spotted envy. Or worse.

"I've got news," Desiree said. "Bad news."

She watched Desiree's reflection in the mirror as the dark-haired woman continued speaking. "One of the girls overheard Gladdy say the theatre's been sold to some new owners and we're closing." Her mouth turned downward.

"What?" Juliet's heart nearly stopped. "What do you mean, closing?"

"You think you're some prima donna or something?" She laughed as if she'd told a great joke. "It happens to us all. We get hired, we get let go for whatever reason. You should be glad you've lasted this long without getting canned or worse. Count your blessings."

Juliet felt the blood drain from her face. She'd thought her troubles were over, at least temporarily. She stood. "I really need to get ready for rehearsal. If you'll excuse me…"

Desiree pulled her silver cigarette holder from a small crocheted bag, dropped in a cigarette, and, holding it jauntily between her fingers, swished from the room.

Juliet headed to Gladdy McBean's office and was ushered in to see him immediately.

Gladdy looked up, obviously pleased that she'd come. "Please, Juliet, sit down."

She settled into a chair opposite him. "I just heard the theatre's being sold. Is it true?"

"It was a recent decision." He settled back in his chair, steepling his fingers. "The Hammersteins weren't looking for a buyer per se, but they were approached with an offer they couldn't refuse."

"How long till the Revue closes?"

"The end of the month."

"That's only three weeks away!"

"It's likely your contract will be picked up by the theatre's new owners. You might have a few weeks off while they renovate. Perhaps all summer."

"Without pay?"

"Of course." He removed his eyeglasses and wiped the glass with his pink handkerchief. Holding them by the crossed earpieces, he tapped them absently on the wooden table that served as his desk. "If it's a job you need before then, most of our players will head west. Hollywood. You might think about that as an option. We tend to look down our noses at the movies, but it would give you a paycheck."

"I just came from California."

"Ah, yes. I remember."

She nodded.

He placed the eyeglasses on his nose, wrapping the wire stems around his ears. "A director from Biograph Studios will be in our audience tonight." He paused as though waiting for her to respond. When she didn't, he went on, "I can introduce you."

"I'm not interested." Dismayed, she quickly calculated the costs of getting the girls back to California. It was an impossible sum.

"If you change your mind, let me know."

"I won't."

That night Juliet shut the world from her heart and mind, putting every ounce of her energy into her performance. She would think about her money problems tomorrow. For tonight she laughed and vamped and sang with gusto. Even though her life was about to fall apart.

At the end of her song, the applause was thunderous. In the front row the patrons stood, clapping wildly. She attempted to leave the stage, only to be called back again for another bow.

The maestro nodded, and she launched into Irving Berlin's *When I Leave the World Behind* in what was quickly becoming her trademark throaty voice.

The beat was slower, and for the first time since she stepped onstage, her worries about tomorrow crowded into her heart. She looked up into the spotlight, wondering if she would ever truly leave the worries of this world behind. Images of her sisters and their hopes and dreams, her responsibilities, crowded into her heart. By the time she finished the second chorus, tears were rolling down her cheeks.

When she bowed, there wasn't a sound in the theatre. The silence was unnerving—she gave a quick bow and had nearly reached her dressing room when a spattering of applause finally broke out. Her heart dropped; it was never good to end a performance on a downbeat. But she didn't care. Her career would be over soon anyway. She didn't know how she could make it through the summer without pay.

Struggling to keep fresh tears from flowing, she changed out of her costume and into her street clothes. She heard the faint crescendos of the orchestra, the flourish of the last song, *Stop and Go,* signaling the end of the show. Thunderous applause broke out again as she put on her coat. Her plan was to slip out the back way without being seen.

But before she could go, a knock sounded. "Miss Dearbourne?"

Surprised, she pulled open the door. A grinning Gladdy McBean stood next to the most handsome man she'd ever seen. She took a step backward and swallowed hard. "Yes?"

The two men entered the bustling dressing room, the second man's presence seeming to fill the place with magic. When he smiled, his tanned face showed two even rows of white teeth, and his vivid eyes, light and lively, crinkled at the edges.

Blinking up at him, speechless, she realized where she'd seen him. The film magazine *Photoplay.* He was predicted to someday become one of the biggest stars of the silent screen. Already he played opposite the likes of Gloria Swanson, Mary Pickford, and the Gish sisters, Lillian and Dorothy.

"This is Stephan Sterling." Gladdy McBean, standing slightly off to one side, seemed to be enjoying her astonishment.

She offered him her hand. "Juliet Rose Dearbourne," she said.

"I enjoyed your performance, Miss Rose." Instead of shaking her hand, he lifted it and kissed her fingertips. He laughed lightly. " 'Miss Rose.' I like the ring of it. If I can convince you to come to Hollywood, we'll drop the 'Dearbourne.' "

Juliet was too stunned to speak. He continued, his silvery voice full of self-confidence. "Rarely have I been as touched by a rendition as I was with your final number. The emotion in your face, your eyes, was quite impressive."

She pulled back her hand, feeling her cheeks redden. "Thank you," she managed.

Gladdy cleared his throat. "You may wonder why we stopped by—"

"I think I've just guessed," she said, regaining her composure. "I assume Mr. Sterling is the Biograph director you mentioned before the show."

Sterling laughed again. It was the sound of a man certain of his place in the world. "And?" he chuckled.

"And you've come to lure me to the silver screen." And *lure* was the appropriate word. There was something tawdry about the movie business and those caught up in it. It was one thing to act in a Shakespearean play or in the Revue, quite another to be part of the world that magazines called "decadent." It was difficult enough to keep her life with her sisters separate from Broadway. But Hollywood was a different matter. *Screenplay* told of the wild parties, the use of alcohol and narcotics. Juliet wanted no part of it, for herself or for her sisters.

His gaze flickered over her. "Your honesty is refreshing. Most women I know would give their eyeteeth to be asked to consider such a move."

"I'm not most women you know," she said. "I have no interest in Hollywood." She buttoned her coat. "And I really must be going. It was lovely to meet you, Mr. Sterling."

Sterling and McBean exchanged questioning glances. Gladdy excused himself, and Sterling stepped into the hallway to hold open the door for Juliet. "I would like to see you again, Miss Rose."

"I'm not going to change my mind."

Several of the Revue players, who were now removing costumes and replacing props, turned toward them. A few recognized Stephan and called out greetings. He seemed to enjoy the attention and waved heartily. "It's not to change your mind, my dear," he said, turning again to Juliet. "Believe me. I would simply like to spend more time with someone so refreshingly honest. Someone who can make me laugh."

She stopped at the stage door leading to the alley. "I'm afraid you'll be disappointed. And I rarely make people amused, Mr. Sterling, except when I'm onstage. Besides, my life is very full right now. There simply isn't time for anything else."

His hand covered hers as she reached for the door handle. "I hope I can change your mind, Miss Rose. Will you allow me to try?"

She met his intense gaze. The man was persistent, she had to give him that. And *Juliet Rose* did make a wonderful stage name.

"A smile at last," he said softly. "Now that was well worth the wait. You are beautiful, Miss Rose, when you smile."

She rolled her eyes, shaking her head slowly.

"And that's even better! Maybe it is I who can make *you* laugh when you're not onstage."

They stepped down the stairs to the alley. By now the other players were heading past them to the front of the theatre to catch cabs and carriages and trolleys home. "May I escort you someplace?" he asked when she stopped at the curb. "I'll be happy to drive you home. My car is just around the corner."

"No, Mr. Sterling. I will see myself home. But thank you."

He bent to kiss her hand again. "Then it is farewell, my dear Miss Rose. Mark my words. When I set my cap to see something accomplished, I seldom take no for an answer."

She lifted her chin. "Then you've never met up with the likes of me."

"Nor you with the likes of me, Miss Rose." He raised a brow as he kissed her fingertips, letting his lips linger a half-second too long. When he looked up, his eyes were warm. "We will meet again. Perhaps next time you will be persuaded to see things my way."

She didn't answer.

"Did I mention that the offer I am prepared to make on behalf of Biograph is quite lucrative? That it would be a starring role?" His eyes crinkled at the corners. "And that—though I did not want to say so in front of my friend Gladdy—I'm not referring to a mere hiatus. I mean to sign you to Biograph long term." He bent low, bowing as a prince would to his queen. Then standing upright, he whispered, "Sleep on that tonight, Miss Juliet Rose."

She stared at him dumbfounded.

A motorized cab pulled forward, and he opened the door to help her in. "Sweet dreams, Miss Rose," he said, then closed the vehicle's door. "We'll talk again."

TWENTY-THREE

Two weeks later Juliet looked up to see Clay MacGregor striding toward her as she was leaving the stage-entrance door of the theatre. The narrow brick alley was filled with the players on their way home from rehearsal, but Clay MacGregor, with his big-boned height and brawny shoulders, stood out from the crowd.

She was surprised at the warmth that seemed to invade her heart as she watched him draw near. It mingled with other emotions she was starting to feel about this man, emotions that disturbed her. She'd watched his gentle ways with her sisters, the quiet joy that seemed part of his manly strength, his ruggedly handsome face with the touches of humor around his mouth. She had also noticed how his attention often fell on her like sunlight, how his eyes flickered with interest when her gaze met his. But she had no time or inclination to wonder at the rapid thudding of her heart when he was near. Her life had no room for him or any other man. She refused to be distracted by romantic notions.

Yet when he planted his feet squarely and blocked her way at the foot of the rear door stairs, her resolve came close to melting.

"Clay, what brings you to the theatre district?" She kept her tone cool, determined not to reveal her joy at seeing him.

"You," he said, arching an eyebrow that completely disarmed her.

"Me?" The pale golden hue of his face in the late afternoon sun further caused her resolve to falter. "Me?" she repeated softly, not wanting to admit how pleased that last word of his made her feel.

"I came by to invite you and the girls on an excursion. It may be one of the last we'll have together." She caught her breath and frowned. He had become as much a part of the family as Mairia had. The thought of his leaving caught her off guard, and for a moment she couldn't speak. "One of our last times together?" she finally managed.

He gently placed her hand in the crook of his arm and escorted her down the alley toward the boulevard. But before he could answer, a familiar voice called from behind them.

"Miss Rose! There you are!" Stephan called as she turned. "I've been looking everywhere." He picked his way through the other actors and musicians until he reached the front of the theatre where she now stood with Clay.

Stephan had eyes only for her. "Miss Rose," he said with great affection. "It's good to see you again." She frowned at his proprietary tone.

"May I introduce Clay MacGregor?" She cast a glance at Clay, whose eyes had turned the shade of a stormy sky.

Stephan stuck out his hand. "Good to meet you, Mac. If I may call you that, old boy." He laughed heartily while deftly attempting to turn Juliet away from Clay.

Juliet held her ground. "If you'll excuse us a moment," she said to Stephan, whose expression darkened as he stepped back to wait in the shade of the marquee.

"Mac?" Clay muttered when they were alone again. The warmth had left his eyes.

"He's merely an associate," she protested.

Clay turned away from her, apparently to watch for a cab. She followed his gaze. It seemed that chaos reigned around them: the almost deafening discordant noise, the people and vehicles frantically hurrying from one place to another. Strangely, it had once seemed exciting, full of bustling energy.

But now, standing here with Clay, a man who belonged to the wild California land as much as she did, she had a sudden longing for the quiet of home, the Big Valley, and the call of birdsong so sweet it hurt her heart.

She looked up to see that Clay was now studying her. "About that excursion," she said. "We would love to accompany you." She felt warmth flood her cheeks as she added, "*I* would like to accompany you."

He quirked a brow. "*You* would, Juliet?" His voice was husky and low. He gently turned her away from the marquee where Stephan was standing.

"I would."

Clay lifted her chin with one finger and smiled again, finally, into her eyes. She didn't care if Stephan or anyone else was watching. For an instant she cared nothing about her earlier resolve to keep him at a distance. It was as if the sun had just risen in her heart.

"Then I'll pick you up on Tuesday."

"Tuesday then."

He grinned and stepped toward a waiting hansom taxi. "Your, ah, business associate waits," Clay said, nodding toward Stephan. Somehow he didn't seem to be too concerned as Stephan once again strode toward Juliet.

"Miss Rose," Stephan said again with great warmth, reaching out both hands for Juliet's.

Juliet swallowed a smile as she glanced back at the cab. For the life of her, she thought Clay rolled his eyes as he stepped into the cab. She decided she couldn't wait to see him again.

"I've come to convince you that I'm right about your future," Stephen said, his expression warm.

Juliet laughed, enjoying the man's persistence. "I told you before, I'm not interested."

"And as I said before, Miss Juliet Rose, I seldom take no for an answer." He smiled into her eyes. "And this time, I've brought the one thing you need. A contract with terms you can't refuse." With a confident chuckle, he patted his vest pocket. "I guarantee this time you'll listen to reason."

Something in the intensity of his expression caused Juliet to shiver, even in the fading evening sunlight.

⊰⊱

The following Tuesday, Mairia Garden strode down 28th Street toward the Fifth Avenue Theatre where she'd made her debut back in '77. She'd been young then, vulnerable, naive. It was a theatre where performers such as Lily Langtry, Edwin Booth, and Eleanora Duse ruled the stage.

She stopped in front of the structure, rebuilt after fires ravaged the original and its successor. The facade was the same, but the theatre was now in decay. Once the center of the theatre district, the old girl was now in the wrong place. *Just like me.* Stepping closer, Mairia craned her neck to look upward to those rooms behind the dark windows where she had first discovered that life was less than sunlight and hopeful dreams.

With a shudder she turned away, feeling the old, familiar darkness return. Her throat ached for a drink, just as it did every day with nearly every breath. She swallowed hard and wondered where she might find a quick swallow of whiskey.

There were two more places she must visit before her journey into the past was complete. She knew the old Enemy would hound her with every step, vying as always for her soul. It frightened her, even though she was ever aware of the One who walked beside her.

Redemption had come years before. Oh yes! When she had believed there was nothing of herself left to rescue, God had gathered her into his arms while she was still wrapped in tattered, filthy rags—both on her body and in her heart.

Mairia walked briskly away from the decaying theatre, the demons of her past at her heels. When she reached the trolley stand and found her seat on the car, she was surprised to find her face wet with tears she didn't remember shedding.

She stepped from the trolley at 34th Street, directly in front of the Manhattan Theatre. Walking slowly, she moved her gaze up the tan-and-white brick facade to the brownstone trim. The years she called this place home skipped through her mind. Though she'd lost her innocence, her soul, at the Fifth Avenue, at the Manhattan she began her dark journey, building all the while an impenetrable shield around her heart. But it hadn't been enough to dull her pain. She quickly discovered that only alcohol and narcotics could make her forget.

Oh yes, she'd built her name until there was no rival. The Queen of the Manhattan Opera. The toast of the town. And in the process, what little remained of her heart turned to stone.

Across from the Manhattan was the Songbird Saloon. Mairia turned and stared at her old haunt. The wasted hours, the friends—if one could call them that—the dark despair come morning, flooded into her mind.

She was surprised to hear the same music drift into the street. A siren song, it had always been. It was still.

Stepping off the curb, she dodged a trolley and stepped aside for a Stutz Bearcat, then walked to the entrance of the Songbird. Wondering if any of the old crowd might still be there, she pushed open the door.

Juliet and Clay ushered the children onto the Staten Island Ferry. The summer day was brilliant, the sky bright blue and cloudless. Annie and Abby took the young ones upstairs to the observation deck, while Juliet and Clay stood near the starboard railing, watching the city float by.

The wind caught a thick tuft of Clay's hair, lifting it straight above his forehead. For an instant Juliet wanted to smooth it with her fingertips.

The ferry rocked gently, waves lapping with a small smacking sound. The water sparkled in the sun, and sea gulls called as they circled and swooped and rose again on flashing wings. "I was hoping you might return to California with me," Clay said, looking out to sea.

She studied his profile for a moment. "Can you keep a secret?"

"Of course."

"I've been in contact with a surgeon. Have seen him twice—"

"You're not ill, are you?" He turned, looking worried.

She laughed. "Oh, good heavens, no. It's for Gillian. And she's certainly not ill."

A slow understanding dawned in his eyes. "Gillian!" He seemed unable to stop smiling.

The Statue of Liberty was just coming into view, and they both turned toward it. "I always wondered what prompted you to come here," he mused, almost as if to himself. "I was told you were canned at the New Globe, but I wasn't convinced by Cornelia's explanation."

"Someday I'll explain," she said quietly. "For now you'll have to trust me. I must keep a confidence of my own."

"That I understand," he said, his gaze still on the magnificent statue. "You were going to tell me about the surgeon." He turned toward her. "Knowing you as I do now, I think I've guessed. It's Gillian's foot." He shook his head, still smiling.

She nodded. "I've not wanted to breathe a word of it to anyone— not even my sisters—until I know for certain that the surgeon can help her. I've seen Dr. John Allen Wyeth three times. Gillian's seen him once. He's head of the Polyclinic Medical School and Hospital on 34th Street. He's a busy man who normally doesn't see patients himself, but we've convinced him to make an exception with Gillian."

"*We* have?"

She laughed lightly, again realizing her mistake too late. "Client confidentiality."

"Does Gillian know why she was taken to him?"

"She thinks it's for a new leg brace. We can't get her to wear the ones she's been fitted for in the past. Her foot is twisted but not in such a way that she can't get around. We are worried, though, that she'll have back problems later on if we don't do something now. She's a determined little girl. We've never coddled her because of her foot, and she's the better for it. She doesn't feel sorry for herself. She's just made up for not being able to run and play with other children by becoming quite the little bookworm."

"I've noticed that she's got a mind quicker than a deer can run."

"She does," Juliet agreed.

"When will you know what Dr. Wyeth can do for her?"

"He's taken all her bone measurements and studied the skeletal structure of her foot and ankle. His medical school makes use of the photography method known as x-ray."

"I've heard of it."

"He says he'll tell me next week."

"I'll pray for his wisdom," Clay said simply.

His words touched her, and she was reminded of how easily her mother and father promised such prayer to each other and their children. Their faith was so much a part of their lives that she sometimes imagined every breath was a prayer.

Clay's faith reminded her of her parents'. She'd noticed it in a dozen different ways since he'd become part of their family. His booming voice speaking to God before meals, thanking him for each child by name, even thanking him for something unique each had said or done that day.

Or when he looked up at the stars during their buggy rides and uttered thanks to the Creator for the one true "greatest show on earth."

Or when he knelt beside her in church and breathed a prayer of such intimacy with his Lord it made her eyes tear. To think that Clay would bring Gillian's surgeon before God, praying for his wisdom, that he would lift little Gillian into her Father's care, touched Juliet's heart to the core.

She met Clay's gaze. "Thank you."

"I understand why you can't leave."

"When do *you* plan to return to California?"

He grinned at her. "My report to your relatives was posted two weeks ago. I haven't heard back, but I can't imagine they're worried."

"I've written to them as well, letting them know where we are. I should have done it long ago." She looked out at the statue, now growing closer. "I suppose I let my anger with them keep me from writing. First, that they didn't trust my judgment, my love for my sisters. And second…" She grinned up at him. "Second, that they saw fit to hire an investigator to haul us all home."

"As for me," he said, "I'm glad they did."

The way the sunlight slanted against his eyes, the way they crinkled at the corners when he laughed, the rugged roll to his shoulders, made her want to know how it might feel to be in his arms.

But she had no time for a romance with Clay MacGregor or anyone else, she reminded herself. Her sisters, her career, and her determination to see Gillian through her surgery occupied all her time and attention. And lately a new thought had pushed aside the others to make a space of its own. As soon as she had money ahead—after paying back Mairia's loan—she planned to launch a search of her own for her father and brother.

No, there was no time for romance. Not a spare minute.

Obviously Clay hadn't a clue what she was thinking because, before she could protest, he bent over her and drew her into his arms. Juliet had only the beat of a heart to let out a small gasp before his lips touched hers.

The kiss was as brief as a gull's cry.

"Oh, my," she sighed, once he had released her. She looked up into his eyes to see him studying her. Stepping back, she imposed an iron control on herself. "I haven't time..." she began, then faltered when a shadow crossed his face. "You see, my life is full right now. I have responsibilities."

He held up a hand. "You're thinking of me as just another responsibility?"

"I simply don't have time to add anything, anyone, to my life right now."

"You're afraid I'll derail your career like a fallen log on a train track."

"That's not fair. I have my sisters to think about."

"You also love the limelight. I see that in you."

She lifted her chin stubbornly. "Every stage has a limelight. It's by her nature that an actress must love the spot."

"You know what I mean."

The captain blew the whistle as the ferry headed around the Statue of Liberty. For a moment the crowd, including Juliet and Clay, fell silent in awe of the magnificent figure.

"Give me your tired, your poor," Clay murmured. *"Your huddled masses yearning to breathe free..."*

"Send these, the homeless, tempest-tossed, to me..." Juliet continued, joining in reciting the memorized verse at the statue's base. *"I lift my lamp beside the golden door."*

"Our country's symbol of our freedom," he said, still gazing upward. He turned back to Juliet. "And you, Juliet? Do you know freedom?"

"How can I?" she scoffed. "I work to care for others. My sisters still hurt from our tragic losses. I'm trying to fix their ills, nurse their heartaches, teach them what they need for the future. On top of that, I still miss my mother, so much that I think I might die myself if I dwell on it too much. And I want to find my father and brother, and I'm scared they may be dead too. Jared and I lost the land entrusted to us. I didn't know how much I loved it until it was gone. I suppose loved ones and home are much alike in that regard.

"Freedom?" she said. "How can I possibly know the meaning of the word?"

She stared up at him through a shimmer of tears, surprised at what lay behind the hedge she was attempting to build around her heart. Silently Clay gathered her into his arms and held her while she cried.

That wasn't what Clay meant at all when he asked about freedom. He meant freedom from the chains that bound her to earth, chains of helplessness and sorrow, pain and guilt, worry and fear. He longed to tell her that there was One who walked beside her to share her sorrow if she would let him. Take the burden of her heartache if she would give it to him. He would turn the darkness in her heart to brilliant light.

But Clay simply held her, resting his cheek against the top of her head. And he prayed that, when the time was right, he could tell her.

━━◆━━

Mairia entered the Songbird and peered into the musty darkness. In the corner a piano played a tinny song just like the old days. Mairia took a seat near the window where she could see the Manhattan Opera House across the street.

She remembered the sound of applause, the glory of the music, the soaring voices of the singers, the magnificent design of the sets, the costumes. Those were the days.

For nearly ten years she was the star, the Voice everyone came from Paris, from Rome, from Boston, to hear. She'd gloried in it until her golden voice betrayed her. Some said its cause was the drink. Or the occasional powders she took. Still others believed the rumors that she partied for days on end and her body finally gave out.

The success was fleeting. It hurt her pride to let another voice become the star. Within a period of months she had moved from top billing to the insignificant chorus line. Finally she was let go because she couldn't squeak out a note without coughing. She had left the Manhattan and looked for other work. Her savings paid her bills for a time. Finally the drink and powders caused her to miss rehearsals, then performances, even when she was getting top billing. She walked away from her penthouse before the creditors came. She moved to the streets, to dirty and dangerous back alleys, and changed her identity, hoping never to be found again.

"What can I get you, lady?" the barkeep called to her.

Her throat still ached with the need for alcohol. Surely just one wouldn't hurt. "Whiskey," she said, "straight up."

The glass appeared on the table in front of her with a slosh of liquid down one side. She paid the man, then sat staring at it, imagining the pleasant sting it would leave as it trailed down her throat. Her hand trembled as she reached for the glass, lifted it, and swirled the pretty amber liquid.

Twilight was falling now, and theatre patrons crowded along the walk leading to the Manhattan Opera. Bejeweled ladies, some in fox and mink even though the weather was mild. Top-hatted gentlemen in fancy spats. She wondered if any remembered her name, remembered her voice. Or cared.

She stared again into the whiskey. She played with the glass, dipped her finger in the liquid, then circled the rim with it until it sang a note.

Slowly she stood, almost reluctantly. She gave the drink one more glance, then nodded to the barkeep.

"Hey, lady," he called. "You didn't touch your whiskey."

"I didn't need it after all," she said and stepped through the door.

She strolled down the avenue to the trolley stop. In a half-hour she would join Juliet and the girls for supper. Her heart lifted at the thought of them, and she quickened her pace.

A gathering of sparrows sang from the branches of a spindly-limbed, nondescript tree. "You've called me," she whispered heavenward. "I don't know why you pressed it upon my heart to attend the *Ramona* pageant the night before Juliet's mother died. I don't know why you pressed it upon my heart to encourage her to come to New York. Or to follow her here for that matter.

"I don't know what I can offer her that someone more qualified than I couldn't give. I'm a has-been actress and gravel-voiced ex-opera singer, an alcoholic who has no business poking her nose into a decent young woman's life. I suppose if you pressed into service those who loved you when you were on earth—an ex-prostitute, a tax collector, a friend who denied you when you were about to be nailed to a tree—then why should I complain about being the cracked vessel I am?"

The trolley rattled off without her, so she hailed a cab instead. She gave the cabby the address, then settled into the seat with a sigh. The cabby flicked the reins over the swayback's rear, and the hansom moved forward into traffic.

"Juliet's road may not be easy, Father," she whispered. "I see myself in her. And I fear for her because of it. She hasn't faced the hard decisions about her career that I faced. She hasn't yet had to choose the light or dark of it."

Mairia remembered the man at the Fifth Avenue who offered her the world behind those dark windows she'd looked up at earlier. She shuddered. She had chosen wrong and had nearly lost her soul in the process.

"Maybe that's why you've pressed me into service," she breathed, looking up at the stars in the twilight sky. "Because I know the difference and our Juliet doesn't.

"But I'm not perfect, Lord." A sudden chill traveled up her spine. "I could stumble again. And fall. Next time I might pick up that whiskey. Sit in the Songbird or someplace worse until I lose everything once more…perhaps even my redemption."

She contemplated how close she might come to doing just that. "Help me, Father," she said instead.

"Help those you've given to me and to whom I've been given."

TWENTY-FOUR

Gillian sat primly beside Juliet in the doctor's office, her gloved hands folded in her lap. She glanced around the waiting room, letting her gaze rest on the framed certificates hanging on the walls.

"What are those?" she whispered to Juliet.

"Dr. Wyeth's certificates of graduation," Juliet told her. "And some are those belonging to other doctors and nurses who work with him at the clinic."

"How long does it take to be a doctor?" The child studied the certificate nearest to her, then stood to run her finger over the name at the bottom.

"You'll have to ask Dr. Wyeth when he examines you."

"Why is it taking so long for him to fit the brace?" She glanced down at her twisted foot as she sat down again.

"He wants to get it just right," she said, then added, "and he has some other ideas to make you more comfortable."

"I'm already comfortable," she said and shrugged. "And I don't want to wear an ugly brace. I'm quite fine the way I am." She stuck out her chin stubbornly.

"We'll wait to see what ideas Dr. Wyeth comes up with."

Gillian's name was called a moment later, and Juliet held her sister's hand as they moved down the hallway.

A smiling nurse ushered them into an examination room.

"I'm gonna be a doctor someday," Gillian said seriously to the nurse.

"Oh, honey," the nurse said with a laugh, "little girls grow up to be nurses, not doctors."

"Why?" Gillian demanded.

"Well, let me see. We get to wear these lovely uniforms." She touched her small pouf of a hat, obviously trying to appeal to Gillian's feminine nature.

"I don't care about hats and uniforms or even pretty dresses," Gillian said, "but I've decided, I am gonna be a doctor. How long does it take?"

The nurse laughed again as she put Gillian's chart on a table near the doctor's chair. "Much too long, sweetheart. You'll want to get married and have babies before you would be graduated." Still laughing to herself, the nurse bustled from the room.

"Is that true?" Gillian demanded when they were alone. "Do I have to get married and have babies?"

Juliet caught her sister's hand in hers. "What a thing to worry about now. You have years to decide. Besides, once you fall in love, you may not want to wait a minute longer than necessary to be a bride."

The child looked down at her foot with a worried look.

"Nobody would want me," she said quietly.

A sting caught in Juliet's throat as she hugged Gillian's shoulders. "You are beautiful, sweetheart. Don't let anyone ever tell you otherwise. And do you know what I heard Clay say the other day?"

"What?"

"He said that you're quicker of mind that a deer is of foot. And you remember how fleet-footed a deer is, don't you?"

"I remember from home. I used to watch does and fawns from my window. Sometimes a buck."

"Then you think how fast they run when you dream of becoming a doctor. You've got a mind that will allow you to be anything you want to be."

Gillian pulled back her shoulders and folded her hands. "Maybe I'll come to Dr. Wyeth's medical school when I grow up," she said. "Yes. I've decided. I'll come here."

Dr. Wyeth opened the door and, after a glance at his chart, sat down across from them. "How are you, young lady?"

"I'm going to be a doctor like you when I grow up. I just decided."

He didn't laugh, which pleased Juliet immensely. "Good," he said, "but you must realize that it will take lots of hard work."

"I don't mind hard work, do I, Ettie?" She looked to her sister.

"Not a bit," Juliet agreed.

"Good," Dr. Wyeth said. "Now, how old are you?"

"I'm eight."

He knitted his brow in thought. "All right then. That mean's you'll be ready to return here in 1926 and enroll as a freshman student in our graduate school."

Gillian's mouth dropped. "I can?"

He nodded seriously. "But you'll have lots of work to do between now and then."

Her eyes were big. "I will?"

"Yes. You'll need to study hard in school. You'll need to work especially hard at ciphering numbers, and the sciences. Study plants if you can. You might have your sister find a used microscope for you."

Gillian's eyes were shining when she turned back to Juliet. "Oh, I will," she sighed.

"And you can check in with me from time to time and let me know how your studies are progressing. Will you promise to do that?"

Gillian nodded vigorously.

"Good. Now then, I need to talk to your sister for a moment. Will you mind waiting in the outer office?"

"No." Gillian scooted off her chair and stuck her hand out to Dr. Wyeth. He shook it solemnly.

"I'll be seeing you again soon. I think you'll be pleased when we meet again."

Gillian frowned, puzzled, then gave the doctor a big smile as if he could say anything, anytime, puzzling or not, and it would be all right with her.

When she'd left the room with the nurse, Dr. Wyeth turned to Juliet. "The x-rays show that surgery on Gillian's foot has a good chance of being successful." He removed his eyeglasses and rubbed his eyes before replacing them. "Her ankle is in such a position that the nerves will be difficult to avoid severing. There is a risk that even if we straighten the bones—after we've broken them and installed the metal pin I told you about—the severed nerves might cause paralysis."

"Would she be worse off than she is now?"

He frowned. "Technically, no. But as you know, the greatest danger of surgery is the anesthesia."

Juliet let out a pent-up breath. "You're saying her foot can likely be straightened so she can walk normally."

"There will be rehabilitation, of course. She's never learned to use her leg muscles properly."

"All this is a possibility?"

He smiled gently. "I would say, a probability."

Juliet sat back with a wide grin, then the smile faded. "What will be the cost of the surgery?"

"Yes. There is the matter of cost," he said, looking down at the chart. "As I mentioned, the angle—and degree—of abnormality will be difficult to reverse. The surgery, plus the weeks of rehabilitation, of course, all add up to a considerable sum."

"And that is?" she said, knowing her heart was about to twist in two.

"Perhaps as much as five hundred dollars."

She looked at him helplessly. "That's impossible for us at this time," she finally said. "Perhaps in the future…"

"There's another option. This is a teaching hospital. If you want to wait until the students reach that segment of their studies, the cost would be significantly less. And you would be helping the students—"

"I will not allow my sister to be a class project, Dr. Wyeth," she cut him off. She then hesitated, drawing in a deep breath. "But you can be sure you'll see us again—and before 1926. I'll find the money somehow. I swear I will."

Without another word, she strode from his office, collected Gillian, and headed home to the brownstone. Gillian chattered the entire way about becoming a doctor. Juliet barely listened. Her only thought was how she could find the money for the operation.

———◆———

Four days later Gladdy McBean and the Hammerstein brothers called the cast together after rehearsal and announced they had reserved a room at Delmonico's that night for a farewell gathering of all the members of the Revue.

Stephan Sterling caught Juliet's eye just after the announcement. He headed toward her.

"May I have the honor of escorting the most beautiful member of the cast?" He was more charming than she remembered.

She held up her hand to say no, then hesitated as Gillian's little face flashed into her mind. Perhaps she shouldn't dismiss the Biograph role so quickly. "I was about to say I couldn't possibly go. I have responsibilities at home."

"And now?" He lifted a well-formed brow.

She laughed. Perhaps Gillian might have the operation sooner than planned. "I would be delighted to attend with you."

He looked extremely pleased. "Where shall I pick you up?"

She smiled and gave him her address.

"I'll see you at seven," he said, his hand protectively resting on her back.

———◆———

"You can't leave tonight," Annie pouted an hour later. "Clay is coming over to show us how to fix spaghetti. He said he learned from the Italians in his building. He's bringing sausages and tomatoes and everything."

Juliet winced. She'd forgotten their plans, one of their frequent family evenings that Clay seemed to enjoy as much as the rest. And she knew there wouldn't be many more before he was gone for California. A stab of regret touched her heart, but she quickly put her thoughts about Clay from her mind. She'd told him, hadn't she, that she had no time for romance. Surely he would understand that she hadn't set her cap for Stephan Sterling. This was business, a farewell party. That was all. Business related to her career.

"And Cornelia said she's gonna bake a pie for uth." Willow played with the spot where a big new tooth had finally appeared on her shiny gum.

"Cornelia doesn't cook very well," Gillian said.

"She says she wants to learn," Emma Grace said importantly. "She told me that it's her new hobby. Baking pies for us."

"Last time she forgot the sugar." Abby made a face.

They all groaned.

"You did very well though," Juliet said with a laugh. "You each ate your helpings and thanked Cornelia for the treat. I was proud."

"Stay, Ettie, pleath…" Willow whined.

"I can't, sugarplums," she said as she stepped into her dress.

They all hovered as Gillian fastened the row of buttons on the back. Just as the child finished, a knock sounded at the door.

"It's Clay!" squealed Emma Grace, racing from the bedroom.

Willow ran faster and pushed ahead of Emma Grace, who fell against the door as Willow pulled it open. "It's not Clay!" she yelled to the others. "It's somebody new." Her voice sounded disappointed.

Past the edge of the bedroom door, Juliet could see Emma Grace craning up at the man. "Who are you?"

Juliet stepped into her shoes and headed to living room. "Emma Grace, it isn't nice to ask someone who they are. You need to wait to be introduced." She smiled up at Stephan. He swallowed hard, looking a bit bewildered.

Emma Grace was scowling, her bottom lip protruding. "But where's Clay?" she asked to no one in particular.

"He's bringing us spaghetti," Willow said to Stephan. He apparently didn't know what to say because he didn't answer.

Gillian stared at him, her expression matching the twins', whose eyes were narrowed in suspicion.

"Girls, I would like for you to meet a new friend of mine. Come here, all of you."

Stephan Sterling, dressed to the nines, moved inside the room, making it appear smaller and more impoverished than it had the moment before he arrived.

"Sugars, this is Mr. Sterling.

"Stephan, these are my sisters—Annie, Abby, Gillian, Willow, and Emma Grace."

The girls stared at him without blinking for a long moment. Then Abby gasped. "Good heavens, I've seen you before. On a poster." Wide-eyed, she turned to Annie. "Do you remember? That time in Los Angeles…?"

Speechless, Annie nodded slowly, still gaping.

Willow puckered her brow. "But where's Clay?" She obviously wasn't impressed by his star status.

"Stephan is my friend, and we're going to a party together." At the child's look of disappointment, she added, "I won't be gone long. You make certain you save a piece of Cornelia's pie for me." She winked, and the girls giggled.

"We will, Ettie," Willow sighed.

Stephan looked uncomfortable. He let his gaze travel slowly around the room. The worn furniture, the stacks of picture books, the scatter of toys. Emma Grace's naked doll lay in a heap on a table, its cloth limbs akimbo, its face smudged with sticky kisses. A game of checkers was half completed in the middle of the floor, and a doll's highchair lay on its side nearby.

"We should go, darling," he said to Juliet.

She took in the sad little faces, then glanced back to Stephan. "I really shouldn't leave until Clay gets here."

"Not the Peter Rabbit one," Emma Grace explained to Stephan. "He's *Clay* MacGregor."

"He'th not the mean, mean one that made Peter Rabbit sick," added Willow. "He's a nice Mr. MacGregor."

As if on cue, Gillian let out an impatient sigh. "I keep telling you, Peter made *himself* sick, silly goose."

"Girls," Juliet said, "I want you to pick up your toys before Clay—"

A loud rapping interrupted her. Gillian, Willow, and Emma Grace squealed with joy and ran to answer it. Stephan stepped aside just in time as the door flew open and they hurled themselves toward the tall cowboy.

Grinning, he stooped to greet them, set the sack of groceries he'd been holding on the floor, then opened his arms to the little girls.

"He's here!" yelled Willow. "Clay's here!"

Clay swooped Emma Grace up. She wrapped her arms around his neck and gave him a loud smack on the cheek.

"I wanna play checkers tonight," Gillian said.

"It's my turn." Emma Grace's lower lip was sticking out, her brow puckering. Just then Clay's eyes met Juliet's. His gaze moved to Stephan, and Juliet swallowed, trying to think of what to say. How to make Clay understand that Stephan was truly a business associate.

"Girls, wait just a moment," Juliet said, "so I can make the introduc—"

"I'll do it," Willow said, interrupting Juliet. "Mr. MacGregor, this is Ettie's friend, Mr. Sterling. Ettie is going to a party with him tonight. Mr. Sterling, this is the *good* Mr. MacGregor. Not the bad farmer." With each *s* sound, a small spray erupted from her mouth. Stephan blanched visibly and took a step backward.

By the time Willow finished the introductions, Emma Grace and Gillian had pulled Clay to the center of the room. He gazed at her, a look of stark disappointment and betrayal in his eyes.

"Well, I suppose we'll be going then," Juliet said. She wondered if it was the stuffiness of the crowded apartment or her surprising feelings about Clay, the memory of being in his arms, that caused her face to flush.

Clay seemed to study her for a moment, then headed into the kitchen with the girls. She heard him ask Annie to put on a pot of water and Abby to pull out the iron skillet.

Just as she stepped through the door to the hallway, Mairia Garden headed down the hall toward them. With a smile, Juliet made the introductions, expecting Mairia to charm Stephan with her elegant demeanor and impeccable manners as she did everyone else.

Instead, the older woman assessed Stephan with cool reserve, and Juliet thought, for just a heartbeat, that there was recognition in her eyes.

Still puzzling over Mairia's behavior, she followed Stephan down the stairs to the street. A whisper of a breeze had kicked up, and when they walked to the hansom cab, tendrils of hair lifted from Juliet's face.

Beside her in the cab, Stephan now seemed more relaxed as he settled against the upholstered fabric. He assessed her with his gaze. The horse clopped on the pavement, and the carriage bounced along in rhythm with the steps.

"Each time I see you, Juliet, you are more beautiful," he said.

She flushed and changed the subject. "Do you usually come to New York this often?"

"Only when there's a reason." His eyelids were half closed, his expression unreadable.

She studied his handsome face, took a deep breath, then plunged ahead. "I have some questions about the Biograph role you mentioned."

He gave her a knowing look, a half-smile playing at his lips. "Fire away."

"Hollywood has never held much appeal to me. I've seen very few films." She shrugged. "To be very blunt, it's not the glamour, the promise of stardom or notoriety, that would draw me to such a life."

His smile broadened as if he had just won a game. Or perhaps a battle. "Let me guess. It's the money."

Her face heated again as she considered how her dreary little living quarters filled with her five noisy sisters must have appeared to him.

"Yes, my family's needs are pressing." She leaned forward earnestly. "And to be truthful, if I accept your offer, I will need a sizable advance."

A still, small voice seemed to speak to her from the darkness of her soul, saying *No!* A warning perhaps. Or maybe fear? She pushed it from her mind.

Stephan watched her. A moment later, the vehicle turned toward Delmonico's Restaurant. Juliet swayed with the carriage, then righted herself again.

"I'm certain an advance can be arranged," he said.

She breathed easier. "I have other concerns of equal importance." Then, taking a deep breath, she explained about Dr. Wyeth and the surgery for Gillian. "I will need to remain in New York for the surgery and also for her rehabilitation."

"The time in New York might be a problem," he said thoughtfully. "We're scheduled to begin work on the first film within the month."

"If it can't be arranged, then we have no contract," she said, turning to look out at the passing traffic. Her pulse was beginning to beat erratically, and she didn't know which she feared more, that he might say no or that he might say yes.

He lifted her hand and kissed her fingertips. "Given those options darling, my answer is, of course, we'll rearrange the shooting so that you can have your time here," he said. Then he chuckled. "And tonight when you lay yourself down to sleep, I want you to think about two things. First, my dear, whatever financial woes have plagued you in the past are over forever. And as we discuss the, ah, arrangements of our business relationship, think on this…"

He leaned forward and placed his fingertips beneath her chin. Looking deep into her eyes, he said softly, "I intend to make you a star."

She blinked again and tried to ignore the warning that came from the depths of her heart.

"You tell me what you and your family needs," he continued, "and it will be done. Surgery for your sister? It will be done. Rehabilitation? That too, even if we must bring someone from New York to work with her in California." He grinned at her.

She studied his handsome face and consciously put aside her fears. She had earned the right to be financially secure. Hadn't she done everything in her power to keep her family together? Hadn't she met all their needs—for food and clothing and health?

"Well…?" Stephan said, studying her from across the hansom cab.

"When can I sign the contract?" She swallowed hard and stared into the bleak night, trying to keep Gillian's little face before her.

Stephan moved closer to her, his arm draped across the seat behind her. "It just so happens I brought a copy with me."

Mairia waited up until Juliet arrived home. It was well past midnight. There were stars in the girl's eyes, the faint odor of alcohol on her breath, a whiff of cigarette smoke on her clothing. She chattered nonstop about the music, the delicacies, the conversation. Mairia knew, without a word from Juliet, all about the giddy thrills of being with such a crowd, the laughter and song, the trade secrets shared when the booze flowed and tongues loosened. The feeling of being set apart from the rest of the world, elevated somehow.

Mairia stood then to return to her own apartment, but Juliet stopped her.

"There's something I need to tell you," Juliet said.

"About Stephan?"

Juliet nodded. "Yes, about Stephan." She paused as if she knew something wasn't right about what she was about to divulge.

A chill traveled up Mairia's spine. "What is it?"

"He's made me an offer."

"To star in his pictures. I thought you'd dismissed that weeks ago."

"I told him yes tonight."

"Because of Gillian?"

"I knew you'd understand."

"God's ways aren't always our ways, child," Mairia said, feeling the room spin a bit. She sat down. "He tells us clearly that we're to stand ready for battle, but the battle is his."

Juliet laughed. "This isn't war. It's merely providing surgery for a child to walk again. I needed the money. Biograph seemed the only way to get it."

"Do you think God doesn't love Gillian more than you do? That he doesn't have a plan for her?"

Juliet's face heated. "How can you know that this isn't his plan? The money is right. The timing is right."

Mairia couldn't answer. "Perhaps it is," she said quietly. "Did you listen to your heart before you signed on the dotted line?"

"How did you know I signed?"

"I know how powerful men in New York operate—Hollywood is likely worse. My guess is that Stephan had the document in his pocket for you to sign after you'd been wined and dined."

A flicker of apprehension crossed Juliet's face. "You seemed to have already met Stephan when I introduced him tonight."

Mairia studied the girl sitting across from her on the worn sofa, looking so hopeful, innocent, and hardened all at once. "I've met many like him," Mairia told her. "Handsome, suave. Most without scruples, without heart."

"You can tell all that after a few minutes?" Juliet tossed her head with another laugh. "I can take care of myself. Haven't I already?"

Mairia stood wearily and walked to the door. Then she turned. "Don't lose yourself, Juliet. Too easily the promise of riches, no matter the good cause they'll be used for, can turn a young woman's head." She paused, her hand on the doorknob. "Don't lose your heart to the wrong promise."

"You've been speaking in riddles since the day I met you." She gave Mairia a quick hug. "Someday you'll have to explain what you mean. But for now, we both must get to bed."

Mairia stepped through the door, then stopped and looked back at Juliet as she added, "I nearly forgot to tell you. Clay said to tell you good-bye."

Juliet looked puzzled, as though she'd forgotten he was leaving.

"He boards the eleven o'clock bound for Los Angeles tomorrow," she said in response to the unasked question.

When she left, Juliet stood alone in the hallway, feeling as if a precious ray of light had just been extinguished.

TWENTY-FIVE

"I must get my father back to the States as quickly as possible," Sully said to Reverend Fleming and Vala Deverell.

The three sat in Reverend Fleming's office, located in the front of the sanctuary just behind the wall bearing the rough-hewn cross. Reverend Fleming was seated at a small, worn desk, with Sully and Mrs. Deverell sitting in chairs to one side, near the room's single window.

"I have six sisters and a brother at home who need him." He leaned forward earnestly. "My father wants me to return alone, but I am going to insist that he come with me—if you'll agree to my plan."

Vala Deverell, a wiry woman with piercing, bespectacled eyes and a small twist of gray hair at the nape of her neck, studied him. "Because you've invited me to join this conversation, I assume your plan involves my daughter," she said.

Sully rolled his shoulders, frowned, and leaned his elbows on the chair arms. "My father needs medical attention. Right now, around the clock. I can take over some of his care. But I think his chances for survival will be greater if a nurse goes with us to administer his medication and continue with his rehabilitation."

Reverend Fleming leaned back in his chair, steepling his fingers. "Rebecca is a very capable young woman, but this journey you're proposing is a dangerous one. We must consider her safety." He sighed heavily, looking worried. "And there's the problem of leaving us short-handed."

"I realize that," Sully said, "believe me. I've thought this through a dozen different ways, trying to figure the most logical, the most expedient way to get him home. I don't often cross my father's wishes, but I feel compelled to take care of some financial business in Iquitos, then leave as quickly as possible."

Mrs. Deverell spoke up, her gaze on Reverend Fleming, her voice thoughtful. "Two things occur to me, Collin. The first is that we've prayed that God would provide a way for one of us to leave on furlough. I hadn't considered that it might be Rebecca who would go." Her voice dropped slightly, as though she was speaking to herself. "She is so young. And yes, I am concerned about her safety. That's a long, arduous journey he's proposing. How well we know it." Then she turned again to Sully. "Has she told you about her translation project?"

He shook his head.

"When we first arrived here, my husband—her father—began translating the Bible into the Yagua language. He was able to complete the New Testament before his death. For many years the project languished—largely because no one else had the time or skill to devote to it. Rebecca came across his papers one day two years ago and began translating the book of Psalms."

Reverend Fleming smiled. "And a wonderful job she's done of it. Many a night, after working at the clinic all day, she burns the midnight oil, poring over her work. We use her translation in our services. She's made Scripture come alive to our people. It's not a stuffy translation, believe me. So natural you can almost hear God's voice."

Mrs. Deverell nodded in agreement. "She's written letters to churches and denominations, asking for funding for our work—especially for the translation project. Some money has come in but not nearly enough. We've always felt that if only people could hear her speak they would understand her passion. If they could hear her read just once from the Psalms in the musical Yagua, they might be moved to help complete the translation and publication of the Yagua Bible."

"But is this the proper time?" Reverend Fleming mused, moving his gaze to the window overlooking the compound.

"She *would* have Sullivan's protection," Mrs. Deverell said as if trying to convince Reverend Fleming herself.

Sully blinked and sat up straighter. He half expected Rebecca's mother to laugh at her own joke, but instead she continued to study him in utter seriousness.

"I need to head to Iquitos before we begin this journey," Sully said.

Reverend Fleming drummed his fingers on his desktop. "I suggest that when you leave Iquitos, you continue on down the Amazon. There's no reason to return here." He paused. "It will take several days to ready the dugouts and gather supplies."

"How long will the trip take? I mean, the entire journey to the States?"

"You'll be on water the entire way. The first leg will be nearly two thousand miles by river, most of it downstream on the Amazon until you reach the Atlantic. Then you'll travel by ship to the Caribbean, through the Panama Canal, and up the coast to California. Because we're now in the dry season, getting through the Amazon headwaters will be more difficult. You may have to portage your boats—especially difficult because of your father's weakened condition."

"There's really no other way," Sully said. "I must get him home."

"When my husband and I first came here from the States, Sullivan," Mrs. Deverell said, "it took us nearly a year of travel. Of course, that was before the Canal was completed."

A year. Sully's heart dropped. He thought of his sisters and Jared. His worry must have shown in his face because Mrs. Deverell reached for his hand.

"Just as God is here with us," she said, "he is with your family—your sisters, your brother. Whenever I fear for someone, I think of Deuteronomy 33:12." She quoted the verse, "The beloved of the LORD shall dwell in safety by him; and the LORD shall cover him all the day long, and he shall dwell between his shoulders."

Her eyes softened. "What a beautiful image that is! Our Lord carrying his beloved near his heart. What greater peace can there be than that?"

Reverend Fleming nodded in agreement. "Why don't we take some time right now to pray for God's guidance in this, that God would truly direct our paths. Carry us all between his shoulders." A moment later, his head bowed, Reverend Fleming's voice resonated through the room. He spoke to Christ as if he were standing there with them, their dearest Friend, who cared for them and their loved ones.

Sully felt a deep peace settle into his soul. Here in this place at the utmost ends of the earth, he felt as though he'd touched Christ's robe, and Jesus' Spirit covered him as at no other time in his life. A presence so real that it was almost a fragrance...or a light...or a warmth inside him.

He was surprised when he lifted his head to find his cheeks wet. But there was no shame in his tears, only awe at the wondrous discovery within himself...and about the God he belonged to.

Quaid squinted as he looked up. Sully stood in front of the window by Quaid's bed, and the way the light streamed over Sully's shoulders, he seemed more apparition than reality. Perhaps Quaid was dreaming again.

"Father...?" Sully stepped closer and took hold of Quaid's hand. His grasp was warm, solid. Flesh-and-blood real.

"I'm here, son. The question is, why are you? I thought you were going to head to Iquitos."

"You don't sound too happy to see me." Sully grinned as he pulled up a chair and settled into it.

"I thought we'd settled on your course of action."

"We've had a change in plans."

Quaid tried to lift his shoulders to get a better look at Sully's face, but he was still too weak for the effort to make much difference. He lay back, breathing hard. His son stood and propped the pillows behind him, angled his shoulders to a more comfortable position, then sat again.

"And these changes are...?" Quaid didn't try to disguise his disappointment, his irritation with his son.

"You are coming with me, first to Iquitos, from there to Belém, from there to California."

Quaid fell back against the pillows and lifted his gaze to the ceiling. "I can't do that. You know I can't. My plan is the one we'll go with. I insist."

For a moment the only sound in the room was that of the jungle. The cries of birds, the fluttering of palm fronds in the breeze. Quaid turned toward his son again. There was a stubborn set to his chin that Quaid hadn't seen before. He looked years older than his eighteen summers. A new confidence seemed to have taken over his body.

"I'm sorry to go against your wishes, Father," Sully said. "But I am the one who must insist that you come with me." He moved to the window, pulled back the gauzelike covering, stared out at the compound for several moments, then turned back to face his father. "I've given it a lot of thought…also a lot of prayer. We must both go home," he said quietly. "I made a mistake in insisting we come to Peru, and for all the wrong reasons. Now it's time to retrace our steps—together."

"Carting along a sick old man will slow you down." Again he attempted to swallow his irritation. "How long will it take if I go with you?"

"As much as a year. Perhaps as little as six months, depending on the rains and the boats and boatmen we can hire in Iquitos. We'll catch one of the transport boats from the rubber plantations."

"Without me how long would it take?"

"It doesn't matter because I'm not leaving unless you're with me." His son's chin jutted out, and his shoulders settled with the certainty of his conviction.

Quaid chuckled, a low rumbling sound. For once he didn't slip into an exhausting fit of coughing. "I suppose I have little choice in the matter."

"None whatsoever," Sully said, lifting a brow, "so no more argument." A sense of pride filled Quaid. "Tell me the details."

"We will leave just as soon as our supplies are ready for the trip to Iquitos. That's the first leg. There, we'll take care of the bank draft as you suggested. We'll buy the remaining supplies in Iquitos and continue on from there."

Quaid lay back against his pillows, tired, but with a lighter heart than he'd had in a long time.

"There's one more thing," Sully said. "We'll have a nurse accompanying us."

"A nurse?"

Sully nodded. "Yes. Rebecca is coming back to the States with us."

Quaid studied his son's face for an instant, then chuckled again. "Ah, yes," he said closing his eyes. "Truly a fine plan, son. Truly it is." A few minutes later, he slipped into a deep and restful sleep.

⫘

Two weeks later, two dugout canoes made their way toward the small city of Iquitos. Quaid and Rebecca were in the lead canoe, a Yagua Indian at the rear. In the second dugout were two large trunks and several burlap sacks filled with supplies and Sully with a second Yagua.

Iquitos rose before them, a smattering of gleaming, tile-roofed buildings nestled beside the river. In the distance he could see the city's famous two-story iron building, a miniature Eiffel Tower, designed and built by G. Eiffel himself. The closer they drew, the more astounded Sully was by the bustling, modern look of the city. Women in fancy dresses, shaded by their parasols, strolled along paths by the river, their male escorts in high collars and frock coats. Rubber barons, Sully assumed, and their ladies, looking much the same as any rich folks in the States.

Once they had docked, Sully hired a cabby to take them by horse-drawn carriage to the Palace Hotel. An opulent establishment, the Palace Hotel had a traditional red Spanish-tile roof and facade, and ornate iron balconies gracefully beckoned the weary traveler. After they secured their rooms and Quaid was safely deposited in his bed, Sully and Rebecca left for the center of town.

Within minutes they were in the colorful Plaza de Armas. Around them the bustling city seemed alive with scents of pork and chilies roasting on outdoor fires, the sounds of vendors calling to each other from their fruit and flower carts, and the laughter and shouts of children darting in and out of the plaza.

Beside him, Rebecca laughed. "I've always been charmed by this city," she said. "When my father was alive, we came here often."

They ducked from the road to the sidewalk as a mule-drawn wagon clip-clopped toward them, wheels creaking. On either side of the open area stood more financial institutions than Sully had ever seen on one city block, even in the heart of Los Angeles.

"If I can't cash in my bank draft here, I don't think I could anywhere," he said.

"You've brought me along to translate," Rebecca said, "but I daresay you'll have little difficulty." She laughed again at his quizzical look. "Most of the bankers are from England or the States. Even a few from Australia. When the rubber barons moved into the area back in the seventies, the bankers soon followed."

Rebecca strode along beside him, her skirt swinging with each step. She looked as fresh as a rose blossom despite the city's heavy, warm climate. Her face glowed with pleasure as they passed flower carts and food vendors. Cages of parakeets lined the walkway, the bright-hued little birds squawking and chirping and beating their wings as they passed. A macaw watched them warily from his perch near still another vendor's shoulder.

Rebecca stopped near a cart with a colorful array of vegetables, fish, and breads. After she said something to the vendor in Spanish, the small, dark man grinned and handed her two trim bundles wrapped in long, husklike leaves. She handed one to Sully and began opening hers right there on the sidewalk. Sully followed her lead and unwrapped the hot and steaming, pillowlike cake.

Sully bit into the fragrant, honey-flavored delicacy, and his eyes popped open with pleasure. Watching him over the top of her own little bundle, Rebecca giggled. When she finished, she licked her sticky fingers and promptly ordered two more.

As they passed the next flower cart, Sully stopped and pointed to a clump of pink tiger lilies. He paid the vendor and presented them to Rebecca, who blushed as she took them from his hands.

They strolled toward the British National Bank of Peru, located on the far side of the plaza just beneath a clock tower that looked as though it had been transplanted from the British Parliament in London. Just as Rebecca had predicted, Sully had no trouble exchanging the draft. The efficient bank manager took little time examining it and then counting out half the sum in U.S. currency and half in Peruvian. Sully tucked the money away securely in his money belt.

They made a few more stops before heading back to the Palace Hotel, first at a small telegraph office where he quickly wrote out a short note telling his family that he and his father were on their way home. He placed a few coins in the hand of a rather weary-looking telegraph operator and gave instructions for the telegram's delivery to Riverview, California. Standing beside him, Rebecca translated. The man nodded absently.

Next Sully visited a store, where he purchased garments to replace the thin rags he and his father had worn since their abduction. Rebecca helped him choose some Panama-style khaki pants and lightweight shirts. With a grin he tossed two Puerto Rican straw hats to the shopkeeper, who added up the bill.

Rebecca looked apprehensive as Sully paid for his purchases. Finally she said, "You'd better hope that we won't be portaging our dugouts to the Amazon. I can only imagine the look of you while sloshing through the mud and wet silt."

"I'll save these rags for just such an occasion," he said with a laugh. He sobered at the thought of bearing his father along in a dugout canoe. He looked down at the new clothes, which might seem extravagant. "I hoped we might have a chance of securing a place on one of the rubber plantation's freighters."

"They don't leave daily," she reminded him, still seeming unnaturally quiet. "This isn't the time of year for good transport. The river is shallow. The larger ships wait for high water. There weren't any freighters in sight when we docked."

"We'll find one," he said, taking the wrapped clothing from the shopkeeper. "I haven't come this far to be told it's not possible."

"Are you always this optimistic?" She glanced up at him. Her earlier look of disapproval was gone, now replaced by a hint of admiration. For a moment he thought surely the look was meant for someone else who'd just passed by. But her gaze didn't waver.

He swallowed hard, cleared his throat, and nodded to the doorway.

"Perhaps we should be getting back to the Palace," he said inanely, because those gold-flecked eyes held him captive and his mind was empty of everything except the shape of her lips, the tilt of her nose, the thicket of curls around her face.

Finally he cleared his throat, and they headed out to the street. They strolled along, Rebecca holding the tiger-lily bouquet close to her face as though they were the most precious gift she'd ever received.

Feeling exceptionally brave, perhaps because of the beauty of the day, perhaps because of the beauty of the woman beside him, Sully took Rebecca's hand and tucked it into the crook of his arm.

She glanced up at him shyly, the tips of her lashes catching the glint of the sun. He smiled down at her, knowing with certainty that his heart would never be the same after that moment in that place.

Later, after a siesta, a bath, and a change of clothes, Sully and Rebecca ventured out of the hotel again, this time to find the buildings and offices of the rubber barons and see if there were any freighters due to leave. They were turned away from the first three, but finally, in the fourth establishment, were ushered into the small office of an arrogant underling. Sully noticed that even before the man, Mr. Snowden-Thane, shook their hands in greeting, Rebecca's eyes fluttered closed and her lips moved briefly. It gave him comfort to know she was praying.

"We do have a smaller transport heading to Belém in two weeks," Mr. Snowden-Thane said after they had explained their plight. "The *Lady Caravel* is a luxury paddleboat and moves quite slowly though, especially this time of year. First we have the low waters of summer, which cause us to take to shore often, awaiting rain to fill the rivers. Once the rains come, we can expect weeks of flooding and further delays. And because of the months of travel involved, I'm afraid the cost per passenger is a bit more."

"How much?" Sully asked.

Mr. Snowden-Thane's answer caused both Sully and Rebecca to blanch and exchange a wary look. "You don't understand," Rebecca said suddenly. "Mr. Dearbourne and his father are desperate to return home to their family, who must think they are dead. And I…well, I am on a mission of mercy—first of all, to care for Mr. Dearbourne's father and second, to bring God's word to the Yagua."

Mr. Snowden-Thane gaped at her a moment, then moved his gaze to Sully, taking in his newly purchased, stylish clothes, complete with the Panama hat. Suddenly Sully understood why he had sensed Rebecca's disapproval when he bought them. He looked down at Rebecca's plain brown skirt and high-necked, mutton-sleeved blouse, a style even he knew was at least a decade old. He was suddenly ashamed of his extravagance. Especially when he thought of his sisters and brother waiting at home, likely penniless, likely thinking themselves orphaned.

"What Miss Deverell says is true," Sully said lamely, then glanced into her eyes and found the courage to go on. "This young woman is going to the States to look for funding for her Bible translation project. Her father, now deceased, completed the New Testament before his death. She has taken up the project and finished the book of Psalms. The mission where her mother still resides gets by on a shoestring." He stopped to catch his breath.

Rebecca laughed lightly when he paused. "It sounds like we're begging, and that isn't quite the truth." She lifted her chin. "I have money to pay for passage, but it must be reasonable or we'll find another mode of transport."

Mr. Snowden-Thane chuckled. "I do believe I would give you passage without charge if I could. But the truth is, the choice isn't mine. We are transferring the heads of several divisions back to England."

"I must book passage for all three of us," Sully said, making a sudden decision. "Because of my father's health, we absolutely cannot wait to get him to the States."

Rebecca's eyes looked stormy when she turned to him. "I will pay my own way, Sullivan."

He knew her funds from the mission were worse than slim. He pulled the money from his belt. "My father and I have hired you as a nurse, and of course we will include passage to California as part of what we owe you."

The storm in her eyes hadn't calmed. "If we are indeed booking passage on the *Lady Caravel,* I will see to my own way," she said pointedly.

Mr. Snowden-Thane cleared his throat. "We'll plan for three passengers then?" He headed to his desk and pulled out some papers. He seemed to be smiling to himself.

"Three," Sully said with a sidelong glance toward Rebecca.

"And the names?"

"Miss Rebecca Deverell," Rebecca said. She rummaged through a small crocheted bag and pulled out a number of bills. Shoulders back, head held high, she counted out the money and handed it to Mr. Snowden-Thane.

"And my father, Mr. Quaid Dearbourne. Myself, Sullivan Dearbourne. Two cabins, of course."

Mr. Snowden-Thane finished writing their names in the ledger. "I will give you a private room," he said to Rebecca. "One more thing," he said as they turned to leave. "I'm glad to have you aboard. Yet I must warn you—the people who ride this paddle wheeler have a reputation of rather raucous behavior. There's gambling and drinking and carrying on. They seem to let down their hair for the long weeks of travel between Iquitos and Belém. But perhaps your presence will remind them of their manners."

"I thank you for the compliment, but I also take your words as a challenge, Mr. Snowden-Thane," Rebecca said, to Sully's surprise.

Mr. Snowden-Thane laughed heartily. "Somehow I knew you would. In my way of thinking, you might try to get those heathens to contribute to your Bible project instead of gambling away their families' fortunes."

Rebecca didn't laugh. "I believe that I'll do just that," she said. Then without another glance at Sully, she swept from the room.

<hr />

Pedro, the telegraph operator, frowned at the foreign language scribbled on the slip of paper in his hand. It made no more sense than it had earlier. Maybe his mind was dull from weariness. The night before his wife had insisted on celebrating the birthday of their first grandchild, even though he'd told Elena he wanted to wait until Sunday.

He yawned, staring at the paper in front of him. The pretty young woman with the American had explained to Pedro where the telegram was to be sent, but he'd forgotten to write it down. He set the paper on top of his pulpitlike desk for his boss, Gabe, to handle. He'd handled many of the Brit and Aussie telegrams. Though Gabe knew fewer English words than Pedro did, he would know what to do.

Pedro yawned again and leaned back in his chair. A quick siesta wouldn't hurt while he waited for another customer. He closed his eyes, succumbing to a drowsiness that pulled him under like the currents beneath a dark ocean.

A strange ache began in his arm, slowly working its way to his neck. He sat up with a start, grabbed his chest, then slowly sank to the floor. His eyelids fluttered briefly as a slip of paper floated from someplace above his head and came to rest beside him, behind the desk.

TWENTY-SIX

D r. Wyeth had wheeled Gillian into surgery promptly at six o'clock in the morning. Three hours ago. Juliet paced the floor, trying to keep from checking her watch more often than every few minutes. Her sisters waited with her, taking turns asking questions, voicing worries about Gillian, or whining about being bored. Mairia, who had accompanied them, remained a rock of calm all morning, entertaining the children and leading Willow and Emma Grace in prayers for their sister.

"How long will Gillian have to stay in the hospital?" Willow had asked the question at least a dozen times.

"Two weeks, silly," Emma Grace said. "Dr. Wyeth told us."

"Can we visit her, Ettie?" Annie looked worried as she pulled Willow onto her lap. "They'll let us, won't they?"

"There's a hospital rule that no children can go into the room, though you and Abby may be considered adults."

Abby sat back with a pleased sigh as she thumbed through a magazine.

"How much longer?" Willow asked. "I'm hungry."

"Me too," Emma Grace said, wandering to the doorway. "Here comes that man," she said, looking down the hall.

Figuring it was the doctor, Juliet jumped up just as Stephan Sterling rounded the corner carrying a bouquet of at least three dozen roses.

"Stephan," Juliet said. "I didn't know you were in town again."

He chuckled and placed the roses on a nearby table before turning again to Juliet. "I couldn't let our favorite little patient have her surgery without coming to find out how she is."

"You came all the way from California to see Gillian?" Abby asked, incredulous.

"Partially true," he said, smiling at Juliet. "I had other motives as well." He looked from the dumbfounded girls to Mairia. "Will you excuse us for a moment?"

The girls stared at Juliet and Stephan without speaking, as though putting them together for the first time. As a couple. Stephan as Juliet's beau, or as Emma Grace might say, as "someone to court us." Juliet wasn't entirely displeased with the picture. He certainly treated them well.

"We'll be right back," Juliet said to them all, trying to avoid Mairia's disapproving look. Juliet couldn't fathom her judgment of the man who had given Gillian a chance at a normal life.

His hand beneath her elbow, Stephan steered her down the hall to a courtyard in the center of the hospital.

"I really can't be away for more than a minute," she said. "Dr. Wyeth may finish and come looking for me—"

"This couldn't wait a moment longer," Stephan said. "I've gotten final approval for the script. For your role."

"I thought my role had been approved."

He colored slightly. "Well, technically it hadn't. Though I had no doubt that I could convince the producers to hire you."

"What did I sign then? I thought my contract covered the details of my role in the film."

"Oh, the contract is legitimate, of course, as a part of the production company. But as you recall, the offer to play this particular lead was verbal, not written."

"What if you hadn't been able to convince the producers? What if they wanted Mary Pickford or someone else of her stature, not me?"

"Darling, you must get used to the fact that what I want, I get. I would have simply walked away from my part in the film, both as director and male lead. The producers knew better than to cross me."

"You're the male lead?" He hadn't mentioned that before.

"Oh yes." He rubbed her neck affectionately as they stood near a water fountain.

She stepped back with a small laugh.

"And you'll be happy to hear it's a love story," he went on as if he hadn't noticed. "Dramatic and humorous at the same time."

232

"Did you bring the script with you?"

"I've made reservations for supper at Delmonico's tonight. I'll give it to you then and tell you the finer nuances of your character."

"I can't leave the hospital. I'm planning to stay in Gillian's room tonight."

His annoyance was clear. "Surely you can leave her with Cornelia for a few hours. Once you see that she's safe and doing well, of course."

She shook her head. "I wouldn't dream of it."

Then the look of annoyance was gone, replaced by sympathy. "I'm sorry. I understand. I'm just not used to little children, their needs and wants and all that. Please forgive me."

She had to smile. Before she took over mothering her brood of sisters, she wouldn't have known about such things either.

"I have a better idea," he said. "I'll stay watch with you to keep you company. We can read our parts in the waiting room between your visits to Gillian's room."

"Please, no," she said gently. "I appreciate the gesture, but I must give my attention fully to Gillian."

"I understand," he said. If she hadn't known better, she would have thought his expression was a boyish pout.

"I do have one last newsworthy item to tell you," he said as they turned back to enter the hospital. He held the door open for her, and she stepped inside.

He circled his arm lightly around her waist as they walked down the hall. "I've arranged for a private nurse to accompany us back to Los Angeles."

She halted. "Us?"

He smiled into her eyes. "Oh, yes. You didn't think I was going to let you return alone, did you?"

"Gillian won't be ready to travel for weeks."

"Not entirely true, my dear. I've spoken to experts on our Coast, and the general consensus is that our little princess will weather the journey quite nicely with a private nurse. The same who will also help her learn to walk again."

"Dr. Wyeth's plan is to work with Gillian here in New York. I appreciate the offer, truly. But I must insist that we remain here."

He looked uncomfortable. "You really don't have a choice," he murmured, looking at his shoes.

"What do you mean? Of course I have a choice." Then she remembered the contract. "You promised the producers, didn't you, that if they gave me the part I would start production in two months? As we discussed?"

He looked back at her and shook his head. "It wasn't quite that cut and dried. I had to give in on that point. Quid pro quo and all that."

She stared at him.

"I so admire your concern for your sisters," he said quietly, disarmingly. "I've wanted to help in every possible way. I care about you, Juliet. I see such good things ahead for you. But you're encumbered with enormous responsibilities. I want to make you a star, but without some relief from your day-to-day responsibilities, you'll never achieve your full potential." He draped his arm around her shoulders. "Ah, but we'll save the details for another conversation. For now, let's get back to the others."

She nodded and allowed herself to be escorted back into the small waiting room.

Dr. Wyeth hurried around the corner a few minutes later, his expression solemn. Juliet jumped up to meet with him in the hall away from the others.

"She's come through it just fine for now," he said, then touched her arm as if to steady her.

"And her prognosis?"

"We won't know until the incisions heal exactly what we're dealing with."

"What do you mean?"

"The nerves were twisted and intertwined along with muscle and other soft tissue. It was nearly impossible to keep them intact."

"So you can't tell me if Gillian will walk?"

"We must wait until she heals." He smiled wearily. "But given this child's spunk, I would guess that if there's a way, she'll find it."

Juliet spent the next two weeks sleeping by her sister's bed in the hospital. At the beginning of the third week, Gillian was released. After only two days at home in the brownstone, Stephan's gleaming hired car arrived to transport them to the train station—the six Dearbourne sisters, Mairia Garden, and Dora Blythe, Gillian's young and very pretty nurse, who had eyes for the handsome actor-director.

After they arrived in Los Angeles, Stephan arranged for the travelers to stay in the opulent Beverly Glen Hotel while he accompanied Juliet in her search for living quarters, suggesting certain areas of the city that were more acceptable to the movie industry than others. She finally chose a small bungalow to rent for more money each month than she would have thought possible to make in a year. Laughing, Stephan assured her that with her salary, it was expected. Though she wasn't yet a star, he explained, she needed to live like one.

Within a week she had moved the children into the delightful place, enrolled them for the new school year, and convinced Mairia, after much wheedling and pleading, to live in the small guest cottage on the other side of the rose garden.

One morning a week later, just before rehearsals were to begin, Juliet left the bungalow and journeyed to the Big Valley and home. She hadn't told anyone she was coming. She would see Merci, of course, and Great Aunt Brighid if she was around. But first she wanted to go home. To at least see it, if only from afar.

After Willow, Emma Grace, and the twins left for the school at the end of the block, she fussed over Gillian a bit, making sure she was happy and settled with a stack of books, then gave Mairia a quick hug. "I'll be home before dark," she promised, then ran with pulse-pounding anticipation to the streetcar that would take her to Union Station.

When she walked through the tall wood-slat doors of the Riverview livery, the musty smell of hay and horses filled her nostrils. She halted midstep as memories came in waves, flooding her heart and mind, memories of riding with her mother and father across the Big Valley, the wind in her hair, the sun on her shoulders, her parents' laughter carrying on the wind.

She blinked in the dim light, bringing herself back to the present. A moment later the stableboy opened the squeaking door and stepped inside to help her choose her mount.

Her heart lifted as she rode through the town on a tall gray mare, her mane whipping backward. When she reached the citrus groves on the outskirts, she pressed her heels into the mare's flanks, moving her to a gallop. By the time the groves thinned and the wild lands rolled out before her, she felt at one with the horse, and they rode like the wind across the fields.

The sun was slanting to the west by the time she reined the mare to the top of an overlook above the ranch. From a distance it looked just as it always had. The Victorian house, with its proud turret and gabled windows, was nestled among the groves that spread for miles in every direction. Behind the sweep of the rolling foothills rose the rugged San Jacinto Mountains, the sky behind them a purplish haze, the mountains themselves bathed in the light of the setting sun.

Juliet's eyes ached as she took in the sight. It was beautiful. It was home. Or at least it had been once. She headed the mare down the incline and back to the path leading to the ranch. She knew each boulder, each misshapen tree trunk, and the closer she got to home, the faster she urged the gray to move.

Finally they were there. She told herself not to cry as she walked the horse to the big porch. Someone had nailed a sign to the front door, warning that trespassers would be prosecuted to the full extent of the law.

She swung off the saddle and looped the reins on the front

balustrade. Leaving the horse to graze on a clump of dried grass, she walked up the stairs. Her mother's morning glory that once had cascaded across the entrance was a mere tangle of twigs and vines. Only a few hardy leaves hung, twisting in the breeze.

The wood trim was in sad repair, its paint faded and peeling. She tried the door. The knob turned, but the door wouldn't budge. On closer inspection she found that it had been nailed shut. The beautiful, carved oak door with its oval, beveled glass had been treated no better than a slab of rough-hewn barn wood. Incensed, she headed around to the back of the house.

Under the pepper tree, the rope swing her father had made when she was a child dangled loose in the breeze. Memories of Emma Grace, Gillian, and Willow crowded into her mind, their wide eyes and squeals as their father pushed them toward the heavens, their giggles when he ducked aside as they swung back to earth. She continued around to the back of the house, hoping to find a way in. Every window was boarded; every door was nailed shut.

She returned to the front, raising her eyes to the turret and the gables. The windows on the second story were untouched. Then, smiling, she walked around to the apple tree that grew directly below her bedroom window and looked up again, shading her eyes.

Its branches reached nearly to the roof. One branch, just as she remembered, stretched within a foot of her bedroom window. Without another pondering moment, she hiked up her skirts and tied them with her belt. She placed one foot in the crook of the trunk and swung the other up to the lowest branch.

She continued up until she reached the horizontal limb that swept against the house. Gingerly she crawled across it an inch at a time, not daring to look down, until she reached the window.

Finally her goal was in sight and, breathing a sigh of relief, she swung her legs over each side of the branch that now hung at a precarious angle and reached for the window. It was stuck fast. Frowning, she tried to force it open.

Still it wouldn't budge. Finally she smacked it with her palm, and it gave way. With a hoot of triumph, she lifted it the remaining distance upward and eased her body from the branch into the room.

Dust filled her lungs, and Juliet sneezed twice as she took in every detail. Her bed and dressing table hadn't been touched. She walked across the worn carpet and touched the silver-handled hairbrush that had once been her mother's, then turned to the wardrobe, letting her fingers trail across the clothes that hung there. How quickly they'd had to leave that day.

She took her time going through the other rooms on the second story, first the dormitory room where Emma Grace, Gillian, and Willow had slept, then Jared's room at the end of the hall. She walked across the oak-planked floor, enjoying the creak that accompanied each footfall, and peeked in the twins' suite of rooms. It was just as they'd left it, wardrobe door ajar, dresser drawers askew. It surprised her that the bank officers hadn't yet cleaned out the place and sold all their belongings.

She crisscrossed the hallway twice before finally deciding to climb to the top of the stairs. She was certain that stepping into her father's rooms would twist her heart in two. She had already ignored Sully's closed door, knowing even the quickest look inside would cause fresh tears to flow.

She moved on up the stairs to the third floor and walked through the double doors. It was just as she remembered it, smelling of leather and saddle soap, though now slightly musty from being closed for all those months. Taking a deep breath and ordering herself not to weep, she walked across the threadbare Chinese rug to Quaid's desk in front of the rounded turret windows. To one side, in a pewter frame, was a miniature photograph of her mother.

She picked it up and held it closer, taking in everything about Emmeline, from her sturdy build, so different from Juliet's, to the soft look of her gaze. How Juliet would love to sit down and talk with her this minute, tell her mother about all that had happened in New York, Gillian's surgery, and how the children had grown. To ask her about marriage and how a woman might know if she was in love. Ask her about life and sorrow and how a person could go on when they'd lost their father and brother and home.

She lifted the curtain and looked across the Big Valley toward Rancho de la Paloma, which was shimmering in the last rays of the setting sun. She could almost imagine how it was in the old days when her great-grandfathers first settled in the valley, when cattle roamed the windswept lands, vaqueros sang and danced, and fandangos were held for every family this side of Los Angeles.

A lone figure on horseback headed up the road to the hacienda. Juliet stepped closer to the window, frowning in concentration. Even from this distance, the man looked familiar, the way he hunkered down over his horse. She stared, felt the quickening of her pulse.

Clay! It couldn't be!

Though it very well could, she realized in the next beat of her heart. He'd had business with Merci and Brighid before. He certainly could have business with them again.

Perhaps to give additional details to his report about Juliet and the children.

She frowned. He surely would have done that weeks ago when he first returned from New York.

A minute later she shimmied down the apple tree, taking only two items from the house, her mother's hairbrush and the miniature likeness in the pewter frame.

As she stooped to pour well water on her mother's morning glory, she thought again about Clay's ride to Merci's. She pushed away the ludicrous notion that had planted itself in her mind. Once. Twice. The third time it returned, she decided it might not be so far-fetched after all. Her cousin was a beautiful woman.

Only one way to find out, she decided as she swung one leg over the saddle. She would ride out to La Paloma and see for herself.

⎯⎯◆⎯⎯

As he headed back to Riverview, Clay reflected on what Merci had told him. Juliet and the children had indeed returned to California, the family had learned by a letter dated a week ago. She'd also signed on with Stephan Sterling's picture company. Didn't she know the studios owned their actresses? She might as well belong to the man himself. Clay set his jaw as he nudged the horse over a rise, determined not to let his fuming disappointment spoil the day.

He urged his mare to move faster as they followed the trail around an outcropping of boulders and between some clumps of gray sage, skirting the land that had once belonged to Juliet's family.

He'd ridden a mile or two west when he saw another rider approaching at a gallop, her light hair streaming out behind. He drew his horse to a halt and watched.

"Well, I'll be a monkey's uncle," he muttered, a wide grin overtaking his face. The ire he'd felt earlier melted at the sight of her.

She didn't seem surprised to see him. She drew back on the reins, and her horse danced sideways in little steps.

"Ah, sweet Juliet," he drawled, lifting his Stetson slightly. "What brings you out this way?" He spoke as if they'd seen each other the day before.

"I was about to ask you the same thing," she said with the same airy tone he'd adopted.

Sliding from the saddle, Clay sauntered to her horse, tilted his hat back, and looked up at her. She met his gaze with a smile that seemed alive with affection and delight. As she dismounted, she placed her small hand in his. In that heartbeat of time, he drank in her presence like a thirsty man who'd been weeks without water.

She colored prettily. "How have you been, Clay?" The airy nonchalance was gone.

"I've missed you," he said. "And the girls…"

"We only arrived in town a week ago."

"You could have written."

She laughed and waved her fingertips as if brushing off the thought. "I've been busy, Clay. I begin rehearsal for my new film tomorrow. We'll shoot in just a matter of days. There have been scripts to learn…that sort of thing."

"Ah, yes. I heard you signed with Stephan."

"You've been to see Merci?" Her tone seemed slightly accusing, which surprised him.

He shrugged. "She mentioned it while I was there." He didn't want to admit that news of Juliet was the sole reason he'd ridden out to La Paloma.

She narrowed her eyes. "I had my reasons for going with Biograph, you know. And Stephan has been wonderful to me, to the girls…"

Their moment of magic was gone.

His tone chilled to ice. "Of that I have no doubt." He turned to remount, one boot in the stirrup. "I really mustn't keep you, Juliet. I've got an early-morning shoot tomorrow. Must get the aeroplane to Los Angeles before sundown." He swung a leg over the saddle, staring down at her upturned face.

She seemed unwilling to let him go. "So you'll be in town tomorrow?"

He nodded. "Stunt part with the *Keystone Kops*."

"You must come by and see us. Our new little cottage isn't that far from the *Keystone* lot. The girls will be delighted. Mairia, too."

He wanted to ask, *And how about you, Juliet?* Instead he said, "Tell me, how is everyone?"

"Oh, this is unforgivable," she said, biting her lip and shaking her head slightly. "I was so happy to see you that I've neglected telling you the biggest news of all."

So happy to see me? The day suddenly seemed brighter. "Biggest news of all?" he repeated calmly.

"It's Gillian!" she said. "She may walk normally for the first time in her life!"

"The surgery. She had the surgery?"

"Yes! That's why I signed with Biograph. I was able to get an advance against my salary. Enough to pay for her operation and rehabilitation. Oh, Clay, Stephan has been wonderful. He came to New York to make sure of our safe travel back to California. Hired a nurse, then helped us find a house once we were here."

"Everything is coming together for you then."

She nodded slowly, but a shadow seemed to fall across her expressive eyes.

"It wasn't what I'd planned."

"What do you mean?" He remembered the joy of watching her perform that first time and suddenly wondered if she would experience the same joy in the flickers.

She sighed. "Oh, I don't know. I suppose I'd built it all up in my mind: life in the theatre, that sort of thing. It's really just hard work. And with film, I'm wondering if churning them out like dime novels will suit me." She'd mounted now and walked her horse closer to his.

"You once told me that your real love is for the story itself, not necessarily acting it out." His mare danced sideways, and he reached down to pat the horse's neck.

They continued talking as their horses moved together at a slow walk along the trail. "My mother used to say that very thing to me," Juliet said. "For years I kept a journal, always planned to write a book, a play...something."

"Now maybe you'll have some time for yourself."

She sighed, seeming lost in thought. "But after my mother died and father disappeared, that passion seemed to shrivel up and die. Part of my heart seems to be missing. For a long time I thought it was my desperate need for my mother. Then it seemed due to my other losses, my father and brother. While we were in New York, I thought it was a longing for time away from the incessant clamor and chatter of the girls." She laughed self-consciously, then looked away from him as she fingered her mare's mane. "There's just something missing..."

From that place in your heart where God should be, Clay added to himself.

"Only one other person cared about that passion of mine," she mused, looking out over the sweeping land. He thought he saw her eyes tear, but when she turned back, she was smiling. "Someday," she said, "perhaps I'll find it in my heart to write again." Then she shrugged. "Meanwhile, Stephan is determined to make me a star. It's a way to be financially secure at last, I suppose."

"I suppose," he said, his heart heavy with a strange sadness for her.

"I really must be on my way to Merci's," Juliet said with a toss of her head. The confident ingenue was back. Eyes sparkling. Chin tilted upward. He wondered if anyone else knew of the heartache, the emptiness, she hid. "I want her to spread the word to my family that I've come home."

"It's been good to see you, Juliet," he said.

Then he waited under the canopy of a live oak until she disappeared from sight.

TWENTY-SEVEN

Sully helped his father walk into the mahogany-paneled dining room. The room had been set up for Rebecca's talk, with rows of chairs that would seat at least fifty, a lectern on a platform at the end. During the weeks they'd been aboard the riverboat, Rebecca had won the hearts of passengers and crew alike. It had been the suggestion of the first mate to the captain that she be allowed to speak about her translation project.

The passengers drifted into the room, and Sully exchanged a glance with his father, who was grinning from ear to ear. "I knew she could do it," Quaid said. "She's got a fire inside that won't be quenched."

"A fire for God's Word," Sully said quietly. He gazed up at the platform as Rebecca stepped up and gave him a wide smile, placed her notebook on the lectern, then headed toward the two.

"Pray for me," she said, giving his hand a quick squeeze and meeting his eyes.

The room filled up quickly, mostly Englishmen and Americans, though a spattering of Portuguese, German, or French could be heard from time to time. There were a few well-dressed women, but most of the audience was made up of men. High-rolling plantation owners and investors, Sully knew from observation. Some rowdy, others who kept to themselves.

Rebecca moved gracefully to the platform after her introduction by the captain, and from her first smile, the audience was hers. Her features became more animated as she spoke of her passion for the Indian tribes of the Amazon, her appreciation of their world and culture, her desire to bring them the story of redemption.

Sully sat back, unable to stop grinning with pride. And with emotions for her he'd just begun to fathom.

Her talk was short, no more than fifteen minutes. At the close she looked across the audience and asked if they would do her the honor of listening to a brief passage from the Psalms in the Yagua language. Then she began to read the forty-sixth Psalm. The language was musical, the familiar clicking sounds pleasing to the ear.

Then she looked up again with a smile. "Now, in English," she said, "if you'll grant me a few minutes more.

"God is our refuge and strength,
a very present help in trouble.
Therefore will not we fear,
Though the earth be removed,
And though the mountains be carried into the midst of the sea;
Though the waters thereof roar and be troubled,
Though the mountains shake with the swelling thereof.
There is a river, the streams whereof shall make glad the city of God,
The holy place of the tabernacles of the Most High.
God is in the midst of her…"

The words seemed to describe their journey, Sully thought. God had been with them from the day they sailed out of San Pedro Harbor, through the loss of everything familiar, including his emotional moorings.

Yet there had been a river… What a river! Sully felt like shouting for the joy of it. These waters, more powerful than the mighty Amazon, had flowed from God's heart into his in the least likely of places, and he would never be the same.

He gazed up at Rebecca, wondering again at the wondrous journey that had brought him to her village to find himself. To find his God. And this woman he dreamed would become his wife.

That evening Sully and Rebecca stood on the deck and watched the moonlight cast a rippling glow across the waters of the Amazon. He'd planned carefully how he would ask her to be his wife, from the tiger lily he had pulled from the bouquet on their table at dinner, to the exact spot where they now stood in the moonlight.

He prayed for courage. He prayed he wouldn't make a fool of himself. "I have something to ask you," he said quietly.

She gazed into his eyes, and as if sensing the seriousness of the moment, she became very still, almost as if frozen to the spot. As he reached for her hand, he again prayed that he wouldn't embarrass himself. It felt small and warm and steady inside his grasp.

"Becca," he said finally, "I don't think it's any secret how I feel about you."

She smiled, and the cast of the moonlight on her golden skin made him catch his breath. He loved everything about her—the untamed thicket of hair that suited her better than anything fussy or fashionable ever could, the curve of her lips at the corners of her mouth just before she smiled, the way she walked with grace and strength. Her eager, brilliant look when their gazes met, a look that he hoped meant she loved him too.

He swallowed hard, praying for the strength to utter the words that had been on his heart for weeks. He pulled the tiger lily from the inner breast pocket of his jacket, and with a smile, placed it in her hands.

Taking a deep breath, he plunged ahead. "I love you," he said. "I want to spend the rest of my life with you. It all makes so much sense to me—why my father and I had to endure what we did, the tragedies and tests. All of it was for a reason."

She stared at him, unblinking, her eyes shining in the pale light of the moon.

"God brought us together, Becca. Through my bumbling efforts and near-tragic mistakes, still he brought me to you." Everything was coming out wrong. He sensed it as the words fell out of his mouth, as he watched the expression on her face darken.

It wasn't at all the way he imagined the scene would play out. Her face wasn't filled with the delight and joy he'd hoped to see when he finally uttered the words. She looked confused and flustered.

Still he rushed on, taking her cold hands into his, squeezing them gently to make them warm, willing her to understand his heart even though his words were failing him. "What I'm trying to say, Becca, is that I want to marry you. I want us to be together for the rest of our lives."

She released her hands from his and backed away slightly, still looking up at him. "Don't, Sullivan. Please don't ask me that."

At her words, he thought his heart might never beat again. "I thought I saw love in your eyes."

At first she didn't answer. She just stood there in the moonlight, looking so beautiful he thought he might die. The call of the night birds carried from the jungles, joining with the rhythmic rise and fall of the paddle wheel, the rush of water cascading from each board as it returned to the river.

"I can't marry you, Sullivan," she said at last. Then she turned and ran across the deck back to her quarters.

TWENTY-EIGHT

"Pickford made more than a dozen films last year." Stephan Sterling settled back in the plush leather chair in his corner office at Biograph. "*The Foundling, Poor Little Peppina, The Eternal Grind, Hulda from Holland,* and *Less than Dust,* to name a few. All hugely successful by anyone's standards."

"I'm certainly not Mary Pickford. Her success is greater than I can even dream, Stephan, no matter how many films I might attempt in one year."

"You may not be Pickford, but you've become noticed, even in your smaller films. DeMille has asked about you. Surely that means something. He's hinting that he wants to sign you for *A Moonlight Romance.* If he makes the offer, I think you should take it."

"I can't do more than I'm doing right now," Juliet said. She saw too little of her sisters as it was. But Stephan had been her guide through the labyrinth of motion pictures and everything related to the industry—the breathtaking speed with which films were made, the success or failure of stars because of a fickle public. He hadn't once steered her wrong, and for that she was grateful. "I'm a Biograph girl. Happy doing the stories I choose, working with you..." She smiled at Stephan. "And from everything I've heard, DeMille's strong-willed and opinionated. Even Mary Pickford couldn't get along with him. Why should I think I can?"

"You don't have to get along with him. All you need to do is let him help your career. You wouldn't be in close quarters in a studio. You'd have some breathing space. The film will be shot outdoors on location." He paused. "And the money is good."

"Money isn't everything."

Stephan stared through the window for several minutes. Outside, a

group of actors walked by on their way to the morning's shoot—
Rebecca of Sunnybrook Farm—in Studio A. Two young men carried a
long piece of painted plywood past the window, veering off to avoid a
group of actors strolling in the opposite direction.

Finally Stephan turned to her again. "I would think you'd jump at
the chance for this. It might be your big break."

She laughed. "If the offer is made, I plan to turn it down."

"DeMille isn't someone you want to turn down." He laughed
lightly. "And you know, don't you, why studios allow this? And why I'm
encouraging you to do it?"

"The money you make renting me out?" she said cynically.

"I don't deny that it's lucrative for Biograph."

"I don't like the story—it's not something I could take my sisters to.
I've read the DeMille script. In *A Moonlight Romance,* the hero is married when he falls in love with the heroine."

"His wife is a lunatic," Stephan countered. "Spends years in prison.
Doesn't that count for something?"

She shook her head. "It counts for nothing in my book."

Stephan fell quiet for a moment while a smile played at the corner
of his mouth. "What if I told you that rather than your five thousand
dollars per picture, DeMille is offering you ten thousand per movie?
He's talking about asking you to shoot three films for him during the
next six months." He leaned forward, his eyes never leaving her face.
"Do the arithmetic, Jule. That's thirty thousand in a half-year's time."

She gaped at him, too stunned to speak. "Thirty thousand…" she
finally croaked. Her mind was racing. She'd hoped to save enough to
launch a full-scale search for her father and brother. And buy back the
Dearbourne Ranch before the bank auction. She hadn't dreamed she
would be able to come up with that kind of money. With this offer—
should it be made—she could do both, and soon.

Stephan's gaze drifted from her face back to the window. She could
almost hear him ticking off the minutes in his mind as he waited for her
to comment.

The preproduction bustle of actors, actresses, and animals heading to the *Sunnybrook Farm* set was in full swing, producing a cacophony of noise as extras and stuntmen joined the parade of workers carrying costumes and props. She would need to head to the costuming department within the hour to dress for her starring role as Rebecca. But for now her heart continued to beat erratically as she thought of buying back her beloved ranch.

"Suppose you make inquiries," she said finally, "see whether there's true interest or if it's just a rumor. I'll think about the offer if and when it's made."

He walked her to the door. "Our Saturday night gala is in DeMille's honor."

"You planned it that way?"

He gave her a smug look. "Of course, my dear. It's the way the game is played. It will be the perfect time to see it he's ready to talk about a contract."

She smiled. "I'll be there."

He touched her elbow, his expression affectionate. "I'll send my car for you."

"That isn't necessary."

"I realize that. But I insist."

When she didn't answer, he went on, "I stopped by to watch filming yesterday." He rested his hand on the door handle. "I must say, you make an utterly charming *Rebecca of Sunnybrook Farm.*" He touched a curl that had sprung loose from the cluster at the nape of her neck. "Your public will love you in this one." He tucked the strand behind one ear, and smiled into her eyes.

"My public?" She liked the ring of it.

He let the backs of his fingers trail along her cheek, and she stepped back with a nervous laugh. "I really must go," she repeated. "I can't keep the director waiting."

She rushed from his office, her face flushed. Why did Stephan affect her so? Perhaps it was because of his stature in Hollywood. Of course, his handsome face didn't hurt either. She was beginning to enjoy his harmless flirtations. Not to mention the power he wielded in Hollywood or the attention they received at clubs and restaurants when she was on his arm.

It was heady, she didn't deny it. His inner circle of stars and directors drew her like a magnet. He drew others the same way, but he made no secret of caring for Juliet. Nor should he. Stephan was a good friend and ally, should she need one. He'd already shown his affection for her sisters, especially Gillian and her struggle to walk again.

She entered her small dressing room, surprised at the direction of her musings. It was as if she was trying to convince herself that she could care for him as more than a business manager.

The thought intrigued her.

She was still thinking about him as she pulled on a long gingham dress, lacy pantaloons, and an apron. She watched her reflection in the mirror as the studio hairdresser combed her locks into ringlets and draped them down her back, finally placing a flower-frothed straw hat atop her head.

Utterly charming, Stephan had called her. If she didn't know better, she'd think Stephan Sterling was falling in love with her.

She almost dropped the hand mirror. Why hadn't she realized it before? The signs had been there since their eyes first met in New York.

Just then the lights bore down and the cameras began to roll.

Juliet drew in a deep breath and slipped into her role, attempting to concentrate on her actions and timing, hoping as always to be comedic and dramatic. But in the back of her mind was the smiling, sophisticated Stephan Sterling.

Willow threw open the door when Juliet arrived home at their little Laurel Canyon bungalow later that afternoon. The twins weren't due home from school for another hour, and Dora had taken Gillian to the clinic for her rehabilitation session.

"Ettie, guess who's here?" Willow bounced up and down in her excitement.

Juliet swept her little sister into a warm embrace. "Your *s*'s have nearly returned," she laughed.

Willow stretched her mouth into an exaggerated grin to show her teeth.

"There they are, sawing their way through—two perfectly wonderful big pearls! Are you taking good care of them?"

"I've got another loose one." She wiggled another tooth, just next to those growing in. Then she stopped and placed her hands on her hips. "You didn't guess."

Juliet hung her hat and coat on the hat tree by the door and turned to her sister again. "I give up," she said. "Who is it?"

Emma Grace tumbled into the room and ran straight to Juliet, nearly knocking her over with an exuberant hug. "Guess who's here!"

Juliet laughed. "You two are full of questions. The same questions. Tell me who it is."

Each of the girls took one hand to lead her into the garden room at the end of the hall. Then Emma Grace halted and cupped her hand to her mouth, her signal that she had a secret to tell.

Juliet stooped so Emma Grace could whisper directly into her ear. "It's our very bestest friend. And we've been havin' a tea party with him. Cucumber sandwiches and little decorated cakes."

Juliet frowned, cocking her head slightly. "Who?" she whispered back, thinking it might be someone from their school.

Willow took Juliet's hand again and puffed out her chest, glad to be the one to tell the exciting news. "It's Clay MacGregor!"

Juliet's heart caught, and suddenly she couldn't wait to see him.

"We thought the sandwiches were icky," Willow said, "but Clay liked them. He taught us how to nibble at them with our little pinkies stuck out." She demonstrated.

"I don't like cucumbers," Emma Grace said, making a face as she took hold of Juliet's hand.

The two pulled a quite willing Juliet along to the garden room.

"Clay," she said striding across the room.

He grinned as he stood to greet her. She had the fleeting thought of stepping into his arms, but instead she shook his hand affectionately. "It's good to see you."

Cornelia had set a small wicker table with Juliet's new Chinese Rose tea set—dainty plates and saucers and teacups. It was Spode, imported from England, and the finest china to be had on their side of the Atlantic. Stephan had chosen it, saying she needed something impressive for entertaining her new friends. Beside the plates lay settings of silverware, polished to a glowing perfection.

The look of him was incongruous as he settled into one of the small, floral-cushioned wicker chairs. He was too big, too masculine, for the dainty table set and china.

Juliet had to laugh at the thought of him sitting here with Willow and Emma Grace for their tea party, eating cucumber sandwiches with his pinky extended.

It was certainly something Stephan would never do, no matter how much he liked the new Spode.

The contrast between Clay and Stephan was stark. She was suddenly embarrassed by Clay's seeing the pretentiousness of her surroundings, and she wondered if he knew her well enough to figure out that she hadn't picked any of it for herself.

"What brings you out here, Clay?"

He studied her for a moment. "I've just received my first invitation to a Hollywood party."

"You have?" She grinned at him, knowing how he felt about the people who populated the movie industry. "I'm surprised you didn't burn it," she needled.

He laughed. "I thought about it, believe me. Then I wondered if you might like to go with me."

The thought delighted her. She had missed his company. "I would love to. But you must tell me how you came to be asked."

"Ah, I found myself in conversation with a few of the powers that be during one of the last *Kops* episodes. Seems there's more than one movie mogul that would like some free flying lessons."

"I suppose the flyers' reputation as dashing romantics can affect people of all stations," she said with a chuckle, although she couldn't imagine the sophisticated Stephan in anything but a chauffeur-driven limousine.

"They stood in line, waiting to hear when I might take them up. Since then I've been invited to more galas than you can shake a stick at." He raised a brow. "Did I hear you say you'll come with me?"

"I would love to," she said.

He leaned back in the ridiculously small wicker chair. It creaked under his weight. "You once told me you didn't have time for romantic encounters. Is that still true?" His gaze was steady.

Her cheeks flushed, and she wondered at the few beats her heart skipped. "Yes, I suppose it is," she said reluctantly. "Not entirely by choice though. My schedule is impossible."

"Then I will be happy for the one evening we'll have together." His tone was teasing, but his eyes didn't smile with the rest of his face.

"I'll look forward to it," she said.

"It's Saturday night."

Her heart dropped. "At Stephan Sterling's."

He stared at her for a moment, frowning. "The invitation stated only the address—and that the gala was in honor of Cecil B. DeMille." He hesitated. "You already know about it then?"

She nodded slowly. "Stephan asked me this morning to attend with him."

He stood, folded his lace-edged floral napkin and placed it beside the dainty Spode plate. "I should have realized your dance card would be full," he said.

She walked with him to the door, not knowing what to say.

He turned before heading down the sidewalk. "I think I'll burn the invitation after all. This isn't the world I'm drawn to or want to be part of." He shrugged and started to turn away.

"Are you criticizing me for my part in this world, Clay? You're certainly not turning down offers for your stunt work."

He looked at her with a disappointment that seemed to reach

through to his soul. Without another word, he trotted down the street while she stood watching.

He met Gillian who was being wheeled up the sidewalk by Nurse Dora. He stooped to greet the child, and even from the bungalow porch, Juliet could see his love for the little girl in his expression. Gillian reached her arms around his neck and gave him a quick squeeze, then he stood and tousled her hair.

The gesture brought a quick sting to the back of Juliet's throat.

Saturday night arrived before she was ready. Juliet put thoughts of Clay MacGregor behind her as she weighed the offer that might be coming from DeMille. She stood on the landing above the entry stairs, watching through the window, while Stephan's sleek Pierce Arrow pulled to a halt in front of the bungalow. Even as the uniformed driver strode to the front door, she felt a giddy twist in her stomach.

When Willow opened the door, the chauffeur stooped into a formal bow. Willow's mouth dropped, and Gillian wheeled her chair into the entryway, grinning as he repeated his bow.

"Girls? Have you forgotten your manners?" The warning came from Mairia, who stepped into the foyer just behind them. She had become indispensable to running their household, and Juliet found herself relinquishing her responsibilities into Mairia's capable hands.

Willow curtsied, and Gillian bobbed her head; both giggled.

"I'm calling for Miss Juliet Rose," the driver said solemnly.

Emma Grace raced from the parlor and skidded to a halt in her stocking feet in front of him. "Ah, and here she is now. The famous Miss Rose," he said with a wink to Emma Grace.

The three little girls giggled again. "It's my big sister," Willow said. "She's Miss Juliet Rose Dearbourne."

He laughed and looked up as Juliet walked down the stairs to the entry. She stepped to the parlor to say good-bye to the twins, who were lost in their schoolwork, and kissed each of the little girls. The driver held open the door, then escorted her to the Pierce Arrow.

Soon they were gliding along the road, heading to the Paradise Hills. Juliet glanced down at her embroidered voile dress, smoothed the yoke-top skirt and adjusted the loose-hanging jacket, made of the same pale blue-gray, cloudlike fabric. Her hair was twisted high into a knot of curls, and a few tendrils floated loose in the breeze as the car sped along. She'd never paid such a price for a dress in her life, but Stephan had advised her not to be stingy in selecting her new wardrobe. People judged an actress's popularity and success by the extravagance of her dresses. She knew this gown would please him.

Settling back in the rear seat of the Pierce Arrow, she decided that perhaps she had put the DeMille consideration in too dreary a light. This car was an example of those finer things in life that she could afford after just one picture with DeMille. Her sisters would no longer need trolleys, bicycles, or trains. She would simply hire someone like Stephan's pleasant driver.

All this, of course, would follow the more serious expenditures of buying back their home and sending an investigator to South America.

By the time the vehicle turned into the Sterling estate, Juliet had decided to relax and enjoy the evening, even the inevitable meeting with the notorious director. Only once did it occur to her that she was counting on something that hadn't happened yet, on an offer that hadn't been extended. On riches that so far were untouchable.

The car halted, and the driver came around to open her door. Juliet stepped to the ground in her daring, glass-beaded shoes.

"I'll take over from here," said a familiar voice.

Her heart turned over as she recognized the husky resonance of it. Looking up, she smiled into Clay MacGregor's eyes.

"I thought you were going to burn your invitation," she said.

He grinned. "I changed my mind."

Twenty-Nine

Clay took Juliet's hand as she stepped from the Pierce Arrow. When she smiled up at him, he thought she might surely hear the loud drum of his heart. And when she spoke in that low honey-timbred voice of hers, he sucked in his breath and for a moment couldn't respond.

"Why, Clay," she said, "I don't think I've ever seen you speechless."

"It's not often I see such a vision," he said. And she was, from her knot of golden curls to the sparkles on her toes.

He tucked her hand in the crook of his arm and turned reluctantly toward the two-story mansion.

"Why did you come?"

"I couldn't stay away."

Walking side by side, she dipped her head to his shoulder as though savoring their moment alone. Already a crowd spilled from the house onto the veranda in from of them. "I hated how you left the other day. Had you asked me first, I would have been honored to accompany you instead of Stephan."

"I should be more understanding of the life you've chosen."

"I think it chose me."

"Did it really?" he commented pointedly.

She let her gaze drift away from him, then shrugged prettily. "The flickers certainly can't be considered serious theatre."

"What about your writing?"

"You remembered."

"Of course." He stopped, and she looked up at him. Her eyes seemed to sparkle in the ebbing light of dusk. "You never did show me your stories."

"Life got in the way. There hasn't been time."

"I thought it was something besides time that interfered."

She studied him a moment without speaking. "You remembered that, too," she said softly.

After heading up the stairs to the magnificent entry, they stepped through the front door, only to be accosted by maids and waiters holding silver trays of smoked cheeses and sausages on triangles of rye. In the background, a harpsichord, a cello, and a violin drifted through Joseph Haydn's *Piano Trios*.

Juliet and Clay mingled for a few minutes, winding their way through clusters of stars and others connected with the flickers—cameramen, directors, and storywriters. Tom Mix and William S. Hart huddled in a corner, with pretty women on their arms. Gloria Swanson strolled by with Douglas Fairbanks, lost in conversation. A servant offered Juliet a flute of champagne, but she shook her head. Clay did the same. Mabel Normand caught Juliet's hand and pulled her aside. The two exchanged a few words and laughed, then Mabel spotted Fatty Arbuckle on the far side of the room, waved, blew a kiss into the air, and moved on.

Clay watched her from the sidelines and wondered if she, too, would flutter amongst the important people, trading one starlet for another of higher ranking. But she surprised him by turning back to where he stood, as if she actually preferred his company. He placed his hand protectively under her elbow and guided her to the patio at the rear of the house. They passed a group of young women who giggled as they drained their champagne flutes and cast flirting gazes his direction.

"Does all this seem as meaningless to you as it does to me?" he muttered as they finally stepped into the fresh air again. Dusk was falling, and luminarias were glowing among the palms, casting a flickering light among the shadows. The sky was a vivid violet that faded into an orange glow where the sun had minutes before slipped beneath the horizon.

She looked up at him, her expression thoughtful. "All the parties are like this. Frivolous, lighthearted, not to be taken seriously. You learn to accept them for what they are. Nothing more."

They walked to an artificial waterfall and stood for moment watching the clear liquid splash from one tier to the next, then disappear. "You've done well for yourself, Juliet. Are you happy?"

She looked quizzically at him, her brow furrowed, then laughed out loud. "Shouldn't I be? You saw how we were living in New York. Half the time I didn't know where I'd get the money for the girls' next meal. We no longer worry about living hand to mouth. It's a relief."

She reached down and plucked a frond from a fern, as though something troubled her.

"A relief, yes. But you didn't answer my question."

"I suppose I'm happy," she said. "Once you get caught up in this business, it's hard to keep from wanting more. A year ago I would have been happy to find myself making films; today I'm making films, but I want to be paid more." She laughed. "I suppose tomorrow I'll be making more but not be satisfied until I've reached a certain rung on the ladder of fame."

Her words alarmed him, but before he could comment, she rushed on, "How about you, Clay? Are you happy?"

"There are things I want in life," he said, "that are elusive." He took in the groups of laughing and talking guests, then looked back to Juliet. "This isn't real life. All that making a movie entails—from the first story idea to what people watch on the screen—is an act."

"Now you're getting philosophical," she said. "I'm working because I need the money. Period." Her words were adamant, but there was something about her expression that told him she was uncertain.

"And if you were able, would you be content to go back home, to the life you had a few years ago?"

"I don't know what I want, Clay. And that's the truth." She met his gaze for an instant before turning away. "I suppose I'm typical in that the more I get, the more I want—and I'm being completely honest here—whether it's money or fame. Or both."

Fragrance from the burning luminaria candles and a night-blooming shrub wafted toward them. For a few minutes they didn't speak. Their silence was broken only by the trickling water, spattering of laughter, and the music of Haydn.

Then she gazed up at him, her eyes now merry. "And what is it you want, Clay?"

How could he tell her that all he wanted in the world was a beautiful woman to love who loved him back, a spot of land where a man could lie on his back and stare into the heavens without a pinpoint of manmade light obscuring his vision? that he wanted a passel of children to laugh and carry on and grow up, all the while filling his heart with love? that he wanted to someday fill up an entire church pew with his children and grandbabies? Maybe two entire pews? That was all he wanted.

He laughed and looked away from the intensity of her gaze. He raised his eyes to the darkening sky with its pale spangle of stars. "I like to fly," he finally said. "I suppose for now that's enough." *And being with you, here, tonight,* he added silently.

"I remember seeing your machine. It's yellow as a poppy."

He grinned. "I thought you might have peeked beneath the canvas. Would you like to fly with me sometime? The children could come watch. Perhaps take turns flying. I have extra goggles." When she didn't respond, he rushed on, "Meet me at Meadows Field tomorrow following church. Do you know it?"

"Yes, of course. Near Pasadena."

"Will you come?"

She hesitated, but before she could answer, a male voice called out from behind them, "Jule! There you are. Jule!"

The transformation was immediate. Something akin to dread filled her eyes as she looked over Clay's shoulder to the man who had called out. When he turned, he recognized Stephan Sterling and the elegant, distinguished Cecil B. DeMille striding across the patio.

"Jule, my darling," Sterling said without so much as a glance Clay's direction, "I've been searching everywhere for you."

Juliet laughed lightly and looked up into Sterling's face as they turned away from Clay.

"I told Cecil that you were eager to discuss his ideas." His hand beneath her forearm, Sterling spirited Juliet toward the wide veranda and doorway leading into the house. "You may use the library. It's private there."

Clay could no longer hear their words, and Juliet didn't so much as look back at him before disappearing inside the house amid the laughter and conversation, the ringing crystal glasses, and the dreary drone of music.

Juliet was escorted into the library, where two silk-damask gentlemen's chairs had been pulled together near the fireplace. Stephan's assistant bustled in to start the fire, flicking a match toward the kindling beneath a perfectly laid stack of logs. It was so like Stephan to pay attention to such detail.

DeMille sat down opposite Juliet and studied her carefully for a moment. "I have a reputation for being difficult," he said without preamble.

She laughed, already liking him for his honesty.

He didn't laugh with her but leaned forward earnestly, all business. "Have you read the story I'm proposing we do together, Miss Rose?"

"I have questions, serious questions, about the part you're offering to me."

"It's the lead. I thought you'd be pleased." His voice was gruff.

"It's not the part itself. It's the story. It…" She faltered and could feel color rushing to her face. "It's just that the moral side of the story doesn't meet my standards."

He cocked his head as if not believing what he was hearing. "You're a novice, my dear. You have no way of knowing what the public wants. I suggest you leave that part of filmmaking to the experts."

"I know what I can and can't do," she said, wiping her damp palms on her skirt. "And I can't play this part in this story."

He guffawed. "My dear, let me remind you that you are no Mary Pickford. She may command story rights, but she has the power and prestige to use as leverage. You have neither."

Juliet let out a sigh and folded her hands to listen.

"If you cannot play this role as is, then I suggest we end this meeting right here and now."

She couldn't believe he was dismissing her. She sat stunned, unable to make herself stand.

"I have a compromise to suggest," he said when she didn't leave, obviously mistaking her shock for stubbornness.

"I'm listening," she managed to squeak.

"If you will do this one film as it is written, I'll be willing to discuss the morality of the next two in the contract. Will that appease you?" He leaned forward again, his eyes commanding her to pay attention, to do his bidding. He was a man who was used to having his way. Used to having the power to make a career. Or break it.

Juliet's heart pounded. She knew she should stand up right then and leave the room. But instead she merely nodded. "Yes."

His eyes were bright as they fell on her. "I wouldn't be here talking with you now if I hadn't seen something in you that could be developed. Some potential for greatness."

She moistened her dry lips.

"It's a hard business, and not many make it to the top. I'll be honest. You probably won't either."

She flushed again.

"But you've got a sparkle in front of the camera, Miss Rose. The audience will grow to love you, if you're guided in the right direction. From everything I hear, you're determined, you work hard, and you're willing to go the extra mile."

"I am all those things," she said, "but now I must ask you, do I have the talent it takes to go to the top?" She couldn't help herself. Just sitting here listening to him whetted her appetite for more. Becoming a Mary Pickford. Or better.

He seemed to assess her, then nodded. "We won't know until we try, now, will we?" He chuckled. "But that's what this is all about. Trying you out. See how the public likes you as a DeMille favorite." He steepled his fingers as if weighing his next words carefully. "My attorney accompanied me tonight. If you will wait, I'll send him in to make the final arrangements."

"A contract?"

"Yes, yes, my dear, a contract."

Juliet waited alone in Stephan's plush library. She remembered what Mairia had told her when she signed with Biograph. That these things happened when one was wined and dined.

She strolled around the room, trying to quiet the voice inside her that said she'd given in, trampled her principles. That she'd just lost something integral. She pushed the bothersome thought aside and scanned the titles lining the bookshelves, and she stood in front of a fireplace that was more for artistic show than for the comfort of its embers.

On the walls hung grand paintings of English hunting scenes. She gazed at each one as she moved around the room, unable to sit, to relax. A French door gave way to the veranda and gardens at the rear of the house. She stepped closer and pulled back the heavy damask drape.

There in the moonlight, away from the revelers, strolled a solitary man. He seemed lost in thought as he looked up into the heavens. Incongruous, considering where he was—in the midst of raucous laughter and boisterous voices, louder now that the liquor flowed even more freely than before.

He turned toward the house, and the kind planes of Clay MacGregor's face in the glow of the luminarias brought Juliet a strange comfort. She told herself not to run to him and blurt out that she'd like nothing more than to soar through the heavens in his flying machine…perhaps never to return.

A rap sounded at the door, and she turned away from the window.

Twenty minutes later she lifted the fountain pen to sign her life over to Cecil B. DeMille for the next six months.

━━◆━━

When dawn tinged the sky, Juliet pulled on her dressing gown and slippers and padded downstairs to the garden. The scents of damp soil and evergreen foliage mingled in the air.

This was what she treasured now more than ever. Silence. Solitude. A new day when she hoped her heart might at last find peace.

The horizon lightened, promising an achingly brilliant day. The leaves and spent blossoms in her garden were now silhouetted against the sky. A flock of sparrows landed in the yard's single oak tree. She watched them flitter back and forth. Their chatter and song made her nostalgic for the Big Valley.

Juliet stooped to lift a dying rose, examining the dark-edged petals.

DEATH MUST COME SO THAT NEW LIFE CAN ABOUND COME SPRING, a voice spoke in her heart.

She stopped dead still and looked around. Surely the voice had been her imagination.

"But I'm the one doing the pruning," she muttered. "It's up to me, no one else."

DEATH MUST COME SO THAT NEW LIFE CAN ABOUND, the voice repeated.

Lips clamped together, she moved through the roses, snapping off the rose hips and spent blossoms, crushing them in her fist.

NEW LIFE IS MY GIFT, BELOVED.

BUT FIRST THE DEAD WOOD MUST BE PRUNED.

"Ha!" she argued with the voice. "I once believed in you," she whispered. "I thought you cared. Then you took everyone I cared for away from me." She looked down at the crushed petals in her hand. "I learned that I can't depend on anyone else—not my mother or father, or even Jared. And I certainly can't depend on you." She drew in a shaky breath. "Only me," she muttered. "I'm the only one I can count on." As soon as she uttered the words, an image came to her of a sticklike tree, ugly and alone, bent on its own destruction.

She remembered her mother once telling her about an experiment she observed in Brazil. A horticulturist raised a grove of trees on a rocky cliff. They were ravaged by the harshest of winds. He'd beaten their slender trunks and purposely withheld life-giving water.

As a little girl, Juliet had cried, picturing the pitiful, half-dead trees. But her mother had laughed and cuddled her close. "Oh, my little darling girl. If only you could have seen them when I did! They were tall and glorious and bore the best fruit in the horticulturist's grove."

"How could that happen?" Juliet had asked.

"They were made stronger because of their pruning, their roots bore deeper into the soil because of the lack of water, and their trunks could withstand the harshest gale while the weaker trees were uprooted. And because of their scarred trunks, no pest or disease could invade them."

Her mother had pressed her close. "That's what God does with us, sweetheart. He chooses only those he knows can survive and, yes, even thrive in the trials he brings our way."

The morning sun rose higher now, touching Juliet's shoulders, bringing her back to the present. She let the rose hips and crushed petals fall from her hand onto the dew-covered grass.

When she felt the gaze of someone on her, she turned to see Mairia standing in the window. The slender woman inclined her head slightly toward Juliet, her expression serene. Juliet had the oddest feeling that Someone had been in the garden with her just now, and that while they walked together, the woman behind the window had been praying. That she too had known of the other presence.

As one the sleepy voices of Willow and Emma Grace called to her. Soon Gillian's voice joined theirs, followed by the twins shouting for quiet so they could continue sleeping.

Brushing off her hands, Juliet opened the French doors. "I'm in the garden room. I've got a surprise for us all."

She waited until all five of her sisters had gathered at the table before bending toward them and whispering mysteriously, "Guess where we're going after church today!"

They all looked at each other, dumbfounded. Then at last Juliet said, "Flying!"

THIRTY

The girls chattered on the trolley all the way from Laurel Canyon to Pasadena. Emma Grace and Willow bounced on their seats. The twins, behind Juliet and Gillian, giggled nonstop about the daring young flyers they were about to see.

By the time Juliet stepped from the trolley near Meadows Field, her heart was turning somersaults in anticipation, right along with her sisters'.

Juliet looked around the landing strip in wonder as they drew closer. Picnicking families lolled on grassy slopes, their children playing nearby with dolls and toy cars and hoops. Little girls with straw hats and long-waisted, beribboned dresses skipped and giggled and darted here and there, playing tag. Three little boys on bicycles rode by, showing off to a passel of little girls.

Above it all putted the flying machines, painted in every color of the rainbow, some with double wings, others triple. Some had engines in back, some in front. They dipped and soared and rolled in loops, disappearing over a clump of live oaks only to reappear minutes later.

"Where's Mr. MacGregor?" Emma Grace demanded with a pouty frown. "I wanna see his aeroplane, not these."

"Missy, where are your manners?" Juliet said. "And you're the only one besides me who's seen it."

Emma Grace turned her pout into a smile. "Clay's is yellow," she said. "I remember from before."

Juliet walked slowly toward a building on stilts at the far end of the field where two men stood on the top level, holding binoculars to their eyes. The girls followed in a cluster, gawking, the younger ones with faces tipped to the sky, the twins watching the field where the flyers milled about their colorful aeroplanes.

266

"They look like butterflies," Willow said, her chin tilted heavenward. "Or bees."

Abby elbowed Annie as one of the flyers walked by and smiled at them. Soon they were whispering and pointing out another young man, who was busy pulling down on a propeller to get it to start.

"There's Mr. MacGregor!" shouted Gillian and waved. "Look, look!" She wheeled her chair toward him. "There, look! I see his aeroplane!"

Juliet halted and shaded her eyes.

"I see him too," yelled Emma Grace, jumping up and down.

Sure enough, Clay was leaning against his bright-yellow flying machine, white cowboy hat pulled low on his forehead. He waved back, then started toward them, his grin widening the nearer he got. The three little ones took off running as fast as their legs would carry them. They hugged Clay hard, and he acted as if they'd knocked him breathless. Laughing, he swept Emma Grace into the air and gave her a big hug, then did the same with Willow. The twins were a bit shyer with him, but their pleasure at seeing their friend again was apparent in their smiles.

As always, he knelt to give Gillian extra attention, asking how her foot was feeling and whether she was keeping up with her studies so she would one day be admitted to medical school.

But when he'd finished his hellos to her sisters and to Mairia, it was Juliet's eyes he sought. "Are you ready to take a spin?" He cocked a brow toward her.

She bit her lip nervously as he caught her hand and pulled her toward the small aeroplane. When they reached it, she walked completely around the little machine, marveling at it and forgetting her earlier apprehensions about flying just by being in Clay's exuberant presence. Then she stopped, caught her hand to her mouth, and laughed.

"You are amused, m'lady, by my insignia? I daresay, your laughter offends the MacGregor heritage." His speech took on a distinct burr.

By now her sisters had followed and were inspecting Clay's flying machine themselves. Willow squealed. "Peter Rabbit! It's Peter Rabbit!" She jumped up and down again. "Look! Oh, look!"

The others stepped closer to see the comical-looking rabbit painted on the fuselage.

"So many of these planes look alike when they're in the air," he explained rather sheepishly. "After Emma Grace asked several times if I was *that* Mr. MacGregor, I decided to add Peter to my paint job." He laughed and gave her left braid a playful tug.

She stood taller and tilted her chin, looking a bit overcome with self-importance.

"He's winking," said Gillian, rolling her chair closer. "Look, Peter Rabbit is winking at us."

Clay stooped between Gillian and Willow and drew Emma Grace close. Gillian traced the outline with her index finger. "I like your flying machine," she said, circling her arm around his neck.

"I painted the rabbit just for the three of you," he said solemnly. Then he stood, looking down at the little girls. "Each of you will soon have a turn to ride in Peter's flying machine. How does that sound?" He glanced across their heads at Juliet who nodded her approval.

"But first, it's your big sister's turn. I want you all to stay with Miss Cornelia close to the tower." He pointed to the stilted building. "You must promise not to wander onto the field while we're gone. You hear?"

The three little ones nodded their assent, but the twins' eyes were still following the flyers readying their machines for flight.

"And I don't want you to worry if we don't come back for an hour or so." He reached for Juliet's hand and helped her step to the wing of the small aeroplane. She seated herself in the rear compartment, sinking low in the wooden seat. Clay handed her a pair of goggles, then held her hair back while she strapped them on. Next came a leather helmet that fit snugly on her head, though her thicket of curls sprang from under it. Then he produced a long woolen scarf, wrapped it around her neck, and smiled into her eyes as he adjusted it. When he finished, he brushed her cheek with the backs of his fingers, sending a shiver down her spine. For a moment his lips were so close to hers, she thought surely he was about to kiss her.

Juliet held her breath as their gazes locked. Half a heartbeat passed, then he touched her nose with his fingertip. "I'll be right back," he said. "I must see to the prop." Then he clambered over the side of the flying machine and disappeared.

She heard two airy *thunks* as he wound the propeller, then another. And another. The engine sputtered and coughed, then halted in stubborn silence. Another *thunk* carried toward her, followed by some muttering sounds from Clay. Something about the aeroplane being headed for the nearest scrap heap if it didn't cooperate.

Juliet grinned. Seconds later a *thunk-thunk-thunk* sounded as the motor caught, coughed, and settled into a smooth purr.

The little aeroplane shook and lurched, causing Juliet's stomach to do the same. She bit her lip and waited for Clay. He didn't disappoint her. Goggles and helmet in place and neck scarf swinging, he climbed over the side of the fuselage. "Now's the time to start praying," he shouted over the noise of the engine. He gave her a thumbs-up and settled into the compartment directly in front of her, disappearing from sight behind the seat back.

She craned to look over the side as he taxied the flying machine to the end of the field. The engine *putt-putted* as they waited in line behind two aeroplanes, one with flames painted on its tail, the other a solid bright red with puffs of exhaust coming from the engine.

They inched to the starting line, and Juliet's heart pounded harder than ever. Seconds later, they were speeding down the grassy field. Just when she thought they might not ever lift off, the little flying machine sailed into the air.

She gasped as she saw the ground drop away beneath her and blinked as a cold wind stung her face. She threw back her head and laughed out loud, her scarf flying behind her.

Up they climbed. Clay turned the craft in a wide loop back to the field and swooped down so she could see her sisters' faces. The little girls waved and smiled and yelled their greetings, though she couldn't hear a word. Then the aeroplane turned again and headed higher into the scattering of buttermilk clouds.

Juliet looked down at the farmhouses and orange groves, clumps of live oaks and sycamores. They followed a road with horse-drawn carriages and Model Ts below. A bicyclist gawked skyward as they swooped near. Juliet laughed and waved when he fell off his cycle.

Soon they headed away from Pasadena. The small village of Sierra Madre appeared to Juliet's left, and she craned over the opposite side of the aeroplane to see. Clay turned east again, following the line of rugged mountains called the Sierra Madre in the old days, now known as the San Gabriel range. They cruised past Mount Baldy, which dominated the terrain. Then for as far as she could see, the flatlands and foothill slopes were covered with miles of orange groves.

A train chugged along beneath them, smoke puffing from its stack. Clay swooped lower until the aeroplane barely cleared the treetops. He cut the engine until he was traveling at the same speed as the locomotive, then waited for a clearing and swooped near the engineer's window, just fifty feet or so off the ground.

The man shook his fist, motioning Clay to pull up. His expression spoke louder than the words they couldn't hear. Juliet giggled, imagining the man yelling something about Clay's being a menace to decent society. Soon they had lifted just beneath the clouds again. They soared along for another half-hour or so, Juliet settling back in her seat and thoroughly enjoying herself. Clay seemed to be taking the plane higher than they'd been before. He pointed the propeller straight into the heavens, and Juliet gasped as her stomach stayed behind.

Before she had a minute to collect her thoughts, the engine stopped its chugging and the craft tumbled downward, settling into a slow nose-down spiral. In the silence of the sky, she heard Clay laughing. "Are you scared?" he called to her.

"Not a bit!" she yelled back.

"Good," he yelled over his shoulder, then laughed again in a hearty guffaw.

She relaxed at the sound of his voice. A hundred feet from the ground, he somehow managed to yank up the front of the aeroplane. The engine rattled to a start again.

And she remembered to breathe. Minutes later she screamed with joy and abandon as they headed into the clouds, looped over and around, then soared heavenward.

At the top of the third loop, during the silence brought on by the stalled engine, Clay called back to her. "Pay close attention to where we're headed…" The rest of his words were lost in the noise of the engine as it caught.

He settled the aeroplane once again into a horizontal purr, and they continued floating east. After a bit, she looked over the side and blinked.

Clay was taking her home.

The San Jacinto Mountains rose directly ahead, the sweeping fields of the Big Valley spread out below. Compared to the terrain near Pasadena, this land was barren and wild. As they neared Riverview, a few orange groves appeared, interspersed among ranches and farms.

After they passed over the city, the land to the east appeared golden, shimmering in the sunlight, its dried grasses waving in the wind.

The plane bumped as it caught a few gusts, but Juliet was too busy craning over the side looking for the Victorian grove house to be worried. Then she saw it in the distance.

"Take me closer," she whispered mostly to herself, knowing full well that Clay couldn't hear her. "I want to go home."

As though he understood, he cut the engine speed, and the little aeroplane dropped lower. They sped over the treetops, and Juliet picked out Rancho de la Paloma on her left and the Victorian on the right. Clay slowly circled both ranches, passing over the century oak in the middle courtyard of Rancho de la Paloma and the land her father kept wild for the deer and bear and coyotes.

The flying machine approached the Victorian, and she drank in the whole of it, the pepper tree by the wide front porch, the turret on the roof, the rows and rows of orange groves.

An empty field stretched in front of them, just between the two properties. Clay headed for the place, then, cutting the engine again, let the little aeroplane drift to the ground and roll to a bumpy stop.

His face appeared over the back of the seat in front of her. Juliet stifled a smile. He was covered with soot from the engine, except for two white circles where the goggles had covered his eyes. He grinned, his teeth white in contrast with the smudges.

"Were those screams of joy or terror I heard?" He stood and brushed himself off.

She stood too, stretched, and laughed into his eyes. "Pure terror," she said.

He jumped to the ground first, then reached up to help her. Placing both hands around her waist, he lifted her from the cockpit. Once her feet reached the grass-tufted soil, though, he didn't let go.

For a heartbeat, they stood gazing at each other, her feet on solid ground, her back against the flying machine. He touched her face with his fingertips then bent toward her slowly. She had enough time to skitter from his arms if she wanted.

Instead her mouth formed his name. "Clay…"

Before Juliet could say anything more, he touched her lips with his. His kiss made her weak with pleasure. His warmth surrounded her as he drew her into his arms. She sighed and reached her arms around his neck, resting her cheek against his chest, close enough to hear the rapid thudding of his heart.

Without words he seemed to understand the bittersweet emotions caused by her homecoming. She took in the landscape around them, the way the sun's slant turned it golden, the feel of the breeze that whispered through the eucalyptus, lifting its musklike fragrance into the air. "All of this has been in my family for generations."

His arms encircled her, and she leaned against him.

"When I was a child, I couldn't wait to get off this land. I couldn't understand the love my parents and grandparents had for it. Now every time I think about the home that's no longer ours, my heart breaks all over again."

He reached for her hand and drew it into both of his. "Home is more than a plot of land or a house."

She turned to him in wonder. "You speak in the same riddles that M—" Juliet caught herself, "that Cornelia does."

He looked puzzled at the slip, but didn't ask what she meant.

Instead, with the Victorian standing tall in late autumn sun behind his shoulder, he cupped her face with both hands and openly studied her. "I see a scared little girl who's been forced to grow up before her time. Forced to guard a place in her heart that was once her home and is no longer."

Hot tears pooled in her eyes. She swiped at them angrily, unwilling to show her vulnerability. But they spilled anyway. With utter tenderness, Clay wiped them with his thumbs, then kissed each cheek.

She backed away from him, from the love that seemed to surround her in his presence. "I'm not that little girl you'd like to believe I am," she growled. "I'm a grown woman who's been lucky enough to discover a career that you disagree with. You and Cornelia somehow have that mixed up with losing my heart. Losing my way 'home,' as you both put it."

She turned her back to him, staring toward the house once filled to overflowing with laughter and joy and voices of love. "I've just signed with DeMille. Only good things can come of it. Who knows what the future holds?" He stared at her silently, his tender expression gone, replaced by a sad, pitying look.

"You have no right to judge me, Clay. Or my business."

"You're right," he said quietly. "I don't."

With a shrug, he glanced to the flying machine. "We should be getting back to Meadows," he said. "The girls must be worrying."

She nodded mutely and followed him to the tiny yellow aeroplane. The day had lost its glow, and instead of looking over the side of the plane with the merry abandon she'd earlier felt, she merely listened to the drone of the propeller until they circled and landed at Meadows Field.

The little ones didn't notice that anything was amiss and one by one took their turns for a ride around the field, laughing and shouting joyful greetings from the passenger seat of the aeroplane.

It wasn't until she was home again that night, her sisters tucked in bed, that Juliet allowed herself to dwell on the day. She stopped in a pool of moonlight and pictured Clay's face, the warmth in his eyes when he held her face in his hands. She drew in a long breath and shuddered painfully. No one had ever known her well enough to point out those things she knew about herself, and feared. It was as if he could read her heart, the sadness of her soul. And still he had kissed her. As if he cherished her more than anything—anyone—in the world.

For a long time she stood in the garden thinking of his kiss.

◆

Juliet was wrapping up the day's shoot on the *Rebecca* set when Stephan Sterling rushed in and signaled for the camera to stop rolling.

He held the morning's edition of *Variety* in his right hand and strode to where Juliet was standing in costume near an old parlor stove. He thumped the paper with the back of his left hand. "Have you seen this?" His eyes were sharp and assessing.

She took the paper from him and gaped at a small article in the bottom corner of the first page: *Rising Star Takes Flight*.

A pen illustration accompanied the article, a drawing showing her sitting ridiculously close to a handsome young flyer as they soared among the clouds. The aeroplane likeness wasn't even close to Clay's. She scanned the article, which was filled with lies about her relationship with the mysterious and daring flyer. Laughing, she handed it back to Stephan.

"He took my sisters and me flying a week ago Sunday. All the rest is a lie."

Stephan's smile had faded. "Since you've signed with DeMille, everything you do will be reported sooner or later. You'll need to carefully weigh any outings where you might be seen, how they could be interpreted."

His gaze probed hers. "From now on, your life outside the studio belongs to either DeMille or me. You should ask me before you attempt any more of these little adventures."

"What are you talking about?" She moved out of earshot of the cameraman and the rest of the crew. "What do you or the public care about my friendship with Clay MacGregor, or anyone else for that matter?"

Stephan sighed, and his expression softened. "Sometimes I forget, my dear, that you are so new to this business. And so very naive." He signaled the cameraman to take a break, then spirited Juliet from the set. When they were near her dressing room, he stopped and turned toward her. "Cecil and I are in agreement that we will bill you as the public's new princess. If you marry at all, it must be someone they see as your prince. Nothing less."

She laughed. "What do you mean? I'm not planning to marry Clay MacGregor or anyone else." She backed away from him, bracing herself against the closed dressing room door.

Stephan continued as if he hadn't heard her, "From now on, every time you are paired with someone, friend or foe, it will be reported. Your behavior is a direct link to how your movies sell. In that sense, you belong to the public."

"For instance." He quirked a brow, grinning mischievously. "Think of the stir *our* alliance would cause among the public."

She blinked, focusing on one word only: *alliance*. "Is this a marriage proposal?" Her tone was as teasing as the look in his eye, and yet she held a measure of disbelief at his words. He sounded as though he *owned* her.

He laughed again and lightly caressed her cheek with his fingertips. "Perhaps, but we'll save talk of our future for a later time. For now, we need to discuss your new contract, how it affects your hiatus from Biograph. I'll send my car for you tonight. We'll mix a bit of pleasure with our business." He gave her a blazing smile, as if he adored her.

"I'll call *Variety*," he said. "Tell them to meet us at Delmonico's for an announcement that will keep the gossipmongers in Hollywood busy for weeks."

THIRTY-ONE

Waking late on a wintry February morning, Clay pulled on his clothes and hurried through his breakfast in the packinghouse and hangar that served as his detective agency office, as well as a place to hang his hat and garage his aeroplane. It was the first day of filming for a new *Keystone Kops* episode, directed by Mack Sennett, on location near Riverview. Clay peered through the window in the room where he kept a cot and wardrobe. The weather was marginal for flying, which worried him some. He figured he'd wait and see if it cleared before taking the machine up.

Heading to the corner newsstand, he bought a paper and tucked it under his arm as he made his way back to the office. He tossed the paper onto a table, planning to read it later, but the banner headline caught his attention. *America Going to War.* Pouring himself another cup of coffee, he sat down to read.

The British had reported that the German Ambassador to Mexico City had been advised to incite the Mexican government to attack their common border with America, in effect distracting the U.S. while the Germans simultaneously began unrestricted submarine warfare against the United States. Clay scanned the article with growing interest.

Woodrow Wilson had campaigned and won the election the year before on U.S. neutrality in the war, but ever since a German sub had attacked the *Lusitania* off the coast of Ireland in 1915, killing American passengers, the sentiment was growing for America to enter the thick of the battle. Clay wondered if Wilson would stick to his guns and keep the U.S. neutral. He shook his head as he read, certain that this country would be drawn into conflict before the end of this year, 1917. His gaze fell on a small column at the bottom of page two.

Flyers Needed for Royal Air Force.

He read the short paragraph with interest, tore it from the newspaper, and tucked it in his jacket pocket. As he folded the paper, another heading in the "Society and Arts" section caught his attention. Frowning, he lifted it closer.

Rumors of Impending Nuptials between Hollywood's Sterling Couple.

His stomach turned.

The article was short, describing how Juliet and Stephan Sterling had been seen at swanky restaurants together, more than once gazing into each other's eyes "as if no one else in the room existed," lifting champagne flutes in a toast, "no doubt to their romance," the gossipy column elaborated. Rumor had it that wedding bells must follow soon.

Clay wondered if it could possibly be true.

He was still seething when he started the propeller and pointed his flying machine into the wind. He kept the altitude low because of the threat of rain, but he was so busy mulling over his displeasure at the thought of Juliet marrying Stephan Sterling that he overshot the filming site by several miles.

Shaking his head and praying for better sense, he cut back on the throttle and turned toward the landing field, where he'd arranged to meet the director and the cameraman. Lacing in and out of rain clouds and their accompanying turbulence as he dropped toward the ground, the little aeroplane popped up and down like a cork in water. Not that different than riding his horse, he thought with a grim smile.

A buzzing drone in the leaden skies caught Juliet's attention. She was dressed as a Midwestern farm wife, her trademark curls tucked into a poke bonnet, her long, plain dress made of blue gingham. Her face was smudged with soil, and she trudged along behind a horse-drawn plow, acting out her latest scene for DeMille.

At the sound of the flying machine, she looked up and shielded her eyes from the rain. She frowned in worry. Even she knew better than to fly on such a day. Heavy thunderheads had formed during the previous hour, and already the word was that filming would conclude within minutes.

"Juliet, let's try that scene again," called her director with weary-sounding impatience.

DeMille was sitting beside him and nodded his agreement. "This time don't look up. I don't care if a thousand aeroplanes fly over in formation."

Sighing, she nodded, then grabbed hold of the unwieldy plow handles. Head down, she moved along slowly once more. Three little boys, her sons in the story, ran across the fields from the nearby farm-house.

DeMille blew a whistle. "Shoot it again! You came in too soon. I hate working with such incompetence!"

Juliet stopped and, hands on hips, glared at him. "They are just children. You've made them shoot this scene at least a dozen times. It's cold, and they need their rest."

The children gazed up at her in wonder. Drops of rain were splatting harder now. One hit her cheek, and she wiped it away. "It's too nasty out here for them," Juliet continued.

DeMille looked angry. "You're not their mother, Miss Rose. If you'll stop hollering at me, maybe we can finish this shot so we can *all* rest."

She didn't budge. "I'm not shooting another take of this scene until the children get a break—out of the rain."

He strode over to her. "You've held up production every step of the way," he said, his voice threatening.

"Because I insist on keeping normal hours," she said quietly as he walked closer.

He looked down at the small actors. "You skedaddle now. Go over to the corner saloon and get yourselves some hot chocolate." He fished in his pocket for some change.

Juliet touched his arm. "A saloon is no place for children." She turned to the boys. "There's a warm café where you can sit and have your chocolate. You take your nickels in there and ask for what you want."

The droning of the engine was more pronounced now, and Juliet looked skyward again, still unable to see the aircraft. DeMille followed her gaze, frowning. "Sounds like someone's in trouble," he said. "Flyer must not be able to see the ground."

"Are we expecting anyone to join us today?" she asked, her gaze still trained on the gray skies.

DeMille shrugged. "I heard that Mack was going to film a *Kops* episode out here today, but it was cancelled because of the weather."

Juliet's heart froze. "Clay MacGregor," she whispered.

DeMille nodded. "Mack did tell me that MacGregor was scheduled for this episode. I'm surprised, if it's indeed him, that he'd even consent to flying on such a day. He knows better than that."

Juliet swallowed hard, turning to follow the sound. It grew fainter, and DeMille grabbed her hand. "I'm certain whoever it is will land it at the airstrip. When he realizes what an idiot he's being."

The director was wrong. The droning came closer, and now the engine sounded uneven, ragged. At the same time, the rain fell harder, and a gust whipped Juliet's skirts.

"We need to get out of here," DeMille said, his gaze still trained on the cloudy skies.

"You go ahead," Juliet said. "I want to see who this is. Give him a piece of my mind when he lands." She didn't add, *if* he lands. Though she wouldn't, of course; the poor flyer was likely in plenty of trouble as it was. But DeMille wasn't leaving either. Juliet held her breath as a whine accompanied the engine's ragged coughing.

Finally the little aeroplane broke through the clouds in the distance. It was traveling too fast to land safely, too near the ground to pull up over the trees. Juliet didn't know much about flying, but that much she had gathered from her ride with Clay months before.

Almost as if in slow motion, the bright yellow flying machine hit the ground, bounced, hit again, and skittered along the muddy field where Juliet had been plowing minutes before. One of the wheels collapsed, and the little aeroplane shuddered and came to a halt, nose down, its propeller stuck in the mud.

Juliet ran as quickly as her skirts would allow to the wreckage and knelt, her heart pounding, near the dented fuselage. She could see the flyer lying with his head on the yoke. When she lifted his scarf to see who it was, she gasped. "Oh, Clay," she cried, trying to pull him out of the seat. "Are you alive? Oh, Lord, let him be alive." Her voice was frantic.

Clay groaned and opened one eye, then groaned again.

Clay kept his smile to himself as he heard Juliet's fussing and murmuring over him. He hadn't landed with much force, so he hoped his flying machine wouldn't take much time to repair. After all, he was under contract for the *Kops* episode, and he needed the money.

"Clay, Clay..." Juliet cried again. "Oh my darling Clay..."

Darling Clay? As curious as he was about the condition of the machine, it was worth keeping his eyes closed for a minute longer. He groaned again.

"Help me," she said, her voice turned away as if speaking to someone standing nearby. If it was Sterling, Clay would play the injured flyer just long enough to get his hands around the weasel's neck.

Juliet climbed into the rear seat and placed her hands under Clay's arms as she tried to lift him from the cockpit again. He couldn't help the laugh that escaped.

There was a moment of stunned silence.

He opened his eyes, to see her face just inches from his.

"Did you just laugh?" she growled.

"I'm afraid so."

She glared at him with reproachful eyes. "How could you frighten me so?"

He tried to sit up, but his head felt as though it had pressed in a vise. He rubbed it, frowning. "It was the 'oh my darling' that got to me," he muttered.

Behind her a male voice laughed. He recognized DeMille from Sterling's party. "Howdy," Clay said pleasantly and tried to stand.

"Juliet, I think I'd better help our fearless flyer from his machine." She stepped back, and DeMille gave Clay the support he needed to climb from the aeroplane.

Juliet still looked pale and shaken, and Clay felt sorry for having scared her. He would have given up flying forever and horseback riding to boot, just to pull her into his arms and hold her close until she stopped trembling. But the burning look was still in her eyes, and he knew he didn't dare.

Rain was falling in sheets now, puddling the mud, but she stood there staring into his face with the forlorn look of a wet cat. At least he could offer her shelter. He reached under the passenger seat and pulled out a woolen blanket. When he held it out, she didn't look quite so angry, and when he wrapped it around her shoulders, he thought he heard her sigh contentedly.

DeMille led the way, and the three waded through the mud toward the far end of the field. "I need a flyer for an upcoming movie," DeMille said as they walked. "After seeing you land that plane today, I think you'd fit the bill."

"Tell me about it." Clay circled his arm around Juliet's shoulders while they walked. She didn't push him away.

"*Cleopatra,*" DeMille said. "I'll need some aerial shots. A cameraman would ride with you. New innovation I want to try."

"You've found your man…providing I'm still in the States when you shoot it."

"Where are you going?" DeMille asked.

"I'm thinking about joining the RAF."

Juliet halted mid-step and turned to face him. "The Royal Air Force? That's English." Her face drained of color, and she sounded worried, almost scared. "Surely you're not considering going…soon, that is."

"I know. My father's from Scotland." He shrugged. "They're asking for American volunteers."

"It's not our war," she persisted.

"I read this morning that it could involve us soon. Could come at anytime." He explained to them both what the article had stated about the discovery of German plans to attack American subs while the Mexicans battled at the borders.

DeMille stepped up and broke the tension between them. "Whatever you decide to do, son, you can always come to me for a job whether it's before the war or after." He stuck out his hand to shake Clay's.

"Surely you can't be seriously considering such a move," she said after DeMille had left them to join a member of his production crew.

Clay grinned at her. "Don't tell me you care whether I'm on American soil or flying over that of the Germans."

"This isn't a lighthearted matter, Clay."

"That, my dear, is precisely the reason I'm going. If not for the RAF, then for the good ol' U. S. of A. as soon as we're in the thick of the fight."

Her face seemed paler than before, but she didn't comment. They had nearly reached the café, and the glow of lights inside beckoned. He guided her through the lush potted greenery at the entry and across the Spanish-tiled floor to the dining room. Minutes later, they were seated by a roaring fire.

"This morning I wouldn't have believed I'd be sitting here with you on this rainy afternoon." Clay wanted to reach for her but restrained himself when she looked down at her hands, folded on the table.

"With your flying machine upside down in a muddy field!" she continued for him. When she lifted her eyes, more than a touch of sadness flickered there. "Do you think it will be hard to repair?"

"I can't tell until I pull it out and straighten the propeller. It may have less damage than it seems."

"Were you scared?"

He laughed. "From the sound of your voice, I think you were more frightened than I was."

She didn't look amused.

His voice was husky when he spoke again. "I thought I heard caring in your voice, Juliet. You even called me darling."

"You're a friend to my sisters and me. That's all."

This time he did catch her hand, and when he pressed it gently between his two, she looked up at him. Her eyes were confused, and yet he thought he saw a flicker of longing there, a wish for something unfulfilled. He remembered the emptiness in her heart and yearned to see her sadness replaced with joy. "Is that all?"

A waiter came to take their order. Clay ordered two hot chocolates and a basket of warm rolls.

"I read something else in the *Daily Mirror* this morning," he said when the waiter had left. "About you and Sterling."

She pulled away her hand. "About the engagement."

"It's true then?"

"He's asked me to marry him." She laughed, but there was a defiant tilt to her chin. "He suggested it for the attention it will garner, the publicity. He said my fans would eat it up."

"He means to make you a star in any way possible." He leaned back against his chair, unable to take his gaze from her face.

"I suppose you could take it that way." She tore her eyes away from his and looked down at her fingers, then fussed with a broken nail. "But perhaps, just perhaps, he loves me." She kept her gaze on the ragged fingernail, worrying it with the opposite hand.

"Surely you don't believe that's his true motive."

"Do you think me unlovable?" She met his gaze again with an expression rife with challenge. "You know that I care about you, Clay," she said, but her tone seemed false. Then she laughed as if embarrassed. It wasn't the honeyed sound he loved but rather a new silvery, Hollywood voice.

"Don't lose yourself to Sterling, or to the movie industry, Juliet," he said.

"There you go again." Her words were scoffing.

"I care, Juliet." He reached for her hands, but she pulled them away. He felt as though she'd struck him.

"Your words, your very presence, conjure up doubts about myself, where I'm headed, even my abilities. After I'm with you I can't sleep for nights on end. Though I treasure your friendship, I can't allow such distractions in my life."

There was a stubborn set to her chin, and he knew she meant it. Her family, her sisters, and even he knew that when Miss Juliet Rose Dearbourne made up her mind about something, there was no changing it.

"I'm sorry," she said, her voice now cool and distant. "But we truly have nothing more to say to each other."

"What about those things you said while I was in the plane? You were worried, you cared. I know you did."

She arched a brow. "I'm an actress. Surely you know that by now."

He closed his eyes against the pain of knowing he was losing her. "Does it occur to you that you can't sleep because you can't bear to hear the truth about who you are and where you're headed? That you've put up a barrier around your heart that even love—real love—can't penetrate?"

"All I know is that it hurts to be with you, Clay." She stared at him for several moments, then stood. "I've changed my mind about the hot chocolate," she said. The blanket-shawl fell from her shoulders and dropped to the floor.

He stood and watched her walk away. She still wore the damp and bedraggled gingham dress and poke bonnet, and her boots were caked with mud. But she sailed across the elegant Spanish tile like a queen. A little girl queen.

It broke his heart.

Juliet ran up the stairs to the suite that was hers during this production, on the fourth floor of the Inn. The walkway overlooked the courtyard and part of the patio dining area. The rain had stopped, and the enclosure was now lit by candles. She glanced down. Clay had moved to a spot beneath the orange tree that Teddy Roosevelt had planted at the turn of the century. The tall cowboy was leaning back in his chair, lost in thought. Juliet couldn't bear the look of him and turned again, this time to head for her room.

Once inside, she opened the French doors and stepped out to the balcony. The city below her had come to life, and the wet streets sparkled in the lantern light. She faced east toward the Big Valley, the snow-peaked San Jacinto Mountains rising in the distance. It saddened her, but she knew that she couldn't go back now. She had a future. A hope. It was time to grow up. Put the childish dreams and fantasies behind her.

Besides, Juliet's offer to buy back the ranch had been rejected by the bank. It seemed that someone else had beat her to it. The bankers hadn't even needed to put it up for auction.

As for her father and brother, Jared had sent word to her that he'd long ago hired a private detective with funds collected from family members. With his missive he included a list of those who contributed: Great-grandfather MacQuaid Byrne; Aislin and Spence Dearbourne; Hallie and Jamie Dearbourne; Sybil and Scotty MacPherson and their three sons, Gregor, Kerr, and Sandy, and their families; Brighid and Songan Rafael; and Merci Byrne.

Bitter feelings of resentment bubbled up from someplace inside when she'd read the list. He hadn't bothered to ask her to contribute. She'd felt excluded, dropped from the family's inner circle. Worse, she hadn't thought to take up a collection among the relatives. Her brother had. He communicated with her only by mail. He had never come to their new home. No doubt he still blamed her for losing their ranch.

She turned from the window and closed the French doors behind her.

But Stephan offered her a different world, one without the sorrowful memories she carried.

He wanted a spring wedding at his new estate in a desert oasis called Palm Springs. He promised the finest of everything for herself and her sisters, from life in his mansion to a European education for Annie, Abby, Gillian, Willow, and Emma Grace. Travels abroad for them all.

They would never want for anything again.

It sounded so inviting. How she wanted the dark shadows of her past to finally disappear. Clay only seemed to unsettle her more. She was tired of the striving, the soul-searching he brought with him. All she wanted was a little peace. A little quiet. A life without such burdensome cares. She walked to the small oak desk and sat down.

Deep down, she knew what she wanted, what was right for her. She had put Stephan off long enough. He was a good man. With time she could grow to love him.

Lifting a pen, she dipped it in the inkwell and began to write.

Stephan,
It is with great honor that I accept your
proposal of marriage.

THIRTY-TWO

Sully leaned against the starboard rail of the paddleboat. He felt a touch on his shoulder, surprising him. He turned, his heart lifting when he saw Rebecca standing there, the wind in her hair, gazing at him with those golden eyes.

Beyond her shoulder he could just make out the sleepy town of Manaus, glistening in the midday sun. The steamboat had been trapped for weeks, waiting for the floods to subside on the upper Amazon. Finally they were on their way. Sully had been told it might take six months to reach home, but it had taken more than that just to travel to Manaus, and there were still hundreds of miles to go.

"Your thoughts are far away from here," Rebecca said gently, turning to watch with him as they approached Manaus.

He caught her hand and, holding it fast, moved closer to her. He followed her gaze out across the wide river. "I'm just thinking about how long it's been since I left home…how much has transpired since my father and I sailed away."

"How long has it been?"

"Over a year." He moved his gaze to the shore where the hills met the river, the green slopes dotted with white, tile-roofed houses. "Strangely, as much as I want to get home, I'm content to be here with you too." He drank in the comfort of her nearness, the beauty of her profile. "I wouldn't have missed being with you on this voyage for all the tapioca in the Amazon valley."

Rebecca had a way of tilting her face down, then looking up at him through her thick lashes. She did it now, and his heart danced. "I think you enjoyed watching me gather funds for my translation project from the passengers."

286

"The gamblers didn't have a chance, Becca, once you met with their wives." He laughed lightly. "Entertaining as that was, it's being with you, watching your face, listening to your laughter, that has made each day a glorious adventure."

She leaned against him, and he rested his cheek on the top of her head and closed his eyes, drawing in her warmth and her faint scent of roses.

"I know I was premature when I asked you to marry me," he said. "I apologize."

She pulled back and crooked her head, her steady, unblinking gaze meeting his. "I can't make a lifetime commitment to someone whose calling isn't the same as mine."

"I understand." They had talked about it at least a dozen times. He'd prayed about it as well, and still he hadn't an answer.

Her voice was low as she continued, "Even this, Sullivan, is wrong." She looked up at him with loving eyes. "I shouldn't be standing here with you." Then stepping backward, she turned toward the river again. "I love you so." She swallowed hard. "I love you so much I'm tempted to throw to the wind everything I'm committed to."

"I don't want you to do that." Sully's heart twisted. "And yet I can't promise something that I haven't felt, something that God hasn't laid on my own heart."

She touched his arm. "I don't expect you to make false promises." Her voice dropped to a whisper. "To be together under those circumstances would be worse than being apart from you."

He bent his head toward hers and sighed. "It hurts me to think about losing you, Becca."

She smiled gently. "I don't want to lose you either. But we have to trust God in this. When the time is ready, he will speak. Then we'll know."

He wished his faith were as simple, as strong, as Becca's. "It's more complicated than just hearing his voice or feeling his nudge. If God calls me to join in your work, I have nothing to offer. You have your medical training, your translation skills. You've probably always felt you fit in the Yagua world. It's all you've known."

"You think that I said yes to God's nudging because it's natural?" She frowned. "That because I'd never been anywhere else in the world, I didn't want to leave the compound?"

He was embarrassed to admit that it had crossed his mind.

"I'll have you know, Sullivan, there's nothing more I would rather do than experience all the things I've missed over the years. I want to ride in a vehicle with an engine. I want to see a flying machine. Do you realize I've never seen such a sight though they've been around for years? I want to see a moving picture. And taste ice cream."

Her eyes filled. "Do you think it was easy for me to answer the Lord's nudging to stay in the jungles and complete my father's work?"

A myriad of emotions flickered through her expressive eyes as she talked. He watched as her face registered everything from passion to expectancy to…fear. Pure, undiluted fear.

He placed his hands on her small shoulders and cocked his head slightly. "Your words are brave, but you're afraid, aren't you?"

She bit her lip but shook her head. Her lips shaped the word *no*, but the sound didn't follow. After studying him for a moment, she whispered, "Yes."

"Afraid that your call isn't strong enough to keep you from the temptation of life beyond the compound?"

Her eyes filled. "How did you know?"

"I can see it in your eyes."

She turned away from him, her gaze on the approaching settlement. "It's all mixed together, Sullivan. Everything out there that beckons."

"And me? Am I a temptation too?" His voice was husky.

"Yes, you. Most of all you." She stared into the rippling waters beside the paddleboat. "Before I met you, I'd only read about love, and now that I know its power, I worry I can't let it go." She turned to him. "I fear that once I'm back in the States, the temptation to stay there— to be with you, to experience sights and sounds and wonders I've never known—will be too great. I can't bear to think that I may be too weak to walk away from something…from someone…when I know God has called me to something different."

"Even our Lord was tempted, Becca. Maybe that's what this is. A test of your obedience."

She frowned, taking in his own words. Then a transformation overtook her. Her face began to glow with wonder, with admiration for his godly wisdom. It surprised him, and he took a step backward. "Of course," he said, thinking he had just talked the woman of his dreams out of loving him, "you know about these things much better than I do. Who am I to suggest what you might be thinking or the Lord might be planning…?" His voice fell off lamely, and he shrugged.

Rebecca broke in before he could finish his thoughts, her eyes still wide. "Sullivan, I hadn't considered my dilemma in those terms. You're right. Christ was sorely tempted for forty days and nights immediately following his baptism, before he heeded his call to ministry."

Sully gaped as she rushed on, filled with enthusiasm and awe. She touched his arm and sighed, looking up to him as though for guidance. "Would you pray for us both, that we might seek God's will for us…for our future? Right here, right now, before we step on shore?"

"Me?" He'd never uttered a prayer aloud in front of anyone else in his life, not since he was a child and said his prayers at bedtime. He swallowed hard and cleared his throat. He tried to remember that he was speaking to his Lord, not trying to impress the woman he loved and hoped to marry.

"Lord," he said in a shaky voice, "Becca and I come before you to seek your wisdom. You've said that you will give us the desires of our heart if we abide in you.

"Remind us daily that we need to stay near you so that your desires for us become our own." He remembered his mother speaking the same words; he wasn't even sure of the Bible reference, but now the images that came along with the words settled into his soul like a balm.

He gained more courage as his prayer flowed. He pictured the two of them bowing before their King, seeking his guidance, his will, for their lives. Sully prayed for the Yagua, for Tildie and Collin Fleming, for Becca's mother and Sullivan's father, for his family at home, mentioning Jared, then each of the girls by name, asking for God's mercy for them all.

When he'd finished, Rebecca studied him solemnly and didn't speak. He wondered if he had blundered somehow.

"I'm not very good at this…" he said again. She reached for his hand. "When you pray, it seems that our Lord is standing here with us." She gazed up at him with that same sense of discovery, of wonder. The paddle wheel churned behind them, its engine humming, the steamboat's wake trailing far behind. A balmy breeze kicked up from the east, lifting Rebecca's springy curls. "I no longer doubt that he will lead us," she said finally. Then without another word, she left him.

Sully stared across the waters, feeling that he was on the threshold of something he didn't understand, something that terrified him. He looked up into the heavens. "Father, you've brought me a long way… but I still have no idea where I'm headed. Becca has more confidence in me than I have in myself.

"And I don't know whether that's good or bad." He let out a rough sigh, picturing the skinny young man he'd been when he left home. He'd now grown hardy and strong, but too often he still saw his courage, his heart, and especially his abilities in as much need of nourishment as his physical self had once been.

"Lord," he said, looking to the heavens with a grin, "I sure do hope you're not finished with me yet!"

THIRTY-THREE

Gillian's gonna try to walk all by herself today!" Emma Grace ran to Juliet's bedroom. "Can we all go wif you?"

Juliet turned from her dressing table and drew Emma Grace into her arms. The last two times Gillian had tried to put her weight on her foot, she'd fallen on her face in tears. The doctors were still uncertain whether she would walk again. If she couldn't take a step unassisted today, they'd told her that she would be fitted for a brace. Juliet didn't want the girls to witness Gillian's heartbreak if she fell.

"This is a special time for Gillian by herself, sweetie. I promise you, though, as soon as Gillian walks, we'll hurry right back here for all to see. And whether she walks or not, we'll buy ice cream to celebrate how brave she's been. And Cornelia said she'll bake a cake."

Emma Grace made a face. "Maybe just ice cream." Juliet raised a brow in reprimand, and Emma Grace immediately added, "I'm sorry."

Juliet pulled her sister closer. "Maybe this time you can help her remember to put in the sugar."

"Last time she left out the eggs. That ol' cake was flatter than Clay's flapjacks." She licked her lips. "I like Clay's flapjacks." She picked up the hairbrush and fiddled with Juliet's hair while she talked. "I like Clay better'n anybody in the world. Better'n all my sisters and Cornelia and Dora and everybody. Better'n that Mister Sterling." She sighed. "I miss Dora though. I liked her a lot."

"Her job was finished here, sweetie. She needed to return to New York."

"I like everybody better'n Mister Sterling." She went back to fussing with Juliet's curls.

With a sigh Juliet turned and took Emma Grace's face in her hands. "You'll like Mr. Sterling better once you get to know him. He likes you, you know. A lot." She planted a kiss on the tip of Emma Grace's nose.

Emma Grace giggled.

Juliet combed her hair into a sweeping knot and set her straw hat atop the mass of curls. "He's coming over this afternoon."

Her sister's eyes were huge in the mirror. "He is?"

Juliet nodded. "I invited him because we have some special news."

Emma Grace loved secrets. Her eyes danced. "What is it?"

"You'll just have to wait, missy."

"Wait for what?" Willow said from the doorway. She enunciated each word, proud that she'd lost her lisp. Juliet missed the sweet baby sound of it.

"Mr. Sterling is coming by for a visit this afternoon after we get back from the clinic."

"He has a secret he's gonna tell us," Emma Grace said importantly.

"Who has a secret?" Gillian wheeled her chair down the hallway. "You're always telling secrets without me."

Juliet laughed and held up her hands. "You'll just have to wait, girls. I think you'll be pleased to hear it." She leaned closer, drawing them into a small circle. "All I can say is that our lives are about to change in wondrous ways."

There was a small gasp from all three, then Willow said in a complaining voice, "But I don't *want* anything to change." None of them looked happy.

"That's all I can tell you for now," Juliet said, then adjusted her hat. "Gillian and I have a very important day ahead of us, and we must be on our way. We'll be home by the time you return from school."

Juliet wheeled Gillian to the streetcar stop and boarded a few minutes later, the conductor helping with the wheelchair.

"I just know I can do it today, Ettie," she said as they entered the Broadway clinic.

Her eyes shining with hope, Gillian bounced up and down in the chair, causing the wicker seat to creak. She greeted each nurse by name and shook hands with Dr. Brown, who'd been overseeing her case since they arrived in California. He knew all about her plans to enroll in Dr. Wyeth's medical school and asked very seriously about her studies each time they visited.

"And how's my favorite little lady?" He probed her ankle, then lightly touched the wormlike scars. "Are you ready to take that first step today?"

Gillian nodded vigorously. "Today I'm going to do it!" She leaned forward as if to stand.

"That's the spirit." Dr. Brown stood to support her on one side. Juliet took her place on the other, just as she had before.

Gillian drew in a deep breath. "This time I am, this time I am, this time I am," she whispered to herself.

Juliet met Dr. Brown's eyes above Gillian's head. Even before they released Gillian, before her leg collapsed beneath her, Juliet saw the sadness in his eyes. That was when she knew that most likely Gillian's nerves had been severed after all. And that no matter the child's hope and determination, she might never walk again.

"I think we'll give that little ankle a rest," Dr. Brown said cheerfully as they helped her back into the chair. "I've ordered a brace for you, and we'll do the final fitting today."

"I don't want a brace," Gillian pleaded. "I want to walk." Her eyes filled with tears. She looked up at Juliet. "Tell him I can do it. Tell him I'm going to walk, Ettie."

"Maybe he's right, Gillian. Your ankle just needs to rest. Then we'll try again later."

"You said my muscles need to get stronger," Gillian said to Dr. Brown, her voice demanding. "You said if I didn't work them hard, they wouldn't get strong enough to hold me up. If I wear a brace, my muscles won't ever get strong."

Juliet knelt beside Gillian and gathered the girl into her arms. Gillian, who never cried, sobbed as though her heart would break. Juliet's broke right along with her sister's.

⟨⟩

The mood was somber at the bungalow when Stephan arrived. He carried a bouquet of pink roses for each of the sisters, a dozen red roses for Mairia, and three dozen white roses for Juliet. There were so many that his chauffeur helped carry them in. The girls watched in wonder as they were placed on every empty space—on lamp tables, side tables, and even the dining table.

Juliet wished they'd show more enthusiasm at his generosity. "Thank you, Stephan," she said, and narrowed her eyes at her sisters, willing them to follow suit.

"Thank you, Stephan," they chorused dully, which was almost worse than saying nothing.

Annie and Abby rolled their eyes behind his head as he took Juliet into his arms and gave her a hello kiss. Willow giggled, Gillian snorted, and Emma Grace tittered. Embarrassed, Juliet stepped back slightly, her face flushing. Stephan's warm smile instantly turned to a scowl of confusion as palpable apprehension filled the room. Mairia frowned, still holding her red roses as though she didn't know what to do with them.

This wasn't going as Juliet had planned, but she couldn't fault Stephan. He had no experience with a family of five girls and a governess who was more of a dear friend than an employee. He laughed nervously, which endeared him to Juliet.

She gave him a confident nod, then looked back to her family. "Let's go into the parlor. Stephan has something he would like to ask you." She took his hand, trying to ignore Mairia's worried stare.

The girls trudged reluctantly into the small room. Annie dropped into the settee, pulling Emma Grace onto her lap. Abby sat near Gillian, who had refused to wear the leg brace Dr. Brown had sent home with her. And Willow perched on a stool near Juliet. She leaned forward, elbows on knees, chin propped on her hands, and watched Stephan with solemn eyes. Mairia settled into a rocker in the corner of the room, her expression as troubled as Juliet's sisters'.

Stephan stood next to Juliet's chair, his hand on the high back. "I've asked your sister to marry me," he said without preamble.

For once in their lives, the girls were utterly silent. The color seemed to have drained out of their faces.

He glanced down at Juliet, smiled, and turned his attention again to her sisters. "Because you're family—and especially since we'll all be family soon—I wanted to ask your permission."

The girls exchanged looks, as if confused. Finally Annie spoke up, "You need our permission?"

He turned red, obviously not used to explaining himself. "Normally in these cases," he said, "I would ask the bride-to-be's father, but... ah..." He stumbled, cleared his throat, and began again. "Since your father hasn't yet returned from South America, you girls will have to do." He'd meant it as a joke, but none of the children laughed.

Juliet stood to help him out. She smiled brilliantly at him and turned to her sisters. "Stephan and I very much want you girls to be part of the wedding—which will be in Palm Springs this spring." She looked at each of her sisters one by one. "If you agree, that is—about Stephan and I marrying, and about being in the wedding."

"I wanna be the flower girl!" Emma Grace broke the ice by running to Juliet and hugging her. "Please, Ettie, can I?"

Juliet laughed. "Of course, pumpkin. I would have no other." She looked to the other solemn faces. "All of you will be my bridesmaids. We'll shop for lovely gowns for us all. How does that sound?"

"Where are we going to live?" Abby stared glumly at Juliet.

"We'll live in my house in Paradise Hills," Stephan answered. "There's a lot more room there for us all."

"It's a museum," Annie muttered.

Abby snickered in agreement, and Juliet shot them a narrow-eyed warning.

"Sorry," they said in chorus.

Juliet settled into her chair again and pulled Emma Grace onto her lap. The child had grown so much in the last few months, her feet now dangled to the floor. Juliet's voice was earnest as she continued, "This is a wonderful opportunity for you all. Stephan has agreed to see to your schooling. You'll be able to attend private schools first here, then abroad."

"Abroad?" Abby choked. "You mean Europe? What about our friends? And you can't mean you're going to send us away!"

Juliet laughed lightly to put their fears to rest. She knew her sisters well. They simply needed time to get used to the new life that lay ahead. World travel, the best private schools, a home where each could at last have a bedroom to herself, servants to wait on them. A real home. Together she and Stephan could give them everything.

She settled back, listening to Stephan explain the delightful opportunities they would have. As they listened, their anxious expressions gave way to curiosity and, finally, anticipation. Pleased he was winning them over—though she was fully aware it would take much time and effort—Juliet glanced across the room to Mairia, who as yet hadn't uttered a word.

Lips in a straight, tight line, she gave Juliet a brisk nod and stood to leave the room.

Stephan noticed her retreat and called to her just as she reached the door.

"Cornelia, you will be welcome at the Sterling Estate as well," he said kindly.

"I'll be leaving," she said quietly. "I'm no longer needed here."

Juliet started to follow her, but Stephan gave her a brief shake of the head. He was right, of course. Mairia could wait—she was a grown woman, able to make her own decisions. And Juliet didn't want her unsolicited advice on how to run her life. She would simply lecture Juliet anyway.

Doesn't she know, Juliet thought indignantly, *that through my own neglect, I lost the only home the girls had ever known? And that now, at last, I can give them another?*

She almost laughed. What a home it would be! Oh yes, this would more than make up for her blundering mishandling of their home in the Big Valley.

———◆———

"Oh, what a colossal failure I've been here, Lord," Mairia whispered as she walked in the garden. "You sent me here to help our Juliet find her way. Of that I have no doubt."

She stepped across the dew-laden grass and looked up at the stars. "Why can't she see you? You're calling her every moment through her heart, just as you continually called me.

"Oh, but I remember how long it took me to listen!" She sighed. "Your whispers are in the wind. Your voice is in a child's giggle. Your touch is in the voice of someone we love. Why can't our Juliet know you're speaking to her through these things?

"And the longing, Lord! Why can't she acknowledge her inconsolable longing for you? It's written on her heart. Written on mine. Oh, Father, sometimes I just want to shake some sense into her head." Mairia laughed lightly. "Even as I say that, I'm certain you must have thought the same about my stubborn will."

She strolled to a willow and touched a ruffled leaf, let it go, and watched as it turned in the breeze.

"Father, I fear she'll never stop running long enough to listen to you. She's too busy substituting all the wrong things for that which will make her whole, make her truly alive for the first time in her life."

Mairia stayed in the garden long after the laughter and conversation died in the house. She watched as one by one the bedroom lights dimmed and at last the Pierce Arrow hummed away down the street.

"Mairia?" Juliet opened the sunroom door and peered through the darkness into the garden. Mairia was scarcely visible in the starlight. "Are you out here?"

"Over here, child," Mairia called.

"You can't leave," Juliet said, walking closer. The thought saddened her more than she could say

"My time here is at an end," Mairia said, though not unkindly. "I've felt it for some time."

Juliet settled onto an iron settee near her. She pulled her knees under her chin, tucked in her skirts, and wrapped her arms around her legs. "You don't approve of Stephan."

For a moment, Mairia didn't answer, and when she did speak, her words came out as a weary sigh. "I don't think you're marrying for the right reasons."

Juliet looked across at her friend in the pale starlight, surprised that it was important to gain her approval. Settling her back against the nubby, scroll-like ironwork of the bench, she chose her words carefully.

"I have to admit, I didn't love him at first," she said finally. "But he's done so much for me and is so generous in what he's offering to do for the girls." She leaned forward earnestly. "Can't you see? He has our best interests at heart. There aren't many men who would take on such a brood."

Mairia studied her for a moment, and her expression softened. "You'll have to determine what's right for you and for them," Mairia said. "I haven't walked in your shoes to know the heavy burden of responsibility or guilt you carry."

"Guilt?" The word erupted, half-squeak, half-scoff.

Mairia didn't change her expression. "Is it not part of the reason for your decision?"

Mairia had guessed one of the secrets of Juliet's heart, her responsibility for not helping to save Sunny Mountain Ranch. "I can give them a real home finally." Her voice sounded small, even to her.

"You've done that from the start, child" Mairia reached for her hand. "And I've been in plenty of mansions that aren't homes. They're mausoleums, nothing more."

"But Stephan's life is filled with friends, colleagues, laughter. Good times. Exciting conversation. We'll all like that, I think."

"What if that's not enough?" Mairia's gaze was challenging.

Juliet knew exactly what her friend meant, but she didn't want to admit it, not to Mairia, not to herself. "No one can know that about another."

"What if you marry Stephan," Mairia persisted, "and he becomes a devoted husband, makes you into the star he's predicting…and it's still not enough?"

Juliet fell silent. A breeze rattled the oak leaves overhead, and from the distance the lonely sound of horse hooves on pavement carried toward them. "Pain pierced your heart long ago, Juliet," Mairia continued softly. "You've put up a shield to guard yourself from being hurt again. But I think as surely as you've done that, you've also barred your heart from hearing God's voice."

Juliet shrugged to hide her confusion. "You always turn the conversation back to my heart—I'm going to miss that. I don't believe it, but I'll miss hearing it."

Mairia leaned forward, as if unwilling to be dismissed so lightly. "Go back to that place in your heart, Juliet, when you were a child and life was full of wonder and promise—before all the pain and sorrow and tragedy. Before you became a mother to your sisters, too busy to listen. Was there a time when you heard him? Think about it, child. Was there?"

Juliet was silent as Mairia continued. "It could have been in the rippling rush of a river, or in the turn of an oak leaf, maybe in the glimmer of sunlight against a hawk's wing. Think about it, child. Know that in those shimmering moments, it was God himself speaking to you. Don't think those moments were accidental."

"Life full of wonder and promise?" Juliet laughed. "When was that? Much too long ago to remember, Mairia. Though I must say I fancy the notion." She fell quiet for a moment before continuing. "Gillian was full of wonder and promise just this morning, wasn't she? Where was his voice when she fell on the ground, unable to walk? When it was clear she will never walk?"

A piercing silence fell between them. Juliet turned her back, and Mairia stood wearily. "It's late," Mairia said, "and it's been a long day." She headed to her little cottage behind the house.

Juliet sat in the garden long after Mairia left. She would talk the woman into staying tomorrow. She had to; she didn't know what they would do without her. If only Mairia didn't go on and on about those heart matters. And now the silly notion of God's voice whispering to her in the wind…or through some shimmering afternoon in her childhood. She supposed it was just the longings of a lonely old heart.

Though if she did imagine such a thing, before the pain and sorrow in the Big Valley, what moment would she pick? The night was balmy as she sat back, reflecting, closing her eyes, enjoying the light breeze. A memory drifted into her mind. She had been five years old. Her father pushed her in the old swing he'd built just for her. She soared through the air, thinking she was surely flying above the trees straight into the sky. His strong arms lifted the swing, then pushed her again. She threw back her head and squealed and giggled, his rumbling laughter joining the music of some frogs in a nearby creek, the hum of the cicadas, the babbling voices of the twins who were just learning their first words.

What if Mairia was right? What if God did choose to speak to her heart through such things…before pain, sorrow, and fear got in the way and made her stop listening?

Juliet looked up at the star-spangled sky and tried to fill her mind with anything but memories of the Big Valley and home. God might have spoken to her there, but now the family home was gone. And so was he. All of it was too painful to think about.

Thirty-Four

Sullivan sat with Rebecca at one of the tables in the dining room. Quaid used his cane to propel himself toward them. They looked up and smiled as he approached. Sullivan pulled out a chair, and Quaid nearly fell into it.

"You're looking better every day, Father."

"And feeling better," he said with a laugh. "Though I daresay, I'm still looking more skeletal than human."

"You look wonderful to me, Mr. Dearbourne," Rebecca said.

They spoke about the approaching port, Belém, just hours away. Rebecca excused herself as she often did when they were together. She seemed to sense that they were making up for lost time communicating as father and son. After Rebecca left, Quaid studied his son. He'd noticed a change in the boy in the past few weeks. At first it was a glimpse of something special, yet recognizable, familiar.

He walked with vigor and spoke with authority. Even his laugh and the way he held his head seemed different somehow. A confidence that belied the boy he'd been only a year ago.

At first Quaid thought it was because of Rebecca, but on closer observation, it was something more, something bigger than he could imagine. Love might have played a role, but Quaid suspected that God had played an even greater role in the transformation. He wondered if Sullivan recognized the difference in himself.

"I was about to go up on deck to watch our approach to Belém," his son was saying.

"I'd like nothing more."

A few minutes later, Sully turned to the city on the hill and held out his hand dramatically. "Belém…at last!"

"Where the Amazon pours into the Atlantic," Quaid mused, "and we've nearly returned to where we started."

"Has anyone said how long it might take to catch a steamer from Belém to the States?"

"This is a major port city," Quaid said. "Should be ocean liners in and out of here weekly." He laughed. "Of course it depends on where they're headed…"

Sullivan laughed easily with him, then let out a contented breath. "Sometimes I want to be home right away, and sometimes I don't care if I ever go back. Is it that way for you?"

"After nearly a year and a half of the worst of conditions, illness, abduction, I must say there's nothing I want more than to see my children again. To hold my little Emma Grace and Willow and Gillian."

A shadow crossed Sullivan's face.

"Sull, this has been the journey of a lifetime, and we've learned a lot. So for that I am grateful. I've realized for the first time in my life how precious and short life is. For years your mother and I were concerned with houses and lands. She wanted groves. I wanted wilderness. We were both wrong."

Sullivan leaned back as if quietly assessing his father's words, weighing them, perhaps against the guilt Quaid knew his son felt. "It's not the land that's important. Instead, it has to do with being near those we love. It has to do with honoring the precious life God's given us. I had a lot of time to think while I was sick. It grieved me that I had left your sisters and Jared at home."

He smiled, knowing he needed to again try to lessen the burden his son still carried. "I was never sorry that we came, Sullivan. Don't get me wrong. I was never sorry that you had the courage and curiosity to send us off on the quest for investing in the rubber industry. I was only sorry that I didn't bring all my children with me on this grand adventure."

Sullivan finally grinned. "Does that mean that once we're home, you're going to pack us all off again?"

Quaid threw back his head and laughed out loud. It felt good, so good, to laugh again. "Perhaps after a bit of a rest."

"We'll send another wire," Sullivan said, his gaze on Belém. "I didn't tell the family when to expect us when I sent word from Iquitos. We should let them know we're on our way. Or we could just surprise them. They're expecting us anyway. They just don't know when."

Quaid imagined the looks on the children's faces when they finally arrived. Little Emma Grace hopping up and down with joy; Gillian and Willow, wide-eyed; the twins, young women now; Juliet, beautiful and capable; and Jared, bold and brash. He sighed, thinking of his children, safe at home, happy and healthy. And he tried to again brush away the nagging fear that they might have lost everything.

When the *Lady Caravel* pulled into harbor a few hours later, it docked at a distance from the main port. A liner the size of the *Lusitania* was anchored north of the city. Leaving Quaid on board to rest, Sullivan and Rebecca hurried down the gangway and made their way to the port authority office, only to discover that the ocean-going liner was leaving immediately for the States.

"He says if we want to take that ship, we must hurry to the tender," Rebecca translated. "We can purchase our tickets on board."

"We don't know if there's room for three more passengers. Ask him if he knows."

She translated, and the man shrugged. "He doesn't know."

"Where in the States? Does he know that?"

Sullivan looked out to the harbor. The smokestacks were already belching. He turned back to Rebecca, who was still speaking in rapid Portuguese. "He says the ship will travel through the Panama Canal, that's all he knows of its destination."

"That's good enough for me." Behind them the whistle blew from the liner, loud enough to rattle the windows even at this distance. Sullivan grabbed her arm to steer her to the door.

"Wait!" she said, and turned back to the port authority. Again they spoke in rapid Portuguese. She looked stricken when she turned back to Sullivan.

"What is it?"

"There's no time. We must get your father and board. There won't be another ship heading to the States from here for quite some time."

"Why?" Sullivan panted as they ran.

"I'll tell you later," she said, her face still pale.

They reached the *Lady Caravel* and raced to Quaid's stateroom. In minutes they had hailed a horse-drawn cab that took them to the tender, and within the hour, they were ticketed and safely housed in their staterooms. It wasn't until supper that night, when leaning across their dining table, that Sullivan asked, "What did you mean about this being the last ocean liner to leave Belém for a good long time?"

For a heartbeat she didn't answer. Quaid and Sullivan exchanged glances.

Then she cleared her throat nervously and said, "President Woodrow Wilson has declared war against Germany. These waters may already be infested with German submarines."

At midnight in his stateroom, long after his father was asleep, Sullivan paced the floor, praying for his family's safety and begging God's mercy to be poured out on America. Still troubled, he finally turned out the light and crawled into bed. Just before he drifted to sleep, he remembered.

There had been no time to send the telegram. Their arrival would be a surprise after all.

THIRTY-FIVE

Juliet settled against the glove-soft leather of the backseat as the Pierce Arrow convertible glided through the village of Palm Springs. On either side of the road slender palms reached into the brilliant spring sky, their fronds glittering in the sunlight. The lush, flowering oasis of a town was an odd contrast to the jagged eastern face of the San Jacinto Mountains that rose above it.

In the seat across from her, Annie and Abby gawked at the surroundings, while Gillian and Willow whined about the long drive out from Los Angeles. Emma Grace had thrown herself across Juliet's lap and now was fast asleep, legs hanging to the floor. Juliet stroked the child's cheek, her heart welling with love.

Stephan had suggested the girls stay home from the tour of the Continent that he had planned for their wedding trip. Understandable, of course. After all, it was to be their honeymoon. The tour was complicated by the news that America had entered the Great War, but Stephan refused to acknowledge that the trip should be postponed. He had connections on both sides of the fighting, he'd assured her. He'd planned it meticulously, using friends in Italy, France, and England to book them in only the most elegant chateaus, under fictitious names and citizenship, tucked far away from the fighting. Still, she worried about the wisdom of the tour, pushing from her mind the inappropriateness of traveling without the blessing of her country's State Department. She'd wheedled Mairia Garden into watching her sisters in her absence; they would be in good hands, but she would miss them terribly.

Stephan's home loomed on a stark knoll in the distance. It looked like a small castle carved from the desert rock.

"There it is, girls. That's where the wedding will be." *Tomorrow,* she added silently. *Tomorrow.* And she wondered at the chill that traveled up her spine.

Her sisters craned to see the estate, the home that would be their second when Stephan or any of them became bored with the first. He laughed often about the glorious option of having two homes and talked about building a third, overlooking the ocean.

Juliet settled against the warm seat as the car rolled toward the estate. A mockingbird sang its warbling song once, twice, three times. Another bird answered from a clump of ocotillo a distance away.

The sound didn't match the darkness in her heart.

"Driver?" she called.

The man turned with a lifted brow. "Yes ma'am?"

"The Desert Inn. Do you know it?"

He nodded. "Yes ma'am. Everyone knows the place."

"Take us there. Please."

"But, Ettie, I thought we were stayin' up there." Willow pointed to Stephan's castle.

Juliet whispered a silent thanksgiving. "When we arrive," she said to the driver, "please make arrangements on our behalf. We'll take the bungalow in the rear, behind the gardens near the pool. I don't care what the proprietor must do to secure it, just see to it that it's done." She did enjoy the clout that her position as the soon-to-be Mrs. Sterling afforded her.

Mrs. Juliet Rose Sterling. It had a nice ring.

"Yes ma'am," the driver said.

"After we've moved in, you may take word to Stephan that I prefer to be left alone for the time being."

"Yes ma'am."

She closed her eyes, sinking deeper into the seat as they drove. Her heart had ceased its erratic beating, and she breathed a bit easier.

The driver stopped the car beside the Desert Inn and stepped out. He returned within minutes. "You will have the bungalow you requested, Miss Rose. The proprietor will meet us in back to escort you to your quarters and help with your luggage."

"What's wrong, Ettie?" Willow asked, her voice heavy with worry.

Her little brow furrowed, Emma Grace took her hand. "Why aren't we goin' to the 'state for the wedding?"

"It's tomorrow, sugar." How could she explain her extreme case of prenuptial nerves to a child? "We'll have plenty of time to drive there in the morning."

As soon as the driver left with her message for Stephan, Juliet settled onto a stone bench in the secluded garden beside the bungalow. Willow and Emma Grace had changed into playclothes and raced around the gardens and pools, exclaiming with wonder at each new cactus or bird. Annie was sketching in her notebook, and Abby was leafing through a copy of *Variety* she'd found in the room.

Gillian sat near Juliet, her heavy brace seeming more of a burden to her than ever. As always, a book was in her hands. "Why don't you want to see Stephan?"

Juliet laughed lightly. "I would love to see him. It's just that I needed some time with you girls, time alone. That's all."

Her answer seemed to satisfy Gillian, who now buried her nose in *Treasure Island.*

Leaving Gillian with her book, Juliet strolled over to the fountain. She pulled her hand lightly through the water and let the sparkling liquid drip through her fingers.

She simply needed rest after the long, dreary, hot drive from the city. That was all. Her case of nerves was nothing more than fatigue. Staring into the water of the fountain, she started when a voice called to her from the opposite side of the courtyard.

It was followed immediately by the happy squeals and giggles of her sisters.

"Juliet?" he called again. The timbre of the voice was at once husky and musical. Familiar.

She turned in surprise. She'd half expected Stephan to ignore her plea for privacy, but now she saw Clay MacGregor striding toward her, Willow grinning ear to ear on one side, Emma Grace hopping up and down on the other. When he reached Gillian, he stooped and spoke to her, compassion written on his face. The twins hurried to him, in an animated excitement Juliet hadn't seen for weeks.

He gave them each a quick hug, then headed toward Juliet, giving her a sheepish look. "Please don't be angry with Stephan's driver. When he pulled up Stephan's driveway alone, I wheedled him to tell me where you were."

"I didn't know you were coming out here for the wedding."

"As you remember, my aeroplane opens many doors. I'm actually out here for a shoot in a nearby canyon. One of your guests is in the film. I flew him to town as a favor. Stephan was kind enough to invite me to stay for the festivities."

She tilted her head to meet his eyes, and her heart began to thud beneath her ribs. There seemed to be a liquid warmth, bright and golden, in his eyes. She breathed in slowly to get rid of the lightheaded spin that enveloped her. It was surely caused by her lack of food since breakfast.

"I'm surprised you stayed, Clay. I know how you feel about Stephan."

He moved even closer. "Perhaps I just wanted to see you once more before I leave."

"Leave?" She frowned, though she'd been expecting it since the United States entered the war.

"I've joined up."

"How soon will you go?" She tried to ignore the ache that suddenly invaded her heart.

"I must report before the week is out."

"You will keep in touch." Her words came out like a plea. "I mean, the girls, all of us will be interested in what you're doing."

"I'll write to the girls. You'll be a married woman, Juliet." He raised a brow. "It would hardly be appropriate."

"Then why did you come here on the eve of my wedding? Surely you don't think today is any more appropriate than your writing to me afterward." She tossed out the words just as she tossed her head.

There was a stubborn set to his jaw. He moved closer, she supposed so the girls wouldn't hear. "Perhaps I came to see if I could talk you out of this sham of a marriage."

"How dare you…?" she sputtered. "You don't know what you're talking about."

"Then why didn't you go to Stephan's?" His voice, though still husky, held a challenge. "This makes no sense." He glanced around at the grounds of the modest resort. "Overnight guests have already begun to arrive. I'm certain Stephan was expecting you to get a head start on your duties as Mrs. Stephan Sterling—the grand hostess of the Sterling estates."

At the mention of her married name, his eyes held a naked anguish that tore at her heart.

"I-I was simply not feeling well. The drive is long, tedious." A bird swooped down to drink from the fountain, and Juliet flicked her fingers in the water to frighten it away. "I have a headache."

"The groom's chariot arrives in all its sleek, moneyed glory," he drawled with an arched brow, "only there's no bride."

Juliet swallowed hard, willing herself to look pale and drawn. If she hadn't known it would look too theatrical, she would have lifted the back of her hand to her forehead.

"I have to wonder if the bride has second thoughts. If she doesn't, it's about time she did."

She turned away from him and walked back to the stone bench where she'd been sitting earlier. He followed and sat down beside her. Catching her fingers, he held them in the grasp of his big, warm hand. The gesture made her eyes fill. She blinked rapidly and looked away from his scrutiny.

"Tell me how I can help."

"I think I'm beyond help. And though you think I've changed my mind, I haven't." She met his gaze with a steady one of her own. "I'm merely taking time to be sure. That's all."

He didn't let go of her hand. "I suppose it's typical for brides to have second thoughts."

She nodded again. "I'm sure it's no more than that."

He studied her face, and she felt her cheeks redden under his scrutiny. The fountain splashed in the background, and a whisper of wind caressed the palm leaves. A tendril of hair fell from beneath her hat and lifted in the breeze.

Clay's eyes held a depth and light that she found hard to look upon. It was as if he could look into her very soul. "Don't marry him, Juliet."

"Why?"

He lifted her hand to his lips and kissed her fingertips. "Do you love Stephan?" he asked.

"I just need time," she said, letting her gaze drift from his eyes. "It's a good match."

Clay let out a rough sigh. "What about the girls? Are you certain they're happy about this?" When she didn't answer, he went on, "From the first day I met you, they were the most important people in your life. I suspect you're doing this as much for them as for yourself. But are you sure it's what they want?"

"I care about my sisters," she protested. "I love them with all my heart."

"Don't go through with it, Juliet. Give yourself some time to think, to pray…"

"That's why I'm here, Clay."

He caught her hand. "Let me show you the place where I'm filming." There was boyish excitement in his voice. "It's not far from here. We can take a couple of horses."

"Now?"

"You won't regret it. Believe me." He paused, smiling. "It's a place where you can almost reach out and touch God. Maybe it's just what you need right now."

She grinned up at Clay. "I'll change clothes. You find the horses."

After he hurried from the courtyard, she gave instructions to the twins about watching the younger girls. They ran off to try their new bathing suits in the pool, obviously delighted that she and Clay were going riding. She pulled on her riding clothes and brushed back her hair.

When a loud rap sounded at the door, she almost ran to greet Clay. Unable to stop smiling, she pulled it open.

Her heart dropped. Stephan, his eyes filled with white anger, stared at her.

Clay headed into the sparsely populated town, his heart light at the prospect of a day with Juliet.

He'd been in town during two weeks of filming and had learned about the rich history of the barren but beautiful desert oasis. For the past five years, a few Hollywood stars had been coming to the natural hot springs to take mineral baths and bask in the healing sun. Clay didn't begrudge the practice, only that the Cahuilla Indians were being manipulated out of what had been their land and run further into poverty.

Most stars, like Stephan Sterling, paid little attention to the Indians. Clay knew he was cynical, but the stars' concerns were hedonistic at best, thoughtless at worst.

Still musing as he walked, Clay headed toward a horse ranch tucked against the mountains at the end of town. He wondered if Juliet noticed that Stephan was among those whose thoughtless treatment of others was legendary, whether it was the Cahuillas who worked his estate or the starlets who flitted around him at the studio.

Today, in that glorious place by the falls, he hoped to show Juliet a different world. A world of peace. Where he communed with God. *Oh, Lord,* he breathed, *let it happen. Let Juliet find her peace with you there too.*

With a lighter step he strode around the side of the ranch house to where cattle hands were working some colts in the corral at the back. A few minutes later, he mounted a pinto and, holding the reins of the palomino he'd gotten for Juliet, let the horse take its lead.

The sun was beginning its downward arch above the San Jacintos by the time he reached the Desert Inn. He tied the mounts to a hitching post out front and headed to Juliet's bungalow.

He pounded on the door, grinning to himself as he awaited the sound of her light footstep. He wasn't disappointed. She opened the door a few seconds later.

"Juliet…" He stepped inside, fighting the urge to gather her into his arms.

"Well, well," a theatrical voice boomed from across the room. "A surprise visitor!" Stephan Sterling stood and moved toward the couple.

"Juliet, you didn't tell me you were expecting company." His gaze bored in on Clay's. "I should have figured where you'd come when you left the estate in such an all-fired hurry, MacGregor." He narrowed his eyes, stepping closer. "How'd you know where to find her?"

Clay kept his mouth shut, and Juliet didn't dignify Stephan's accusations with a single word.

Juliet let out a long sigh. "I want both of you to leave me. Now. I made the decision to come to the Inn, hoping for time to think. Alone. And that's exactly what I intend to do. Please go." She shot Clay an imploring look, even as she took Stephan's hand. "Please," she whispered, now looking up at Stephan with the expression of a woman in love.

Clay's disappointment was keen. He nodded slowly, his eyes briefly meeting Juliet's, then headed to the door. She followed him, standing for a moment on the porch as he walked away from her.

"Thank you anyway," she called after him.

Clay lifted his hand in a halfhearted wave, then headed back to the horses. Leaving the palomino, he mounted the pinto and headed down the trail to Tahquitz Canyon. His heart was heavy as the horse followed the streams of water deeper into the gorge. He'd ridden only a few miles when the sounds of the falls carried toward him, its low roar beckoning.

Clay nudged the pinto to move faster.

Juliet was lonely after Clay left. The feeling surprised her. She tried to concentrate on Stephan's words but had a difficult time following his logic. Stephan seemed bent on convincing her that her qualms were normal, in fact, to be expected. He was ready to forgive her and take her and the children to the estate where she and they belonged.

"Darling, nothing has changed," she said finally. "I intend to marry you tomorrow as planned. Just tell our guests I needed time to rest for the big day."

Stephan's demeanor brightened considerably.

Juliet smiled, easing him toward the door. "I have one request."

"Anything." He was so handsome when he smiled, and now the expression warmed his features, dazzling her with his aristocratic dark looks.

"Tell our guests we'll make all this up to them tomorrow."

He bent toward her, but she turned her head and his kiss landed on her cheek instead of her lips. He looked puzzled, then laughed again. "I will leave you to your restful thoughts, my princess," he said.

"Tell me," she added casually as he stepped through the bungalow doorway, "where is *Lost Horizons* being shot?"

"Tahquitz Canyon. A lovely place, I hear."

She nodded. "Have you been there?"

He laughed as though the idea were ludicrous. "It's a grueling hike. Straight up the canyon. When the Cahuilla build a paved road and we can drive, then I'll take you there, sweetheart." He chuckled and stepped down from the porch, pausing. "Why do you ask?"

Juliet shrugged. "No particular reason."

Stephan narrowed his eyes suspiciously but didn't comment. "I'll send my car for you and the children in the morning," he said instead. "Ten o'clock sharp. Don't disappoint me again." He gave her a soft smile that threatened to melt her heart. "Please, my princess."

"I'll be ready."

She followed him at a distance, waiting until his big car slid down the dusty road. Then without hesitation she ran to the hitching post and mounted the palomino. It briefly occurred to her that this might not be the horse that Clay had found for her, but if need be, she would settle up with the owner later.

For now she headed to the canyon known as Tahquitz.

Clay climbed to the top of the waterfall, leaving his horse to graze in the tender spring grass beside the deep pond at the base of the falls. The sun was on its downward slant now, casting a blaze of color across the desert landscape below.

In the canyon the shade was deep and restful. Clay squatted at the edge of a slice of granite, rocking back on his boot heels, a long blade of grass in his mouth. This scene never failed to bring peace to his soul. No matter the frenzied pace of his work or the unsettling activities of those around him, he met God here. Always.

"It's me again, Lord," he breathed, squinting out at the golden sweep of the land in the distance. "I'm always bungling things, and this time it's no different. I felt you nudging me to go to Juliet."

He shook his head, deep in thought. "I truly thought she needed me today, that this was the time when we could talk."

A wind kicked up, churning the cottonwood branches that provided a canopy at the edge of the pond below him. The roar of the waterfall overpowered all else, and it was only by the wind-chime movement of the leaves and the feel of the water's back-spray that he knew the wind blew.

"Lord, I want to follow you in this. A part of me wants nothing more to do with Juliet, the friends she keeps, the mistakes she makes. Then I look into her eyes and lose all sense.

"I don't want to get ahead of you, Father. I don't want to think you're sending me in a direction that comes from nothing more than my overactive imagination.

"She is a little girl lost in a world that's caused her so much pain that I'm afraid she'll never discover love—yours or mine." He considered the thought for a moment. "If it's truly you who's brought me, who wants to touch Juliet in your name, I'm here, Father. I'm here…"

Juliet pressed her knees into the horse's flanks as they wound up the trail. She glanced at the rocky incline, rising to the challenge before her. The heights were dizzying.

She had almost reached the top when she saw Clay, leaning against a boulder, his boots crossed at the ankles, his hat pulled low.

He gave her a nod and sauntered toward her as she approached. He held the palomino's bridle as she slid from the saddle and turned to face him.

"How'd you find this place?" He was smiling beneath the brim of his hat, his eyes light against the tan of his face.

"It wasn't easy." She laughed. "You didn't say whether you'd begun filming. I don't see how a cameraman will make it up the path."

He took her arm and led her to a boulder beside the waterfall. "That's for DeMille to figure out. So far, I've flown over a few times with the cameraman in the passenger seat. He's yet to decide how to handle getting equipment to this pool." His gaze took in the waterfall, the pool below. "It's this that DeMille wants in his film. Not something fake created in a studio."

She followed his gaze. "It's lovely." She looked from the lush palms by the water to the top of the jagged granite outcropping. "You said you come here to meet God."

"I hear him best away from the clamor of the city. Though he's been known to speak to me in my flying machine or on my horse. I guess it doesn't matter where I am. When he decides to speak, I just need to stop and listen. Maybe it's just that I listen better here."

"Mairia says that he speaks from within our hearts."

"Mairia?"

She gasped. "Oh, I don't know what's gotten into me. I mean Cornelia."

"She knows our Lord too." There was a hint of a knowing smile at his lips.

He turned again to her. "I hear him better here than anyplace I've found. I'm usually so busy yammering, I forget to listen. Here the silence is more profound than any word I might speak."

He stepped closer, until he was standing within arm's length. But he didn't reach for her or make any attempt to touch her.

"Other things keep us from listening. Things that are even worse than our own yammering. They fly at us like arrows, slicing and bruising until our hearts can't hear God's voice. Things like a mother's death, a father's disappearance, the terrifying responsibility of raising a family by yourself."

She stared at him, trying to take in the thought, the idea that God might have been speaking to her through the years…since that first time in the swing, drawing her, wooing her, loving her. But her heart had been too bruised to respond.

"We erect defenses against the pain, the sorrow. We might settle for a marriage that holds no love. That way we can't be hurt by death or by others leaving."

She turned away from him. "You've said enough, Clay. How could you possibly know what I've been through?" She expected him to gather her into his arms and hold her close. She wanted to cry as she hadn't cried since she was a little girl and feel the stroke of his hand on her hair. But he didn't move toward her.

"I've had my own taste of sorrow," he said softly. "My mother ran off when I was ten. My father said it was to be with another man. He hated even the mention of her name and forbade me to speak it. I grew up filled with hate and resentment that she had left me with him.

"I was summoned to her side when she lay dying in the slums. It was then I found out it hadn't been the way my father said it was. He'd kicked her out and threatened to harm me if she came back."

"What had she done?" Juliet's heart went out to him. "What would have caused such anger?"

"The other 'man' was her Lord. She discovered a love above all others, and my father would have nothing to do with it. He was embarrassed by her exuberance. She told everyone about her Lord and how she loved him."

He paused. "In his anger, he threw her into the streets without a penny. Told her that if she ever contacted me, he would beat me to within an inch of my life. He was a violent man, known to fight in saloons and such, but he never laid a hand on me."

"You speak of him in the past tense."

"He died a lonely and forgotten man, stabbed in a barroom brawl not long before I met you." He looked away from her. "Right after he sold the family ranch."

"You're not bitter?"

Clay laughed self-consciously. "I have my moments."

"I'm sorry," she said, feeling strangely comforted by his confession.

"I told you that I meet God up here."

She nodded.

"That's why I wanted you to come...to meet him, not me."

"Thank you," she said, honored that he would share something so precious to him.

He took a few steps away from her, and she called his name. He paused, looking back.

She stepped closer. "How did your mother survive all those years? You said you found her in the slums."

Clay propped his boot on a stone and leaned against his knee. "She served others." There was pride in his face. "She dedicated her life to helping orphaned children, the sickly and deformed that no one else wanted. The castoffs from a society that values the beautiful, the perfect. A church has taken over her work." He smiled softly. "They named an orphanage after her. The Tess MacGregor House."

Then he turned and was gone.

THIRTY-SIX

J uliet stayed in the canyon, near the falls, until the sky was streaked with pearly dusk. The roar of the water fed her thirsty spirit. She was too weary to pray and uncertain that she knew the right words anyway, so she just thought about what Clay had said about God being with her.

The wind lifted her hair, and she closed her eyes. In that brief instant she felt as if God was there. Had been there with her for a very long time. She wondered why she hadn't noticed it before. She imagined him carrying her close to his heart when her mother died, imagined him crying because of her heartache.

Her sisters came into her mind, and she realized that she hadn't been the only one caring for them all this time. She pictured Christ sitting with Emma Grace on his lap, smiling as she sucked her thumb and twisted her hair. Or laughing at the precocious antics of Willow, chattering with her lisp. And Gillian. God had carried her in his loving arms with her twisted leg. Had seen her through her surgery. The twins were near him too, both so eager to grow up, to be independent young women. God listened to Abby pour out her heart and to Annie as she told him her own fears and dreams.

Could it be that he had been with each one of them every moment, close enough to touch, to feel his embrace? Juliet would have known his presence—if only she hadn't been so wrapped up in her own sorrows.

Ashamed, she stood and moved to the edge of the granite slab. The waterfall cascaded, its spray a rainbow veil in the slanting afternoon sun. Its roar filled her ears, and she closed her eyes.

She thought of the bitterness in her heart. It had lodged there like a granite stone since her mother's death. And when her father disappeared, when their home was taken from them, her anger had moved in beside the bitterness.

Suddenly those emotions seemed infinitesimal compared to the rivers of joy and peace that her Lord offered. Juliet opened her eyes and stared again into the deep, whirling waters below.

COME TO THE WATERS, BELOVED. The still, small voice in her heart spoke above the roar of the waterfall. COME TO THE WATERS...

Once she'd thought herself so thirsty of spirit that nothing could quench that longing. Once she'd thought her soul so empty that nothing could fill it.

Juliet stared into the pond. "But, Lord," she argued, "how can you offer me this peace and joy when I have forsaken you?"

I WILL OPEN RIVERS IN THE DESOLATE PLACES OF YOUR HEART.

AND A FOUNTAIN OF LIVING WATERS, CHILD, IN YOUR DARK VALLEYS.

She paced along the granite cliff. "You can't mean it, Father. Not after I turned from you. You don't know my heart...the dark fear that lurks. The sadness, the bitterness. I can't just snap my fingers and make it go away. It's who I've become..."

IT IS I WHO FORMED YOU IN YOUR MOTHER'S WOMB,

I HAVE SEARCHED YOU AND KNOW YOUR HEART.

I UNDERSTAND YOUR THOUGHTS...

EVEN SO, I HAVE LOVED YOU WITH AN EVERLASTING LOVE.

"I betrayed you. I should have turned to you, been a better example for my sisters. I've failed my parents. They would have wanted me to teach the little ones about you. I've failed you, Father." Her knees gave way beneath her, and covering her face with her hands, Juliet knelt to the rocky ground. "How can you love me enough to draw me to you?" she cried. "I can't comprehend it."

I WILL MAKE THE WILDERNESS OF YOUR HEART A POOL OF WATER, BELOVED.

AND THE DRY LANDSCAPE SPRINGS OF JOY.

COME TO THE WATERS, CHILD.

She lifted her face, almost afraid to breathe. "Lord, you would have me as I am?"

I WILL TURN YOUR HEART OF STONE INTO A HEART OF FLESH, A HEART FILLED WITH MY LOVE.

"What must I do?" she breathed.

COME TO THE WATERS, CHILD. COME UNTO ME.

"I'm here, Father," she wept. "I'm here."

Juliet didn't know how long she stayed by the waterfall. It might have been a few minutes, a few hours, or an eternity. She only knew that when she stood, everything was new. Her heart felt lighter than it had in years, perhaps ever.

Joy welled from someplace deep inside Juliet. Tears of thanksgiving filled her eyes as she walked toward the waiting palomino, then mounted.

The sky was darkening as she started back down the narrow path. It was almost with surprise that she remembered her upcoming wedding and her earlier jitters. With her newfound peace, it seemed that God was with her in all things, even her marriage to Stephan.

When she reached the bungalow, a welcome fire crackled in the fireplace and lamplight cast a golden glow through the window. She had just started some water to boil for tea when she heard the voices of her sisters from across the grassy lawn.

Throwing open the door, she stooped just in time to catch Emma Grace as she catapulted herself into Juliet's arms, followed by Gillian, Willow, Annie, and Abby, all trying to hug her at once. For a moment, a hot sting caught Juliet behind the eyes and she couldn't speak. She gathered them closer, suddenly not wanting to let them go. Ever. She breathed in the familiar fragrance of soap and puppy dog from being too long in the warm sun.

"Are we still marrying Stephan tomorrow?" Emma Grace whispered in her ear.

She nodded. "You'll be pretty as pictures, all of you. I'm so proud you'll be with me."

"I'm glad I'm the flower girl," Emma Grace said, looking important.

Juliet headed to the kitchen to move the whistling kettle from the stove. "You will have a little basket of flowers to carry, and you'll walk in front of me and throw flower petals."

"I didn't see any flowers except wild ones," Willow said, carefully pronouncing each *s,* now that her front teeth had grown in.

"How about cactus flowers?" Gillian asked. "I saw some pretty ones."

"Maybe we could pick wildflowers in the morning," Abby suggested.

"We'll get up at dawn and take a walk in the fields," Annie said, excitement in her voice. "I saw Indian paintbrushes and bachelor buttons on our drive here."

"And I saw ocotillos and yuccas, but they're not very pretty," Emma Grace said, prompting an immediate argument from her sisters about which flowers were the prettiest.

Juliet stifled a laugh as she pictured Stephan's face when the girls arrived carrying their scraggly bouquets. He had planned every perfect detail for their wedding for the sake of the reporters from *Variety, Silver Screen,* and the *Daily Mirror.* Every faultless blossom from his prize-winning hothouse would be arranged with perfection, especially her bouquet. He might frown for a moment, but later he would laugh with them all at the joy of their contribution. He'd admitted to her that he had much to learn in dealing with their fresh exuberance.

"I think wildflowers are a perfectly wonderful idea," she said, still smiling. "In fact, I'll help you pick them in the morning. We must get up early though."

They promised they would, then Willow looked at her with huge eyes. "When people get married, they love each other more than anything else in the world, don't they?"

Juliet nodded. "Sometimes they love each other more than life itself from the first time they meet. Other times they care deeply about each other, then that love grows and grows till they love each other more than anything else in the world."

"I don't love Mr. Sterling," Willow said, careful of the *s* sound.

"I don't either," said Gillian softly.

"That's not nice," Abby said from across the room.

"Maybe your love for Mr. Sterling is the kind that will grow and grow," Juliet suggested.

Emma Grace ignored her and reached up to cup her hand around Juliet's ear. "I have a secret," she whispered.

"What is it, honey?"

"I feel like throwin' bach'lor buttons right in his ol' face."

Juliet caught her little sister's hands and held them fast. "Why would you want to do that?" she said softly.

The child's eyes filled with tears. " 'Cause he's takin' you away to Europe."

Circling her arm around the little girl, Juliet pulled her close. "That's only for a little while. Wild horses couldn't keep me from coming home to you," she said. "No matter what happens, we'll always be a family." Stephan understood her commitment to her sisters. He'd told her so again and again. Now she just needed to convince her sisters that he had their best interests at heart. But looking down at Emma Grace's upturned, worried face, she wondered about his wisdom in planning their wedding trip to Europe in the midst of war. "It's only for a little while," she repeated.

Stephan sent the Pierce Arrow sedan to collect them at ten the following morning. Juliet's hands lay calm in her lap as they glided once again through Palm Springs to his estate. But her thoughts weren't so calm. She was making a lifetime decision, one that affected them all.

Oh, Lord, she prayed, *if there's any reason at all I shouldn't go through with this, let it be clear. I'm new at this, at listening to your voice and praying for guidance.*

She thought about asking Stephan for time to talk things over a bit more, perhaps even postponing the wedding.

But the guests were waiting. It truly was too late to call off the huge affair.

Her heart thudded wildly, but she closed her eyes and prayed for calm. After all, she and Stephan had a lifetime ahead to talk things over. Things like her newfound faith.

Her eyes flew open. She wondered what he'd think if she told him about meeting Clay, meeting *God,* by the waterfall. Would he understand it?

What if he didn't? What if he ridiculed her?

She moistened her lips. Surely her musings were just those of a nervous bride. Likely all young wives-to-be had the same qualms on their wedding day.

Frantically she glanced around. The palm fronds lining the lane sparkled in the sun as they danced in the breeze. Mockingbirds trilled, and a few feet from the Pierce-Arrow a rabbit skittered across the sandy desert floor.

All was well. She was being ridiculously and unnecessarily jittery. She could, of course, change her mind at any time before the ceremony if she wanted to. She lifted her chin upward, feeling a greater confidence settle her spirits.

Then she remembered the hundreds of guests, those she'd worked with, those she hoped to work with in the future. And among them, those who held her motion picture career in their hands.

She wondered if she truly could walk away.

The girls, dressed since dawn in their best voile and ribbon dresses, were unnaturally quiet and watched Juliet with solemn eyes. She'd thought they would be thrilled to be part of the festivities, but instead they were increasingly glum. Even the twins sulked moodily. She blamed herself. They had obviously sensed her trepidation. She smiled at them, hoping to lighten their spirits.

"When are you gonna get in your gown?" Emma Grace said, playing with Juliet's fingers.

"I told you. After we arrive. Stephan has a special suite where we'll go, and someone to help me dress and fix my hair."

"But I wanted to fix your hair," pouted Gillian.

"Me, too," whined Willow.

"Huh uh. I said I was going to," said Emma Grace, sticking out her lower lip.

The Pierce Arrow slowly moved up the estate drive. Flanking either side of the roadway were manicured lawns, lined by tropical plants of every shape and color. Flowers decorated the beds, blooming in a rainbow array.

As they pulled up to the front, Juliet could see Stephan standing atop the veranda like a prince awaiting his princess. A large crowd had gathered on the front steps of the mansion. Charlie Chaplin stood off to one side near John Barrymore and Gloria Swanson. Mack Swain grinned and waved as the vehicle drew nearer. Behind the group, standing very close together, were Mary Pickford and Douglas Fairbanks. Mary blew Juliet a kiss.

Everything was going according to plan. Stephan hadn't wanted the guests to see Juliet in her wedding gown until she walked down the aisle. He'd known everyone would be awaiting her arrival. After all, they were Hollywood's brightest couple.

Emma Grace started to cry. Not a silent, weeping little noise, but rather, a loud, bawling sob. It was loud enough to make every one of the guests fall silent and stare as the Pierce Arrow slowed to a halt in front of them.

Juliet frowned. "What's the matter, honey?"

Her little sister's face was red, and large tears rolled down her cheeks.

"Baby, tell me. What's the matter?"

Emma Grace was howling now, her face redder than before.

Juliet gathered the little one close, aware that Stephan was glowering at her from the top of the entry stairs. Emma Grace's wailing definitely wasn't part of his perfect agenda.

The child drew a hiccuping breath, and before she could wail again, Juliet heard Willow and Gillian snickering.

"All right," she said sternly. "What's going on?"

Willow's glum look was gone. She covered her mouth with a giggle, and in her excitement forgot about her *s*'s. "Can't you thmell it, Ettie? Emma Grathe wet her panth." She collapsed into howls of laughter, right along with Gillian, who joined her, shrieking with glee.

In her arms, Emma Grace shuddered and buried her face against Juliet. For the first time in months, she popped her thumb into her mouth.

"Take us around to the back," she called to the driver.

"But Mr. Sterling, he said to bring you here…"

"I don't care what he said. Take us to the servants' entrance immediately."

The car glided away from the entrance, and Juliet waved for the second car to follow. The twins frowned, looking irritated that they'd missed their grand entrance. Abby flopped against one side of the backseat; Annie did the same on the opposite side, folding her arms stiffly. Both scowled, refusing to look pleasant for the wedding guests.

Juliet craned to glare at them, but they refused to meet her gaze. When she looked back she saw Stephan. He'd come down from the veranda and was standing in the crowd, his eyes following her intently. His face had turned crimson, and his lips were thin and pale with anger.

Clay stood in the middle of the crowd, watching the arriving entourage with a sinking heart. He couldn't believe she was actually going through with this sham. He'd counted on Juliet coming to her senses. She was a bright woman. Couldn't she see that this was all wrong? Even the children looked agitated and unhappy. He longed to go to them and tell them everything would be all right.

But everything might not be all right, ever, if Juliet went through with it.

When the cars disappeared around the side of the house, he slowly moved to the gardens and lawns in back of the mansion. The wedding tent truly was a sight one might imagine from a fairy tale. But then, that was what Hollywood was all about, wasn't it? Illusion. From the giant floral bouquets on each linen-covered, silver-adorned table to the ribbon-bedecked cabanas, to the pools and waterfalls and fountains beyond.

Chairs had been placed on either side of a silk moiré runner that covered the aisle Juliet would soon tread. Clay took his seat in the last row. He wondered why he had bothered to attend. Beside a garish, orchid-covered arbor, a full orchestra began to play something from Mozart, then Haydn, and finally settled on dramatic, sappy melodies such as played on tinny pianos or too-loud organs during a love story at the flickers.

He was only torturing himself, he decided, watching the woman he loved marry another man. What kind of fool would put himself through such agony? He slumped down further in his chair, wondering if he could slip out without being seen. Looking around, he saw that the throng of air kissers was making its way to their seats. It was too late. He sighed, settled back, and awaited the show.

The orchestra struck the first triumphal chord of the "Bridal March" as Juliet moved to the back of the lawn, her sisters clustered around her, their faces solemn. At least they weren't crying—except for Emma Grace, who still hiccuped once in a while, her little shoulders jumping with each one.

Stephan stood beaming under the flower-draped wedding tent. Then he moved his gaze from his bride to her sisters.

Juliet realized how bedraggled the little band must look to her groom, who stood handsome and impeccably dressed as he awaited his bride.

The girls clutched wildflower bouquets in their hands, their blossoms drooped and wilted, the stems straggly. Pollen from the flowers had dusted orange streaks on their pretty voile dresses, and Willow had rubbed her face while holding her cluster, causing both a yellow stripe on her nose and sporadic sneezing attacks.

Now Stephan was scowling.

The "Bridal March" continued, and several guests craned in their chairs in obvious wonder at the delay.

A gentle nudge from someplace deep inside told Juliet she should back out. She stared at Stephan, then back to the restless guests. There were smiles and looks of awe as they beheld her in her gown.

Juliet gave them a confident smile, but her knees were shaking now, and she stared at Stephan. She didn't think she could take a single step toward him.

She had to run from this place.

But in front of all these guests? She glanced at them, drew in a deep breath, and moved her gaze back to Stephan.

Now he was smiling, grinning actually, at her—and, of all things, actually chuckling at Willow's sneezes. He made a big show of pulling out a handkerchief and shaking it out to await the child's arrival at the end of the aisle. The audience laughed, and Stephan beamed.

Juliet drew in a deep breath. All was well. She simply had to put aside her worries and get herself down the aisle.

"Is it time?" Annie whispered, quirking a pretty brow.

Juliet nodded and gave her a brilliant, confident smile. "Let the little ones go first," she said.

Emma Grace looked up at Juliet, her lower lip trembling. "I don't wanna go." She dropped her flowers on the ground.

Juliet stooped. "You don't have to, but it would mean a lot to me."

The little girl shook her head stubbornly, and Juliet worried that she was about to howl again.

"How about walking down the aisle with me instead of first?"

"I want to!" wailed Gillian. "If she gets to, I want to."

The others started to chime in, and Juliet held up her hand. "Quiet, all of you."

The orchestra began another chorus, and Juliet drew in a deep breath. "Now then. Let's settle this. We can all walk together."

Three little heads nodded, and the twins shrugged.

"Annie and Abby, you start first. Emma Grace, you'll come with me, holding my hand, and Gillian and Willow, you'll each walk on one side of us."

The twins held their heads high and started walking down the aisle. A collective sigh of delight rose among the guests, and even Stephan smiled, obviously glad to have the ceremony begin. His eyes met Juliet's, and he positively beamed.

Juliet moved to the near end of the silk runner and stopped, her sisters clustered around her. In the front row far ahead she could see Merci, Brighid, and Songan craning and smiling. Merci tapped Grandmother Aislin and Grandfather Spence, who turned and waved. Great-aunt Sybil stood, blowing kisses with both her gloved hands, then waved a hanky. Beside her, Scotty winked.

Her sisters perked up considerably, waving and blowing kisses when they saw the familiar faces.

Then Juliet's heart froze when Clay, sitting in the back row, turned to her. Their eyes met, and she tilted her head to him. Her stomach twisted with misery, a despair so acute she wanted to run to him, to weep and let him draw her into his arms. Instead she bit her trembling lip and continued walking to her groom.

The orchestra swelled as she reached the arbor where Stephan waited. He took her hand and kissed her fingertips. She looked into his eyes, hoping he would understand the frailty of her emotions right then. But he seemed more interested in the production, the reaction of the guests to the show he was producing and directing.

As predicted, he stooped and gave his handkerchief to Willow who blew her nose loudly. The audience laughed, and Stephan gave them a brilliant smile. Then he turned to Juliet with what seemed to be a practiced look of affection.

Practiced! She looked into his eyes, searching for more. Yearning for more. But realizing that that was what it had been all along. Practiced emotions. Practiced words and phrases. Practiced expressions. He had been playing a role, a role of suitor, father to her siblings, grand host and groom at the wedding of the decade.

The robed minister stepped forward and began to speak, but Juliet didn't hear a word he said. She still stared into Stephan's eyes and trembled as if she'd taken a sudden chill. It was as if she were gazing at the scene through someone else's eyes. A groom with a practiced look on his face. Playing for the audience. Of course, that's what they all did.

That's what she was doing this very minute.

She wondered what Stephan was thinking and realized she didn't even know him well enough to guess.

What was she doing? The thought struck her as if someone had pulled back a curtain and she could see herself acting out a part for an audience of her peers. But this was no part. This was her life.

Clay had heard enough. The minister droned on about the sanctity of marriage, and Juliet was staring into her groom's eyes as though she believed every word, as if she loved the man. He almost laughed at his naiveté. To think he'd misjudged her so. She actually loved the man!

Clay waited until the guests were too enthralled with the ceremony to notice, then he stood and headed around the side of the house to the front entry. He sprinted down the long winding drive and through the tall iron gates. He didn't stop running until he reached the Estrella Inn, where he'd spent the previous night. After collecting his belongings, he left for the airfield. Within minutes of his arrival, the prop turned over, the engine purred, and he turned the little machine into the wind.

Stephan looked into Juliet's eyes with a dreamy look on his face as the magnificent Leona Maxwell sang a Mozart aria, accompanied by a full orchestra. When the song was over, there was sniffling from a few female members of the audience, and the minister cleared his throat and began to speak in a loud, clear voice.

Juliet's panic grew. If she was going to stop this sham of a production, she had to do it now. She glanced at the audience, her peers, her friends, her family, and wondered how she could stop everything without making a scene.

She almost laughed. A scene? She shouldn't mind such a thing. This was a Hollywood crowd after all. But again, she reminded herself, this was real life. And if she didn't stop it now, greater scenes of tragedy surely lay ahead. She breathed a prayer for courage.

"Ladies and gentlemen, we are gathered here in the sight of God and..."

Juliet held up one hand. "Please, if I may," she said to the minister. "I need to say something."

There was an audible, collective gasp from their guests, and Stephan stepped backward unsteadily. She wondered if he might faint.

Her sisters were as silent as little voile clouds.

"Stephan, I can't marry you," Juliet said. "I-I just can't." She glanced around wildly, only realizing after she couldn't find him that it was Clay she sought. "I'm sorry," she said to the guests, whose mouths were gaping as surely as her sisters' were. She bit her lip, certain she was about to cry, and again looked to Stephan.

His expression was filled with rage and mortification.

"Forgive me," she said, reaching for his hand.

He shrunk back as though she were a leper.

Her head held high, she gathered her sisters and walked away from the orchid-covered arbor. No one uttered a word.

<hr>

The following morning at the train station, with the girls gathered around her, she picked up the *Daily Mirror.* They boarded the train, and after Juliet settled in her seat, Annie looked over her shoulder from the seat behind her. "Look, Ettie, there's mention of Clay MacGregor."

"Where?" Gillian wanted to know, grabbing for the paper.

"I want to see," Willow said.

"Let me, let me!" Emma Grace grabbed it away from Gillian.

"You can't even read, silly goose," Willow said.

Juliet reached for the newspaper. "I'll read it to you." She scanned the article, her heart sinking. The first paragraph praised the young men who had already signed up for the armed services at the first word of America entering the Great War. It listed the men who would ship out that day. Clay MacGregor was among them.

"Read it to me," Willow said.

Juliet's eyes filled when she read Clay's name.

"What does that mean, Ettie?" Emma Grace wanted to know.

"Clay will fly an aeroplane in a faraway place to protect us, baby. He won't be back for a long, long time."

"The flying machine with Mr. MacGregor's rabbit on it?"

"Probably a different one, maybe one with an American flag on it."

Emma Grace stuck her thumb in her mouth, and Juliet pulled the child closer. It reminded her of the image she'd seen in her mind when she talked to God the day before. How Christ had held her sisters, held her, through their sorrows, even when they didn't know he was there. She pressed Emma Grace close and thought about Clay.

"Hold your beloved son in your arms, Father," she breathed. "Don't let him go."

THIRTY-SEVEN

Juliet opened her eyes to find Emma Grace standing by her bed, staring at her with solemn eyes.

"Good morning, sweetie," Juliet murmured, blinking. She rubbed her eyes and yawned, then pulled back the covers so that her little sister could crawl into the bed beside her.

Emma Grace snuggled close and inspected her thumbnail. "I'm glad we're going home," she said softly.

"Home, yes." Juliet put her arm around her sister. "But we're not moving back to the ranch. You understand that, don't you, honey?" It had taken Juliet less than a week to decide she never wanted to work in Hollywood or New York again. It was time to go home. If not to the family ranch, at least to the Big Valley.

"Uh-huh. We're goin' to Aunt Merci's. But it's close to home."

"It's the old adobe on her property. It will take a lot of work to make it clean and nice for us." Juliet didn't want to think about the critters that had likely moved into the place during the years it had been vacant. "It's by a lake called Mystic."

Emma Grace giggled. "Why's it called that?"

"Because it isn't always there."

Emma Grace turned toward Juliet, her eyes big. "It disappears?"

"When the Big Valley has lots of rain, Mystic Lake is one of the prettiest sights you'd ever want to see. But during the years of drought, it looks as dry as the land around it."

"It will be a pretty place to live."

"It's also the very first place that your Great-grandmother Camila and Great-grandfather MacQuaid Byrne lived in when they first came to California. They stayed there while the big hacienda was being built."

"That was a long, long time ago I bet," Emma Grace said. "Tell me the story."

Juliet smiled at her sister. It was strange how she had dismissed the stories for so many years as unimportant, yet now they'd become part of the fabric of her life, a connection to those things she'd almost lost. Family. Home. She wanted to tell the girls so they would remember. So they would tell their children, and the stories wouldn't be forgotten. Ever.

"Once, a long time ago," she began, "two married couples traveled here from far, far across the sea. One of the men was a sea captain, the other a first mate on his ship. They looked around the whole world and decided that the most beautiful place on earth could only be found right here in California's Big Valley."

"It's pretty," Emma Grace said, her eyes still closed.

"Yes, baby, it is." Juliet sighed, remembering the glorious tales her mother and father and grandfather often told. "One couple, MacQuaid and Camila Byrne, found some land they loved best. They built the Spanish house I was just telling you about, the hacienda. The house was made of adobe, and guess what?"

"What?"

"They built that house around an oak tree, a century oak."

Emma Grace giggled. "Around a tree? Are you sure?"

"I promise you it's true. And that oak tree is still there. It's in the same patio of the house where Cousin Merci lives today."

"Tell me the rest of the story."

"Well, this handsome sea captain and his beautiful Spanish wife raised cattle on their land. They had big parties to which other rancho families would come from miles and miles around, so far that they had to sleep over in the hacienda.

"Three little babies were born to this family," Juliet continued. "Three little girls."

"Almost as many as us."

"Almost. Their names were Aislin, Sybil, and Brighid."

Emma Grace's eyes flew open. "That's the same name our Grandma has."

"It is. She's our grandmother. The house I'm telling you about was hers when she was a little girl."

Emma Grace's eyes were wide with wonder. "Did she play in that tree that was in the house?"

"I remember many stories she told me of sitting in its shade."

"What else? Tell me more stories."

"The other man and wife I told you about?"

"Uh-huh."

"Well, their names were Hugh and Sara Dearbourne. They built a house near their friends, the Byrnes. This family had two sons. Their older son's name was Jamie; the younger boy was named Spence. Aislin, Sybil, and Brighid played with their friends Spence and Jamie all the time." She ruffled Emma Grace's hair. "But when they grew up, Jamie and Spence both loved the same sister and wanted to marry her."

"Oh, dear," the girl said, her eyes closed again. "Then what happened?"

"It was our grandmother they loved, and she had to choose which brother she loved."

"That would be hard."

"It was, because she loved them both in different ways."

Emma Grace opened her eyes. "I know which one she picked!"

"Who?"

The little girl sat up, then dove into Juliet's arms. "It was Grandpa Spence!" Then she fell back in a heap of giggles.

Gillian and Willow joined them. Willow snuggled with Juliet, and Gillian lifted her heavy brace onto the bed, then scooted close to Emma Grace.

"What happened?" Gillian asked. "Why are you laughing?"

"I'm telling your sister our family stories."

"I want to hear too," Abby called from the doorway.

"So do I," Annie said as she pushed aside Abby and plopped onto the bed beside the other girls.

Now her sisters were perched like little morning birds, waiting to hear the story of their ancestors. Juliet caught them up to where she'd left off with Emma Grace.

"Then," she said dramatically. "Remember the brother that Aislin didn't choose?"

"Jamie," Willow whispered.

"He fell in love with a woman whose heart was solid gold."

"Really?" Gillian, Willow, and Emma Grace asked in chorus, their eyes big.

"That means she was kind and generous and loving, silly gooses," Annie said.

"Geese," Abby corrected.

"Her name was Hallie, and she was a widow woman with a tiny little girl named Emmeline."

Their eyes widened.

"Our mama?" asked Gillian.

"The same. When she grew up, she came to California—before that she'd been living in the east with Jamie and Hallie. Anyway, she came to California and fell in love with Aislin and Spence's son, Quaid."

"Our papa!" shouted Emma Grace, standing on the bed and jumping. "This is the story of our mama and papa. It's like a fairy tale."

Juliet swallowed hard and caught her sister's hand. "That's hard on the springs, baby. You'd better sit down." She looked at their expectant faces as they waited for Juliet to go on, but the heaviness inside was nearly too much to bear. She remembered the stories she'd heard so many times, about her stubborn mother and her orange trees, her cowboy father and his endless patience. And she missed them. Clear enough.

She looked into each little face, in which she could see both Emmeline and Quaid. It wasn't fair that they couldn't know their mother, and their father would soon become a distant memory.

She decided right then that she wouldn't let that happen. She would keep them alive for her sisters through her stories. She would tell them daily, if need be, how much their father loved their mother, how their grandparents fell in love. She would tell the little stories as well as the sweeping stories. She would ask Merci, Brighid, and Sybil to tell their tales. She would write to Jamie and Hallie in Washington, D.C., and ask them to write down their memories and send them to her before they were forgotten forever.

When the girls were older, Juliet would tell them about the tragedies, too. For without the darkness, they would never understand the light. God had brought them through so much, had taught them of his unfailing love through the years in the midst of suffering. It was a legacy of faith meant to be passed along. "It was the land," she said after a minute, "that brought our ancestors here nearly seventy years ago. They called it the Big Valley, but they thought of it as the Promised Land."

"Just like in the Bible," Willow said solemnly.

"They believed God brought them to this place."

"That's in the Bible too," Gillian said, looking important.

"That's why our land is so important to us. That's why we're going home. We can't live in the house that our parents built, but we'll be nearby."

All the silver, crystal, fancy lamps, sofas, and chairs that Juliet had acquired with Stephan's direction had been sold. She'd tucked away the money for the expenses ahead, for the repair of the century-old adobe and to buy furnishings more practical than crystal and Spode.

Without a twinge of regret, Juliet had locked the small bungalow and headed with the girls to the trolley stop, then the train station.

As the train made its way to the Big Valley, the six Dearbourne sisters stared through the window at the passing scenery. The tall buildings of Los Angeles gave way to smaller settlements.

"Ettie, tell me when we get close to home," Willow said when they reached Pasadena.

"It will be a ways yet, pumpkin. Nearly another hour."

Gillian, sitting next to Juliet, was unusually quiet that morning and seemed lost in thought. Juliet leaned toward her. "Is everything all right?"

Gillian didn't look up. "I don't want to be in this dumb ol' brace anymore. I wanted to walk when we came home."

Juliet reached for her sister's hand. She wondered if setting the child's hopes too high with the operation had been another of her colossal mistakes. She certainly had made her share of them while raising the girls.

"You know, baby, I haven't given up." *Oh, Lord! Don't let me give her false expectations,* she prayed silently. But she so wanted to see Gillian's face light up with hope again. "Maybe now that I have more time, we could exercise it every day. It can only help strengthen your foot."

Gillian laced her fingers through Juliet's and gave her an adoring look. "Can we start tonight?"

Juliet laughed and gave her hand a squeeze. "We will. And I think that all the hard work and scrubbing we'll do at the adobe will help it too."

"Is it as big as our old house?"

"It's got only two rooms."

Gillian shrugged. "That's as big as our apartment in New York."

Emma Grace, who was listening from across the aisle, broke in. "Our real house was big."

"Really big," Willow agreed from behind them. "I want to go see my bedroom. I might have left some dollies by mistake."

"Can we, Ettie?" Gillian asked. "Can we go look? Maybe I left something there too."

"It's not ours," Juliet explained patiently. "The house has been sold. But once we meet the new owners, then we can ask if we might visit sometime."

"I don't want anyone livin' in our house," Willow whined.

"Me neither," sniffed Gillian.

"What if Daddy comes home and someone new is living there?" asked Emma Grace. "He won't know where to find us."

"We'll leave word with the new owners," Annie said gently with a glance to Juliet. "They'll tell him for us. Besides, he'll ride over to see Merci right away. She'll tell him."

Annie and Abby were growing up. It seemed to have happened overnight. She smiled at Annie and mouthed, *Thank you.*

Abby nestled her arm around Emma Grace, pointing out landmarks along the way—Meadows Field, where they'd ridden in Clay's flying machine; Sierra Madre, the pretty little village near the mountains; Mudd Springs, where the mountain man Jedediah Smith had once camped. She helped her sister sound out the words on each train depot they passed.

Juliet leaned back against the seat. The girls felt it; she felt it. They were truly going home. Maybe not to the old home place, but home nonetheless.

If she needed to work in a packinghouse, she would. It wouldn't be so bad. And at night, she'd already decided, she would write. All the words, the phrases, the poetry, the stories, that had been pent up for too long hammered at her heart to be released.

Now it was at last time to answer that cry of her heart.

Oh yes! It was time.

Jared stood on the platform, waiting when the train pulled in, just as he had promised.

For a long moment they stared at each other, then Jared held out his arms. Juliet ran to him, her younger sisters crowding in beside her. His big arms spread around them all. Everyone seemed to be talking at once, catching up on hugs, declaring it had been much too long.

Juliet apologized for being so stubborn. Jared said it was his fault for not visiting them in Los Angeles. The girls hugged him again, and Willow said he looked like their father now.

With that, he met Juliet's eyes above their sisters' heads. For a moment he seemed too moved to speak. He pulled out his handkerchief and wiped his eyes.

"Ettie says it's her fault we haven't seen you," Emma Grace said. "She didn't think you wanted to see us. This morning at breakfast she said she should have insisted."

"It's not quite that simple," Juliet said.

Jared agreed, still grinning. "Right now it doesn't matter. I'm just glad we're here, together." His sisters clinging to his arms, Jared led the family down the street to his farm wagon and the drive to Merci's and the waiting family.

"Do you have any idea who bought our place?" Juliet asked when they passed the turnoff to Sunny Mountain Ranch. Though her mother and father had renamed it years before, right now it struck Juliet that it would always remain Rancho Dearbourne in her heart.

Jared shook his head. "The sale took place months ago." He glanced down at her. "I'm sorry."

They rode along without speaking for another few minutes.

"I'm sorry I didn't try to help you save it, Jared."

He reached over and took her hand. "I don't think it would have made a difference. You were right about that."

"I should have tried."

"Someone else is living there. I drove by out of curiosity a few weeks ago. There was smoke coming from the chimney. It looked like someone had been working in the groves."

"I don't know if I want to see someone else on our land," she said quietly. "The girls want to have a look at the house, but I don't think I can bear to meet whoever is there."

"It's not ours anymore." Jared's face held more sadness than she thought possible.

"It meant more to you than I thought."

"It was part of our heritage," he said. "And I suppose now that Father and Sully aren't coming back…" He didn't finish.

"You've heard then from the investigator you hired?"

He nodded, keeping his eyes on the road. "They left no trail when they disappeared into the jungle."

Juliet stared across the sweeping lands of the Big Valley to the mountains in the distance. A hawk caught a thermal and rose high above, the fading sun glinting on its feathers, turning them amber, then gold.

Thirty-Eight

The weather was bad that morning. Frigid cold. Rainy. Clay fastened his leather helmet as he climbed into the cockpit and peered out at the cloudbank while Andy Little, his gunner, climbed in below. Clay had a fixed machine gun, a Vickers, up front that he operated, but the gunner below did most of the shooting with his free-mounted Lewis guns.

The prop turned and the engine revved, causing the Bristol to shudder, then settle into a smooth roll as he headed to the runway. The plane was one of the great combat aircraft of the war, a two-seater with an observation port below. He'd been with this plane for four weeks now and knew it nearly as well as he did the bi-wing at home. He'd shot down his share of Germans, six as of yesterday, and Andy had taken to calling him Hotshot MacGregor.

At liftoff he headed straight to the Channel, and by the time he was over France, he'd hit ten thousand feet. Drop any lower, and he was in danger of taking shrapnel from the ground. And no matter where he was, he had to keep from facing the sun. If he was blinded by it for even a moment, it could mean his life.

No danger of getting caught today, he thought, as the Bristol hit turbulence and shuddered briefly. Clay scanned the cloudy skies for signs of the Germans. Gusts of wind and rain periodically hit his windshield, and he strained to see through the gathering storm.

It was times like this that he wished parachutes hadn't been banned from use. The war departments of both countries said it made cowards of the pilots. He'd thought about ordering his own private model as some of the others had, but he hadn't gotten around to it.

Andy had just looked back to say something over the engine's noise when a roaring shadow shot through the clouds. Clay looked up, immediately on the alert at the sound of rapid fire. A German plane was directly in front of him. Before he had a chance to react, he felt a stinging sensation in his chest and leg. The engine coughed, sputtered, then whined as the plane headed in a spiral downward.

Clay was aware of the smell of smoke and the blast of flames. Seemed to be coming from the rear of the aircraft. Smoke filled the cockpit. He choked. Coughed. Now his eyes streamed.

Still the plane spiraled.

He yanked back on the yoke, then pushed forward to get out of the spin.

But the little bird kept spinning. And spinning. Nose down, wing over wing.

Dizziness dimmed his thoughts, slowed his hands on the controls. Trying to think clearly, Clay thrust the nose forward again with the yoke, desperate to level the nose, to stop the deadly spin.

The aircraft shuddered, straightened briefly, then continued to fall.

Seven thousand feet, six thousand, three, then two. Clay glimpsed trenches below, the battlefield of Flanders. But he wasn't sure which side he was on.

The screaming roar was deafening, the heat and flames unbearable. The ground came up fast now. He heard Andy Little cry out. Or was that his own voice?

Then all was dark at last.

※

One morning a month after moving back to the old adobe, Juliet was sweeping the rickety porch when she looked up to see the approach of a Tin Lizzy in the distance. "Are you Miss Dearbourne?" the balding stranger said, raising his hat in greeting. "Miss Juliet Rose Dearbourne?"

She nodded, wondering what possible business anyone could have with her out here in the near-wilderness. "Yes, I'm she," Juliet said, stepping down from the porch.

"Name's Daniel Rivers," he said amiably. "Of Rivers, Webster, and Kenyon in town."

She recognized the name as a law firm in Riverview. "Pleased to meet you," she said. "What brings you way out here today?" She set the broom against the side of the adobe and turned to face him.

He propped a foot on the lowest of the porch stairs. "I have some business to discuss. Is this a good time for you?"

She wiped her hands on her apron and gave him a nod. "As good a time as any, I suppose. I'm sorry I can't invite you in." She laughed lightly. "There's really no place to sit. We're in need of furniture, but we've been too busy cleaning and fixing to worry about places to sit quite yet."

"This will be fine, but I do have some papers for you to sign." He nodded to the stairs.

"We can manage without a desk," she said. She settled onto the top step, and he stood near the post at the bottom of the stairs. He looked apprehensive. "I suppose there's no easy way to tell you why I've come."

A knot of fear caught in her throat, but frowning, she waited for him to continue. In the distance, the children's voices drifted on the wind from where they were catching frogs beside Mystic Lake. She could see Annie sitting on a small stump and Abby stretched out in the tall grass by the edge of the water.

"I've received word of a death that I've been asked to report to you."

She gasped. "My father? Sully?"

He shook his head. "I'm sorry, but it's someone else."

"Who, then?"

"Clay MacGregor was shot down over enemy lines in France."

"Clay…?" she whispered hoarsely, feeling her world spin around her. "Not Clay.…Please, not Clay!"

"I'm sorry," Mr. Rivers said again. "I truly am." He shook his head sadly. "Clay MacGregor's body was never recovered, but those who saw the fiery explosion of the aircraft say there is no chance he survived."

Tears welled in her eyes. "They can't be sure, can they? Please tell me it's a mistake."

"There were eyewitnesses to the aeroplane's explosion. The War Department is certain, Miss Dearbourne." He patted her hand. "They are careful about erroneous reports of death, believe me. A full investigation is done in every case such as this."

"Why have you come here?" she managed at last.

"Clay MacGregor had no next of kin. He gave the War Department your name. And of course, instructions to contact me in the case of his death. My job is to carry out his final wishes."

Juliet couldn't speak. She stood, went to the end of the porch, and looked out across the Big Valley. *His final wishes.* She supposed Clay wanted her to take care of a special request for burial. She shuddered, unable to think about his grave.

She remembered the last time she saw him. How he turned to look at her as she walked down the aisle on her wedding day.

Then he'd left before he knew she had changed her mind.

"He thought I was married," she whispered, her gaze still fixed on the peaks of the San Jacintos. "That I'd become Mrs. Stephan Sterling. How did you find me?"

"He signed his will more than three months ago. Would that have made a difference?" He hesitated, "And of course, the deed."

She whirled. "What are you talking about? His will, the deed?"

"He signed a last will and testament before he enlisted. He's left everything to you, Miss Dearbourne."

She leaned into the porch railing, knowing her legs wouldn't support her much longer. "He didn't have much," she said. "He lived frugally."

The balding man smiled gently and stepped onto the porch. "You now own a hangar that was once a packinghouse."

"And the aeroplane?" She wanted to cry. The lovely poppy-colored aircraft with a rabbit on the side.

"There's something else," Mr. Rivers said. "He made a purchase several months ago. A house."

She frowned. "I can't imagine why he would have wanted a house." Unless it was because he'd planned to ask her to marry him. She'd broken his heart instead.

"It's quite large, hundreds of acres attached."

She looked at the man in shock. "What are you talking about?"

Sudden images flooded her mind. Clay bending down to talk earnestly and affectionately with Gillian. He taught them how to cook spaghetti in New York. Clay taking them on rides in his flying machine. The *good* Mr. MacGregor, according to Willow.

Clay at the waterfall, the night he reintroduced her to her Savior. She blinked back her tears and turned away from Mr. Rivers, gulping in huge breaths of air. Then she forced herself to breathe slowly, trying to keep the ache in her heart from doubling her over.

"I didn't know Clay had the means to buy property," she finally said.

Daniel River's eyes were kind, understanding. "His father sold his property to developers some time ago," he said. "Apparently that money was kept in a trust for Clay until the older MacGregor's death."

The attorney pulled a folded document from the breast pocket of his jacket. He studied it a moment, then handed it to Juliet.

As Juliet read first about the trust that was now in her name, her gaze then fell on the property description, and her eyes filled. "Leave me, please," she managed to say.

"You'll need to sign the deed," he said. "And then I'll be on my way."

Through a shimmer of tears, she scribbled her name at the bottom of the document.

A moment later, Mr. Rivers's motorcar rattled back down the road.

Juliet sank to her knees on the porch and covered her face with her hands. "Oh, Clay," she whispered, "I thought you would come home to me. Houses and lands don't matter. It's you I've wanted all along. And now it's too late.

"It's too late!"

THIRTY-NINE

From the first moment Juliet stepped into the family Victorian, her heart told her she had come home at last. She looked around in wonder, walking from room to room, touching doorjambs and mantels, realizing they were more precious to her than the finest furnishings from Daten-Dunton in Boston.

But it was the early mornings spent in her mother's overgrown and dying garden that touched her spirit in the deepest way. She spent hours on her knees, pulling weeds until calluses hardened her palms. She carried water from the well, a bucket at a time, pouring the liquid between rows of hollyhocks and trellised sweet peas and clumps of rosemary.

At first she thought the morning glory that cascaded across the porch roof was beyond resurrection. But after carefully pruning the dead wood from the vines and removing the dried and yellowed leaves, she noticed tiny shoots of new growth. She dug around its roots, mixing into the hard soil a soft, fragrant loam from the river. And now she could see the pale green leaves emerging, the first promise that her mother's legacy would not die out. While she worked in her mother's garden, she talked to her Lord in a way she hadn't done before. She poured out her heart, crying through her sorrows about her mother, father, and brother. And Clay. Always Clay.

She asked for forgiveness for her headstrong ways and praised God for bringing her home. For bringing all of them home.

Peace at last settled over her like a blanket. While the aching for those who'd been taken never subsided, it was bearable because she wasn't alone.

After the peace of her morning reveries, her days were filled with overseeing the activities of her sisters. She soon settled into a pleasant rhythm, directing the cleaning and repair of the Victorian like a drill sergeant.

At least that was how Jared teased her, and their sisters added saluting and marching with stiff arms to their giggles and grumbling every time she barked an order. Jared attacked the groves with his own military precision, hiring a cadre of men to help him. It would take years for them to recover from the months of neglect to make a profit.

This time, if money ran out, she assured him, she would happily go to work in a packinghouse.

The glass-winged pests were moving north, it had been reported, and great strides had been made by the Department of Agriculture experimenting with new methods to fight them. By mid-June her orange trees were beginning to show the results of spring rains, pruning, and weeding—they were glorious.

Memories of Clay never left her. Every time an aeroplane putted across the sky, she looked up. The yellow bi-wing was still covered with a canvas tarp in the center of Clay's hangar. Unable to bear even a glimpse, she hadn't yet visited the place.

Jared came to her one night as she was sitting in the parlor, knitting socks for the soldiers.

"I haven't wanted to tell you my plans until we were settled." He leaned against the mantel, crossing his ankles.

She looked up at him wordlessly. She'd known for weeks what he was about to tell her, and she dreaded the words that would follow.

He gazed at her with eyes so like their father's, filled with strength and kindness "I can't put it off any longer."

"Is it done then?" She bit her lips together, telling herself not to cry. "You've already enlisted?"

"Yes."

"When do you leave?"

"A week from Saturday."

"Independence Day." She turned away from him, suddenly angry that she was about to lose another brother. "I suppose you think you're going off to fight in this glorious effort—"

He interrupted. "I have no illusions, Juliet. War isn't glorious."

She dropped her head in her hands and felt the pressure of her brother's hand on her shoulder.

"I'm sorry to leave you here alone with the girls. There's still so much to be done…" His voice faltered, and he cleared his throat.

"It's not that, Jared." She raised her head and took in his solemn face and eyes. "I've lost one brother," she said. "I can't bear to lose another." And of course there was Clay.

"Just because I'm going doesn't mean that I won't come home."

She grabbed his hand. "I am proud of you, Jared. Don't ever forget that."

The next day when they told the girls, Juliet proposed that they have an Independence Day celebration, a proper send-off, she said, for Jared. They would invite all their relatives, those at La Paloma, those in Monterey, and Grandmother Aislin and Grandfather Spence from the Valley up north.

"We'll even wire Grandmother Hallie and Grandfather Jamie in Washington," she announced. "They'll have time to travel here by train in time for the biggest celebration ever."

"I know, I know!" Emma Grace squealed, startling everyone in earshot. "Ettie, you told us one time about the parties at the ranchos in the olden days.

The ones with bull and bear fights," Emma Grace said. "Remember, Ettie? You told me about them. They roasted cows and chickens and corn, and everybody made pies, and we could even make ice cream."

Juliet laughed. "Fandangos?"

"That's the ones. Fandangos." She looked proud that she'd remembered it.

"Yuck," Gillian said. "I don't want any bull and bear fighting around me."

"Girls!" Juliet said with a laugh. "If we're going to hold a fandango, I think we'd better get busy planning, instead of fighting. And I can tell you, there will be no bull and bear fights."

"Papa says there aren't any bears left in these here parts anyway," Gillian said with a sigh.

At the mention of their father, each of her sisters seemed lost in her own sad world.

"When's he coming home?" Emma Grace asked, studying her thumb.

Juliet pulled her close, wondering as always if it was time to tell them that their daddy and brother weren't ever coming home again.

Quaid leaned against the railing and looked out to sea. After several delays due to rumored sightings of German submarines, the ocean liner had passed through the Panama Canal and was finally making its way up the California coast. He let his gaze travel along the distant terrain. Mostly he saw the barren and gold coastal range, spotted with a few live oaks, but once in a while in the distance, he could see jagged mountain peaks, some still topped with snow.

He couldn't get enough of it, this beloved land of his fathers'. He remembered the tales of his grandfather, how he felt when first sailing into the Los Angeles harbor, how he'd said until the day he died that he knew he'd come home the moment he laid eyes on California.

Sullivan stepped up behind him and laid a hand on his shoulder. "We'll be there in days," he said quietly, reverently.

Quaid suspected his son's awe and connection to this place was as strong as his own. He also knew that Sullivan was increasingly pulled to another world. He thought he knew where but said nothing of it. Sullivan would tell him when the time was right. It would be a sacrifice to leave the only home he'd known, but serving the King without sacrifice of heart meant nothing.

Rebecca was standing on the other side of Sullivan now, and he saw the fresh awe on her face as she looked at the skyline, the mountains and oaks and green-gold valleys of early summer. She would make a fine wife for Sullivan. Quaid knew from the way they gazed into each other's eyes that a deep and abiding love had enveloped them. There was a spirit of watchfulness, yet also great patience, in them both. Quaid had no doubt that God was doing something of wonder in their lives.

"I've figured the sea days remaining," Sullivan said.

"When do you think we'll sail into harbor?"

"The Fourth of July," he said with a grin. "Do you think we should wire the family from Los Angeles or just board the train for Riverview?"

Quaid grinned, imagining the hugs of his children. His voice choked, and for a moment he couldn't speak. He looked out at the lace and sparkle of the whitecaps and cleared his throat. "I want no further delays—not even to look for the nearest telegraph office. Let's just head there as fast as we can."

Sullivan chuckled. "I only hope someone's home."

Juliet threw herself into the preparations for their old-fashioned fandango. She asked Brighid, Songan, and Merci for their help getting the word out to all the aunts, uncles, and cousins. Jamie and Hallie had already replied by telegram that they would arrive a few days before the celebration to help with preparations.

Songan found some ancient vaqueros who lived in the Olvera Street section of Los Angeles to entertain with rope and riding tricks. Spanish guitarists had been hired to play through the afternoon and evening.

Three days before the Fourth, Juliet looked up to see a hired motorcar heading down the driveway. She threw down her apron, called to her sisters, and ran into the yard.

Grandfather Jamie and Grandmother Hallie stepped out of the vehicle and held open their arms. Juliet flew into them, followed by her sisters. They hugged them each in turn. Their eyes were filled with the deep sorrow of their losses, but there was joyful acceptance in them as well.

The following afternoon, Grandmother Aislin and Grandfather Spence arrived.

Juliet stood back as the four embraced and cried with joy at their reunion. Grandfather Jamie spent a great deal of time ribbing Grandfather Spence about his Model T. The two elderly couples rolled up their sleeves and helped Juliet with everything from food to entertainment. The little girls were constantly at their sides, watching the older folks with awe and asking incessant questions about the old days and life on the ranchos.

The day of the fandango dawned bright and clear. Never had the mountains looked more elegantly etched against the purple-blue sky. The late-spring storms had left the mountains with caps of snow, and the recent Santa Ana winds had cleared the air of its summer haze.

The guests began to arrive, friends from Riverview and neighbors from the county's hinterlands, some in newfangled motorcars, others in wagons drawn by horses. Children from Merci's school and their families drove up in wagons, and soon the air was filled with their shouts and laughter.

Sybil and Scotty MacPherson arrived just before noon in their convertible motorcar. It was long and sleek and at first reminded Juliet of Stephan Sterling's Pierce Arrow. But she couldn't stop smiling when she saw the figure in the rear seat. Great-grandfather MacQuaid Byrne, shoulders back, his hat pulled low over his forehead, looked like royalty. In a way he was, she thought, the patriarch of their clan.

She ran to greet him as Scotty helped him out of the vehicle and into a wheelchair.

Later Sybil pulled Juliet aside as the younger woman withdrew a tray of biscuits from the oven. "Darling, I want you to know I forgave you long ago for all you put us through. All our worrying over you youngsters."

Juliet swallowed her retort and said sweetly, "I hope it wasn't too difficult for you." But Sybil was already chatting with Willow and Emma Grace and asking Gillian a dozen questions about her surgery.

Gillian caught Juliet's eye and grinned before she turned back to Great-aunt Sybil. "Ettie's been helping me with my exercises. Every day she helps me lift my leg and put it down again. Over and over. It's getting stronger." She hobbled across the kitchen to help Juliet, favoring the leg with the heavy brace.

"I'm sure it is, honey." Great-aunt Sybil patted her on the head and moved on to visit with her sisters, Aislin and Brighid, who had just stepped through the back door.

"There must be a hundred people here," Grandmother Aislin said. She wrapped her arm around Juliet. "You've done a beautiful thing, honey, getting us all together. It's been much too long."

"It has been too long," Juliet agreed. "If I could do everything over again—"

Her grandmother shook her head slightly. "All of us would do things differently if we were given a second chance. That's the good thing about grace…God's mercy on us, and ours for each other."

"Thank you, Grandma'am," Juliet said, reverting back to her childhood name for her grandmother.

They walked outside to where the tables were set under the trees. In a clearing just beyond a cluster of chatting neighbors, Songan, Scotty, Grandfather Jamie, and Grandfather Spence, all with frilly aprons tied around their waists, arranged the sides of beef and pork on a large ironwork grill dug over the barbecue pit.

"I hold dear what you've done for your sisters," Grandmother Aislin said. "How you've kept them together, taught them some good things about this family's spunk and grit."

Juliet put an arm around her grandmother's waist. "I've had some good examples set before me."

Grandmother Aislin let her tender gaze rest on Juliet for a moment before nodding. "My sisters and I do have some stories to tell," she laughed. "Oh my, but we do." For a moment her eyes seemed to dance at some distant memory.

They walked toward the pepper tree where Annie was pushing Emma Grace in the swing their father had made so many years ago. The child's delighted squeals rose in the air, joining the music of the other children's laughter, the squawk of jays in the overhead branches, the murmurs of old friends visiting on the porch beneath the morning glory.

"I plan to write the story of our family someday," Juliet said to her grandmother.

Aislin didn't speak but looked pleased. "If I can help, I would love to."

"I want to hear your stories, and those of Sybil, Brighid, and Merci, too. Grandfather Spence, Grandfather Jamie. Everyone."

"Not all of our stories are happy ones, child," her grandmother said. "We've known our share of tragedy."

"I want to write them all."

"Good," Grandmother Aislin said. "The tragic stories add meaning to the triumphant ones. They must all be told."

Gillian and Merci were sitting on the porch stairs just beyond where Aislin and Juliet were talking. Juliet caught her sister's smile with one of her own. She thought of Gillian's life, the suffering she'd endured even at her young age, and that of Merci and her own years of pain. Gillian removed her brace to show Merci her scars, and Merci touched the little foot. Even from a distance away, Juliet could see the tenderness in her touch.

"Here comes someone else," Emma Grace called from the swing. "When I'm up as tall as the trees, I see 'em comin'."

"We'll have people arriving all day, silly," Annie said, giving her another push.

"It's another Model T like the one that Grandmother Hallie and Grandfather Jamie came in."

"How can you tell that from here?" Juliet laughed.

"It's the same color."

"They're all black, honey."

"Well, I just know it is." She squealed as Annie pushed her higher. "They're getting closer," she yelled.

Now the sound of the Model T chugging up the road leading to the house grew closer. A small cloud of dust rose behind it.

"Here it is!" Emma Grace yelled. "It's a Model T. I told you so!" Then she screamed. "Stop me, Annie. Stop me! Let me down. Hurry!"

The conversation around the yard ceased. All was utterly silent until Emma Grace yelled again.

"It's Daddy! It's Daddy!" She took off running for the road.

Juliet was sorry for the misunderstanding that would bring such pain to so many this day. Emma Grace wasn't old enough to clearly remember her father, and the resemblance of a neighbor or friend must have triggered a hidden and desperate hope. She started to apologize to her grandmother, but the look on Grandmother Aislin's face made her pause and look back to the vehicle.

Three doors swung open. A young woman exited from the rear seat and stood back, as if uncertain what to do next. She had short curly hair, a slight build, a pleasant face. Juliet didn't recognize her.

Two men stepped from the Model T at the same time, one on either side of the car.

Juliet bit her lip, afraid to believe what she saw. She heard a choking sound from Annie, then a cry from Willow, followed closely by another from Abby. Someone yelled for Jared to come quickly.

By the time Emma Grace had been swept up in her father's arms, Juliet was running as fast as she could to join them. Behind her, she heard the voices of her sisters and Jared.

"Father!" she cried.

Holding Emma Grace with one arm, he opened the other to Juliet, then the others crowded in, first hugging their father, then Sully. Everyone seemed to be talking at once, and crying, and embracing one another so fiercely it didn't seem they would ever let go.

Then Quaid stepped back with a frown. "Where's Gillian? Has something happened to her?"

Juliet's heart dropped. She'd forgotten about her sister. Gillian had taken off her brace, so she couldn't have hobbled across the lawn to meet her father. In the excitement—and the crowd of relatives and friends who'd gathered around—no one had thought to bring her.

Juliet raced back to the porch, but Gillian wasn't there.

Then a collective sigh seemed to rise at once. Juliet turned to look back to where her father and brother had been standing. Clusters of friends and family stood silent, Sybil and Scotty on one side, Brighid and Songan on the other, Spence and Aislin near them. No one said a word.

Juliet moved closer.

Her father and Sully knelt, her father's arms spread wide. Just a few feet away, Gillian walked toward him. On her own, without a brace, without support. One wobbly step at a time, gazing up at her father, she walked toward him.

"Daddy!" she said at last, tumbling into his arms. "You're home!"

FORTY

December 1917

Juliet had plenty to be thankful for. Her father and brother had come home at last. And Sully—or Sullivan, as they all now called him—was getting married! Everyone, from Emma Grace to Grandmothers Aislin and Hallie, was taking special delight in planning the wedding, which would be held at Sunny Mountain Ranch on Christmas Eve. The little ones had taken a special shine to their newest "sister," Rebecca. They'd begged and pleaded until they were finally allowed to tag along with Sullivan and Rebecca as they drove to area churches, speaking about the needs among the Yagua Indians.

Juliet tried to remember to smile as she went about planning the rest of her life, a life she had once dreamed of sharing with Clay Mac-Gregor. But he was gone now. Killed in that horrible war. Why hadn't she told him of her feelings? Why hadn't she realized her love for him before it was too late? Now all she had were memories of their brief time together. And the ranch. His generous gift had given her family hope for the future. Though the house and lands were legally hers, she had eagerly stepped back to hand over the running of the big Victorian and the surrounding lands to her father.

Yet, surprisingly, it was Clay's gift of the large building that housed his aeroplane that brought her the greatest pleasure. Once she had convinced herself to go, it was there that she felt closest to Clay. Every time she entered the cavernous structure, she was reminded of the first time they had met, and she missed him more than ever.

Today, as she did nearly every day, she rode her mare into town to oversee the work she had commissioned for the building with the money he had left her. From down the lane, sounds of hammers and saws, shouts of crew members to each other, carried toward her. Shading her eyes against the sun, she fixed her gaze on one thing only as she drew closer. A new sign had been installed just the day before. Her heart caught as she studied it now.

The MacGregor Theatre. It was written in terra cotta relief above the two-story arch, which was wide enough to accommodate the theatre's entrance and large window. The result was a flood of light in the box office lobby that was sure to welcome and warm visitors. She had designed the doorway herself, patterned after the Regal Theatre in New York: four double French doors beneath the steel and glass marquee.

With a deep sigh, she dismounted and stepped inside, nodding her greeting to foreman Charlie Kent, a burly man whose loud bark was far worse than his grumpy bite. He stopped his work at the far end of the room and sauntered toward her. Without preamble, he pulled out a roll of plans and unfurled them on a makeshift plywood-and-sawhorse table.

"You gotta decide about the design for the balcony fronts," Charlie said. "The artist is coming by this afternoon. You want the same swags and laurel wreaths we've added to the box seats?"

She glanced around at the partially finished auditorium with its ionic pillars and pilasters, the coffered ceiling arches. It would take a year to complete, but already she could see the grandeur of the finished product.

"Yes, let's use the same design," she said. "I've seen it done in New York, and it will fit in well here."

"Seems awfully fancy to me," Charlie grumbled as he rolled up the plans.

She swallowed her smile as she headed toward the staircase. She had taken only a few steps when he called to her. Standing on the bottom stair, she looked back.

"There's something else you gotta do right away. You've gotta get that flying machine outta here." Charlie jerked his thumb to the corner of the room where they had rolled Clay's small aeroplane. "Two weeks from now we'll be closing the side opening. Once we do that you'll never be able to move it. Unless that's what you want." He shrugged.

"You're not far from wrong. I plan to make a monument of it, a memorial to the man it belonged to. And in honor of others from Riverview who've died in the Great War."

Charlie lost his expression of bad humor and his eyes crinkled in kindness. "That's commendable, miss. A nice gesture."

"Thank you."

"Shall I ask the artist to design something with the aeroplane in mind?"

"I'll ask him myself. Tell him I would like to meet with him after you're finished. For now you can push the flying machine outdoors. Just make sure the canvas covering is replaced." She continued ascending the stairs, her heart considerably heavier. The thought of the small aeroplane with its wheels sunk into concrete twisted her heart. Bound to the earth forever. She wondered if the monument might be enough without the aeroplane. Perhaps she should sell it after all. She pushed the thought from her mind to deal with later.

She walked briskly to Clay's office and sat down behind the desk. Leaning forward, she tapped a pencil on the blotter and stared through the window. As busy as she was, overseeing the work on the theatre and working on her script, *Promised Land,* she found herself sometimes lost in memories. And there, sitting where Clay had sat, she missed him. When she heard the sputtering hum of a flying machine overhead, her heart would ache so desperately she thought the agony of her sorrow would never end. That she would never get past the vivid picture of him in her mind's eye, the way he touched her heart with the husky warmth of his voice, the music of his laughter. The light of love in his eyes, until they turned to dark granite the day he watched her walk up the aisle to marry Stephan Sterling. She had been so blind not to see his feelings for her. So foolish to let him walk away.

She opened her notebook, dipped her pen in the inkwell, and wrote two lines of dialogue and a stage direction. Then she crossed it out and rewrote the lines. She read them aloud. They were more stilted than the original. She tore the page out, tossed it in the wastebasket, and repeated the process two more times.

Staring at another blank page, she considered the plot, the three women characters, the weaving of generations and theme. Then placing her pen in the well, she stood and walked to the window.

The early December day was cloudless and brisk, a perfect day to ride to the lookout above the Big Valley. It was the place her family's history came to life, all those stories told her by her grandmothers, her great-grandfather, her aunts, and cousins. Already they formed the rich texture of the story she was attempting to tell.

It wasn't a lack of material that caused her to stare at the blank page. Quite the contrary, it was the abundance of it.

And Juliet sat for hours with MacQuaid Byrne, her great-grandfather, as he spoke of his childhood in Ireland and of his life as a sea captain, traveling the world. He told her with damp eyes about the love of his life, Camila, the great-grandmother who died before Juliet was born. The beautiful young woman had left both country and sad memories to sail into the unknown as the captain's bride. Yet she'd come to love the rough-hewn captain and had borne him three daughters: Aislin, Sybil, and Brighid. Though born into aristocracy, she hadn't been afraid of hard work. With her husband, MacQuaid, she'd helped build Rancho de la Paloma into one of the finest and largest ranchos in all of California.

Juliet smiled as she looked toward the mountains, thinking about the hours she had with Grandmother Aislin, who told her about the two brothers who had each touched her life. Jamie and Spence. The old woman still cried when she spoke of her love for both, telling how they played together as children and how the family always assumed it was Jamie her heart sought. Then Juliet had taken the train to Monterey and listened while Sybil told of her romance with Scotty MacPherson. Laughing, her great-aunt related how she always wanted to marry a gent and live in New York in the height of fashion and riches. Then she met Scotty, poor as a church mouse, but she was so head over heels in love she never noticed.

Juliet saved Brighid and Merci's stories until last. She had known about the "terrible times," as the family referred to both stories, but she hadn't known until now the extent of the dark sorrow and heartache the mother and daughter had endured.

She spent days with them as they explained what had happened, especially how God had turned their bleak tragedies into joyful redemption.

Oh, the rich stories her family had to tell! How could she have ignored them for so long?

Juliet gazed from Clay's office window, once again looking across the landscape and toward the mountains. She smiled to herself. Perhaps *Promised Land* could come to life as she gazed across the valley of her ancestors.

Without a backward glance, she dropped her notepad and writing implements into a small satchel.

"I thought you were staying to meet with the artist," Charlie Kent called as she breezed by.

"I'm heading to the hills," she tossed over her shoulder. "Tell the artist I'll speak with him another day."

She mounted her horse, patted the neck of the young mare, and nudged her forward. Soon they were on the east side of Riverview and heading deep into the Big Valley. She let the mare take her lead, relishing the feel of the brisk wind against her face. They passed rows of lush green groves, laden with winter fruit.

The terrain changed as she neared the property belonging to the Byrnes and Dearbournes. Except for the portion that comprised Sunny Mountain Ranch, the land was wild, just as her father had wanted it.

Sage, beaver-tail cactus, sycamores, and live oaks dotted the land. It lay golden in the late fall sunlight. She remembered how often Aislin, Sybil, Brighid, Merci, even her mother, years before, had spoken of the land as though it were alive, as if it had lived through the stories of their lives, as if it had a story of its own to tell.

Juliet pressed her heels into the mare's flanks, urging her to a gallop. They sailed across the wind-swept fields, past the old play fort where Aislin and Jamie once pretended they were ancient Celts. She let the mare slow as they neared the San Jacinto range, and soon they were winding their way upward along the trail that hugged the mountain. When they reached the place where the rock slide had taken her mother's life, Juliet halted the horse and slid from her saddle.

For a moment she stood in silence, thinking of Emmeline's strength, rejoicing that such a woman had come west to prove her gumption. That such a woman had set an example for Juliet and her sisters to follow. That such a woman had loved her.

She picked a tuft of pine needles, held it close, and breathed in its pungent scent. "Mama," she whispered, "I never told you how much I loved you, how much I needed you. I know you can't hear me, but I need to say it anyway.

"I've come home. I've finally come home!"

She placed the pine branch on a boulder near where the slide had been cleared from the trail, then remounted. She let the mare again take her lead on the steep trace. Small stones and clods tumbled downward behind them, but still she climbed.

When she reached the top, she headed to the lookout. The mare knew her way and picked up speed on the level ground. Now they were in the pine forest, dense and deep green. The luscious smell of decaying pine needles and loamy soil filled her nostrils. A couple of jays scolded from the bottom branch of a pine, and a mountain bluebird skittered along the base of a manzanita.

With a grin, Juliet halted the mare and, leaving the beast to browse in a tuft of winter grass, ran to the bald mountain at the end of the trail. The sun beat on her shoulders, and she turned slightly, arms outstretched, letting her gaze travel from one end of the Big Valley to the other.

The land of her fathers, as much a part of her heritage as the blood that ran through her veins. How could she ever have wanted to leave?

She settled onto a flat boulder, and arms propped behind, lifted her face to the sun.

When Merci had told Juliet her story, she'd quoted the third chapter of Habakkuk. Now it came back to her.

Although the fig tree shall not blossom,
Neither shall fruit be in the vines...

the flock shall be cut off from the fold,
and there shall be no herd in the stalls:
Yet I will rejoice in the LORD,
I will joy in the God of my salvation.

Juliet thought about all the tragedies of recent years. It had taken until now to realize that truly God was her strength. He'd made her feet like those of a deer. And he'd brought her at last to the place where she could walk on the high hills.

Her heritage was that of those who'd gone before her, their tragedies and triumphs, their loves and losses, their walk with God.

Smiling, she leaned forward, her eyes on a bird soaring in the wind. It was at such a distance, it appeared as little more than a speck in the clear sky. An eagle, perhaps? Or hawk? All she could make out from here was the golden glint of the wings.

She pulled out her notebook to record her thoughts. The stories poured from her heart. She wrote furiously as the words of the Dearbourne and Byrne women came back to her, stories of triumph over all odds, of humor and joy and tragedy.

Tears filled her eyes as she wrote. The play took form. Three acts. Three generations. The land as backdrop. The land as character. It was constant—along with God's providential care. Why hadn't she seen it before? She scribbled on, her head bent down, her mind working faster than her fingers could write. Hours passed almost without notice, so lost was she in the story.

A sound carried from the distance, interrupting her thoughts. Soft at first, then growing louder. A low drone. A motor. A foreign sound that shouldn't have been allowed to interrupt her silence. *Shouldn't be allowed to blend with the music of the wind in the pine trees.* She laughed to herself. She was becoming more like her environmentalist father by the day.

Without looking up, she continued to write, ideas still flowing.

The drone grew louder. It putted along, alone in the sky. She glanced up. It was coming from where she'd earlier noticed the eagle or

361

hawk soaring on the wind. Only now she knew the small winged object hadn't been a bird at all.

With knees trembling, she stood as the small plane drew closer. The wings of the bird hadn't been golden either. They'd been the bright yellow wings of an aeroplane. A biplane.

She shaded her eyes with her hand, afraid to hope. It had to be a similar aircraft. Just because it was the color of California poppies didn't mean that it was Clay. She was being ridiculous. It couldn't be Clay! He'd lost his life in the Great War. His plane had gone down in flames. He couldn't have survived.

She was torturing herself, standing here like a fool staring into the sky at a small yellow aeroplane.

It was closer now, swooping downward just above the treetops. She stepped backward as the pilot circled and returned once more.

This time she gasped. The silly rabbit that Clay had painted on the side was clearly visible.

Anger and dismay flooded her whole being. Someone had stolen Clay's flying machine out from under the noses of Charlie and the other workers. She never should have allowed them to wheel the machine from its safe place in the cavernous building.

The flaps were down now, and she heard the power cut back on the engine. The pilot was readying to land.

In the Big Valley, not far from Sunny Mountain Ranch. Just a couple hundred yards from the Victorian. Angry more at the trespass on her heart than the taking of the plane, Juliet mounted the mare and nudged her forward. The horse seemed to sense Juliet's urgency and hurried along the rocky, dusty trail.

When they reached level ground a half-hour later, Juliet brought the mare to a gallop. They came to a rise, and she could see a figure leaning up against the fuselage of the craft.

She narrowed her eyes, planning to give the thief a piece of her mind as soon as she was within shouting distance.

The slope of the man's shoulders, the way he was leaning back, feet crossed at the ankles, arms crossed at his chest…the way he was grinning at her as she approached…all made her heart stop.

She halted the mare and blinked to be sure.

No, it couldn't be! It was merely a cruel hoax.

Then Clay opened his arms. With a cry, she slid from the saddle and ran to him. Tears poured unchecked from her eyes as she flung herself into his arms. He gathered her close, and she buried her face against his warm chest.

He was trembling as he laid his cheek against the top of her head and clung to her as though he would never let her go. For a moment that seemed to stretch into eternity, neither of them spoke.

"I love you," Clay finally said. "Oh…" The single word was an aching groan. "Oh, how I love you."

She tilted her face back to welcome his kiss, tasting their mingled tears. "Oh, Clay, I should never have let you go," she whispered when she could breathe. "Oh, my love!" But she started to cry again before she could ask how the miracle had happened. "I thought you were, we all thought…"

He touched her lips with his finger. "I was injured behind enemy lines, then unconscious for weeks in a field hospital, without identification. There's much, much more to the story, and I'll explain it all later."

Then he smiled that crooked grin she loved. "Just as you'll have to explain how my hangar got turned into a theatre." Again, she started to weep, thinking her heart couldn't possibly contain the surprise of joy. "Oh, my darling, how I missed you!" he murmured, then leaned down to kiss her once more.

"How did you know…?" she began, but her voice choked. "How could you have guessed that I loved you?… The wedding. Stephan. I walked down the aisle. The last you knew I was about to marry him." She shuddered, even now remembering.

"I figured you had gone through with it," he said, his voice gruff with emotion. "It ripped my heart in two, Juliet. Ate at me the whole time I was away. But when I arrived at my packinghouse and asked what in blazes all those workers were doing to my hangar, they said, Juliet Dearbourne was the boss so I'd better talk to her. Not Juliet Rose. Not Juliet Sterling. And I was sure that Stephan never would have allowed you to stoop so low as to build a theatre in humble Riverview." He grinned. "Especially a theatre with my name on it."

She looked down, her cheeks flushing suddenly.

He laughed softly, and with the crook of his index finger, lifted her face to his once more. "I couldn't know for certain, but there were some moments when I dared to dream." His intense gaze was making her heart melt. "Such as the day you ran through the mud and rain to my crumpled biplane, thinking me dead or at least injured beyond repair." He chuckled. "You called me darling, and I dared to hope…at least for a few minutes…that you meant it.

"And there were those times when you met my gaze over the top of Willow's head when she'd said something in her sweet lisping voice, or over Gillian's when she was trying so hard to walk, or Emma Grace's when I was helping her stir the sauce for spaghetti and she'd splattered it all over us both. It was as if we were connected somehow, that our love arched over their little heads, including us all in its wonder. I had hoped and prayed that you felt it, understood it. Then along came Stephan—" His voice broke off.

Juliet's eyes filled with tears again. "It was you all along, Clay," she whispered. "Just you. I didn't see it then, didn't understand the first thing about love. The wonder of it."

She drew his hand close and kissed his rough fingertips. "You've been right here in my heart, Clay, from the first day I met you. I may not have understood all that meant, but even when I thought you weren't coming home, you never left this place."

He kissed her eyelids, each in turn, and she opened them to gaze up at him. He drew her into his arms again, pulling her close. She shut her eyes, feeling the strong, steady beat of his heart against her cheek.

"And you'll be in *my* heart forever, my love," he murmured into her hair.

From the distance, she heard Emma Grace cry out, "Willow, Gillian! Somebody's holding Ettie by an aeroplane. And it's yellow!"

Then shouts and squeals and giggles blended as the girls took off across the field that separated them from Clay and Juliet.

A rumble of laughter sounded in Clay's chest. "Shall we go tell them the *good* Mr. MacGregor has come back?" he said. Before they could move, Willow, Emma Grace, and Gillian raced toward them, calling out and laughing with joy. Two more voices carried on the wind from the porch beneath the morning glory as Annie and Abby yelled after their younger sisters, asking what the commotion was all about. In a heartbeat all five of her sisters were running toward Clay and Juliet as fast as their legs could carry them.

Juliet pulled back to look Clay in the face. "Welcome home," she said and kissed him on the nose. "Welcome home, Mr. MacGregor!"

Epilogue

Spring 1923

Sara Camila MacGregor snuggled in her daddy's lap as the curtain parted in the middle and opened to both sides of the stage. Around them sat her whole big family, her aunties Emma Grace, Willow, Gillian, Annie, and Abby. Uncle Jared was at the end of the row with his new wife, Jane Elizabeth. Her other uncle was somewhere far away with Auntie Becca and their new baby, so they couldn't come home for her mama's play.

She giggled and waved to Cousin Merci who was sitting in front of her. Merci had kind eyes that laughed at the corners. Sara Camila liked that. Then she waved to Great-grandma Aislin, sitting beside Merci, who smiled and put her finger to her lips to shush Sara Camila.

But Sara Camila didn't like to be shushed. She put a hand over her mouth, showing she was trying to be quiet.

Her daddy frowned and whispered in her ear. "Mama's play is about to begin. Listen and watch, baby. *Promised Land* is just for you."

"For me?"

He nodded, but his attention was on the stage. She reached up and, with one hand on either cheek, turned his face back to her. "Why?" she demanded.

He grinned at her. "It's how you fit into the story of Mama's family."

"How 'bout our new baby that God's givin' us?" She whispered so she wouldn't disturb anybody, but people were clearing their throats and shushing her anyway.

"It's about his family too, sweetheart," her daddy whispered back. "We'll bring him next year."

"Mama says our new baby might be a girl." She had forgotten to whisper, so she clapped her hand over her mouth and looked around to see if anyone had noticed She dropped her voice again. "And he'll still be a baby next year. He'll cry."

Her daddy laughed softly and held his finger to his lips just like Merci had done. "Watch now," he whispered, and turned Sara Camila to the stage.

She settled back against her daddy's chest, peering at the big family that sat all around her. They filled up three rows, they did. The people onstage had the same names as her aunties and uncles and cousins. She laughed at that. But Mama had explained that they were playacting, that they were pretending something called "roles."

People came and went on the stage, and sometimes Sara could hear soft crying from Cousin Merci and Great-aunt Brighid. Some of the others in the big theatre cried too, and they didn't even belong to her family.

The curtain came up and down twice with long times between, and just as Sara Camila's eyes were about to drift closed, she heard the sound of her mama's voice on the stage. Sara Camila sat up to watch. She almost didn't breathe. Her mama was dressed in clothes like Great-grandma kept in her attic trunk.

Her mama was looking at a man she called Quaid, just like Sara Camila's Grandpa's name, only it didn't look like her grandpa. And the man named Quaid was calling her mama Merci.

She frowned. It was confusing, it was. Then her mama began to speak in a low, clear voice. She almost sounded like Cousin Merci.

"God rescued me," she said to the man. "I was lost and didn't know where to turn. I saw only darkness, but he was there in my darkest night. Through it all, he was there."

"It's the story of our lives, of all our lives," the man said. "He carries us when we can't take another step."

"I heard a voice speak from the depths of my heart," Sara Camila's mama said. "He told me that my face was before him when he died. He said that I who had no father, could call him *Abba*."

"*Abba?*" the actor named Quaid repeated, his voice nearly a whisper.

"It means 'heavenly Father...Daddy.'" Her mama breathed the word as if it was the holiest sound in the world, like words from the Bible. "Imagine that."

Her mama fell quiet for a moment, then she turned again to face the man. "And even as I speak it now, I remember the sound of his voice in my heart. Though it wasn't really a sound."

She turned and walked across the stage, seeming to think about what she'd said. "It was more like music—the music of the seas and the earth and all their creatures and the stars in the heavens singing together. Yet it came from someplace deep in my heart with a feeling so pure and filled with love, I could scarcely contain my joy." There was silence for a moment, then her mama said the word again. "Abba."

A hush fell over the auditorium.

"Abba," Sara Camila whispered, but nobody turned around to shush her. "Abba, Daddy." Snuggling into her father's arms, she decided she liked the sound of the word. "Abba," she said again.

"Don't you see?" her mama said from the stage. "Our heavenly Father was there all along, with my mother in her terror and pain. He was with me as I wandered in despair and darkness.

"He's with us all...each child that is born on this land, into this family. He was with Camila when, heartbroken, she ventured to the New World, married to a sea captain she hardly knew. He was with Jamie in the Civil War prison, and he was with Spence when his father betrayed him.

"He's been with us all, each step of the way. All along, through the darkness, through the light, he was bringing us to the Promised Land."

"The land of our fathers?" the actor named Quaid asked.

Sara Camila's mama shook her head. "Not the Promised Land you might think," she said. "Not the portion of earth he gave our fathers." She paused now, looking into the audience.

"He was bringing us, step by step, to discover the place in our hearts where he would meet us. That deep place within us where passions and dreams reside. Where he heals our fears and sorrows. He was bringing us to the place where we hear—and recognize—his voice.

"The music of our souls," the man said.

"That's our Promised Land," said Sara Camila's mama. "No matter what happens to the plot of earth we call our home, the real Promised Land will last through eternity."

Sara Camila sighed and stuck two fingers in her mouth, just as she always did when she was sleepy. With the other hand, she twisted a small lock of hair above her forehead. Her eyes drifted closed.

Her mama was still talking about the family and those who would follow, the fresh miracles of lives and loves as God led each one to the Promised Land. She didn't understand the words, but she liked the sound of her mother's pretty voice.

With the thud of her father's heartbeat against her ear, Sara Camila thought about the wonder of such a place. A place where God's name was Daddy.

She opened her eyes again when people started clapping their hands so loud it sounded like thunder. Then her daddy lifted her and carried her between his shoulders, in that place just above his heart. Her mama was close by now, and her daddy had his big arms wrapped around them both.

Then the others came, her grannies and great-aunties and aunties and even Great-great Grandpa MacQuaid, who lifted his arms out to Sara Camila.

Smiling, she reached to him. Her father gently placed her on his lap in the big chair with wheels. She giggled as somebody pushed the creaking thing down the aisle toward the door.

"Five generations…" her mama said as she walked next to Sara Camila.

Suddenly the whole family was staring at her in the wheelchair with Great-great Grandpa MacQuaid.

Great-grandma Aislin laughed from someplace behind the wheelchair. She was joined by the deep rumbling chuckle of Great-grandpa Spence. "And oh, the blessings poured out on each one," he said.

Sara Camila peeked around the corner of the wheelchair and saw them looking into each other's eyes. Her great-grandpa did the silliest thing she ever saw. He kissed Great-grandma right there in front of everybody. Great-grandma's cheeks turned pink and pretty, and she giggled just like Emma Grace and Willow and Gillian sometimes did when they were talking about boys.

With a sigh, Sara Camila settled back against her great-great grandpa. Her eyelids were heavy again, and she let them close.

The family's voices faded as she fell asleep, dreaming about the land her mama had talked about in her play. It was a bright place with breezes that tickled Sara Camila's face and made her throw back her head and laugh with joy.

It was a place with distant hills the color of sunlight, with fields of grass, dancing with butterflies and humming with grasshoppers.

Up in the sky, higher than Sara Camila could ever imagine, a graceful bird soared without flapping its wings. When it turned, its feathers caught the sun and seemed to shimmer with golden light.

She smiled and stuck her fingers in her mouth. It was a good place, this Promised Land.

Beloved Friends,

We've come to the end of our travels with the Dearbourne and Byrne families. I hope you've enjoyed the journey as much as I have.

What an adventure this has been! In *When the Far Hills Bloom,* we traveled from California in the 1860s to the New Mexico highlands with Aislin and Spence and a band of wild horses. We tramped across the country with Jamie after his escape from a Northern Civil War prison and delighted when he found Hallie. In *The Blossom and the Nettle,* we cheered as the fireworks began between Emmeline and Quaid, the next generation to inherit the land, and we wept with Merci on her journey toward grace. In *At Play in the Promised Land,* we ached as the headstrong Juliet and the reticent Sully headed their self-centered ways even as we remembered their parents' and grandparents' hopes and dreams. And we understood at last, as did Juliet and Sully, that their true inheritance had nothing to do with the land after all.

Even as we leave the families in *The California Chronicles,* a new cast of characters is being born. Please watch for *Heart of Glass,* which will release in 2002. Ivy Lockwood already walks across my computer screen, whispering her story to me as she goes. Because of Ivy—a hurting woman who chooses to remain "dead" to her family after she disappears in a storm-swollen river—*Heart of Glass* has already captured my writer's heart and imagination in a way no recent story or character has.

What a joy for me to weave tales filled with threads of faith and joy and grace! Thank you, beloved readers, for your affirming letters about the stories I write. This year *The Sacred Romance* by Brent Curtis and John Eldredge had a tremendous impact on me personally and in my writing. In chapter 1, the authors quote A. W. Tozer: "Thirsty hearts are those whose longings have been wakened by the touch of God within them."

May our hearts always thirst, my friends, and long to wake to our Lord's sacred touch. I deeply appreciate you all.

Blessings and love,

Diane

Diane Noble

Photography by *Filoe*

Diane Noble is the award-winning author of a dozen novels, three novellas, and three nonfiction books. Last year she was a double finalist for the prestigious RITA award, given by Romance Writers of America for Best Inspirational Fiction of 1999. *When the Far Hills Bloom,* the first book in the California Chronicles, was a 1999 finalist for both the RITA and the HOLT Gold Medallion, honoring outstanding literary talent. She is a past nominee for the Romantic Times Career Achievement Award and has twice won the Silver Angel for Excellence in Media.

Diane lives in the mountains of southern California with her husband Tom. Their nest is mostly empty except for Kokopelli and Merlin, two beautiful but neurotic felines who helpfully drape themselves over computer monitor and writing desk while Diane works.

Please visit Diane's Web site at http://www.dianenoble.com, where you can catch up on the latest about her new releases, works-in-progress, and photos of her travels to the settings for her books. You can also win a free, signed book by entering her seasonal contest. Stop by for a visit soon, and come again often. You can write to Diane at:

Diane Noble
P.O. Box 3017
Idyllwild, CA 92549
E-mail: diane@dianenoble.com